ARE YOU MINE?

ARE YOU MINE?

ABBY FRUCHT

GROVE PRESS
NEW YORK

Grove Press
841 Broadway
New York, NY 10003-4793

Published in Canada by General Publishing Company, Ltd.

The chapter "Throne of Blood" appeared, in slightly altered form, in
The Ontario Review, 1990, and in the anthology *Ohio Short Fiction*.

Library of Congress Cataloging-in-Publication Data

Frucht, Abby.
    Are you mine? : a novel / by Abby Frucht. — 1st ed.
    I. Title.
PS3556.R767A74   1993
813'.54—dc20   92-36468
    ISBN 0-8021-3385-1(pbk)

Manufactured in the United States of America

Designed by Ann Gold

10 9 8 7 6 5 4 3 2 1

For Alex and Jess, and to Lynn Powell, Yopie Prins, and Wendy Kozol—with endless cheers for our nights and days in Oberlin.

ACKNOWLEDGMENTS

For their exuberant readings and idiosyncratically thoughtful responses, I thank Carolyn Frucht, Howard Frucht, Yopie Prins, Wendy Kozol, Mary Grimm, and Michael Zimmerman. Cathy McCormick's and Eric Cowley's advice on various scientific and medical matters was indispensable. Tom Hart, my agent, has remained a trusted reader and supporter; Walt Bode, my editor, has become one.

This book was completed with the help of a fellowship from the Ohio Arts Council; the author thanks that state for its generous and intelligent funding of the arts.

CONTENTS

THE GIFT   1

THRONE OF BLOOD   31

KILLER   53

A FACE IN AIR   69

THE SECRET   203

O IN THE MORNING, O IN THE EVENING,
    O AT NIGHT   219

THE
GIFT

❧   ❧   ❧

Once, Douglas nearly told Estaban about the woman who died of a heart attack when she and Douglas were in bed. This had happened years before. Not an older woman but young, twenty-one like Douglas, and not a noisy attack but quiet, quick and so painless it seemed to blend easily with the pleasures of the moment. She was moaning; the sound faded, intensified, then faded again. Her eyes were wide open and grew only a little wider. She was on top, her long hair swaying glossily across his tensed nipples; he wasn't surprised when she collapsed on top of him the way she did because she was a dancer, prone to exaggerated physical gestures that tried to compensate for shallow emotional ones but couldn't. He and she didn't know each other, really, at all; mainly they had flirted from across crowded rooms—cafeteria, lecture hall, a party once, although that might not have been her, and if it was, she was with someone else and looked more tenderhearted than Douglas ever saw her before or after. With Douglas that first-last night she never let down her guard. Even naked in bed she flirted so hard he had to stop himself from looking behind him for the man who must still have been appraising her. One minute she was a Jewish-American-Princess-Prima-Donna-Cock-Teasing-Quasi-Intellectual who sucked him until he was pulsing before performing a sequence of *grand pliés* on top of him, and then a minute later she was dead. One minute she was pulling her bodyshirt up over her ears with such airy, ethereal style that he wouldn't have been shocked to see her head become detached from the rest of her and float toward the ceiling, and the next minute she was an apparition. One minute she was begging him to consent to masturbate behind a lit-up screen onstage so that the swelling, writhing fountain of his shadow would backdrop her cat-suited solo, and the next minute she was a corpse.

One minute he didn't love her at all but the next minute maybe he did.

He could see some beads of moisture inside her nose, and on her lower lip a faint toothy imprint where she must have bitten down during sex.

He draped her in her poncho before dialing 911. He didn't know CPR, but he searched for a pulse and found nothing, then laid his hand where her heartbeat should be and couldn't bring himself to push. He might kill her if he *did* push, kill her if he didn't, it didn't matter if she was already dead. He couldn't feel any breath, and when he lifted her eyelid to study the white underneath, it was like gripping the wing of a dead butterfly; no tremor, no flutter, but when he let go, his fingertips were dusted with a glitter of purple shadow. As he waited for the ambulance, her ordinarily olive-complected face turned gray and then nearly transparent so he could see the violet tracery of blood vessels in the half-moons of soft skin under her eyes, and maybe the few minutes between the time her skin turned transparent and the time they wheeled her out the door was when he loved her even though he was distracted by the cops. Two policemen had arrived just ahead of the ambulance and another just after, although it seemed all they needed was to ask him some questions. Name, number, address, that kind of thing.

"What happened exactly?" one cop asked.

"She fell over," Douglas answered.

"Fell over where? I would have thought, under the circumstances, she would have already . . ."

"She was on top," said Douglas.

"Anything else you can tell us?"

"Her eyes sort of . . . opened," said Douglas.

"Heavy breathing?"

"Well, yeah, but we were—" he gestured toward the tangle of sheets at the foot of the bed.

The cop smiled. "I'm sorry."

"Is this hard for you?"

"Is she your wife?"

"No," said Douglas.

"Girlfriend? Significant other?"

"Not exactly," said Douglas.

"Friend? Prostitute? Second cousin? Help us out a little."

"Not a prostitute," said Douglas. "A dancer. At the university, I mean. A student. In the dance department there."

"Which university?"

Douglas told them.

"What's her name?"

Douglas said her name was Julie but that he didn't know her surname, where she lived, whether or not she had a job and if she did, where. He knew she ate a tossed salad every noon in the snack bar and that after her meal she stood up, clasped the seat back as if it were a barre in a dance studio, and stuck first her right leg and then her left straight up at the ceiling, her baggy warm-ups slipping into the cleft of her leotard. He told them that he sometimes caught sight of her, from across lanes of traffic, bicycling west along Big Bend Boulevard, but that he'd never caught sight of her bicycling east. As he spoke he watched the medics crowd around her as they carried her out the door, and in his state of blank confusion he imagined they were crowding just to get a better look at her face. Dead, she was no longer theatrical, only beautiful and sad-vulnerable looking. Maybe that was what he loved about her, suddenly— the loneliness that would have embarrassed her had she only known about it. When she was gone, when the cops and the ambulance had vanished, the loneliness seemed to have stayed behind, in the way Douglas's curtains wouldn't quite close and in the dull paper shine of his Pink Floyd poster. He'd never noticed it before; he wasn't lonely, only solitary, he liked his privacy. But now the quiet drove Douglas into the street, where he walked for an hour or two with his hands in his blue jeans pockets, feeling overawed the way he did sometimes after a movie. It was simply too much to take in. He didn't feel grief. He didn't feel sorrow, just percussion in the rib cage, under the skin. Had the dancer not died, had their lovemaking gone on as it should have, and ended as it should have, and had they parted as they would have, and had he walked the streets afterwards and felt such a knocking, he would have thought it was the thrill. He would have thought it was bravado. But now he thought it was love, and that was a funny thing. It made him wonder how often he'd been mistaken before, how often he'd mistaken love for thrills and bravado. But he was only twenty-one. His mistakes didn't matter, they hadn't piled up behind him, they didn't push him around. What mattered was now, this feeling, this woman, this night. That she was dead only made it more urgent that the feeling survive. He walked home in the cold, his thin shirt flapping, his body tense with concentration like a child in an egg race, the egg balanced on a spoon, the love knocking at the inside of his heart. There was a thought that he had to keep pushing out of his mind—that he had climaxed inside her the second she died—in order to keep the love whole, unbroken. In fact, he didn't know if he had climaxed at all. He couldn't remember, there was so much going on, her sudden collapse and the weight of her on top of him, not breathing, and her bottom in the air as he tried to free himself. When he sat up, she flopped over, a hand in the air. Then the hand dropped onto her still-flushed breast, the nipple erect, her fingers sliding over it as if in absent caress, the way they might have done even had she been alive. Her belly taut as a drum. Had she been living and looking so lonely he might have laid his head on it and listened for gurgles. Then they both would have laughed, her laughter less shrill than he'd heard it before. Already he was chiding himself for not having noticed earlier these things about her that would have made him give some-thing in return. When he got back to his room and saw the bed with the mixed-up sheets, he couldn't lie down on it, flip on the radio, and put his hands behind his head as usual. He sat in his chair instead and put his feet on the cinder block table and waited for the phone to ring so he could tell somebody what had happened. He would say he was in love but that he'd never told her and now he couldn't. But the phone didn't ring and he never told, and it is this that he most wants to say to Estaban, *Isn't it strange that I never told?* Or in Estaban's manner of speaking, *Isn't it psychotic?* Because, of course, had someone—had any-one—phoned him that night years ago he would have told, he would have spoken, he would have opened a sort of floodgate, Douglas has led himself to believe . . . and now imagines that by telling Estaban about the girl who had the heart attack, he might break the ice and free himself to tell Estaban all the things he wants to tell him about his wife, about Cara. Cara this, Cara that, Douglas could talk about Cara forever.

*I*nstead he tells Estaban the usual Monday morning stuff about what he and Cara and little Georgie did together over the weekend, delivered in a frenzy of shouts and lost phrases as he and Estaban cut through the wind of the tarmac toward the already spinning propeller of the helicopter.

"We hiked the towpath," shouts Douglas, aware of the absurdity of his necktie whipping this way and that around his neck, and of the wings of his sports jacket flapping around his tee shirt. He likes this costume although it no longer feels like the radical statement it used to; now it only feels quirky—his one, safe quirk. "And then we found a spot under the trestle and watched indigo buntings and waited for trains, and the longer we sat there the sleepier Georgie got, so—"

But Estaban is shouting in return, gesturing past Douglas at a single sheet of lined paper tumbling gracefully away from them over the blacktop; Douglas's notes for his impromptu calendar of the day's best-kept secrets to be woven with some degree of mischief into the morning's traffic coverage. It's a small city, and the hardest part about keeping radio listeners abreast of its underground culture is that there is no underground, really, to speak of, just as the main problem with doing the traffic report is that there isn't any traffic. It was Estaban who thought of combining the two, but it was Douglas who came up with the idea of the "lake analysis" to be delivered when there's not enough traffic to fill in the gaps in the skimpy calendar—what the lake looks like, skittish or calm; what the lake *feels* like, cool or foreboding; what kind of mood it appears to be in. For that, he doesn't need notes; half the time he makes it up, off the top of his head or more often straight out of his morning with Cara.

"Water's amorous," he'll say, with a sidelong glance at Estaban.

"Water's sleepy."

"Water's fretful."

"Water got out of the wrong side of bed."

"Water's all arms and legs," he says first thing this morning, the minute the copter gets airborne, the swells of the shoreline not even in sight. That's a risk, but still, he's not embarrassed to see, when they're hugging the lake, that the water's a blank, flat and motionless. No arms, no legs, no sighs even. It's as milky and dull as the eye of a fish on ice. It most often is. It's a placid, uninteresting body of water, once poisoned, now sanitized. Actually, Douglas doesn't need the notes for the calendar, either, really, because it's changed just a little since yesterday, and the day before, and the day before that, but he ran to catch the paper anyway and now, once they're over the city, fights his impulse to scan it. Instead he gazes down at the smooth morning rush of the streets, reporting the unhindered traffic, the inevitable, sensible movement of cars across space, like milk up a straw. A blocked lane here, a detour there, a characteristic bottleneck at West 92nd. So what? On the morning of the day of Georgie's birth, over three years ago, when Douglas was in the hospital with Cara in labor, coaching her in the breathing techniques that she suddenly claimed to find so ridiculous, there was a chemical spill on I-71, a huge semi jackknifed under a spume of spreading, drifting toxins, traffic halted all around, the National Guard called in to evacuate although evacuation was nearly impossible with so much fume and panic and conflicted, disorganized effort at rescue and control. The next morning, when Douglas was back at work, everything was peace-and-quiet again, more peaceful than usual even, if such a thing was possible.

Douglas didn't care.

"Water's dopey today," he reported euphorically on the morning after the birth of his first son, Georgie; Cara hadn't slept all night long, she didn't want to, she said, but she was drifting, fading, *dopey*, the mews of their new baby dilating around her as he nuzzled and sucked her into lapsed consciousness. Douglas didn't regret having missed the big spill, for he trusted such emergencies would happen again. Sometime later one did, not a spill but a small plane crash-landing at 7:40 A.M. on I-480 within sight of the airport runways—six ambulances, eleven fire trucks, the pilot's collarbone broken, the driver of a swiped pickup truck hysterically screaming into a policeman's bull-horn—or so Douglas was told, for he missed that, too. Georgie had croup, and his midnight attack of seal-like barking, amid the general chaos of steaming bathwater, open-and-shut freezer doors, and hurried telephone calls to the pediatrician, so agitated the dog that she paced nonstop for an hour after Georgie was finally sleeping, back and forth, back and forth, her toenails clicking on wood, her whine plaintive and revved-up and never-ending until Douglas caught her by the collar and held her nose gently but firmly against the plush of the bedspread, shutting her up, by which time Cara was oblivious under the blankets, so when Georgie woke again, not barking this time but in need of a good hard rocking, Douglas didn't wake Cara but rocked Georgie himself. At six o'clock he phoned Jenny and took his first sick day ever.

"Croup," he replied, when Jenny asked him what he had, so later, when the plane crash-landed, Douglas was snoring in the rocking chair with Georgie in his arms and Jenny was in the helicopter gazing down on the big event with Estaban. Next morning, when Douglas was back in the cockpit, eager and fresh from his day off at home—and yes, jittery, bored, wanting disaster, wanting anything, even if someone had to break another collarbone in order to make it happen—then the streets were calm again, clean as if they'd been swept, glittering, safe as could be.

"It's you," Jenny joked. "You're a jinx, an un-jinx, whatever. I'd like to have you at my wedding when I get married. If I get married. Wherever you go, it's peace on earth forever."

"She's right, sort of," Cara said a little skeptically.

"He's an angel," said Estaban's mother the very first time she saw him, her plump fingertips reverent and smelling of gardenias as they plucked at the highlights in Douglas's red hair. "Such blue eyes, too. You *are*," she said. Her name was Annunciation, and her manner of speaking—the vowels resonant from under a profundity of flesh, the flowers on her dress trembling as if with an echo—suited the word. "And you should know it. If you're an angel you have to know it."

*I*n his flight jacket and black jeans, Estaban looks like what he is, a pilot, and why this should fascinate Douglas he doesn't know, unless it has something to do with the fact that Estaban, who in his late thirties must be about five years older than Douglas, still lives with his mother. This curious fact provides Douglas with a reason for not ever telling Estaban what he wants so much to tell him about Cara. Concurrently he wonders, why shouldn't Estaban live with his mother? They get along alright. Estaban's mother would be alone if not for Estaban except on Saturdays and Sundays. She has five daughters, three sons, and not even Estaban knows how many grandchildren who crowd into her house on weekends. On weekends her house is too small; on weekdays, too big. Estaban's father is dead just three years. A generation ago the family moved from Haiti to Miami, then from Miami to Chicago, then from Chicago to here, where Estaban's father made a living as a cook, in, of all things, a Thai restaurant. Not even Estaban's mother knows how her husband learned to cook Thai, but his preparations were exquisite, and the family grew up on leftover spring rolls, lemongrass soups, and a concoction of tiny meatballs stewed gently in coconut milk that was Estaban's father's own special creation and that no one anywhere on earth has tasted in the years since he died.

All of this Douglas knows about Estaban, along with the fact that the radio in Estaban's mother's bedroom has been tuned to the same opera station for as long as anybody can remember and that one of the reasons Estaban's sisters and brothers gave for marrying as early as they did was to escape the murky crescendos of that music. Douglas knows this not because he and Estaban even try to talk about these sorts of things in the helicopter above the impossible noise of the engine but because he once interviewed Estaban on his afternoon radio show. Estaban's interview was in fact a test case, the producer being uncertain that Douglas's plan to interview ordinary people about whatever they wanted to talk about would carry, but when thirty-six listeners phoned the station suggesting recipes that might duplicate the flavor of Estaban's dead father's meatballs, the show got off to an okay start and is now a local phenomenon.

"Douglas has a way with people's hearts," Jenny said. "He makes everyone good. He brings out the best, whatever it is, no matter how hidden or worn-out or forgotten or ignored or beaten down or—" Jenny had a boyfriend whose goodness, as she put it, had been trampled so much it was afraid to show its face; it was her boyfriend she wanted to be talking about.

"I wish Douglas would make *me* good," Cara joked.

"I wish you would make *Cara* good," said Douglas's sister, Susan, on the phone from California one day last month, not joking at all.

"I wish I could make *you* good," retorted Douglas.

"Maybe you do," said Susan. "Maybe you do bring out the best in me and maybe I'm just a bitch."

"Maybe," said Douglas.

"Am I?" asked his sister. "Do you really think I am? Because some people do think it, I know, so if you do, you won't be alone. But do you? Think it, I mean? Am I?"

It was a tender moment, made tenderer yet by the fact that in all of that asking—Do you? Am I?—Susan hadn't been able to bring herself to use the word *bitch*. It was the most genuine avowal of feeling that his sister had had to offer since the time she sent the infant Georgie a musical windup pig, and Douglas was shocked and not a little chagrined to think that he had been the one to elicit it.

"Maybe not," he said gently. "I don't know, Susan. If you were redheaded like me, people would call it your fiery nature," he added, recalling what their mother had said to him when she was in the hospital with what would be a final round of kidney failure. "Watch Susan for me," said Douglas's mother, her hand clutching a cup of water, and Douglas clutching her hand so it wouldn't let go. "Make sure she ends up with somebody nicer than she is. You know, Douglas, someone like you, someone good for her, someone to draw out the kindness in her, wherever it sometimes is. Because Susan is not a nice person. You know that, Douglas, don't you? Your sister Susan is not a nice person."

"What do you call it in Cara?" Susan was asking.

"What?" said Douglas.

"Cara's a redhead. What do you call it in her? Her fiery nature?"

"No," said Douglas. "I call it . . . I don't know," although they'd been through this before, Susan's monthly inquisition, a knot of questions designed to unravel in Douglas hints of what Susan liked to suppose was his own growing unhappiness with Cara. "Has Cara visited her old roommate in Buffalo again this year?" Meaning, *Has Cara left you again just so she can waste a weekend getting stoned with the people she used to go barhopping with?* "Has Cara applied for any new jobs?" Meaning, *Does she really want to spend half her life being a job counselor for people who walk in off the street not even knowing what a job is, let alone being able to keep one?* "Have you found someone to clean the house?" Meaning, *Does she do the refrigerator? The fruit and vegetable bins? Because last time I was visiting I found that stalk of liquid celery stuck to the bottom and something, I don't know what, growing in there.*

And Douglas would need to remind Susan that the last time she visited, the time she screamed upon opening the vegetable bin, was just after Georgie was born, and the dog was sick, too, waking them pissing and crying in the middle of every night, so neither Douglas nor Cara had slept in two weeks, and that maybe the nice thing would have been to clean the vegetable bin rather than to screech about it. Then Susan might ask if Cara had gained any weight or was she still too full of herself to let herself be anything but skinny, to which Douglas could only answer that Cara wasn't skinny, she was slender, and anyway, what does that mean, *full of herself?* Because to call Cara full of herself is like calling the sun full of itself. Because she loves herself, yes, but the love radiates, it's warm, there's extra, she gives it away, she shares, she lavishes it on the planet.

"And how's Georgie?" Susan would eventually inquire, as loyally, as dutifully as if their mother had pulled her aside in the hospital room and asked that she watch over Georgie, which was impossible since Georgie hadn't been born yet and Douglas hadn't even laid eyes on Cara. And of course this last question was a trick question, too. *Is Cara taking care of him alright? Has she ever thought of buying him those cute Band-Aids since he's scared of the usual kind? Does she help him with puzzles? Because once on the phone, when I asked him, he said that she didn't.*

Georgie gets more love than you could imagine if your whole life depended on it, Douglas thinks but never says.

Cara would say it. More precisely, Cara would be unable to stop herself from saying it.

"Georgie gets more love and more affection than you can begin to imagine," Cara might say, but in that tone that takes the edge off the hurt of what she's saying, as if it's not a judgment but a fact, and not only a fact but an awesome one. Cara simply speaks out, which is one of the things about her that Douglas's sister seems to find so objectionable. Always, Cara is blunt, abrupt, and truthful. You can count on Cara to tell you when your fly is down or when you need a mouthwash, just as you can count on her to tell you how good you looked this morning in your just-washed blue jeans and that she wants you to come home and fuck her right now. Cara can make the word *fuck* sound not only affectionate but downright elegant. With her high, insistent voice, and with the way she has of throwing the weight of her whole body and heart and intellect into everything she says, Cara makes the phrase *Fuck me hard* sound like *I'm so glad you're the man I'm spending my life with, I'm so glad you're who you are, I'm so glad I'm who I am and that you love me and that we met and that we were lucky enough to be born into a time of relative peace when we can be together and make a life and raise Georgie, and now I want to have another baby. Do you?*

Cara made it sound like that last night, in fact. With her hands, she gripped his shoulders, with her thighs she gripped his hips, with her voice she grabbed hold of every bit of his concentration and made him focus it on what she was saying. Fuck me hard. *Do you want another baby?* Cara's questions don't implore; they command. Douglas paid attention. He didn't speak. He knew the diaphragm was in a drawer at one side of the bed and that he and Cara were on top of each other on the other side of the bed and that she expected him to answer in one of two ways—either slide into her, or stop and roll out from under her and reach for the birth control. So she gave him his choice and he took it; he slid. Their lovemaking last night had the serious beat of intense instrumentals, the kind of music Jenny's late late show includes because, as Jenny puts it, the only people listening at two in the morning are people who want a good hit of bass, people who would insist that if the world ended at midnight they don't want to have to hear about it until morning.

This is what Douglas would talk about with Estaban if he talked about these kinds of things with Estaban at all. How Cara's legs invited his answer, how the whole of her body seemed to welcome the introduction of his response, and how, had his answer been no instead of yes, and had he reached for the diaphragm, filled it with jelly and maneuvered it up inside her, taking a moment of almost clinical care to be sure it was fitted correctly behind the hump of her pubic bone—how even then she would have welcomed him but ever so slightly differently, because the choreography of their life together would have taken a different turn. With Cara every feeling had a pantomime attached to it; she had only to enter a room for him to know what kind of mood she was in. When she was mad, her bag was open when she threw it on the chair, and over it would tumble, and out everything would come; when she was sad and kicked her shoes off, they fell apart like weary hands, soles up; when she was happy, in the midst of all the other noise she made she'd pause, stock-still, before telling him, "I swear I can *see* molecules, I can see them bumping around right there in your tee shirt." And then, if she felt love welling up—pulling Georgie to the floor, kissing his tummy, his knees, his ankles, making him promise always to love her even when he became a teenager and hated her guts, and then, suddenly terribly serious, taking his three-year-old face firmly between the palms of her hands and staring him hard in the eyes, with her nose just an inch from his nose, and saying, "And Georgie, always take care of yourself. Listen to me. Some children have guns in their houses. Their parents keep guns, and the children find the guns, and when they find the guns, they show them to their friends. And sometimes they make mistakes, because a child never, ever should hold a real gun, but sometimes they do, and sometimes the gun goes off. Because sometimes the guns have bullets in them. And a bullet comes out. And it hurts one of the children very, very badly. So Georgie, if anybody ever shows you a gun that's not a toy, or if you think it's a toy but you're not really sure, here's what you should do. Don't look at it, and don't say anything at all, just turn around and walk out of the room and find the mommy or the daddy or the grown-up in the house and tell them you want to come home, right now, and don't go back into the room with the gun in it, ever. Will you promise me, Georgie? Will you promise me that's what you'll do?"

And having told her he promised, and having meant it, because that was the kind of earnest child he was even at three, Georgie might try to coax Cara back into hilarity again, but it wouldn't work because she would be suddenly businesslike, standing up, heading off for the kitchen, opening cabinets, measuring rice, weighing onions in the palms of her hands, exclaiming, "No one come near me or even talk to me right now because I have to make dinner and if I get too distracted by your gorgeous little face and whatever cute thing you have to say to me then we'll all go to bed starved."

Cara's forthrightness was one of her charms, and the fact that she knew it was one of her charms, and if Douglas's sister didn't see it that way, then that was Susan's problem, Douglas would have said to Estaban had he and Estaban talked about things like that. If you were one of the people who was in love with Cara, Douglas might say, then her very narcissism was one of the things you loved most. So, for instance, if a bunch of people went with Cara to a Chinese restaurant, it was understood that as soon as everyone began studying the menu, Cara would begin making politic suggestions, like trading chicken for shrimp if already there was too much chicken, and cashews for peanuts if already there were peanuts, and hot for mild, and never more than one dish of broccoli, so that by the time the waiter appeared for the order, the selection would resemble something very close to what it might have been had there been six Caras sitting around the table and not Cara and five of her friends. But still nobody objected, because the meal was always perfect, a blend of flavors and textures that would not have been achieved had everyone simply ordered what looked good without considering what everybody else was getting. For this was Cara's domain—making sure that everyone, including herself, ended up happy, nourished, satisfied—and she guarded it with a passion that Douglas knows he can't properly communicate to Estaban even when they've left the helicopter and gone into the radio station for a mug of coffee and a game of darts.

The dart board hangs crookedly on the wall in the rear of the storage closet between stacks of computer paper and cartons of unopened reels of tape. Their games open as volleys, the darts overlapping, their trajectories intercepting, then quivering side by side not quite in the bull's-eye. Because Douglas is left-handed and Estaban right-, sometimes their elbows bump. If they talk, it's about plans for the station, including whether or not it makes sense to ditch the helicopter and do the traffic by computer if they continue to do traffic at all. Douglas says yes, Estaban no. This is their only point of contention. At issue isn't traffic but the helicopter itself. Estaban loves flying, every morning and at dusk, and that's that. It is here, when they hit on this subject, that the darts start whizzing with more ferocity until the two men fall into place for standard tournament, keeping score on a box of promotional balloons.

At twenty minutes to ten, nearly time for the news, Douglas fishes out a balloon, inflates it, considers popping it but instead lets the air out and sticks it into his pocket for Georgie, wishing at the very least that he had managed to tell Estaban what he plans to get Cara for their approaching fourth wedding anniversary. He has one hundred dollars he can spend comfortably, meaning once he lets go of the money he'll be able to put it out of his mind. So he'll spend two hundred, and worry and be vigilant for maybe a month, even though he has plenty of money these days, worrying is only a habit, he knows that, but still . . .It's a mirror Douglas wants, oval, swingback, sixteen inches in height, the frame a Fijian wood with a bi-color, marbleized grain, chocolate and blonde, the two colors tumbling under the gleam of the finish, the base a trio of halfmoons arranged this way and that, Douglas can't quite remember, he hasn't seen it in a week, what if it's sold? The price was two hundred and eighty dollars and Douglas knows that's what he will end up spending probably on the very eve of the anniversary because he knows that's what he wants, that and nothing else—that very mirror, that appears taller and more slender than the other mirrors lined up on the shelves beside it, whose gleam is more silvery, more luminescent, whose grain more mysterious, whose posture more graceful—and that any other gift, any other mirror even, would be a mistake, a regret. When Cara looks into it, when she sees her image floating in the high, satiny oval of Fijian wood, it will be like looking into the eyes of one of those old-fashioned, formal, sepia portraits of someone who by virtue of the fact that she is there, staring back at you, has become immortal.

Even when Cara is quiet, her silence has a presence sometimes gentle, sometimes fierce; last night, after fucking, her silence had a patience and a watchfulness about it that made him lie very still so as not to disturb it. She was waiting to conceive, or, more specifically, waiting to see if when she did conceive, she would feel it happening. Several women had told her they'd felt it, but Cara was skeptical. Georgie's conception had been a surprise, although in retrospect they'd taken pains to identify the precise moment in which it must have occurred, and had recollected an uncommon tingling following an episode of lovemaking on a too-small, lumpy motel bed in a room crowded with a space heater in use even in summer, for they were in the mountains that night. They had taken the dog out west for a month in the summer so she could lose weight chasing bears. That was how Cara and Douglas posed the trip to their old friends around the country, whose dogs all needed to go on diets. None of their friends were thinking about having babies or even puppies; the female dogs had all been spayed.

The male dogs humped them anyway but never penetrated or even positioned themselves correctly, which made for laughable scenes that took place under the dinner table and made the soup bowls jitter and slide.

Through the window of the motel room they could see the giant shapes of the Colorado Rockies rising darkly against pale moonlight, and when Cara leaned out of bed, reaching the width of the tiny cabin to open the door, they got a sharp breath of spruce trees that gave Cara the shivers. At least they *thought* it was the spruce trees that gave her the shivers, which lasted only for a minute, anyway, before Kato realized the door was open and snuck out quick as a whippet. Kato was a hound, dark colored, impossible to locate in the night. They both pulled on their jeans and ran out to chase her, Cara wrapped shawl-like in the scratchy hotel blanket, forgetting all about the tingling she had felt for a moment inside. When months later they got past the surprise of the pregnancy, Douglas found himself faced with a new surprise, this new woman that was Cara and yet not the Cara he had known, who had had a horror of the very idea of women's bodies—their ankles, breasts, and bellies—swelling up to accommodate pregnancy.

"Never," she had said to him, more than once. "Not me. No. Ugh. Gross. Forget it."

Yet here this new Cara lay, tracing dreamily with the tips of her fingers the strange dark vertical line that had appeared between her pubic hair and belly button. "It's the *linea nigra*," she said to him challengingly. "It's not a vein. It's not feeding the placenta. It's not leeching out poisons. It has no purpose, it's just a change in pigmentation and it doesn't go away, ordinarily; it will be here forever. So, what do you think about that?"

"I hadn't noticed it," answered Douglas truthfully.

"Well, notice it. Now. Then tell me what you think."

"It's just a line," Douglas offered.

"It's crooked."

"A little," said Douglas.

"So what do you think of it? How do you feel about the fact that it will never go away?"

"I don't mind," said Douglas. "It doesn't bother me one way or another."

"Does it distract you?"

"From what?"

"From me."

"It *is* you. It's part of you. How could it distract me *from* you? Does it distract *you* from you? What do you think of it, Cara?"

"I love it," said Cara. "I consider it a mark of distinction. I don't like my nipples turning dark, though. That I could live without. How about you?"

"I can handle it," said Douglas.

"You won't split up with me because of it?"

"Not unless you keep talking about it."

"You won't divorce me?"

"We're not married yet, Cara." They were to be married in a week by a justice of the peace, no ceremony, just a signing of the necessary papers. Douglas was surprised Cara wanted the baby. He even doubted her, at first. But soon he was convinced. Her vanity, her self-absorption, had a new, tender, delicate object. He could see it in her face and in the way she drank her milk, dutifully, ounce after ounce although she hated the taste of it. And in the way she ate her spinach, which she called her "folic acid." And in the way she examined the darkened blood vessels in her breasts, critically, fascinatedly.

After Georgie's birth, those veins disappeared, but the *linea nigra* has not. It has faded a little, that's all. The pregnancy filled out her ass, broadened her shoulders and hips. It left no stretch marks on her belly. And she had been so thin before. She is statuesque, now, in her still-slender, still-bony way. From holding Georgie on her hip, propping him up, there are stretch marks on the pale undersides of her forearms of which just a mere caress causes Douglas's cock to swell. Also, new lines around her eyes, from lost sleep, exasperation, laughter, tears, adoration, fury. And now she wants another baby. Douglas wishes this were something he could bring himself to tell Estaban. But the phrases dissolve on his tongue, like sweets. Nor can he make himself say what he guesses—what he

20

knows—Cara will say when she sees herself in that new, swing-back mirror.

She will say, with a sly curve of a smile, a sly, bright glint of the eyes as they peer at her face in the glass, "This is the most beautiful thing I've ever laid eyes on, Douglas, isn't this the most beautiful thing you've ever seen in your life?"

And then a guffaw, and then slapping her knees, and then, after that, "Thank you, it's beautiful, I love it, Douglas, you always know what I love, you absolutely do," and then kissing him in that way she has, that Estaban wouldn't understand unless Douglas told it all from the beginning, when he and Cara were still in St. Louis just starting out, just getting to know each other. Cara was a student then, studying her philosophy texts on the beat-up vinyl couch in the game room of the union, where Douglas hung out during sets of First Hits on the station down the hall. When the show was underway, he wandered down to the game room and played Scram. He was station manager, which meant he served as technical and artistic advisor to the fledgling student producers, but the students that year were arrogantly self-sufficient so he humored them by making himself scarce, then appeared mid-emergency when they were desperate for his help. Scram was a game for two players, but Douglas played against himself, right hand against left, scorer against stopper. He was proud of his coordination, proud of the way his left hand maneuvered to stifle the options of his right. To this day he can't imagine why Cara studied in the game room, although she's told him that she did it because the sight of his two hands' amiable competition made her want to go to bed with him. He doesn't believe this for a second. At the time of their meeting, she appeared not even to realize that she was a woman and he a man. It was a frustrating couple of weeks, Douglas remembers. She was taller than he was, and Douglas couldn't figure out why he was so comfortable standing before her until he saw that her eyes were level with a bull's-eye, exactly five feet, eight inches from the floor. So it was easy to find himself staring sharply, pointedly into them, without feeling that he was being too forward, too abrupt. Cara seemed not to notice his desire, anyway. On their dates they played Ping-Pong and took walks and went to movies and talked, and at the end of the evening she'd kiss him in the exact way he had seen her kissing the eraser of her pencil while she studied her philosophy texts—distractedly, thoughtfully, incidentally.

And when he opened his mouth and slid his tongue into hers, and lapped and sucked and wanted—what a surprise that seemed to be to Cara, who appeared not to think of herself as a sexual being or of themselves as two people who might want to do such a thing with each other.

And when they made love, the pleasure seemed to come as a surprise and even, somehow, to strike Cara as funny. Because sometimes she burst out laughing between moans of pleasure as they rolled and sucked, which made Douglas think over and over of the phrase *fun in bed*—so that was what they were doing, they were having *fun in bed*. Except her laughter seemed more serious than that, it wasn't play, it wasn't fun, it was joy and mockery at the same time, for she was laughing *at* herself, at this vision of herself with his penis in her mouth, at this vision of their spread legs, clutching arms, lolling tongues, sweating backsides, unconscious cries, grunts, whispers, silences, at all the separate parts of lovemaking that when she saw them one by one were laughable, and she was laughing as well at her laughter, because it was embarrassing, it *was* funny, to find herself bursting out laughing in the middle of an orgasm and then going ahead and having the orgasm anyway because she couldn't help herself.

Douglas had to admit that at the beginning he found this a little perplexing. A little humiliating, in fact. He even wondered if she was putting him on, or if she was sick or perverse or plain crazy. But she didn't seem crazy. She laughed at herself having sex just the same way she laughed at herself clapping after the concerts they went to, such a primitive impulse, *banging your hands together*, so helpless and physical when we think we're being civilized, she said to him later, like the rituals having to do with food, look at waiters, look at fancy silverware, look at people getting dressed up to go out for pork roast when really all they're doing is stuffing a dead pig into their mouths and chewing and swallowing and digesting like a dog with a bowl full of Alpo.

"Dogs like Alpo," said Douglas. "People like pork roast. *You* like pork roast."

"I love it," said Cara, grinning. "I like the crispy parts best. Charred adipose deposits in candied plum sauce."

"And you like going out for dinner," said Douglas.

"I love it," said Cara matter-of-factly.

And she loved sex, too. He could tell that she did. Every time, it amazed her. And frightened her, too. And having put it all together—the eating, the sex, the applause—Douglas understood what the fascination was. It was the thought that the body had a life of its own. Desires, needs, hungers, instincts— whatever. Cara didn't want to believe that. Which was why, when she was washing the windows, for instance, on that eighty-degree morning so long ago, she was able to take off her jeans and step out on the roof in her tank top and underwear with no thought of being gaped at, scoffed at, ogled at, by the people passing by on the street. Which was what she was doing when Susan, Douglas's sister, first laid eyes on her.

Douglas had picked Susan up at the airport in St. Louis, he was driving her home for a visit, there was Cara on the sloping roof outside their second floor apartment wearing only a tank top and a pair of rose-patterned, white cotton underpants. From below on the street, just to look at her through the windshield of his car, Douglas could tell how Cara felt; she felt weightless, impulsive, free of convention. She felt above it all, full of sun and power.

But that wasn't how she looked. She looked sexy. She didn't mean to. Her hair, then as now, was cut rather raggedly at the shoulders; it gave off a fierce, orange, energetic winking.

"My God," said Susan. "What in God's name does that person think she's doing?"

"She's washing the windows," said Douglas.

"You know her?" said Susan.

I'm in love with her, thought Douglas, and led his sister upstairs and introduced her to Cara, whose face was smudged, who made a joke about being on the rag and then took them on a tour of the just-washed glittering windows before offering sun tea, which she had to step back onto the roof to get, by climbing out the living room window. The backs of her legs were smudged, too, and the soles of her feet black as night. A loose thread trailed from the crotch of her panties and wafted behind in a gust of heat.

"Charming," said Susan.

"Oh, Susan, cool it," said Douglas, as Cara climbed back in the window carrying the jar of tea, which she poured into three tall glasses with ice and sprigs of fresh mint that Douglas knew she would have had to climb down the fire escape to pick. By now, Cara must know that her apparent innocence turned him on, he thought. Which meant that it was no longer innocence, then. So what was it? She didn't seem to be flirting. She just seemed proud. She was the same way with birth control. She used it, but she scoffed at it, too, as if she didn't think it mattered one way or another. She didn't actually believe that her body was capable of pregnancy. Until it happened. And then her first response was laughter. And then amazement. And then devotion. And now she wants to have another baby and do it all over again.

The check, after Douglas's attempt to bargain, is for two hundred and seventy-five dollars, postdated so Douglas can get to the bank in the morning and cover it. The mirror's base folds against the frame so it can be carried flat, wrapped in bubbles and a sheet of the artist's own handmade marbleized paper. The funny thing is that once the mirror is wrapped up under his arm, the money doesn't bother Douglas the way he thought it would. He isn't worried at all, only eager to give her the present and thinking maybe he'll do it tonight instead of waiting for tomorrow. Tomorrow is too far away.

When he gets home he can see how her day has gone. On calm days there'll be a jigsaw puzzle set up on the floor, or on the table a plate of cookies that she and Georgie baked and maybe nearby a neat stack of her papers with a pen lying on the diagonal across it. But today there's an unopened package of corn tortillas lying on the living room floor next to one of her shoes, and the other shoe on the counter in the kitchen with one of Georgie's trolls sitting inside it like someone paddling a kayak. Her briefcase is unopened and the telephone off the hook. On the stove is a pot of potatoes, already boiled and now cooling in the water, and a frying pan with nothing in it yet but oil and two browned cloves of garlic. He finds the beans, the green peppers, the Monterey Jack, all lined up on the cutting board on the counter, her way of telling him she wants help with dinner. He slices the peppers and the potatoes along with an onion, and fries them gently while grating the cheese, then hunts down the black olives she's left in the pantry along with the jar of salsa. Since he's forgotten about the tortillas, he has to tear them and fry them separately before adding them in with the rest. When he's done, she and Georgie are still in the shower. If he stands at the base of the steps he can hear them playing hippopotamus. Georgie prefers showers to baths because then he doesn't have to watch the water turn gray and know how dirty he must have been. He's a purist, Georgie, even when he's a hippopotamus. He wants his mother's moist nose against his, he wants his thick white towel, he wants plain milk, not chocolate, in a glass, not a cup, and his own hot buttered tortilla, which Douglas has forgotten, he has torn them all to pieces and fried them in oil, mixed with the garlic and hot sauce and chopped vegetables. A problem. But then the dog appears at the top of the stairs with a ball in her mouth. She bows her head, releases the ball, watches it bounce toward him step after step with a series of wet thwacks. Having caught it with his foot, Douglas kicks it gently under the couch. The dog comes downstairs sideways, sidles past him, sticks her nose under the couch, then turns and watches him happily, wagging her tail. This is their nightly greeting, modified over the years from a far more spirited game of Slinky.

"Hi, Kato," says Douglas. "Come into the kitchen. I have to make Georgie an omelet."

But Kato doesn't come, and when Douglas has put the egg

on, he follows her down the hall past her food- and water-bowls to the bed in the tiny playroom, to read the newspaper and stroke her nose. Every night he makes a point of doing this, just a few minutes of stroking and petting to remind her that she is part of their family, although the bond, sometimes, seems no more substantial than the space between her eyes, his fingers absently exploring the silk warmth of it. By now the shower water has been turned off and Cara and Georgie are drying and combing their hair and taking their sweet time about it so that by the time they come downstairs, dinner will be ready and the table set so Cara won't have to do it herself. This is their secret, and he can hear them giggling about it conspiratorially behind the closed bathroom door, although possibly it is just Cara's way of getting Georgie to agree to have his fingernails clipped. Life is never boring, Douglas thinks, even the simplest moments are full of convolution, his hand on the dog's nose, Cara upstairs, Georgie crying for a second, then stopping, then starting again, then laughing; the newspaper trembling on the mattress beside him, the smell of searing, crisping omelet drifting through the hallway.

When he's flipped the omelet and opened the broom closet for a can of food for the dog, he discovers Cara's gift to him propped against the wall behind the vacuum cleaner. It's in brown paper wrapping with her handwriting on it in a big, loose spiral that Douglas doesn't read because he knows all at once what her present to him is as surely as if he'd opened it and held it in his hands. He doesn't need to pick it up to feel the frame or the glass, or peel the paper away to see the portrait looking back at him or to know what its expression will be; mischievous, proud, and affectionate, the way Cara looks in all of the photographs that Douglas has ever seen of her, even the candid shots, the ones when she is tying Georgie's shoes or washing the dishes or just then stepping into a room. Perhaps Douglas will tell Estaban about this, how for their anniversary he gave Cara a mirror while Cara's gift to Douglas was a photograph of herself, and how eventually Cara will make a joke about it, their own "Gift of the Magi," telling it over and over with a mixture of embarrassment and pure, blushing enjoyment, for the fact is, she'll insist, she loves to look into the beautiful unchanging frame of that mirror as much as Douglas loves to be caught off guard by the eyes of the photograph she gave him; how they catch him, hold him unblinking for a moment as if in a contest of will.

And she will be right, he *will* love the photograph, he'll love it so much he can swear he hears his heartbeat echoing in the kitchen even as Cara thumps downstairs toward the smell of scorched butter and black, rising smoke and the brittle, ruined omelet.

*W*hen they've opened the gifts, and stood them opposite each other among the remains of dinner on the kitchen table so that the two faces, Cara's and Cara's, stare mischievously, angrily, affectionately into each other's eyes, Cara turns to Douglas and says, "Remember last night, what I said last night, what I said that I wanted when we were—" and then she leans closer, looking sideways at Georgie sitting there in his mixed-up pajamas, the pants on backwards and inside out, the top misbuttoned. Through a straw, he finishes the drink Cara made for his dinner in place of the discarded omelet. The drink is pure as can be, one ripe banana blended with yogurt and milk, no sugar, no chocolate, not even a sprinkle of nutmeg, and on the side, a letter G made of oyster crackers.

"When you were what?" Georgie asks, froth on his lip. He drops the last of the G on the floor, on purpose or not, for the dog.

"You didn't come right out and say it," Douglas answers.

"But you knew what I wanted. You know you did."

"Maybe," says Douglas.

"What?" says Georgie, patient as always.

"Kissing," says Douglas.

"A brother," Cara says simultaneously.

"A brother or sister, you mean," says Douglas, feeling his groin tingle at the mere mention of it. He has finished clearing the table; now he scrubs the omelet pan as Cara rearranges

Georgie's pajamas, nearly losing the towel she knotted around herself after her shower, her blue jeans on underneath, her hair a thick fringe at her shoulders as usual, redder than blonde but not red enough to be red unless you catch it in the sunlight, although she's had it tinted red in the photograph, so faintly it seems to be blushing. The photograph is black-and-white just barely—slyly—touched with colored pencil.

"For who?" Georgie asks.

"Do you want a new brother or sister?" asks Douglas.

"If you do," Georgie answers with caution.

"You'll be older. You'll be nine months older. You'll be four years old already, Georgie."

"No, don't get him thinking," says Cara, nuzzling Georgie, kissing his forehead, a halo of kisses. "I got six new clients this morning, two weeks of practically nothing and now who do you think everyone needs at once, but I did a lot of thinking in the middle of it, on and off. I changed my mind, Douglas, I think," she says, laughing the way she used to laugh in the middle of sex, because of what she said, that she *thinks* she's changed her mind, she isn't sure, she hasn't made up her mind about whether she's changed it or not.

"Anyway . . . ," she concludes, shrugging. Her bath towel slips free but she gets hold of the corners before it falls, then keeps her hand on her sternum as if pledging truthfulness. And he can see that she really is truthful. It doesn't come as a surprise. How could it? She is as truthful now as she was truthful last night, *Fuck me hard, I want to have another baby, now I don't, now I do, now I don't.* It's her truthfulness that causes her to change her mind, and it's her changing of her mind, as well as her truthfulness, that is loved by the people who love her. He should know. He loves it, too. He loves the way each moment seems to multiply before her and become a kind of prism of replicating moments, of dancing, shifting possibilities. Late at night, if she runs a bath, she sets a candle flickering on the rim of the tub in a ritual further adorned by the fact that there is always a moment, a long, drawn-out, complicated moment when she can't decide which scent or color candle to light; blackberry or honey, jasmine or sandalwood. To Douglas all the candles smell equally heavy and dense—he doesn't like perfume or incense or even the smell of honeysuckle unless it comes from the blossoms themselves—but still the sight of her standing naked before the row of candles, the match flaming between her fingers as she lowers it not quite to one wick and then not quite to another and another, fills him with delight and with intense, quivering respect. How she concentrates, choosing, changing her mind! It is beautiful to watch. She knows it. She watches it, too. She is watching it now so doesn't notice the depth of his own disappointment or his own surprise at how much it hurts. He should have known this would happen, he should have been ready, he should never have let himself fall in love with a baby that hadn't yet been conceived. He should have known he was in love, already, and then stepped back and kept his distance for a while. He can see the fine red fuzz on the new baby's skull and between its shoulder blades. He can hear its little cries. He can feel its tight fingers close around his thumb. He can see himself looking for signs of Georgie in the new baby's face and demeanor and being equally pleased and astonished to find them present or not present. He can see the four of them romping on the bed together on long Sunday mornings amid toast crumbs and sheaves of newspaper and the stink of unchanged diaper. He remembers the night, last night, Cara bent to sniff his penis, his balls, his scrotum, his hair, her tongue probing the head of his penis, the pinched mouth of it, all in an attempt to locate the exact chemical and physiological source of its peculiar, characteristic, funky, soapy smell. The smell grew less distinctive as the penis swelled, she remarked scientifically, and then she pulled herself on top of him and rolled them both over and said "Fuck me hard" until he knew what she wanted, where they were going, where they were headed, what they were after. And that must have been when he started wanting it, too. He wanted it so much he swore he could feel the blood stop moving inside of him. Now he waits for it to start up again, drying another few plates and cups. At his place at the table, coloring stars on an erasable placemat, Georgie remains quiet. He is always quiet at the times when they most need him to be quiet. When his crayon snaps in two he ignores it and goes on coloring, gold and silver, the only colors he'll tolerate for stars. He won't climb out of his chair before either one of his parents leaves the room, even to look for the dog. The dog and Georgie have never offered each other much solace. Instead they sidestep each other with polite discretion. A brother or sister would be different, but Georgie is far too tactful to come out and say this, and for a moment Douglas imagines that this is what he might tell Estaban, that his three-year-old son has more tact, more sympathy, than any adult he has ever met in his life.

"I started realizing what it would be like for there to be four of us, suddenly," Cara is saying mischievously, proudly, affectionately, with a face like the face of her photo in the mirror.

"It wouldn't be suddenly. It would be nine morths," says Douglas.

"Yes, but—"

She swings her arm around to finish the sentence. It's a gesture she makes often in one or another circumstance, and Douglas prides himself on knowing exactly what it means each time she does it. But now it cancels him out, and Cara's hand seems to know this; it pauses midway, hovers, then sinks to the glossy wood frame of the mirror, tracing with a fingertip a small blonde storm in the grain. From the corner of his eye, Douglas sees the filled dog food bowl where he had set it on the counter when the omelet started burning, and the bottle of heartworm drops nearby. Has he put the drops in yet or not? He can't remember. And the dog needs to go for a walk. She sits at the front door, wagging her tail. How simple that is, how clear its demand, the sound of Kato's tail on wood, its blunt, anxious thumping.

And how simple the response—to slide the dried plates distractedly back into the sink under the murk of dirty dishwater from where Cara will have to fish them out again, to wipe his hands on his blue jeans, to raise his eyebrows at Georgie. He fills the dropper with a half dose of heartworm medication, squirts it into the bowl, pours water on top, goes in silence to the dog to give her everything she wants.

30

THRONE
OF
BLOOD

*I*t was early evening on the day of the birth of Cara's second child, Max. Max was born at noon, and at suppertime Cara was still waiting to fall in love with him. She didn't love him the very instant he was born, as many women say they love their babies, or during pregnancy, as other women do. In fact her inclination all along had been to ignore him entirely, so that the changes in her body during pregnancy seemed to her to be just that, changes in *her* body, not in anyone else's. She barely thought of the baby at all until the labor began, and then her recognition of him was clouded by pain. By suppertime, she hadn't forgotten the pain, as women say they do, but she was trying to forget it. Still, she kept hearing someone down the hall in the throes of it, screaming, "I can't do it, I can't do it, I can't do it," until Cara's entire body clenched in agonized, convulsive sympathy, and only on reflection could Cara say to herself, "I did do it, I did do it, I did do it, it's over."

Cara's gown did not fit properly. Either that or she was wearing it wrong, because it didn't cover her. She couldn't have cared less. She had license to be half-naked, lazy, depraved, steeped in strange, uncommon relief. She was feeling quite pleased with herself, and she was pleased with her baby twitching in sleep on the high, wheeled, glassed-in cart at the foot of her bed, where she could gaze at him as if through a window. He was knobby and pink, unconscious, detached. She hadn't counted his fingers or toes, as mothers are said to do, but she knew they were all there because the nurses would have said something if they weren't, and she knew he was breathing. She could see the uneven rhythm of it through the blanket, unless that was his heartbeat, so fierce in so tiny a body. No matter what, he was alive. She had said to Douglas several times since the delivery, "He's alive, he's alive," meaning, *I'm alive, I'm alive, I'm alive.*

Cara had been out of bed just once all day and knew she'd be expected to get out again soon, to go to the bathroom. The nurses insisted she move her bowels. Now that the labor was done, that was what scared her the most. She might split apart, pushing it out. She had stitches where she tore and where they cut her. Besides, she felt shaky even now but nothing like when he was born. Then she'd been afraid to hold him she was shaking so hard, and her breath had thumped under her ribs. She could see that they were holding the baby above her, still wet and unwashed, bloody, with the white, pasty stuff still on him, but it had not occurred to her to take him into her own long arms even when her fingers parted as if to receive him. When the nurses lowered him onto her chest she said to Douglas, "Hold him there, don't let me hold him." The baby was warm and wet, and she didn't welcome the feel of him the way women are said to. It was too distracting. She wanted only the sensation of the pain being shaken off of her, limb by limb.

"I feel like I'm going to die," she had said.

Douglas had smiled. "Well, you're not."

"Yes, I am. Look at this." She held up a hand that was shaking so hard its outline was blurred. Beyond it she could see the nurses clustered around the baby on the cart against the wall, cleaning him, clipping him, tapping here and there and examining. Then the doctor was sitting between Cara's propped-apart legs with a needle and thread, peering critically at the ragged edges needing to be mended. So calmly, so confidently did the doctor thread her needle that she might have been sewing on a button. She gave Cara a shot of novocain meant to last five minutes, but the stitching took five and a half. Douglas held Cara's hand, but how eerie it was, because the hand was not part of her body. Rather, she *had* no body. She was all system, no flesh, all blood rushing this way and that in narrow, endless, humming channels that seemed never to reach her brain. When someone cranked up the head of her bed, it was only like a change in the weather as if after a rain, when the air thins out. Cara thought she might stay that way forever, all effect and no substance, even while the nurse palpated her belly to make sure her uterus was shrinking.

"That's very good," the nurse had commended, as if Cara had anything to do with it. This is not a bad way to be, Cara had thought—buzzing, buzzing—but already it was starting to fade. For a while she was all pins and needles, and then she was only someone lying on a too-small bed in a hospital room. One elbow stuck out past the edge of the mattress, and both feet did, too, when her knees weren't bent. Now the pain was like a ball of yarn unraveling, as if the nurse across the room were drawing it to her to be wrapped up and taken to the neighboring room, where the next woman lay in labor. Cara's room was large and pleasant, with salmon-hued walls and a dense mauve carpet. Over the sink, a mirror reflected Cara propped up on pillows, and she could see the baby there, too, looking more remote than ever. There was the bathroom, which she avoided looking at, and just next to the bed a table with a water pitcher on it. She was reaching for a cup when Douglas said, "I can get you some ginger ale or juice from the hall," startling her because she hadn't seen him in the mirror. He was sitting in the armchair with his newspaper and pencil, solving the Cryptoquip.

"You were asleep," he said.

"No, I wasn't."

He raised his eyebrows.

"Ginger ale," she said, "and a toothbrush, please."

Douglas said he'd help her to the bathroom.

"Never mind," Cara said.

"It's okay. I can walk you."

"It's not that."

"What?"

"It's what I'm supposed to do when I get there. I can't."

"That's okay. You don't have to."

Her feet were bare, and she laid them flat on the floor all at once, just to feel the ground against the soles, before putting any weight on them. In the bathroom she didn't look at the toilet but took a moment to look in the mirror, where she noticed how vivid she looked; how dark her lips, how red her hair, how pale her skin, like an electric Snow White, only her gown had fallen wide open so you could see her pubic hair and the elastic belt around her hips, which held the sanitary pad. It would have to be changed. It was heavy with blood and hung loose between her thighs, and as she took it off she got blood on her fingers and on the toilet seat. She rolled the pad into a ball, wrapped it in a strip of toilet paper, and was dropping it into the garbage when she realized that she didn't have another. She called out of the bathroom to Douglas, but he was getting the ginger ale. Instead there was a nurse in the room, hovering near the bathroom door.

"I don't have any pads," said Cara.

"Did you go?" said the nurse.

"What?"

"Did you go to the bathroom? Have you moved your bowels?"

"I don't have to," said Cara.

The nurse brought in a stack of pads and a squirt bottle, which she filled with warm water at the sink.

"You clean yourself with this," said the nurse, gesturing with the bottle, "and then pat yourself dry with these," holding up a bag of cotton balls.

Cara said nothing. She was in awe of all the blood, as she had been years ago after Georgie was born, when they had made her wash herself with Betadine. Now water was the thing, apparently. It had run down her legs, and when she wiped it, the soaked cotton turned immediately scarlet. No man can ever bleed like this and still be healthy, she thought, but she didn't say it to Douglas when he came in carrying the can of soda. He would think she was insulting him, and maybe she was. She climbed gingerly back up on the bed, then took the straw in her mouth and sipped, concentrating hard until she thought she could feel in her body the very spot from where the blood began to flow, like the start of a river. It was like sun beating down on ice, and the ice clopping off in big chunks that released just a drop, then trickled, then gushed. It was like sitting on hot ice. She was reveling in this when a nurse approached the baby and stood hovering over the cart. The baby was waking, the edges of his blanket beginning to tremble, a high wail escaping. Douglas reached the baby first and brought him to Cara, but the nurse had started taking Cara's temperature. After that there was the blood pressure to be taken again, and the palpating of the uterus, the baby mewing all the while as Douglas rocked him. Cara hadn't put him on the breast yet and thought of letting Douglas feed him with a bottle; they made a snug-looking pair, and she would keep a safe distance and watch them together, today, and maybe tomorrow as well, and maybe the day after. But Douglas put him in her arms before she had a chance to speak. What a shock it was; Max was practically weightless, yet in a moment he managed to find her nipple, all by himself.

"He has a strong suck," Cara said after a while.

Douglas bent close to the nipple and said he could hear the stuff coming out of it; it made a sound like the fizz of champagne.

"I could go buy us some champagne," he said. "But I'd rather stay here if you don't mind."

"I don't mind. I want you to. Can you bring me a couple of pillows? Put your finger in his hand; see how he grabs hold."

"He's really cute."

"He's so small. When's the doctor going to come and look at him? He's tinier than Georgie ever was. And look how dark his hair is."

"So was Georgie's. It'll change."

"He looks like Georgie as a baby. He's so red all over. I wish . . . Oh, look, he's opened his eyes."

"He's looking at you," said Douglas.

"You take him and feed him with a bottle and then he'll look at you," Cara said boldly.

"I'm not worried," said Douglas.

"I am."

"What?"

"I am worried," said Cara.

"Because why?"

"I don't want to say it."

"Don't worry. It'll happen."

"What will?"

"You'll fall in love with him," said Douglas. "Soon enough. You said the same thing with Georgie."

"I'm not just saying it," said Cara.

"I know. I mean the same thing happened. It took a while."

"It's already been an hour!"

"No, it hasn't. It's been five. You're exhausted, Cara. You're too tired to fall in love."

"But what if I don't?"

"You will," said Douglas.

"You will," said the nurse, who had been there all along, stacking towels at the edge of the sink.

The timing of this second labor had been the same as the first; Cara had wakened at three in the morning and given birth at noon. At three-fifteen the first time, she woke up Douglas; now she'd waited until quarter to four.

"How far apart?" Douglas had asked, both times.

"Fifteen minutes."

"What do they feel like?"

"Like fists clenching and unclenching." She got up on one elbow and looked at the clock. "I don't know. Fourteen minutes that time. And they don't really hurt. It's just pressure. It's just a squeeze." She was thinking it was probably false.

"That's what it felt like the last time," said Douglas. "It didn't hurt at the beginning."

"It's premature."

"It's two days before the delivery date," said Douglas.

"I know. But I was planning on being late. Remember?"

"Well, doesn't look like you're going to be late."

"I don't know. I don't think this is it. Fourteen minutes again. Shit."

"Did that hurt?"

"No. Listen."

It was the dog. Whenever anyone woke up in the middle of the night, she woke up, too, and needed to go out. She was sitting at the base of the steps, shaking, tail thumping on the floor. Douglas sighed and climbed out of bed. Cara made a fist and hit the pillow, her way of kicking the dog.

"You'll be okay for a couple of minutes?"

"Sure," Cara said, and then she watched him get dressed in the light from the hall. Half in and half out of it, his nakedness glowed and dissolved, glowed and dissolved. He had a flat, narrow belly and pale, gangly legs, yet a way of stepping gracefully into his jeans, toes pointed, a little wiggle to the hips when he pulled them up. Last night there'd been a party in the park down the street—high school was out for the year—and she knew he'd try to gather up the thrown-around beer cans and then drop them, get mad, give up, then collect them again.

"Don't hurry up," she told him. "Just have a good walk."

The dog yelped excitedly when Douglas started downstairs, and Cara thought she heard their other child stirring in the room across the hall.

Other child, she thought, horrified, already I said *other child*.

There was a window above the headboard of the bed, and when she pulled herself up and looked out, she felt the fist again, sharper than before. She nearly yelled. But she looked at the clock instead. Fourteen minutes, same as always. Not much later, she heard Douglas drop the empty beer cans on the porch outside the door, then kick his sandals off his feet. "There's some water in your bowl," he said reasonably, and the dog tick-ticked to her bowl in the kitchen. Not since the birth of their first child had Cara said even that to Kato. Long ago she used to sing to her, and lie on the floor with her head on the dog's soft ruff while stroking her paws. Now Kato was just an animal needing meager helpings of affection that Cara doled out begrudgingly if she had a little extra. Cara wasn't one of those big-hearted women like the one who lived just down the block. If you knocked on her door it was opened by children and dogs all sizes, shapes, and colors, not one at a time but all at once, ten or eleven of them, crowding the steps and front hall. After visiting there, Cara felt stingy with love. She was worried she would use it up. Pregnant, she kept looking at her son, thinking, what will happen to us? Even then she kept getting lost staring at him. He was already four, already a ponderer, already learning to read, and she needed to examine him in order to know whom he was changing into, so she would love him for who he was now, and not who he had been before. These days he was Bilbo Baggins on his way to Murkwood. Despite the summer heat, he wore Cara's giant fuzzy slippers and a magic ring she had made out of foil. The ring was supposed to make him invisible, so she would pull him onto her lap and pretend she didn't know he was there. "Bilbo! Bilbo Baggins!" she'd call, and set him down in the chair and get up and go from room to room looking for him, from closet to closet, all the while hearing him giggling against the arm of the chair until she came back in and sat down right on top of him saying, "Forget it, I can't find him, he must have gone to Murkwood." Ordinarily he was playful, but once he grew very still and worried there underneath her so that at last she got up and took his head in her hands, exclaiming in an adoring voice, "Oh, you're back, I've found you," taking a risk and calling him not Bilbo but by his name, Georgie. He didn't want to let go. They stayed in the chair as the room glowed with sunset, and let the rice scorch on the stove. She could feel the baby hiccupping inside her in jumps and starts as it did every day at this time. Her son seemed unaware of them. Cara conducted an experiment; she told herself the hiccups were a baby that she needed to love, and she sat there and loved it and felt how much love was left over for her son in her arms. Almost none. It was terrible. When she wanted to start loving Georgie again, she had to stop loving the hiccups.

"I called Georgie our *other child*," she said to Douglas when he'd come upstairs.

"How are you feeling?" he asked.

"I don't know. It's still every fourteen minutes."

"You still think it's fake?"

"No."

He unbuttoned his shirt and in that same graceful, unconscious fashion let it slide from his body. In bed, he put his hand
on her belly so the cool temperature of it was like a balm on top
of the next contraction. She took his hand in her own and
moved it in widening circles around her navel and then up over
her breasts to her neck and chin. She was scared about the labor
because she hadn't read any books this time and had forgotten
the breathing techniques. Throughout this pregnancy—early
on when she was tired, then later when she'd felt so high and
buoyant—Cara had insisted, had believed, that this delivery
wouldn't hurt. But now she knew that it would. She was being
made to prepare herself. It was like some hand reaching in,
grabbing hold of her guts, squeezing hard, withdrawing, only
later it wouldn't withdraw, it would knead and twist, it would dig
in with knuckles and nails.

"That was nine minutes," she said after a while. "They're
getting harder. I think we should call the doctor. I'm taking a
shower. You should wash your hands, they smell like beer."

In the shower she shaved her armpits and her legs although
that was difficult because her belly was in the way and because
she didn't want to be already doubled over when the contraction came. Soon her son padded into the bathroom, unfastened
his drawstring pajamas, stepped to the toilet, peed, climbed up
on his step stool, washed his hands, climbed down to dry them,
climbed up again to get a drink of water out of his cup, all this
with his pajamas down around his ankles.

"You're all grown up," said Cara, who was drying herself
while standing in the tub.

"I know."

"Get Daddy!" said Cara, but Douglas was in the room already
with a pile of clothes that he helped her get into.

"What should I put in the bag?" he said breathlessly.

"Get breakfast for Georgie. Call Deena and tell her to come
by for him. I'll get the bag. I'm okay. I should call my mother,"
said Cara, who when the contraction faded felt cool, organized,
able. She packed her caftan, two books, three pairs of socks,
and the engraved silver hair clip she always meant to wear and

never did because no matter what, it never seemed appropriate. She forgot underpants, a toothbrush, and everything else. The next contraction took the breath out of her and forced her to stand absolutely still as if to acknowledge its presence.

"Okay, okay," Cara said to it, and then, to herself, "If they stay like this I can make it. I can deal with this."

The hospital was just down the street five blocks, and she imagined she and Douglas might stroll it together in their almost-matching sunglasses, arm in arm along the sidewalks, stopping every seven minutes to look at the pigeons on the telephone wires. But then she found she'd put her sandals on and was standing at the door, waiting, her hands on her belly, her bag packed but upstairs where she'd left it. She was like someone trying to stay calm in an air raid. But for the sake of what? It was only going to get worse. When Georgie had kissed her three times good-bye, she made straight for the car without so much as a glance at Deena leading him away. In the car she announced, "I'm not going to do up my seat belt." There was nobody else on the road just then, and Cara had the feeling that everything in the world was being put on hold so that she could have her baby. She felt singled out. The windshield was free of the bird droppings that always fell on it during the night, but she didn't think about her husband having found a minute in their hectic morning to clean it. She only stared at the glittering hood of the car as it brought her closer to the hospital.

"This might not be the real thing," Cara said to the nurse examining her. "They seem to be subsiding. I think if I go home and rest, get in my own bed, read a little or something, clean up a little, do some . . ."

The nurse said that Cara was four centimeters dilated, that it was certainly the real thing, that the baby might hold on till evening, and that if Cara felt she would be more comfortable at home in her own bed or on a lawn chair in the shade, then she could leave the hospital and come back around five.

"What do you think?" said Douglas, in such a way that Cara knew he was thinking of Georgie and of how fast that had happened, faster than the nurses had predicted.

"I don't know," said Cara. "Why don't I sit down a minute and we can wait a while and get my breath and see how things go, and if I'm okay for a while we'll go. You can make lemonade."

There was an armchair recliner in the corner of the room, big and sturdy-looking with just the right amount of yield when she put her weight in it. Just as she relaxed there was a contraction long and painful, not like the ones before it.

"This is a really bad one," Cara said, and no sooner had she said it then she felt something pop and then a gush of fluid. Cara was astonished, but the nurse was unconcerned.

"Well then. You better go to Admitting," she said to Douglas before mopping it up, then changing Cara's gown. "Here. You're okay. But it will speed things up if you walk around a little."

"I don't need to speed things up," said Cara.

"It distracts you a little, if you walk around."

The nurse fitted some paper slippers onto Cara's feet, then took her arm and led her slowly out into the ward. It had been a busy weekend, so the ward was nearly full. The nurse led Cara to the window of the nursery, where together they looked in at the babies, all sleeping except for one, who stared back through the glass.

"I'll take that one," said Cara. "Oh, no."

"Just relax. Breathe deep. Look at me." The nurse took a long breath, then let it out just as slowly.

Cara inhaled, her eyes on the nurse's eyes, her arm linked through the nurse's arm. When it was over she could remember from the other delivery this same childlike awe she felt for the nurses, who looked wise and even lovely in their white costumes, and whose sensible calm was their greatest virtue along with the fact that they all seemed to know precisely how much it hurt. They never made apologies or told you to be brave or said it would be over soon if it wasn't going to be. They said things like, *Let me know if you think you're about to faint,* or if you urinated on the delivery table, *Don't worry about that, that's nothing compared to what's coming.* They never showed worry or impatience, and they might at any minute walk straight up to you and stick a thermometer under your tongue in such a way that you didn't even flinch. Then there you'd be with the thermometer in your mouth while a second nurse began taking your blood pressure and a third cranked the headrest one notch higher. They were like Gypsies, Cara thought as she lay there among them; one of them could pick your pocket in a second. Except the gown didn't have any pockets. It was white with black medallions, so soft and loose she barely noticed it was there, which was fine because then she didn't notice so much when it wasn't. Twice it had slipped off her shoulders, and now as she lay on the delivery bed, it fell open over her breasts. She didn't know for how long she had been lying on the bed, knees up, head raised, Douglas stroking her arm the way she liked during foreplay, shoulder to wrist with just the barest touch of his fingernails. The contractions were back-to-back with no more than a minute between them in which to drink a little water and tell him to keep doing what he was doing, although she knew very well he would keep doing it anyway. Another thing she said, when she had the time, was, "You don't have any idea what this is like."

"You're right," said Douglas. "But I can imagine."

"No, you can't imagine," said Cara.

"We called the doctor," said one of the nurses. "She said she needed to do a few things and then she'd be on her way over to check up on you. Hang in there."

"A few things!" said Cara.

"Shhh," said the nurse. "Breathe. Good. Slow. Slow. That baby won't be out for another two hours."

"Yes, it will," said Cara.

"You're doing fine," said Douglas.

"I'm doing terribly," said Cara.

"You'll forget about it when it's over," said one of the nurses, which was as close as they ever came to downplaying the pain. Serene as glass, Cara thought reproachfully, looking at the nurse. It was a challenge.

At once she yelled, "I'm pushing!" and gripped the edges of the mattress.

"No pushing!" said the nurse and Douglas at once.

"I have to," said Cara.

"You won't."

"I'm going to!" she yelled. She had to. If she didn't she would split apart. Rather, the thing that had become her would split apart. For it was no longer her body. It was hers and the baby's together. The two of them were like a padlock trying to get itself open. And there wasn't a key. They were steel. The nurse had taken hold of Cara's wrists and was staring her straight in the eyes saying, "No, you *will not push. It is not time to push.*"

"It *is* time to push," Cara protested, knowing all the while that she wouldn't push, that if she did, she would split apart, just as surely and horribly as she would split apart if she *didn't* push, so that the only thing to do was scream at the nurse and thrash at her husband and so keep herself locked in this noisy limbo between not-pushing and pushing, between pushing and not-pushing, between splitting apart and splitting apart again.

The nurse was no longer serene; that battle was won, anyway.

Near eleven-thirty the doctor came, tugging on some gloves and whipping her hair up into a cap. Then she was between Cara's knees, pushing them gently apart while gazing firmly and sympathetically at Cara's face. Cara screamed, "I can't do it!" and then, "I want drugs, I want drugs, I want drugs. Douglas, I want drugs," turning victoriously toward him as if he were the reason she hadn't said anything about drugs in the first place. He wasn't. Cara had had no thought of drugs, ever, during either this pregnancy or the last, and the very idea of drugs now was so amazing and so surprisingly, unexpectedly welcome that she nearly burst out laughing in the middle of her screams.

"Demerol!" she cried, "Demerol, Demerol, Demerol," while Douglas raised his eyebrows at the doctor. The doctor frowned. She pulled her hand out of Cara, then stood up and called for a gown.

"Not quite," she said, and then something that Cara didn't hear because Cara was screaming again at the words *not quite.* Not quite *what?* she wanted to know, screaming and screaming, in the back of her mind still thinking about the breathing that had worked a bit with Georgie's delivery and that had seemed,

for a while, to be working with this one except that the screaming seemed more responsible, somehow. It was like being hit by
a train; you didn't lie there deep-breathing if you'd had your
legs run over, did you? No, you screamed, and everybody
accepted it, and if you didn't they'd be begging you to do it.

"I want Demerol!" she yelled, "I can't do it! I'm pushing!" and
then something happened, at least Cara thought that it happened, although she couldn't quite believe it. That is, the
doctor did or didn't place the tip of her index finger directly and
purposefully on Cara's clitoris creating such a shock of pleasure,
like a slap in the face of the pain, that Cara quit screaming all at
once for the second that it lasted and locked eyes with the
doctor in a gaze so intense that between them it made a
tightrope that the baby might walk across from one to the
other. Then the doctor said, "Okay, Cara, you can push."

"*I* have to tell you all that I screamed," Cara confessed to her
friends during visiting hours that evening. Elizabeth had
opened a box of chocolates, and they were passing it around.

"You're excused."

"You look beautiful."

"You're glowing. Your hair, it's like a halo, and your face is so
pale. Translucent, practically."

"I mean I didn't just shout. I *screamed*. The breathing didn't
work, or else I didn't want to be bothered. I couldn't help it. I
wasn't even embarrassed."

"Oh, they don't care."

"They're used to it."

"Did you have an episiotomy?"

"I tore, and then I had an episiotomy."

"I've never heard of anyone who hasn't had an episiotomy,
personally."

"Oh, I have."

"Really, Cara, he's so beautiful. He was the only one in the
nursery who wasn't asleep."

"He was the only one who wasn't crying."

"He was the only one who really seemed to know what was
going on."

46

Her friends all laughed giddily. Cara laughed, too, but she knew that her friends didn't understand quite how loudly and persistently she had screamed during the labor. That was okay, only she didn't know if she should be ashamed or not. Maybe just a little. From down the hall where that other woman was in labor came screams more guttural than Cara's but with that same shocked pulse as if every second of pain were somehow unexpected. Cara could hear through the wall the way the moaning reached a pitch and then tabled out, and then the other moments when the woman began arguing as if with the pain itself, with the clutching, tearing hand, saying, "Oh no, oh no, oh no." How perplexing it was, to be listening like this, and to be sympathizing but not feeling, as she had before, that sympathetic, agonized contraction. For a moment, for the third or fourth time that evening, she considered describing for her friends what the doctor had done, or what the doctor hadn't done although it felt like she did it. Cara could swear that she did it. But then again . . . it was unbelievable. Wasn't it? One of her friends would believe it, one of them wouldn't, the third would be entirely skeptical. And Cara didn't feel up to a debate about it or an analysis of why, since the doctor was a woman, the gesture was magnificent, but had the doctor been a man, it would have been obscene. She was happy being chattered at and admired. She got nervous when the nurse came in announcing visiting hours were over, because that meant she would get the baby back. Visiting hours he had to stay in the nursery, the rest of the time he could stay with her. Not that she wasn't impatient for him. She was, for his tiny soft warmth right up against her through the thin cotton of the gown, and for his strange smell so similar to the smell of sex. But she wasn't in love with him yet, at all. In fact, after Douglas went home to eat supper with Georgie, Cara fully resigned herself to the notion of not ever really loving this child but getting simple comfort from his smell and proximity. "I'll be a good mother to him," she supposed. He'd never know. No one ever would. She'd stroke him, nurse him, teach him, show him. But not as she did with Georgie. Never in a whirlwind of need and sensation. Inside her would be only patience, and fortitude, and this same, resigned magnanimity.

Cara's bed was equipped with padded metal armrests that could be pulled up on either side of the mattress or dropped down. Cara had pulled both of them up. She'd asked the nurse for extra pillows to be propped against the armrests, although their bulk made it harder to get in and out of bed. Indeed, when the baby awakened needing to be held, she had to pull herself down to the foot of the mattress before sliding off the edge of it, her stitches tugging at her crotch, and when she'd picked the baby up gently and carried him back to the bed, she found it impossible to pull herself back up the length of the mattress while holding onto him. But if she put the baby down at the top of the bed and then shimmied up after, she'd have to swivel around and pick him up without falling on top of him first or knocking off the pillows, and then she'd be stuck halfway up and half down, anyway. It all seemed so impossible. And the baby was wailing. Down she sat in the armchair to nurse him, hoping that one of the nurses would come take him away from her so she could get back into bed. But the nurse didn't come. Through the wall, Cara heard the heavy, angry panting of the woman in labor, but the sound left her curiously empty and unimpressed by anything but her own after-pains spreading over her inch by inch. She began to cry, purposefully at first and then helplessly so her tears fell on the baby's arm and slid under the loose plastic of the bracelet printed with his name.

Max, Cara read, in a moment of lucidity.

"Look at me, Max," she instructed.

But the baby didn't look. Instead he grunted, squeezed his eyes shut, and defecated. The stuff filled his diaper then oozed like tar into the folds of his blanket and onto Cara's arm. When at that moment Douglas walked into the room, Cara held the baby out to him with every bit of strength saying, "Here. This was a mistake. This was a terrible mistake."

Wide awake at last, the baby gazed at Douglas, who explained to him who and where he was and how he got there.

"Your name is Max, " said Douglas. "You have a brother, who isn't here right now. And a dog. This is a room in the hospital. Your mother did all of the work, and that's why she's so exhausted and disoriented that she forgot how to get back in bed."

"I didn't forget how to get back in bed. I told you that. I just can't get back in bed when I'm holding him because I won't be able to grab hold of the armrests and pull myself up without splitting myself open, Douglas. I want the doctor. Oh, God I haven't talked to my mother."

"Cara, I've never heard of a single woman splitting open from having a baby. I'll stay with him, you go take a sitz bath. You remember how good it felt last time."

"I know," said Cara, chastised, because this was the first time since she'd gone into labor that Douglas appeared to find it safe to infuse, into his usual measure of tenderness, his smaller dose of sarcasm. She got out of the chair, then climbed slowly, ever so slowly, onto the bed, knee by knee, hand over hand, like someone climbing onto an inflated raft in a swimming pool. "That hurt," she said, just as the nurse came in with a fluted paper cup. Cara downed her medication before reaching out her arms for the baby. Holding him, she found that the head of the bed was too high, so she gave the baby back, lowered the bed, then took him into her arms again. He was cross-eyed. If Cara moved an index finger back and forth above his upturned face, one eye stayed put while the other tried to follow, lagging behind and then skipping ahead. Gradually he closed his eyes and was asleep in such a way that he appeared to be just hovering on the surface of his own unformed consciousness. Cara watched him awhile, aware of her own eyes closing and of Douglas getting up out of the armchair, kissing both her and the baby, shutting the light, and leaving for home.

"Douglas," she said.

"What?"

A pause.

"When can I see Georgie?"

"Tomorrow at lunch, I'll bring him," he answered.

"Douglas."

"Yes."

"Another pause.

"I'm still not in love with him."

"Just go to sleep, Cara."

"Good night."

"Good night."

"Good night, Max," said Cara, relieved that the room was not totally dark, that there was still a dim light over the sink and a little from the hallway through the half-closed door. Then she slept, too. First she felt the pleasant warm weight of the baby on top of her, but soon she was spinning in a dizzy fatigue that made their two bodies seem to clasp each other equally as if falling together through space.

At three o'clock that morning, when the nurse came for Max to check his heartbeat and temperature, Cara wouldn't give him up from his place against her under the blankets. There was a sleepy tug-of-war before the nurse finally took hold of Cara's fingers and gently but forcibly dislodged them from their hold on the baby. "Go back to sleep," she said. "When I'm finished with him I'll bring him back all clean and diapered and you can wake up and nurse him. He's due for a feeding. When did you feed him last?"

"Eleven," Cara guessed.

"How long on each side?"

"Five minutes," Cara answered, although in fact she had no idea. The nurses insisted on five minutes per breast and that you had to rub lanolin onto the nipples to keep them from cracking.

"Have you been using the lanolin?" asked the nurse.

"Yes," said Cara. She hadn't at all, but now she found it in its tube on her night table, next to the ginger ale. It smelled like sheep in a barn, and when the baby was brought back for nursing, he first nibbled at the breast experimentally, licking and tasting. Then when he tried latching on, he slipped off, over and over again. It's like getting a rocky start on sex, Cara thought, before they finally settled into a good rhythm. At last he sucked firmly and hungrily. The nurse told her to please put the baby back in his bassinet after feeding and not to sleep like that with him lying against her chest, and Cara nodded gamely but knew she'd keep him with her. For one thing, in order to put him back in his bassinet she'd have to climb out of bed again, and then, once out, she knew she would have to go to the bathroom. If she stayed put, she'd be able to hold it in. For how long she couldn't calculate. She might talk to the doctor about it. She was wondering about this when the baby stopped sucking and lifted his face openly toward hers as if to say, *Here I am*. He was utterly, unfathomably calm.

*T*hroughout the very early part of the second day, the nurses kept bustling in to ask if she was alright and occasionally to take the baby away from her. Each time before giving him back they took pains to make some comment about the soaps and shampoos and lotions in the basket in the bathroom, but by nine in the morning they had stopped coming in so much. Cara ate breakfast while the baby observed blissfully and then blankly and then thoughtfully every move of her hand as it traveled from plate to mouth.

"This is orange juice," she explained. "This is a muffin. I'm taking a bite."

Max lay in a thin kimono on a pillow on her lap, and she imagined that to remain like this and watch him drifting in and out of awareness would be enough for the rest of the day if she didn't need to learn how to bathe him. She'd forgotten how to do it. There were parts of him—his umbilicus, for one, his fresh circumcision—that seemed too vulnerable even to be looked at. Also, his breathing was somewhat uneven: one-two, one-two, giving way all at once to a speedy vibration or else stopping altogether for two or three seconds during which Cara placed the palm of her hand on his rib cage and waited, patiently. In the mirror across the room she watched herself unmoving under the blanket—knees up, hair brilliant and uncombed, one shoulder unclothed. Then one arm snaked out and found the silver hair clip on the table near the bed. She swept her hair into a knot and clipped it in place, then undid the knot and refastened the clip behind an ear. It looked romantic either way, but in the end she took it out and laid it back on the table with care. Her eyes were bright, her face was pale, she wore a coy, cool, secretive smile. She hadn't mentioned to the nurses that her baby stopped breathing occasionally. Simply, there was no way to say it without making it sound horrible when really there was something delicate and necessary about it, as if it were his way of coming to grips with the fact that he was now, whether he liked it or not, part of the world.

Just before noon, the nurse drifted in and asked hopefully if Cara had moved her bowels.

"I haven't had to," Cara lied.

"It would be a good idea. You don't want to get constipated. We might give you an enema in an hour or so if nothing happens, before the doctor shows up. Are you planning on having a shower before your husband comes?"

Cara said no, thank you, she was perfectly comfortable.

"I'll change the linens, then," continued the nurse, who held a stack of fresh sheets already in her hand, white as could be, and a thin yellow blanket.

"Oh, really, don't bother," said Cara, sliding deeper into the bed until she no longer could look past her knees to the mirror. The nurse, making a face, dropped the clean sheets onto the armchair and, before turning to go, pulled open the blinds on a window revealing a damp-looking courtyard with nothing in it. Only then did Cara begin to wonder, and to notice the smell. She'd grown accustomed to it, sitting in the middle of it for so long; in fact, it had become rather interesting in the way certain wild animal smells are interesting if you can be objective about them. Cara sat for a while just taking it in before she noticed the strange texture of the sheets underneath her, which were sodden and crusty at once, while between her thighs the big sanitary pad felt as dense as a sausage. Looking under the blanket, she could see that the pad was black all through but no blacker than the sheets she'd been sitting on. Everything was saturated with blood, and everything smelled. Even a corner of the blanket was stiff with blood, while the hems of the pillowcases propped here and there were soaked through as well with a fresher, redder color. The only thing not stained was her ill-fitting gown, which had ridden up completely over her hips. Now she pressed a corner of it gingerly between her thighs, and having satisfied herself that the blood was thick and crimson, she held the baby desperately, kissing him and kissing him.

KILLER

*L*ater that same morning while Cara slept and Georgie was at Deena's and the nurses were busy completing charts at their desk or fussing in the nursery over the baths and feeding schedules of the other newborns, Douglas rocked gently in the chair in the birthing room, explaining to the baby's restless eyes and ever-changeable mouth the rules of Killer. Max was snug in his arms. Killer was a game that Douglas had played years ago while living briefly in London before the onslaught of video games, when darts was still the rage in all the pubs. Killer was big in the pub he hung out in, so he had played it nearly every night for weeks, but now it was hard work remembering, dredging up its complexities. The game was best played with at least four players, each of whom was assigned a sector of the dart board depending on where the dart struck when they threw with their bad hands, and then everyone started with no lives but had to end up with three or more, or else started with many lives and had to end up with none, depending on which version of the game was being played that night. But if you earned three lives, Douglas vaguely recalled, then you became a killer who by entering other sectors could steal an opponent's life, or two or three of their lives, depending on whether you'd thrown a double or a triple. That was pretty much all he came up with— all words and no instinct, so that he couldn't be sure whether if he were to find himself suddenly in the same pub with three people and the same pocked, peeling dart board, he would know what to do. The proprietor of the pub was a tall Irishman named Jim Bourke, who prided himself not on darts or even on liquor but on the skeins of dulcimer and fiddle that spun away from the speakers all night among the rows of dark bottles, a sound mournful and pure. The pub was tiny and sepia-colored, with a map of Dunedin on one wall on which Jim had pasted a photo of another pub for which he was homesick. Douglas blew into Max's ear while he told him this, letting his lips roam over the warm peach of the baby's skull then down past the opposite ear to the fold of flannel papoose that the nurses had fashioned so quickly and mysteriously out of a rectangle of blanket. What he remembered most clearly about those pub weeks in London was that he ended each night with either one life or six, depending on which version he had very nearly won, and that he often went home afterwards with a woman named Francine, who played better than he did even though she was drunker than all the other players put together. Francine was in her fifties, bony and small with a voice like a young man's, scratchy with beer. Years later, remembering, Douglas still admires the flexibility of her drunkenness; the way she barely managed to stay upright on her barstool, but then, when it was her turn to play, the way she sobered up at once for the time it took to kill. She was the same way in bed, or on the couch, to be exact, he confessed to the curled tunnel of Max's fist. They always went to her flat, up flight after flight of a stairway so dark they couldn't see each other, past the mildew-smelling bathroom in the hall outside her door. Inside, she bypassed the bedroom by pushing him drunkenly into a lopsided coffee table. The couch was pilled and harsh to the touch of bare flesh, and the rug underneath it was worn through in spots to the floor. Pulling open a corner of Max's flannel wrapping, Douglas put his lips to the baby's sternum and described how the messy spectacle of Francine's drunkenness turned sharp and nearly technical the second he pulled off his blue jeans. Her mouth was a tight, moist pucker, and her blow job a delicate, suspenseful affair sustained by the precise, yellowed edges of her tiny teeth; each time, holding back, not allowing himself to thrust past the sharp limits of Francine's control, Douglas was surprised by the way such apologetic nibbling seemed to swallow him up. She neither wanted nor expected any pleasure in return, and when he flipped them both over and slid down the short length of her body until his face was flush with hers, he could see that she was drunk again, as drunk as if his semen were another mug of beer, her mouth slack, her eyes half-closed, half-drowned under watery pools. The last time, as he was climbing off of her, she slid from the couch and landed *thump* on the rug, then pulled herself up on both elbows and said distinctly, "Lost lives cannot be won back," before fading out again. That was one of the rules of Killer, but the fact that she'd said it at that moment made Douglas wish that he could fall in love with her at least for the night. He was twenty-four years old and willing to imagine that because he was in London, he might fall in love with squalor as long as it was squalid enough. The bedroom door began to beckon from the other side of the couch; perhaps behind it Francine kept hidden some secret—whips, he imagined, or a trembling, transvestite lover dressed in wet-look polyester— that would inspire him to tell Francine about the girl who had the heart attack and died. He hoped she might have something wise to say about that distant, troubling episode, or even something funny. When she was safe asleep, her snores a soft murmur, he put his hand on the bedroom door, which swung easily, silently open. Inside he found a cluster of creamy, beige throw pillows on a bed made up neatly under a circle of light from a reading lamp. The room was spotless, chaste, and private; there was a vase of dried flowers and a book of nature poems marked with a ribbon. He was shocked and ashamed. Humiliated. He got out of there fast, nearly tripping on the sleeve of her drooled-on herringbone coat.

The baby drooled, too, he tells Estaban in the copter much later that day, having told him nearly everything else as well— the thrill of Francine's sober teeth on his body, the rules of Killer, the baby's scary, pink color, but no mention of the girl who had a heart attack in bed—but the baby's spit was sweet and milky and translucent as pearls. Douglas felt himself dissolve into the sheen of it. He was floating in a halo, he says to Estaban; he and the baby were the halo above the sleeping, indifferent Cara. Cara did look angelic. Transformed. Her awful blood-stiff sheets had been replaced, and she had finally taken a shower when no one was around, having waited just long enough that the nurses stopped mentioning it. From the bathroom drifted a steamy scent of soap and shampoo, and from Cara the perfume of a fresh, laundered gown. Douglas wondered why the laundry at home never smelled this good. At home their clean sheets never had an aroma at all, while here in the hospital the pillows rose under the touch like bread in an oven. He sat rocking in the middle of the comfort of it, watching Cara's detached-looking face, then the baby's ever-fickle, ever-searching expressions, then Cara's remote one again. Asleep, eyebrows raised in a dream, Cara seemed to be gazing past a horizon. "At this moment in time I am the only person in the world who truly loves you, Max," Douglas said, and then regretted having said it, and then said it once more in order to convince himself that the baby didn't understand a word of it, and that Cara, asleep, couldn't hear it. The baby smiled the kind of smile the nurses fondly called *gas*, then stuck his finger up one tiny whorl of a nostril and started whimpering. Douglas pulled the finger free, kissed it, tasted salt, and whispered, "There." Max drew a deep breath and screwed up his face until his lips turned purple. Douglas put the finger in Max's mouth. Max began to howl. Douglas replaced Max's finger with one of his own, felt the clamp and frantic suck of Max's hunger just below his first knuckle, sank into the rhythm of it like someone pulled by a current, allowed himself to drift, would have drifted right over the howl of Max's anger if Cara hadn't wakened and said drowsily, "You can go to the nurses' station and they'll give you a bottle of formula. I thought we had one here but we don't." But simultaneously she was reaching for the baby, her gown open at the breast, the breast lavender with the first of her milk, the nipple luminous. She took the baby in her lap, he quieted and sucked, the room hummed with the pulse of his sucking like the spin of a miniature planet. Douglas was dizzy with awe. Cara raised her knees, then lowered them, the baby settled in her lap, the sheets fell away from it over her opened thighs. Already—it was the most amazing thing, he says to Estaban—her stomach was back to what he knew he would eventually think of as *normal*. Gone, vanished, was the pouch of the pregnancy; she must have willed it away, till in its place was but a ripple of softened flesh and a changed sinuosity in the valley between hip and belly. The skin was satiny smooth, and he could see himself fitting his whole face among the curves of it some morning in the future when he would know them all by heart. He could see that her hips hadn't broadened with this second pregnancy the way they had with the first, and that her shoulders and back were as graceful as ever. Her butt was heavier; that would go away. But the belly would stay changed, and so would the new crease between her eyebrows that had deepened during labor, and so would that new, barely noticeable tremor in her lips as if they were always caught somewhere between kissing and frustration. He believed he could see into the future, looking at Cara. He could see a future moment when he would know her changed body as intimately as he had known it before.

The nurse came in with two bowls of Jell-O, one lemon, one lime, as Cara had requested. She was scared of what she called "real food." Lunch would arrive later on—cranberry juice, a turkey sandwich that Cara wouldn't eat, a third dish of Jell-O that she would eat, no coffee, of course. When the nurse left the room with a handful of curled flower petals swept from under a vase on the table, Cara said insistently, "He's the sweetest baby I ever saw in my life."

"Except for Georgie," corrected Douglas.

"Except for Georgie," repeated Cara with a mischievous smile.

"So it's okay, then," Douglas said.

"What is?" said Cara.

"What you were worried about."

"What was I worried about?"

"Forget it," Douglas said, because he knew she would deny

she'd ever said it. But then he said it anyway, testing his knowledge of her. "About not being able to love Max," he said.

"I never said that."

"Oh, yes, you did."

"But not really," said Cara.

"But yes really," said Douglas. "Unless you mean you didn't say it once. You didn't. You said it seven times."

He actually had counted, in preparation for this moment. Cara seemed unimpressed. Douglas was exasperated, but that was one of the things that the people who loved her loved most about her, he tells Estaban—the way she exasperates.

"You're so gullible," she said. "Where's Georgie?"

"At Deena's."

She didn't ask about Kato, the dog. Which was just as well because Kato was still tied to her tree outside in the drizzle. Douglas had let her out before six in the morning, then left the house having forgotten to bring her in. Her ass would be soaked, her paws, the pinkish edges of her ears, but she wouldn't be crying, not yet, she'd be thumping her tail in that nervous way she had of wondering if they had forgotten her, if she'd be out there dripping rainwater forever. Either that or she would have escaped, snaked out of her collar, taken off along the mud-puddled sidewalks, stopping now and then to tease an earthworm with her nose. He'd be late for work if he had to go looking, but that was okay, because he'd already missed what there was to miss, a spill of laundry detergent on Route 2 at I-90. That had happened early yesterday while Cara was in labor. A convergence of fire trucks, attempting to hose the road down, had created a dune-scape of eye-watering lather high enough to ski on. They had to call in the snowplows to shovel it up. When the wind blew, bits of froth pulled loose and somersaulted airily over the pavement, and then the whole dune rolled over like a whitecap, and then the rain came in and they had to close the road, which was too bubbly to see, too slick to walk on. All in all, from their place in the copter, Jenny and Estaban had waxed too poetic for Douglas's taste; this, too, he admits to Estaban, apologetically, of course. No matter what, he doesn't regret having missed all that soap. How could he? Had Cara not been giving birth, had Douglas not been with her at the hospital but doing traffic instead, then the spill would not have happened at all. This was a fact, and Jenny made sure that the whole city knew it, going on and on about it in her bighearted way. Years ago on the day before Douglas took the job, when it was only Estaban and another announcer in the copter, two teenage girls drove their Buick the wrong way down an exit ramp, killing themselves and three other people, and that was the last, Jenny said, the last rush hour traffic worth crying about. "I have the newspaper here to prove it," is what she said, joking, crackling some papers, snapping some paper over the mike as if she were settling down to read right there in the copter, although of course she didn't have the clipping, she couldn't possibly have. " 'Parents and classmates of Ulli Gerchak and Rhonda Mil'—let me see—'gathered together on the sun-drenched lawns of—The two girls were shopping for a carpet for the new student lounge to—said Rhonda's brother, James Mil—' I'll tell you it was a shock to find this newspaper clipping in my files, because I can never find anything in my files. No. But anyway these girls died, these two beautifully ordinary girls. Think of them just for a minute. Think of what they'd be doing right now. Maybe one of them a mother, maybe one of them a doctor, maybe one of them a mother *and* a doctor or a secretary like you or a newscaster like me. Except that Douglas wasn't there. Douglas wasn't in the sky, and that's the tragedy left out of this newspaper clipping, that's the accident, here. One day and he would have been up there, one day and they wouldn't have died. I don't know. Call me sentimental. I am. I admit it. Call me crazy. No one ever said I wasn't. Call me anything, but don't get in your car unless Douglas is up in the air. I don't," Jenny finally concluded, just a little tongue-in-cheek, just a little embarrassed by her certainty that it was true. And maybe it was, and maybe it wasn't, but anyway it was creepy when it wasn't boring, Douglas thought, switching off the radio. He didn't let himself out of the car quite yet, he just sat there and breathed, watching sunlight glint on the wet hospital roof. Cara had not reached transition yet. He'd run out of the birthing room for a soda, then down the hall past the nurses' station and out of the building to the car, to learn what havoc his absence had caused the morning's commuters. Soap suds. A blizzard of citrus-scented *cleaner, brighter* highway. The thought of it made him perversely happy, as did the notion of sitting here in the hospital parking lot while Cara gave birth to . . . it occurred to him then that if he weren't in the delivery room when it happened, Cara might give birth to something unspeakable. A monster. An idiot. Triplets. Or that something might go wrong—the birth might be breech, the neck wrapped in the umbilical cord, the baby's genderless feet turning bluer and bluer as the doctor urged Cara on. Before he knew it he was out of the car, urging himself to stay calm, to cross calmly and reasonably the expanse of the parking lot so that anybody watching wouldn't think something was wrong and then their thinking make it so. *I am not superstitious*, he said to himself, but the parking lot was huge, suddenly, and when he reached the glass doors, he was sure they would be locked. When he reached the maternity ward, he was sure they would have rushed her to another wing in the hospital. When he reached the delivery room, he was sure they would be frantic, all of them, the doctor, the nurses, Cara especially, for his return. He would say he had been on the phone with her mother, he would close the door gently behind him, take his place at the edge of the bed, *be an angel.* If you're an angel, you have to know it, Estaban's mother had said. He didn't know what this meant, exactly. He thought maybe it had something to do with reverence. With feeling awe. Yes.

Except they hadn't noticed he was gone, Douglas tells Estaban.

Both men are wearing their earphones; Douglas's lips just barely brush against the mouthpiece that is like an invitation, that seems to want him to go on talking recklessly forever. He had promised himself he would open up to Estaban, but he hadn't known when it would happen, or exactly what he might say. Even now he can't be absolutely sure of what he's saying, because the boundary seems blurred, if there's a boundary at all, between thinking and speech, between tongue and memory. Just speak and remember, remember and speak, the ribbons of memory furling, unfurling, alive on his tongue so it's all necessarily convoluted, fragmented, unexpected, true as can be. He's not used to convolutions; he doesn't do them on the radio, he's surprised by how fun they can be, how rewarding. They're like trails in a forest; just choose one and follow. One of the nurses was taking Cara's blood pressure while the other fiddled with some implements on a cart in the corner of the room, he says into the mouthpiece, to Estaban. Cara was between contractions, looking anxious, but no more anxious than she had before. That was what she was waiting for, the next contraction, not for Douglas. The sphygmomanometer sighed as the dial spun round, and then the nurse pulled it free and hung it businesslike on a rack. The funny thing about this room was that its blend of home and hospital should be so reassuring. Despite the odd, high-necked curve of the spigot over the sink, it looked serene and oddly lived-in; some snapshots of babies up on the wall, the blanket folded on the armchair, a wall clock softly ticking. The Rose Room, it was called. Across the hall was the Blue Room, identical except for its blue walls and carpet and the fact that, for now, it was empty. The Rose Room might as well have been entirely empty, too, for all the attention they gave Douglas when he walked into it. They hadn't missed him for a second. But there was more to it than that, to the feeling he had, that he couldn't quite fathom. The dim blush of the room, the light sifting pink through the curtains, the drifting sound of nurses' footsteps and the murmurous hum of their voices—all bestowed on Cara's bed the air of a sanctified region, like a temple, almost, that could be cranked up and folded back and wheeled to and fro but never violated, never quite touched, never entered. There was Cara on top of it, sublime in her pain, and Douglas below, of no consequence. "Useless. Utterly," he tells Estaban. He might stroke her arm from elbow to wrist with the tips of all five fingers the way she liked during foreplay, but this wasn't foreplay, she didn't shiver or sigh, and if she moaned, it had nothing to do with him, or with the washcloth he held now and then to her lips. That washcloth, he confesses to Estaban, the way it wetted her lips, made her look, of all things, so sexy. A sheen of water came away on his hand when he brushed his knuckles across her mouth. He sucked it onto his tongue, and swallowed it.

When the nurse measured Cara's cervix at eight centimeters dilated, Douglas began transition-breathing. He meant to keep Cara company, to guide her, to help her remember. One two three four and a long, drawn-out five, he demonstrated, then put the washcloth to his own forehead and closed his own eyes. He had this notion that if Cara were to shut her eyes, too, then maybe the wild look would go out of them. One two three four fiiive, he repeated. When he opened his eyes he could see that Cara had locked eyes with one of the nurses and that she wasn't breathing the way he was at all, her breath came furious and ragged and through it she was swearing at him to keep the fucking handkerchief away from her. He didn't tell her it was a washcloth, not a handkerchief, or that he'd only meant to clear the sweat from her eyebrows. He took it over to the sink, wrung it out although it wasn't dripping, folded it over the curve of the spigot, and looked up to see Cara in the mirror, on the other side of what seemed an impassable distance. How detached she looked, how unreachable, framed in the mirror's reflection along with the stray hand of one of the nurses that had found its way into the mirror the way the arms and legs of strangers find their way into the photographs you take when you're a tourist. He felt dizzy in the ankles, as unsure of himself as if he'd glanced down during a tournament and seen his own shoe inching over the toe-line. Sometimes, playing darts, his feet cheated on their own, toe by toe. Now he wondered if they might carry him right out of the room. But then the doctor blew in with her unbuttoned lab coat wafting around in the breeze she made, and positioned herself efficiently between Cara's knees. When Douglas stepped to the side he could see the baby crowning and then a jagged line of scarlet where Cara's skin began to tear between vagina and anus, and then a sudden straight edge of scarlet where the doctor took a scalpel and finished it off.

Douglas cried out.

The nurse flashed him an unpleasant look.

Cara appeared not to feel the cut at all.

*E*staban, when Douglas tells him how he'd witnessed the baby's head get sucked back in and swallowed up again, grips the controls of the helicopter tight, then aims the bird into the sun, which has just then emerged from behind a sheen of clouds. Estaban's playing; he takes his playing very seriously, as every pilot does. The sun's rays fan across the windshield from a bright spot in the center that turns black when Douglas looks at it too long. When Douglas tells him the baby's name—Max, not Maximilian—Estaban swings the copter low over the park, then up again, then down nearly to the tops of some sycamore trees. Such discreet, playful sympathy is precisely what Douglas might have expected of Estaban, who is subtle, indirect, and respectful of the fact that Douglas has never talked like this before. Instead of talking in return, he lets the copter respond. There are bike trails down below, the copter follows them around. Today is their last day up in the air. The station hierarchy has been in flux; both Estaban and Douglas, it appears, are suddenly in charge. Even Estaban agrees that the thought of the two of them taking off every morning and evening to tell private jokes about the lake while scanning the city's traffic for anything worthy of comment is not a great way to go about revitalizing the shows. Besides, there've been too many accidents lately all over the world—too many medivacs, too many traffic copters down. So they're taking it slow, relaxing. They've done their evening report, now they're drifting, heading back. They've got plenty of time. Jenny's at the station doing her new show, "Eerie." A pun. She does have a disturbing ear, Jenny. Who else could mix carnival music with audio clips from Nintendo games and come up with something sounding like the Roches singing "The Star-Spangled Banner"? That's the point of her show, to guess what she's synthesizing. Whoever guesses gets two free passes to Peabody's Down Under. Last week she did the echoes in a gymnasium where a bunch of people were shooting baskets—the squeak of the court shoes, the sudden tunneled exclamations, the resonant whisper and thump of the ball—it was mesmerizing. Nobody guessed it. The angle of the mike, and Jenny's genius for mixing, made it sound far too creepy to be something so ordinary. One caller guessed Gregorian chants and another guessed it was what you'd hear through a stethoscope if you were listening to the lungs of a patient with pneumonia.

"I'm not saying I wouldn't do it over again," Douglas goes on. "But you have to be prepared. To feel like a prop. The daddy. The husband. The coach she doesn't listen to. The nurses know it. The doctor, too. She let me cut the umbilical cord, I felt like a little kid, so grateful, so ridiculous, like when you open a door and the kid says, 'No, I want to do it,' so you shut the door just so the kid can open it himself. They humor you. Still . . . Cara has a friend who saves her umbilicals. Umbilici? They turn brittle and dry, little flat bloody dry corkscrews. She keeps them wrapped in tissue in a box with the child's name on it. When the kid turns twenty-one, they get it back. That's the kind of ritual, the kind of crap, actually, that makes me turn cynical without wanting to."

Estaban grins.

"I have nothing against umbilici," Douglas goes on. "And I can see where another person might get philosophical about them."

Estaban cracks a smile.

"Severing the tie," says Douglas, enjoying himself. "Baby and womb, baby and mother. Apron strings. No. But it amazed me to touch it. It was like slippery rope, but it was warm. Somehow I hadn't thought it would be warm. It was actually steaming. I saw it. Steam."

The copter is headed for landing. For a moment Douglas wonders if he's going too far, saying too much, scaring Estaban off. Douglas knows he's not good yet at this business of opening up, he hasn't had enough practice, it seems entirely plausible to him that what he's saying sounds crass, shallow, stripped of emotion. The thought makes him nervous—all that love, all that fear, all that hope, gone to waste. It's like sap in a tree, rushing this way and that, sticky and sharp. Overwhelming. Maybe he should shut up. Or should he say this, too, to Estaban? Admit his discomfort, apologize, then go on talking? And he's forgotten the dog, again. When he drove into work, straight from the hospital, he never stopped at the house as he'd planned. She's still tied to her tree in the moist, steaming grass. Nothing to drink or eat but grass. She could vomit to death out there, he says to Estaban. If she were dead, he would miss her. Odd, but had he not been talking, he would not have thought of that. Surely people who make a habit of talking make a habit of this kind of knowledge as well. They talk, then they know. When they say it, it's real. Touchable. It's not like talking on the radio, talking like this. Until now he viewed talk as one of his radio skills, a talent for filling time, for inventing entertainment, for asking of interviewees the kinds of straightforward questions that paradoxically inspire elaborate answers. On the radio he talks as a way of buying time to keep quiet. Now it startles him to hear his real life becoming words, sentences. Kato might have escaped, snaked out of her collar, trotted off to McDonald's to hunt in the trash near the dumpster, got hit by a car. Dead. He would grieve. He loves that damn animal. He had thought he was only loyal; now he knows that he loves her because she is part of his life with Cara. What else has he missed out on knowing in all these years of not-saying? He can only imagine.

This, too, he says to Estaban, his words unfolding around the velvety disc of the mouthpiece just after the helicopter touches down. It's an apt phrase, *touch down*, for such a gentle, muted gesture, the tarmac all at once humming underneath them while the thump of the propeller begins to slow. Douglas wonders if he'll get nostalgic about flying. Estaban will. But Estaban only looks puzzled, shrugging, removing his headphones, letting them drop around his neck. At once, Douglas hears the music drifting out of them, if you can call it that. Music. Jenny's show.

Estaban's been listening to "Eerie." It takes Douglas just a moment to realize that if Estaban has been listening to "Eerie," then he, Douglas, has been talking all this time to the atmosphere. To no one. To a coil of wires and plastics. The sound from the earphones is tinny and intense; the two men sit motionless in the clinking, fading crossfire of it until Estaban asks, "So, what is this? You always seem to get Jenny's stuff figured out."

"It's a duel," says Douglas evenly, unblinking. "A fencing match. You know. Swords."

He climbs out of the copter, ducks his head, follows Estaban's black flight jacket into the building and down the rubberized stairway to Jenny's office, which smells familiarly of stale coffee and just-misted Boston ferns. Jenny is wearing her purple eyeglasses today, the ones she wears when she is trying to be in a good mood even though her boyfriend just did something awful. The tape she'd doctored for her show *was* of fencing, she tells them; Douglas is right, as usual. She shakes her head; her earrings are blinking holograms of Janis Joplin's open mouth. Jenny flashes her *Why can't every man be like Douglas?* smile, while Estaban gives Douglas a slap on the back that nearly knocks him off his feet.

A
FACE IN
AIR

1 ⚹

*E*ighteen months later, Cara was pregnant again.

The funny thing was that she suspected it as early as she did, just barely into the pregnancy, before her period was due, on the eighteenth of January on a cold, clear day, the icicles bright, the grass bristly but damp, the children out on the sidewalks with boxes of chalk. Georgie was out there with some of his friends. He was lying on his back, spread-eagled, flat on a slab of cold limestone. Another child hunkered over him and outlined him in chalk, starting with the mitten of one hand. It was an odd place to start, Cara thought to herself. She was watching from the window. Max was in her arms, and he wanted to go out, too. He was banging on the window and laughing delightedly.

"Shhh," Cara said.

A body doesn't start at the hand, she thought, unless you are a child, and then it can start anywhere you want it to. A body starts at the belly, she thought, and then she went to the phone and dialed Douglas at the radio station.

"Did I have my period last month?" she very nearly asked the secretary who answered the phone. When Douglas came on she said, "Suddenly I can't remember my period last month. Whether I had it or not, I mean."

"You had it," said Douglas. In the background she could make out one of the broadcasts, a call-in show, she guessed, from the impatient, bantering tone of the exchange.

"I can't remember it."

"You had it."

"I did?"

"Yes."

A week went by before she called him up again to say she wasn't feeling right. They often had these kinds of talks on the telephone, when Georgie wouldn't hear and Max was calm in her arms and not so distracted by the welcome sight of his father. On the phone, Cara and Douglas could be private and alone, just the two of them with the humming space between. Sometimes they focused as much on that silence as on what was being said, as if, ear to ear, they might absorb each other's thoughts.

"What's the matter?" asked Douglas.

"Nothing's the matter. I don't mean I feel wrong. I just mean I don't feel *right*. For this time of month, I'm talking about. I feel good. *Too* good. I feel perfectly healthy. But I don't feel anything beginning to come on."

"Wait a while," said Douglas.

That Sunday evening, when Cara was walking the dog, she stopped at a store she often went to on the farmost edge of the square, a bakery, really, that had groceries, too, amid shelves of sundries. In the window were giant trays of jelly beans, and on the scale near the door was a dial that spun to your personality type. Cara had stood on it once, but it told her the wrong thing. It said she was generous to a fault.

"*Something* to a fault, maybe, but not generous," Cara had joked.

"Honest to a fault," said Douglas behind her.

"Honest with myself, anyway," Cara said.

The cashier there knew her. He was a teenage boy, Hispanic, good-looking and especially attentive to Cara. He always knew that she wanted one dollar and twenty-five cents worth of milk chocolate, and that sometimes she bought sweets for her husband and children and sometimes she didn't, and he knew that it was her dog leashed to the bike rack outside, nosing under the legs of the sidewalk tables even in winter, when nobody ate out there. He knew that she often paid in pennies, one hundred and twenty-five pennies exactly, and he remembered a joke she once told, that she was buying the chocolate only to get rid of all the pennies she and Douglas had collected for years in a jar. He knew that she walked over a mile to get there and a mile back and that that's why the chocolate didn't make her get fat, and that sometimes she bit off a piece of chocolate for the dog and sometimes she didn't. He didn't know how much she didn't like the dog, and he didn't know she sometimes smoked cigarettes, maybe a pack every month and a half, because when she bought them, she never bought them there. She was careful to buy them at places where nobody knew her.

But tonight she was planning on buying a home pregnancy test, and it amused her to think of him ringing it up and not saying a word about it even though he always chatted with her at the register, cupping his hands exaggeratedly for her flood of small change. He'd put the test in a bag even though he knew she never wanted a bag, but he would meet her eye as usual when she said good night.

Except there wasn't a home pregnancy test anywhere on the shelves, not even low down with the tampons where you wouldn't see it unless you were looking for it, and not on top with the baby things, either, the nipples and the bottle brushes. Cara was incensed.

"So wholesome and puritanical and so goddamn all-American they think you go from tampons to nipple brushes with nothing in between," she said much later to her friends. "And it's not as if there are any other stores open that late at night, without having to drive out to Drug Mart."

She drove calmly, though, despite a great sense of purpose, which she muted when she got there by choosing other things first—hair conditioner, a pack of razor cartridges, a new toothbrush for Georgie and on reflection a smaller toothbrush for Max as well, his very first, with a picture of Winnie the Pooh drifting skyward on a bunch of balloons. The home pregnancy tests were in back on some shelves beneath the pharmacy counter, along with the racks of condoms and the douches and other things you were supposed to feel conspicuous about buying. There were several varieties of pregnancy tests, and she knew she would be a long time choosing, reading each and every label to see if she could find one that did not require first-morning-urine. She couldn't, which was too bad, because she didn't want to have to wait that long. First-morning-urine meant any urine collected after five hours of sleep, so she thought she'd drive home, climb into bed, and tell Douglas to wake her at two in the morning. She wondered if you really had to have been asleep for it to count, or if being in bed without eating or drinking was enough, and she wondered what happened to the women who were so worried about being pregnant that they couldn't fall asleep at all. It interested Cara that rather than having imagined women who were too *excited* about being pregnant to fall asleep, she had imagined women who were too *worried* to fall asleep, but she decided that this did not mean that she was worried rather than excited. She didn't know which she was. She was as excited about being worried as she was worried about being excited, she finally said to Douglas, which caused him to raise his eyebrows. Douglas didn't want another baby, ever. And neither did Cara. They'd discussed it several times in light of some people they knew who were having a third, and there was never any question. Two was enough. Two, in fact, was perfect for the way that they wanted to live, and they were living that way now. One pair of arms for each child, and then, when the children were occupied or asleep, four arms between the two of them unless one of them needed to be alone, and then they always could be, or almost always, anyway. Time together, time apart. Last summer they drove long distance, grandparent to grandparent, uncle to aunt, and in the car it seemed to Cara that their foursome made a tiny, sealed universe on wheels, not counting the dog, of course, who lay amid stuffed toys beneath the window of the hatchback, on top of the duffels and bags. To Cara their little world seemed as secure as the corners of a square; herself in the driver's seat, and Douglas nearby, and behind them the children buckled in place, asleep, or listening to tapes, or one or both of them crying, wailing, even, with misery and heat and boredom, it didn't matter in the scheme of things because of the comforting shape they made traveling through space, together. And then when they stopped the car for food or the night, Cara got out of the car and opened Max's door to get Max, and Douglas climbed out of the car and opened Georgie's door to get Georgie, and then while Douglas and Georgie played ball on the lawn of the motel or wherever they could find a strip of suitable grass, Cara carried the baby to the shade, where she changed him and fed him, so that before the general aggravation of dinner or bed there was always this moment of order and peace and pastoral sensibility. Or if not one moment, several. On either side of the highway was the distant sweep of farmland—cornfields, grazing pasture, wheat fields—above which the highway exit with its strip of restaurants and gas stations seemed lofty and high. Sometimes if the motel had a swimming pool, they went behind the chain link fence and along the bristly indoor-outdoor carpet and pulled off their sandals and sneakers and socks and let their naked feet dangle in the turquoise water. Eight feet, forty toes, and Cara always took care of her own feet first and the children's after, because she thought of what the flight assistants said during the safety demonstrations on airplanes, that when the oxygen masks dropped, you were always to fasten your own mask first and your child's mask after, which seemed callous until Cara realized why it had to be that way, and then it seemed a good rule for just about anything.

"It's for sanity," she told herself, "I have to keep sane, if I'm going to keep them sane. And I have to get comfortable, if I'm going to get them comfortable. And I have to be happy, if I'm going to make them happy."

And then she breathed deeply the smell of the warm asphalt parking lot and listened to the noise of the traffic in the distance and of the other parked families unloading their cars, until against such anonymity her own family seemed luminously independent, its four parts bound by the force of its singular motion, except for the dog, who would need to be let out of the car, of course, and allowed to wander for a while beyond the well-kept lawn into the unruly grass, where always found some evidence of *something*—something that smelled bad, or something that looked like it shouldn't be eaten even by a dog, or even a whole other dog that, having been led to the car, looked dazed to be free of the thistles and weeds. Even one dog was too much, Cara thought, shooing the new one off to the dumpster, and there was never any doubt about *that*.

The test Cara bought was an e.p.t. Stick, chosen finally from among the shelves of other tests because it contained the least amount of disposable plastic. At least that's why she told herself she chose it, but when she got it home and examined it she recognized it as the same kit she had used more than two years earlier to see if she was pregnant with Max. At the time, she and Douglas had been trying just two months to conceive, and Cara was two and a half weeks late, and the little kit held so much sudden, easy promise that she'd found herself drifting now and then into the bathroom only to gaze at its array on the counter—the vial, the test tube, the white stick gleaming in moonlight. It was this memory that she blamed for her present state of contentment—not worried after all, and not excited or impatient any longer, but strangely, calmly objective. Tonight she slept deeply and undisturbed, curled protectively in a circle around her belly, sure and maternal. And in the morning, in place of the trepidation she had expected, she was so relaxed upon uncorking the little vial that she nearly flooded it with urine, ignoring the instructions that at the last moment Douglas pointed out to her. Five drops of urine, read the instructions, and then cork it, and shake it, and uncork it, and slide the stick in, and wait.

And when ten minutes had passed, the very end of the stick was pink, just as Cara had known it would be, a sight that shocked her so much she could barely get her breath to say to Douglas, "It's pink," even though he was standing right behind her staring at its pinkness over her shoulder.

After that they turned the tap on and held the stick under the cool running water, and when it still was pink they turned the hot tap on, too, and let it stay under that for a while, and when it still was pink they read the instructions again to make sure they had it right.

Then Douglas said, "Well, what are you going to do?" and Cara said, "I wonder if there are any people out there dumb enough to think that if it's pink that means they're going to have a girl."

After that she walked Georgie to the bus stop for school, with Max in the stroller and the dog on the leash, and all the while she wanted more than anything to be at home in her seat near the telephone in the kitchen, to let it all sink in.

But Max didn't want to go home right away. Max wanted to climb up and down the set of brick steps that led to the walkway of one of the houses on Forest Street, the same steps he wanted to climb every day, the same house whose owner came running out, yelling and gesticulating every time the dog so much as squatted on the grass, no matter what time of day or night it was, as if he sat there all day just waiting for a dog he could scream at. Still, the owner never seemed to get upset about Max on his steps, up and down, up and down, and when, one day, Max yanked a loose brick out of the steps and Cara froze with her eye on the front door, nothing happened. Today she tied the dog to the stroller, and set the stroller squarely in the middle of the sidewalk with its back wheels locked, and then sat herself down on the lowest of the three brick steps, her face in the morning sun. On the sidewalk was a newspaper wrapped in orange plastic through which she could just read the headlines, something about medicaid, and something about Lithuania. Cara didn't know where Lithuania was, exactly, up near Eastern Europe or closer to Armenia, or maybe in Siberia, but certainly in the U.S.S.R., that much she did know. Also that there was revolution and that it might or might not succeed, and that it might or might not have something to do with what was going on in Armenia, where the violence was ethnic as well as political. She didn't wish to know more, but still she was chagrined and a little ashamed by what she considered to be her sympathetic but hazy understanding of the rest of the world, which she couldn't help but think of as throngs of people, masses of humanity in kerchiefs and mustaches, waiting in line for food, or shaking their fists at someone on a podium, or else she thought of people nearly starving in a desert, but always in clusters the way you saw them on the news—legs, arms, bellies, pairs of eyes, pairs of slack, depleted breasts. In spite of her better intentions, in spite of trying, really *trying*, Cara found it nearly impossible to imagine any one of these people, separate from the rest, going through life and having the same kinds of hopes and regrets that she had.

Sometimes it surprised her to look around herself and see the utter peace and quiet of her surroundings, as if things really *shouldn't* be that way, as if there shouldn't be people like herself who went through life untouched by disaster or grief or even hard times. She felt blessed, and at the same time, blameless. She couldn't help being lucky. It wasn't something she sought after any more than it was something she had earned. But she tried, at least, to deserve it. She and Douglas sent money to all the right places, and never griped about taxes except for defense, and never never drove drunk, and used cloth diapers, not disposable, and recycled all of their glassware and plastic and paper and aluminum, and turned off the lights when they left a room. They didn't eat a lot of meat, and they shopped with the aid of a booklet called *Shopping for a Better World: A Quick and Easy Guide to Socially Responsible Supermarket Shopping*, although Cara *had* begun to buy grapes again after all these years, because the thought of never eating another grape . . . and the thought of her two children never tasting a grape, and there were those new grapes now, so crisp on the outside, so wet and explosive with sweetness on the inside. . . . "So anyway I'm not perfect," she said to herself, and she still didn't know how she felt about capital punishment. She only knew that if anyone laid a hand on one of her children, she'd slit his throat.

And now here she sat on the step in the sun, where, having named for herself all her deeds and contributions, she was pleased to find that she didn't feel smug, no, she felt only gentle and felicitous except for a tight spot in the palm of one hand, which had clenched up when she thought about capital punishment and having to slit somebody's throat. If there were days when she doubted herself, when she told herself her good deeds were nothing more than insurance to protect her family from the bad things that happened to everyone else's, then there were good days, too, when good intentions seemed enough. She was thinking about this when who should walk by but the director of one of the private, grade-school-level "academies," a woman who included personal notes along with Cara's invitational brochures, brochures that Cara always skimmed then threw away because the word *academy* irked her and because she and Douglas were committed to the public schools even if they were falling apart. Well, not falling apart, but threatening to. Still, from a distance Cara admired this woman, who had a certain starched earthiness, neat as a Pilgrim. Even now, rushing, obviously late for work, her briefcase bumping against her leg, she gave Cara one of her usual looks—gracious but remote, kind, and at the same time somewhat censorious. Cara had spoken to her a couple of times, once about a family of barred owls that appeared to be roosting in the neighborhood, and another time about a book they had both been reading. This morning, when they said hello, and when the woman took a precious second to pause and play with Max, Cara wanted very much to tell her she was pregnant. After all, there had been the usual hellos and how-are-yous, and when someone asked you how you were and you were pregnant, it seemed almost a lie not to tell them so. But Cara only said she felt good, with a sly, triumphant smile that the other woman seemed to take note of. Then, when the woman hurried off, Cara followed at a distance with Max in the stroller, and by the time she reached home, she felt unrestrainedly proud. She phoned Douglas at once, but he was in a meeting, so instead she phoned one of her friends from what they called Group, a bunch of women who made a point of getting together every month or so and hashing things out.

"Can you talk?" Cara said.

Simple as it was, this was a signal. It meant there was something important that needed to be discussed, privately, one-on-one for the time being anyway.

"I'll be over in a minute," said Wendy.

"We'll have coffee," said Cara, who, having hung up the phone, felt headstrong and a little manipulative, having chosen to phone among her friends not only one of the few who worked at home but the one most patient, circumspect, and least likely to tamper with what Cara knew in advance would be her own monologue, a monologue consisting of the very thoughts, ideas, and feelings that had been churning since morning underneath her repose. She just wanted to speak them aloud, in order to know more precisely what they were, and she wanted somebody who would sympathize and not interrupt, and who would deliver her most provocative insights with decency and restraint, and who would form no hasty judgments, and who would take care of Max while Cara was talking, who would pick him up and bounce him on her knee and let him play with the buckles of her overalls or else give him his bottle or make funny faces so that Cara wouldn't be distracted. Someone who while neither adding to nor subtracting from the sum total of Cara's feelings would merely help her arrange them in the most sensible, pleasing, comforting way.

Wendy was a fabric artist, a sculptor. She arrived at Cara's carrying her basket of materials, from which she pulled, when she sat down with the coffee on the bed in the playroom, where Max was stacking blocks, a single broad heart-shaped leaf of green velvet, a needle, and a spool of blue thread. She bit off a length of thread, threaded the needle, and began tracing in neat, minute stitches the veins of the leaf. Cara could see the rise and dip of the needle reflected in the lenses of Wendy's big eyeglasses, along with the patient, listening attitude of Wendy's posture. Purple thread would be better than blue, Cara couldn't help thinking. Secretly she didn't like Wendy's work; the colors were unbalanced, the compositions unwieldy and too confessional. But Wendy was a trusted listener, overweight and unexcitable. Cara often hoped, when she was talking to Wendy, that what they said to each other might somehow find its way into the cloth and improve the design of the sculpture.

"I'm pregnant," Cara began.

Wendy pulled a tin box out of her basket, opened it, chose from its contents a tiny white natural pearl bead, strung it over the needle and onto the thread, then sewed it—a dewdrop? a teardrop?—onto the leaf. Then her hand with the needle kept stitching but her eyeglasses flashed a question, just as Cara had expected they would.

"I don't know," said Cara. "I don't know, I don't know, I don't know. The thing is," she added after a moment, "it's such a surprise. Not the pregnancy, Douglas and I are so goddamn fertile, but still you never let yourself expect it to happen, that's for sure, but that's not the surprise I'm thinking about. The surprise is how happy I am to be pregnant, and how protective I feel, and how secure in this pregnancy, and how proud of it I am. I'm more proud of this pregnancy than when I was pregnant with Max, when I first found out. When I was pregnant with Max, I was scared. As soon as I knew he was coming, I didn't know if I had it in me to be a mother to anyone other than Georgie, I thought I'd love Georgie more, I thought I'd be torn. But I wasn't, you know? Not for more than a day, maybe, a day of kidding myself that I was. And now there's this rush of elation and joy and serenity. . . . You know how, some days, you're at peace with your body, and some days you're not? At least that's how it is with me."

Wendy nodded. "Like that," she said, pointing her needle at Max, who lay on his back with his legs in the air like a dog waiting for its belly to be scratched.

"Right," Cara said. "There are times when your body fits perfectly, and other times it feels like an accessory you have to lug around. And today I feel at home in it. I feel proprietary."

Wendy nodded again and sipped her coffee, and ran her thumb back and forth over the velvet of the leaf and the hard lumpy gleam of the pearl, and told Cara that since she herself had never been pregnant, she didn't know exactly how it felt, but that she thought she could imagine. She told Cara she looked different than usual. "More settled," she said.

"That bloom that pregnant women are supposed to get, well, I don't usually buy that, but you have it. Except, yours looks kind of pained, somehow," Wendy continued.

"I think that's part of the bloom ordinarily," Cara said. "The pain of it. Because it's not easy to find yourself loving another person all of a sudden, or facing the prospect of having a whole person in your house who you'll respect, and who you'll need, and who you'll worry about."

"And who'll need you," Wendy said.

"Right," said Cara. "And now we get to the meat of things."

Wendy grinned. Max padded over, took a sip of Wendy's coffee that Wendy held out on a teaspoon, and shook his head vigorously no.

"Because I don't know if I want another child," Cara said. "Or, to be exact, I *did* know two days ago that I *didn't* want another child. And now, today, I *do* know that I *don't* want another child, but at the same time I want *this* child."

"You do want this child . . ."

"I want *this* child. I don't want this *child*."

They both laughed because it made sense, and because Wendy understood so absolutely.

"Three children is a lot," Wendy said.

"Three children is too much," Cara said, laughing. "Not to mention three pregnancies, although, like I said, sometimes pregnancy feels so good, so stupidly high-and-mighty, but I don't want to talk about that right now, because it's too dangerous. I mean, the thought of not being pregnant right now feels like emptiness to me. I'd be a void. I'd be hollow. And if I really feel that way, which I do, at least I think I do, then that means I might as well get pregnant for the rest of my life, over and over again. I could have twenty kids and be happy. And I don't want to be happy like that. I'd rather be happy like this, the way I am now. And who can say what it would do to my life, to our lives, to have even one more. Besides, you know, I'm not one of those women with endless patience. I'm not one of those motherly types—"

"You're the best mother I know," Wendy interrupted.

Cara blushed. She knew she was a good mother, and it gave her great pleasure to hear it. "But I don't know if I would be a good mother of three. I have a temper, you know. I lose it sometimes. With Max I thought I could handle it, and it turned out to be pretty much the way I expected, and just recently everything's started getting back to normal, we're on an even keel, you know? Everything's under control."

Wendy nodded.

"And with this one I just can't imagine. I can't even begin to imagine."

"Max might still be in diapers," said Wendy.

"Probably. He would be two and a half, or something, and Georgie would be six. No. Yes. Six, in first grade already. And I was just starting to think about maybe changing jobs; well, I mean just starting to think about thinking about it, because there are times when I'm restless where I am, you know?"

Wendy raised her coffee in salute.

"You?" Cara said. "You're restless?"

"No," Wendy said. "But sometimes it seems like I should be, that's all. Think about it. You do a construction, and it's really great, and if it's really great, someone buys it and hangs it on their wall and you never see it again. And then you sew another construction, and then you sew another, like breathing."

"Well, I envy you, and people like you," said Cara, "having something you love to do. Every time I come to your house you're sitting on the same couch sewing some person or other and I think how I'd like to be sitting on my couch sewing a person when somebody visits me."

Wendy frowned.

"I mean not that I think it's so easy. No. Not that I think your life is easy, that's not what I'm saying," said Cara.

"What are you saying?"

"That I don't have a chance to think," said Cara. "That if I have a free moment I have to choose between thinking and doing, because if I try to do both at once I get lost in the middle and then Max wakes up and I've accomplished nothing. Nothing. So I usually choose the doing, because it's better to get no thinking done than no doing done, and somebody has to do all the stuff around here."

"I have days when I feel like I've accomplished nothing, too," said Wendy.

"Yeah, but that's because you need a break every once in a while, to sort things out, to get things organized. Half my life's a break and still I never get things organized."

"Yes, you do."

"No, I don't."

"You seem pretty organized to me. And sometimes I envy you, too, you know."

"I know," said Cara. "Smile, Max."

Max bared his teeth and lifted his chin as high as it would go. That was his way of smiling on command. He did it for photos and on the street when people stopped to admire him, whenever Cara said, "Smile, Max."

"Now dance, Max," said Cara.

Max threw two blocks on the floor, then picked them up and stacked them on the windowsill.

"Anyway, I thought you were pretty busy at the office," said Wendy, "doing those seminars and things."

"And things," said Cara, getting up for a fresh cup of coffee. "But it's not really work anymore. It's too easy. Like you said, I'm busy. It's busywork, not real. And it's only part-time, which is okay for now, but later . . . I need to counsel myself. I need to tell myself what to do with the rest of my life."

It was a big joke among Cara and her friends that even though she'd spent eight years as director of Career Counseling and Placement in the vocational office at the Community Center, she "didn't know what to do" with her life.

"It's *choice anxiety*," Cara liked to say. "Too many options all laid out in front of me. All the prerequisites, all the requirements, all that endless apparatus."

By apparatus she meant the tests and questionnaires and computer programs people played around with in order to figure out what kinds of jobs would best suit them. Cara, amused, had filled out nothing, answered nothing, figured out nothing, in all these years. When Georgie was born, she took a leave, thinking she might never go back. But then she did go back. And after Maxie was born, she put him in day care, too, and went back half-time. And though she never stopped caring about her work or her clients, sometimes she wished that she would. For it was so exasperating, so frustrating, to care, especially about the most discouraging cases, like Betty. Not that Betty cared, herself, whether Cara cared about her or not. Betty was shrewd and indifferent. Cara was to meet with Betty today, actually, for the eleventh time, exactly. Betty needed to take a test, whether she liked it or not. For months she'd been coming to Cara needing a job, but Cara had begun to despair. Betty had no skills, for one thing, and for another, she kept turning down the few offers Cara managed to arrange. Then, when she *did* find work for Betty, running errands for a printer, Betty failed to show up after only a week, claiming loyalty to her unhappy brother, Sam, and to her own bruised ego.

"We need something more interesting," Betty had insisted. "Sam and I, we're not suited for this."

We, Cara had thought, amused, bewildered, shuffling papers at a loss.

In the meantime, Sam and Betty got by. They went to lectures, to readings, to performances, to gallery openings, to open houses, to anything, in fact, that was free and that included spreads of food. They lived on cookies, wine and cheese, raw broccoli slathered with dip. They went to all the happy hours, too, Cara had been told. They were the local eccentrics, indigent but refined. In Cara's eyes this way of living suited them fine, and she imagined a revised Strong Inventory Test that would include a category of employment like Sam and Betty's—Resourceful Intellectual, it might even be called. They claimed to be brother and sister, they seemed to live in their car, they were fifty and fifty-five years old, they were crazy. They were nervous and defensive about Betty taking the test, because they thought it would get them listed on an FBI file. They wore matching knitted caps. Betty's fitted like a helmet, and Sam's floated on top of his Einstein hair. Betty was small and obnoxious, and Sam was big and shy. Together they were smart, eye-catching, unreliable, uncooperative, argumentative, awkward, and thus far, unemployable.

"I might quit altogether," said Cara to Wendy, "and then, when this baby is born, and when it turns two or three, and when I'm ready, I'll go back to my office and beg them to test me and find me a new career. And I won't take just anything, either. I'll be picky, like Betty and Sam."

"In three years you'll be thirty-six," Wendy said wistfully, "and you'll have had three children, and you'll be starting a whole new life, and in three years I'll be thirty-five, and I'll have sewn eighteen more people, as you say, and if I'm lucky maybe I'll be in love with someone again, although I doubt it, and if I'm really lucky maybe it will be a man, although I doubt that even more. You know, it's ludicrous to me, it's really ludicrous, sometimes, that of all the billions of people in the world, each of us should be expected to fall in love with just one of them. But it's even more ludicrous to me that I can't. But anyway, maybe somehow I'll decide to have a kid, and then when I'm forty with a baby, your kids will be grown and you'll have your freedom, and when I come to visit, you'll be sitting on the couch with a book, or whatever, and when you come to visit me, I'll be changing diapers. Little hand-quilted diapers with appliquéd shit. I'll be the one who'll be crazy."

"So you think I'm going to have this baby," said Cara.

"Why? Oh. I said three children, didn't I. I don't know," Wendy answered.

"I don't know, either. . . . Do you think I should? The really funny thing is that there are so many people out there who would tell me what to do, right off the bat, so if I really didn't want to have to make up my mind, I could walk up to someone in the street, at random, someone I've never seen before in my life and will never see again, and they'd think nothing of it, they'd just throw their damn politics right in my face, as if they knew better than I did, as if they live with me in *my* body. Imagine that. Someone telling you what you have to do with your body, someone telling you you have to sit in a chair for nine months and not move, or carry a heavy box around for nine months and not put it down, and someone telling you you've got to start making milk again, and having breast abscesses and swollen ankles and cramping fingers, and then telling you you have to hold another baby in your arms for another two years and fall in love with it and do it all over again—that kind of thing, it's so horrifying, but it's funny, too, it's hilarious, that there are people out there who would tell me that. So let's play a game. You pretend you're one of those people, and tell me what to do. I begged Douglas to do that this morning, but he wouldn't."

"I won't, either. I'm not one of those people," said Wendy with a frown and a sad glance at Max in which Cara discerned, however faint and unspoken, Wendy's revulsion at the very idea of abortion. But was Cara reading this correctly? She didn't quite want to know. Instead she said, "Thank God. Because I hate those people. I hate their damn stupid guts. That's almost a good enough reason just to have an abortion right there. Just to throw it in their faces. But I won't let them do *that* to me, either. I don't understand this. I already feel bonded. It's the strangest, strongest feeling. It doesn't even have a name and already I'm so in love with it I could die. It's such a joke. How did I get pregnant, anyway?"

"I don't know. How did you?"

"Diaphragm," said Cara.

And later she phoned another friend, oddly enough another Wendy, but an academic one, a beautiful, scholarly, philosophical one, from the Netherlands, who would say something that Cara couldn't predict, who would catch her a little off guard. What Cara hoped was that this other Wendy's very learned remark, whatever it was, would make Cara say something, by way of reply, that Cara hadn't expected to say and, in fact,

hadn't even thought of. Talking, she reasoned, was like thinking out loud; if she talked long enough, she would know what
to do.

"And I'm really happy with my life right now," she was saying
to this other Wendy, who was at work but who was able, always,
to stop, and listen, and give of herself. "I mean finally I feel I'm
getting on an even keel, and work's going fine, and everything's
under control. But to think of all the changes a new baby would
bring, that I wouldn't know about until they happened, that
could change my life completely, forever . . ."

"But your life might change forever tomorrow anyway," said
Wendy, in her beautiful, deep, airy voice. "Or today. It might
change when you walk out the door. Anything could happen.
You never know, Cara."

"It already has changed," said Cara. "No matter what I do, my
life will be changed forever. Either I'll complicate my future, or
I'll complicate my past. Either my life will be chaos, or I'll grieve
for this baby. I'll have a *regret*, suddenly. I'll be a person with
regrets. Because I would grieve for this baby, you know," she
added, surprising herself just as she'd suspected she would.

"Oh, Cara," said Wendy.

"I know," Cara said. "Goddamn, fucking diaphragm."

"I got pregnant on my IUD," sighed Wendy.

A little later, at work, when Betty was as usual ten minutes late
for their meeting and Cara sat in her office, waiting, gazing at
the photographs she kept on her desk, it occurred to her just
what Wendy must have meant.

"Your life might change when you walk out the door," Wendy
had said, but what she meant was that someone could die.
Douglas or one of the children.

And if one of the children died, thought Cara, then she
would need to have a third, because one child wasn't enough.
Because she had learned to live with two. Simply, her capacity
for loving had accommodated itself to two, and the house was
big enough for two, and her arms were big enough for two, and
too big for anything less than two.

So she might as well have the third one now, she thought to herself.

Just in case.

"I know it's neurotic," Cara said to another friend, Elizabeth, a legal aid attorney whose office was several doors down from Cara's. Cara had stepped out into the hallway and seen her at the water fountain. The two of them did most of their talking like this, in the hallway at odd moments between clients and conferences. "But so what if it is neurotic? Big deal if it doesn't make sense. Do you understand what I'm talking about?"

Elizabeth had two children of her own. Seven years ago, while nursing the second, she'd conceived a third. She'd been rooming with a midwife, who performed a saline abortion using a giant syringe. To open Elizabeth's cervix, the midwife had plugged it with a wad of seaweed. The plug had swelled overnight, and in the morning the cervix was open.

"In retrospect, it seems like a stupid thing to have done," Elizabeth told Cara. "In my own home, on my own bed, the risk of infection . . . I could have gone to a clinic, but she did it for free. And it actually worked. That's something I still can't believe. But we were hip, and that's what we were doing. Strange, stupid things."

"But what I was saying," pressed Cara, "about having three children so you'd always know at least you'd have two . . . Do you ever wonder what you'd do if anything happened to one of them?"

"I'd die," said Elizabeth, stepping over to the alcove and pressing buttons on the junk food machine to see if anything would fall out. Once, something actually had, and now they made a habit of seeing if it might happen again.

"I'd die, too," said Cara. "And then I'd need to have another. Do you think you would, too? Have another, I mean?"

"I couldn't even if I wanted. I've had my tubes tied," Elizabeth answered gently. "You should know that, Cara. We've already talked about that, a couple of times."

And it was true, Cara realized, embarrassed, just as Betty showed up in the hallway. They had.

✈

Just over six hours had passed since the e.p.t. Stick had turned pink, but Cara felt she'd done six days of talking. Not that talking, for Cara, was anything new, but at this pace and this intensity it felt like a workout, like aerobic exercise, something to shape up the heart. But Cara's heart only ached. The thing was, all this talking had begun to seem reflexive, like a habit. It reminded her of times in public restrooms when she'd heard other women talking about things you wouldn't think people talked about in public at all. Although of course women did, and each time Cara heard them, she felt a grateful sense of belonging. Once, at a dance concert, during intermission, she'd heard an older woman talking about her bladder problem to someone who might have been her daughter, and once, in a restaurant restroom, she'd heard two women discussing what sounded like a case of cervical warts. Women talked about their bodies, Cara decided, as if the talking was *doing*, and as if the listening was *doing*, too. But really it wasn't. Talking was talking. Listening was listening. In the end, you talked in order to get the talking out of the way, so that when the things that needed to be said had been said, and when the things that needed to be heard had been heard, at last you could go on with your life and go forward, and do what needed to be done.

It was when she was thinking about this, when she was saying to herself, *Okay, enough already. Okay, shut up already,* that Douglas phoned her from the station. He said he had some time and that he wanted to talk, but that he didn't want to talk on the phone as usual, he wanted them to be together, and that if Cara could get a sitter after work and drive in to the station, then they could order a pizza for dinner and sit there munching on it like old times.

Later, driving in toward the station, Cara felt vaguely that she had betrayed him somehow. All that time she'd spent talking, he'd been busy at work with his show—the last-minute edits, the quick consultations with Jenny, the too-patient instructions to the fat technicians—while nursing in silence his own qualms and worries, trying to make some fragile sense of them before he called.

Talking with Douglas was different from talking with her friends. It never felt random, unchecked, desperate, or impulsive, for no matter how mixed-up she felt, no matter how tangled her words and expressions, there was always Douglas, who knew what he thought, and stuck to it, and who without coercion or force let her know what it was, so she could weigh it, consider it, accommodate it, maybe.

In this she knew she was lucky, as she was lucky in so much else. For one thing, Douglas didn't talk to so many people, except on the air. He was careful with words, economical with emotions, but he trusted Cara as she trusted him. Also, he *mattered*, and there was no way around it, even if Cara wished sometimes that there were. Therefore, talking with Douglas didn't feel so hypothetical as it did with her friends. In a way, talking with Douglas did feel like *doing*.

So to Douglas, Cara said, "For now I just want to listen. So just tell me things. Just tell me what you've been thinking, okay? But one thing first. One thing I have to say. Maybe I've been a mother too long. Maybe I'm turning sentimental. Already I love this baby. I'm so happy to be pregnant, I can't help it, I had no idea I'd ever feel this way, Douglas."

"It's not easy," said Douglas.

"Go on," said Cara. "Just tell me what you've been thinking."

They weren't sitting at his desk, which was really just one in a trio of cubicles in a narrow, rather chaotic room full of phones and word processors, and they weren't sitting in the conference room, where Douglas had intended they would sit, on one of the couches overcrowded with big embroidered pillows. The conference room was in use. Eldridge Cleaver, in town to promote his new cookbook, was in there eating dinner with the station director in preparation for his stint on the call-in show at eight. Everyone wanted to know how a Black Panther found himself touring the country with a plateful of prizewinning ribs. Cara thought that was silly. Black Panthers had to eat, why shouldn't they like to cook? she insisted, as Douglas led her past the conference room doors. It was Feature News Hour, Douglas explained, and since the stories were on tape, they could sit undisturbed in the recording studio, on the big swivel chairs beneath a ceiling of patchily stapled but acoustically sound green felt. The felt on the walls was green, too, but was fastened with peeling duct tape. Cara had been in this room many times before while Douglas demonstrated to Georgie the panels of controls, the headphones, switchboards, and phone hookups, but never had it seemed to her so arbitrarily, flimsily made. Several ashtrays were overflowing, and the room stank of cigarette smoke and body odor beneath the rich, spicy smells of their pizza. On a chair across the counter sat a stuffed Humpty Dumpty wearing a fireman's hat. Through the filmy plate glass window she could see the technicians hunkering over a tangle of electronic equipment, the cracks of their bottoms showing above the waistbands of their jeans, while from the overhead speaker could be heard the music accompanying the taped news segment. Douglas switched it off, and then turned on the light, and then turned it off again, to Cara's relief. It was nicer to sit in the dark, among the serpentine shapes of the mikes. The mikes were so close she could breathe into them.

"How do we know these are off?" she asked.

Douglas tapped a mike with his finger. Nothing happened, except the Humpty Dumpty seemed to wink at her from under the slick red brim of his hat. Douglas pulled his chair close to Cara's, so they could link arms and knuckles. She draped her legs over his lap, fitting her knees over his.

Suddenly he looked very serious.

He's going to tell me he doesn't want the baby, Cara thought in a moment of resignation. He's going to tell me I'll get over it. He's going to get upset, tell me I'm being unrealistic, tell me we had an agreement, tell me it'll fuck up our life, tell me to get my act together, tell me I'll regret it, tell me I told him one time when Max was screaming and Georgie wouldn't let me wash his hair, "Don't ever let me have another one. If I ever want to have another baby, shoot me."

"One more thing," Cara said. "Something I said to Wendy. I don't want to have this *child*. But I want to have *this* child. Also,

I have a terrible suspicion that the mikes are going to come on when we're in the middle of talking and the whole city will be listening in on us and calling us up and trying to give us advice."

"Mikes don't just come on," said Douglas, "and even if they did, Jenny wouldn't put the calls through."

"Yes, she would," said Cara. "A hot topic like this. How could she not?"

"Well, maybe she would, maybe she wouldn't," said Douglas. "You already talked about this to Wendy? Who else?"

"The other Wendy. And one of the Elizabeths. I'm all talked out," said Cara guiltily. "But not with you."

Douglas tapped the mike again, sighed, looked Cara in the eye, wrapped his fingers around one of her ankles. They weren't eating the pizza, just watching it cool in the box.

"I feel the same way you do," he said. "To an extent. About the pregnancy, I mean. I understand how you feel. I want you to believe this. If for a second you don't believe what I'm saying, will you tell me? So I can convince you before I go on to the next thing?"

"You love the baby, too?"

"It's not a baby yet, Cara." He said this gently, as if he knew none of her friends had said it to her yet. In fact, she'd thought of it herself, but it didn't seem to matter. A clump of cells, a baby, what was the difference? When someone died, you didn't stop thinking of them as a person and start thinking of them as a mass of decaying tissue, did you?

But Cara persisted. "Do you love it, too?"

"I know I'll love it when it's born, if it's born. But I understand you love it now. It makes sense that you do. You're supposed to. It's natural."

"I'm a slave to biology," Cara said.

"You're a product of a hundred thousand years of evolution," Douglas said. "Or however the hell long it is."

"You make it sound like I don't have a will in this regard."

"I'm not sure that you do. Do you feel like you do?"

"No," said Cara.

"But that's not relevant, anyway," said Douglas. "What's important is how you feel. But how I feel is scared. I don't know if we can do it. I don't see how we can. Think of this; we'd both decided that we didn't want to have another child. We were sure of it, Cara, absolutely sure. So tell me what made us so sure."

"We would have to buy a bigger house," said Cara. "We would have to buy a bigger car. We'd always felt four was a comfortable number. We thought it was perfect. You could be with Georgie and I could be with Max, or I could be with Georgie and you could be with Max, or we could all be together and it wouldn't be too much, and everything was manageable, and I was going to find a new job, and we're not short of money, at least we wouldn't be if I started working full-time or at least making more money. And if any of our friends had three kids we would think they were crazy, like they were growing a tail or something."

Having recited this, she sat back smugly in her chair, although she knew that wasn't all. Not quite, anyway. For there was something they weren't quite discussing, and that something was their marriage, their life together. Just last Sunday morning they'd felt it acutely, wakened from sleep at six in the morning, their bodies intertwined in a warm haze of slumber, not wanting to pull apart. It was Max in his crib, crying to be changed, that had wakened them up, and then the dog awoke as well, downstairs, whining to go out. Cara could picture her, trembling, tail thumping, wet nose trained to the crack in the door. And Max would be wet, soaked through as he was every morning these days, his crib sheet a tangle of smells. Smells of shit, smells of piss, smells of dreams, smells of sleep, smells of fresh-laundered quilting on top of it all. Smells of sleep, Cara had thought wishfully. Douglas, beside her, was snoring again, but when she moved he wrapped his leg around her, tighter than before. She felt the swell of his erection against her naked hip, then its hot, gentle throbbing. Max had quieted a little because Georgie was up, tossing toys into the crib. Three toys in, four toys out, but then they tired of the game, and Max was crying for milk, and Georgie was calling, "Mommy and Daddy, Max needs to be changed and he's hungry, he wants his milk."

"I'll be back," Cara had said, and gave Douglas a kiss, and pulled away limb by limb, and climbed out of bed to put on her caftan. She lifted Max from the crib, kissed Georgie where he sat in his armchair, reading, and carried Max downstairs to the now-quiet dog and the pile of dog shit still steaming on the floor in the corner near the window. Cara didn't say a thing, didn't yell, didn't scream, just walked on past, wanting to preserve her sleepiness, her sexiness, her thoughts of the waterbed sloshing and rocking. Max needed a quick morning bath in the sink, and then a cup of dry Cheerios to keep him happy while she patted him dry. But as she laid him on the changing pad he thrashed with the cup and sent the Cheerios flying all over the kitchen—under the stove, and underfoot, and in the basket on the counter where they kept the breads and crackers. And at the sight of it, Cara felt something let go, and felt the pressure of the new day bearing down hard, and screamed at Max with such fury that he screamed back in terror, his face disbelieving. Ashamed, Cara took him in her arms, rocked him, comforted him. She left the Cheerios unswept, walked back through the house past the dog and the mess, climbed the stairs back to Douglas and climbed into bed, setting Max at the foot next to Georgie, who was reading another book. Douglas was still hard when she rolled up against him, and they lay like that unmoving for nearly twenty minutes, until the children left the room in search of cartoons, and then they lay a while longer, waiting for the children to settle. When all was still, they made love finally with the watchful, quiet patience required of them, which after all had its own special appeal and made Cara forget about the dog shit and the spilled Cheerios. And that was Sunday morning, a precarious balance that Douglas was afraid of tipping over. He was watching her closely, waiting for her attention so he could speak.

"And there'd be three sets of doctor's appointments," he told her, "and three sets of parent-teacher conferences, and three coats to put on in winter, and three—"

"Georgie can put on his own coat, now," Cara interrupted.

"And three meals to cook at night if everyone didn't like what everyone else was eating."

"We'd have rules," Cara said. "I wouldn't do it that way anymore. Why would we have to buy a bigger house?"

"Because the one we have isn't big enough. Right?"

"Yes."

"And I don't see how we would do any traveling."

"Other people travel," said Cara.

"Other people have six kids. Other people have twelve. Other people can do any idiotic thing they want," Douglas said with impatience, but then he reined it in, calmed it, kept it in check. "I'm talking about us," he said coaxingly, playing it safe. Cara knew but forgave. "Do you think we could handle three kids?" Douglas asked.

"I think we *would.*"

"Of course we would, somehow, if we had them," said Douglas.

Then there was silence in the soundproofed room, except for the noises being made by the technicians on the other side of the glass, along with the noise of Douglas's heartbeat. She had rested her head on his chest just under the collarbone so she could listen to it.

"Just think how much we'd love it, if we had it," Cara said.

"Very much," said Douglas.

"Just think what it would be like, twenty years from now, to look around the dinner table and see you and me and Georgie and Max, and to wonder who's missing, who's not there."

Douglas said nothing. He only gripped her ankle harder.

"All my life I'd be wondering *Who's not here?* Who's not at the table, and who's not coming in the door, and who's not calling on the telephone, and who's not coming home for Thanksgiving, and who's not here, Douglas, who's not here?" repeated Cara, not only because she believed it so strongly but because she liked the way it sounded; it sounded perfect for the moment, the way certain pieces of music are perfect for certain moments. It was like a kind of prayer, Cara thought to herself,

pulling it deep down into her body, where it seemed to rever-
berate.

Still Douglas said nothing, but he was being very warm. He
had a way of being warm and a way of being cool that had to do
with how his body responded to hers, and now it nuzzled close.
His heart was still beating, she found herself thinking, as if it
were beating only because she'd lain her ear down to hear it.

Finally he said, "Yes, but think of who *is* at the dinner table.
Think of them, too. Think of Georgie and Max, and of what
they would sacrifice if we had this child."

"Children don't know about sacrifice," Cara argued, "because
they don't think of alternatives. They take everything as it
comes. They never wonder, 'What if . . . ?' They adapt much
better than we do, you know. The world is the world, and they
make themselves part of it. Besides, they would have another
brother or sister. Someone to grow up with. Who could say
that's a sacrifice? Sometimes I think we should ask Georgie what
he thinks. Georgie's pretty together. Does he want another
brother or sister, or not?"

"Don't," said Douglas.

"It gets me that I said *sometimes*," said Cara. "*Sometimes I think we
should ask Georgie.* Because it makes it seem like this has been
going on forever."

Douglas looked at the clock on the wall above the doorway.

"Ten hours," he said. "Cara?"

"What?"

"Think of getting up at night. Three, four times. Think of
nursing. Think of feeding schedules. Think of colic. We've done
all that, Cara. We've finished. We've moved on. Think of cleaning the umbilicus."

Cara hated the stub of the umbilical cord. It was brown and
black and stiff, and between it and the baby's belly there was
always some pus, and if you weren't careful with the diaper you
might make it bleed.

"That's a tactical remark, Douglas," she said. "I don't want to
have a tactical argument. I don't want to have an argument at all,
really. I know just how I feel, and I don't know what to do about

it. You want me to tell you? I feel like you're right, that it would complicate our lives, and our life is really good right now and I don't want it to be complicated, but at the same time I feel so protective. And it would be a betrayal. Because the baby trusts me, Douglas. It trusts my body. Are you sure these things haven't come on?"

She tapped a mike with her fingernail, then leaned into it and said, "And another thing, folks. Do you feel like you're part of the *scheme of things*? Because that's how it feels to be pregnant. And if I don't have the baby, I betray *that*, too. And that's a pretty big betrayal, folks. It's unnatural, folks. It's against nature, folks."

Douglas had cupped his fingers over the mike, so Cara spoke this last phrase into his knuckles.

"It's not a baby," Douglas said. "It's a clump of cells."

"It's somebody's future," said Cara. "You know, when I imagine it, when I imagine the fetus, and when I imagine the newborn baby, I can say to myself, I have the right not to go through with this, I have the right not to have to raise another baby again and go through all that. But when I imagine it grown, that's when I think, well, maybe I don't have the right. Because who am I to look that person in the eye and say, *No, sorry, you can't exist. Sorry, I don't want you. Sorry, you can go to hell.*"

"But you'll never look that person in the eye, Cara."

"So what are you telling me? What is the end result of this discussion, Douglas? What's the consensus?"

"I don't know," said Douglas. "But try not to get angry, okay? Don't get sarcastic with me, it's not fair. And two more things."

"What?" said Cara calmly. It was true she was being sarcastic, and true that it wasn't fair. It wasn't Douglas she was angry with at all, but something shapeless and dense that was pushing her this way and that to confuse her.

"That if we decide to have this baby, we'll love it, and it won't be an issue anymore, it will just be one of our children," said Douglas. "But that we have to decide. Because I don't want to just end up having this baby because we couldn't bring ourselves to make up our minds."

"Make up *my* mind, you mean. Right?" said Cara. "Because it all comes down to me, doesn't it?"

"Yes," said Douglas.

"Why? Because I'm the one who has to let them take it out of me?"

"Either way."

"Very funny."

"Because it's your body," said Douglas.

"Thank you. I know. But I can't imagine coming any closer to making this decision, ever. I don't see what's supposed to happen to make me make up my mind, folks."

She said the very same thing to the doctor two days later, after the pelvic and before the sonogram. Medically the sonogram was unnecessary. The doctor had dated the pregnancy at between eight and ten weeks, judging from the size and tilt of Cara's uterus and the condition of the cervix.

"But what does it look like?" asked Cara as she dressed. Douglas handed her a sock from his chair in the corner of the tiny room, behind where the curtain would be if it were closed. Already he had challenged the doctor in his usual skeptical way.

"Eight to ten weeks from conception?" he asked.

"Eight to ten weeks from the first day of Cara's last period," said the doctor.

"But that's impossible," said Cara. "Unless I had a period while I was pregnant. A small one. That happened when I was pregnant with Georgie, I guess. And maybe even while I was pregnant with Max, although we never quite figured that out."

"Then that makes the baby six to eight weeks, not eight to ten weeks," pressed Douglas.

"Yes," said the doctor. "But we date pregnancies, not babies. It's easier that way. It's the standard." She shrugged, grinned, slid the speculum into a bucket. The speculum had been warmed just prior to insertion, and the doctor's gentle cranking and careful, probing fingers had left Cara so relaxed she could barely make sense of their conversation. But it didn't matter to her how old the pregnancy was or how old the baby was if no one could tell her what it looked like. Now the doctor said it looked like a worm with arm buds. She made a little curled up creature with her fingers and held it up for Cara to see.

"It has a heart," Cara said, wondering if she could get up the nerve to ask outright for a sonogram. "If only I could see it," she began, "if I could see what it looks like already . . ."

"Yes, it has a heart," said the doctor. "A tiny heart, too small to hear it beating, probably, but we can try it, if you want."

"Yes," Cara said. She pulled down her jeans again, lay on the table, felt the smear of the jelly on her stomach and then the smooth back-and-forth of the monitor.

"You warm the jelly, too," said Cara.

"Shhh," said the doctor. There was a loud *chugga chugga* like a locomotive.

"Oh," Cara said. She took hold of Douglas's hand.

"That's you," said the doctor sympathetically. "*Your* heart-beat."

"Try over here where it hurts," Cara said. She pointed to the spot on her belly that she'd already shown to the doctor. Last night she'd decided that that was the spot where the baby was attached inside. It felt tender and sore. But the doctor said it wasn't the baby, just a cyst on the ovary where the egg had been released. Very common, she said. In any case she couldn't get a heartbeat on the baby, just Cara's *chugga chugga* and some intermittent sloshing.

"Too tiny," said the doctor.

The doctor herself had three children, and Cara looked at her and wondered if she could bring herself to ask what it was like.

"What's it like with three children?" she heard herself say.

"It's marvelous," said the doctor. "It's like the Fourth of July every minute."

The doctor was tall and lovely in a horsey way. When she left the room, Cara and Douglas both thought about the word *marvelous* and about the fact that of course if you had three children you would say that it was marvelous, because it *would* be, just as if you had six children you would say that that was marvelous, too, because it would be, too. *Marvelous* wasn't the issue, then. Cara wondered what was. She almost wished she were strictly Catholic. She almost wished that Douglas were another kind of man, one who thought he had the right to put pressure on her. But if he were, then she wouldn't be married to him. Besides, she knew what she'd been hoping all morning, as her hand kept exploring the tender spot on her belly that she'd decided was the spot where the baby was attached. She had hoped that the doctor would find it was a tubal, an ectopic pregnancy, painful but short-lived and necessarily doomed.

The doctor came back with a pitcher of water as big as a football and told Cara to drink. She had read Cara's mind. Cara sipped gratefully.

"This and two more," said the doctor. "You take the hallway to the back, cross the parking lot, go to X-ray. I'll meet you there when it's over."

"Can you come?" Cara asked Douglas, who was taking off work. He gave her a look that said of course he'd come, and to stop pretending she was the only one who cared. She knew that he cared, but she knew as well that he wasn't excited like she was about the sonogram, as excited as she'd been when they had done the same with Max, when they had done the same with Georgie. They kept the photos in a book of family snapshots, several black-and-white glossies of fog in a funnel of darkness in which you were supposed to be able to identify the parts, which looked to Cara like the floating parts of a ghost.

Now, while sipping the water, and while crossing the parking lot with Douglas's hand on her elbow, and while being checked in and directed to a little curtained enclave in the X-ray wing, and while taking off her jeans for the third time that morning and stepping into two gowns and some paper slippers, and while walking the hall to the ultrasound, sipping water, Douglas's hand on the back of her neck, and while sitting in the waiting room next to a young woman also dressed in two gowns and also sipping from a pitcherful of water, and while filling out her chart, and while being led with Douglas into the ultrasound room by the very same technician who'd led them in for Max, and while lying on the table and feeling the spread of the jelly all over again, but cold this time, not warm like the doctor had made it—all this time, Cara was certain that now would be the moment when she would make up her mind. It would all become clear, all at once, she believed. There would be their baby on the screen, ghostly, curled up, its bald head tucked into its wormlike belly, its forehead bulging as if with the knowledge it was going to acquire, its two hands waving in an eddy of liquid, its fingers awkwardly open, its legs crossed at the ankles, perhaps, the way Georgie's had been, or hidden by its bottom the way Max's had been. And no bigger than a snail, and hazier than haze, but Cara knew that if she saw it, she would keep it. Douglas knew this about her, too. Yet here he was at her side, not judging, not getting flustered, not suggesting that this ultrasound shouldn't be done, but standing patiently and calmly while the technician searched. On-screen was a mirage of this-and-that inside Cara, for the technician was taking her time, first scanning the ovaries for signs of the cyst, to be sure it was normal. It was. Then she traced the fallopian tubes, first one and then the other, before entering the dark region of the interior of Cara's uterus, up on-screen for them to admire, like the galaxy seen from the window of a space-ship except that there weren't any stars, no heavenly bodies, no nebulae, nothing hurtling toward them, just cloudy, dark space and finally in the farthest reaches of it a thing resembling a lima bean that the technician circled tentatively before saying, "That's it."

It was the amniotic sac. Inside could be detected a faint, rhythmic pumping. Nothing more.

Beside her, Douglas relaxed. He had seemed relaxed before, but now that he really relaxed, she could feel how uptight he had been.

"You okay?" he asked finally, in a whisper.

"I'm okay," Cara said. "I have to pee."

"Go ahead," said the technician, motioning toward the bath-room. "Then when you're empty we can try to get closer. But I've never seen it this early before, I have to say."

"How early?" asked Douglas.

"Oh, three weeks, maybe, tops."

"I must have known it the day that it happened," mused Cara. "I must have felt it, somehow."

"Three weeks from conception, you mean," said Douglas.

"Can you tell the sex?" asked Cara.

Everyone laughed, including Cara, although she hadn't realized when she said it how funny it was. She was thinking that although if the baby had looked like a baby, she would have wanted to keep it, the fact that the baby looked like a lima bean didn't make her want to get rid of it. So her mind wasn't made up, after all.

Later Cara said to the doctor, in the little windowless room to which the doctor had led them, a narrow room with lockers and a cot and a mirror, where the women doctors took breaks in the hospital, "Looks like a blastula, doesn't it?"

She had learned about blastulas in college biology class. A blastula was a tiny globe of undifferentiated, multiplying cells. The only difference between this blastula and the one Cara had learned about years ago was that its heart was beating.

"No, it's not a blastula," said the doctor. "It's much further along than that. Much. But it's not a fetus yet. It's still an embryo."

"It's still *potential*," said Cara.

"That's right," said the doctor. "It could be the little girl who charms everyone to pieces. On the other hand, it could be a little boy juvenile delinquent."

"What about birth control?" said Cara, popping open one of the lockers and looking inside. Askew on the bottom were two open-toe red leather pumps and an unmated black one.

"What *about* birth control?" said Douglas and the doctor at once.

"Is there any such thing as a reversible tubal ligation?" asked Cara. "I don't ever want to have to be in this situation again."

"Not in this country," said the doctor.

"We can talk about birth control later," said Douglas.

"We can talk about it now, too," said Cara.

They did, for a moment. The doctor said there were new low-dosage pills but that links between hormones and breast cancer were still being debated, and that there was an IUD on the market again, a copper one, just recently approved, safe except for extra-heavy cramping if you cramped heavily to begin with.

"I'll try it," said Cara, meaning after the birth of the baby or after the abortion, she didn't know which, but it felt good to be sure about something.

Now, all these long couple of weeks, ever since she'd started to suspect she was pregnant, Cara had had the feeling that the world was going on behind her back, surreptitiously. But when she stepped outside one morning and saw the changes that had happened in the climate and in the yard, she realized that the changes had been made quite openly and that she was the one who was being surreptitious. She was the one who was spying. She was spying on herself, along with all the other people she chose to enlist, meaning to uncover the answer to the question, *What should I do?* It was as if the answer lay buried beneath the many tangled layers of Cara's emotions, but once she chanced upon it, if she ever chanced upon it, it would be recognized at once for what it was, like the needle in the haystack, sharper and brighter than all the other stuff around it, and if you picked it up, it would stick.

Except it wasn't being found.

Which was fine, for the moment, with Cara. For she enjoyed this debate, both sides of which needed to be argued by herself. Wholeheartedly. Spiritedly. Desperately, even. And she had very nearly managed to convince herself, anyway, that the question was rhetorical. She had always had a fondness for rhetorical questions, for questions that need not be answered. They were games, like puzzles, the solutions of which were far less important than the hours spent shifting the pieces around, experimenting, postulating, fumbling, guessing. For instance: If you fold a purple sweater and slip it into a drawer, and shut the drawer, then is the sweater still purple in the absence of light? And the kinds of questions in a book that people were giving for

Christmas one year, a book Douglas hated and refused to entertain, a book with questions like: If you had a chance to go back through time, to a critical moment in your life, and to choose another path from the one you really chose, would you do it even if that new path might lead you to your death and you would really be dead and you could never come back?

Of course, deep down, Cara knew that her debate was different. For it was not hypothetical. It had an answer. And, deeper down, she knew that the answer couldn't be found by searching. For it wasn't a needle in a haystack, really. It wasn't anything that could be chanced upon. It didn't exist yet. It would have to be made. Cara would have to make it herself, and stick herself with it, and wake herself from this dream of indecision.

And she didn't know how to do that. She joked to herself that she didn't have the skills, the background, the training, the knowledge, the expertise. She was underqualified, she counseled herself. She'd have to fake it, if she wanted it that bad.

So for the moment, she posed, and reposed, the question: *What should I do?* and *What should I do?* and *What should I do?*

Which sounded easy enough. It was a question she could ask herself over and over, like a mantra. It was soothing. And the more she repeated it, the further away it retreated, like background music, and the easier it became to put it out of her mind and look at the changes that had happened in the yard and in the climate, and forget about everything else, almost, because it was suddenly summer on the first day of February. Eighty degrees, and all the bulb plants poking up, and the sandboxes uncovered, and the earth overturned in the garden next door, and the air so warm you could lift your face into it and forget. Max liked to sit on the step next to Cara, his small face lifted at an angle complementary to hers, but only for a minute, and then he wanted to play with the birdseed that had fallen from the feeder. He knew he wasn't supposed to eat it; he just got very serious studying it in the palm of his hand and then flinging it uncontrollably before scooping another batch. Every so often he glanced over at his mother, and at the papers she held balanced on her knee, which needed to be tabulated before that afternoon. They were Betty's Strong Interest Inventory of the Strong Vocational Interest Blanks, and since Betty had an appointment with Cara at the community center at three, and since Betty had left two messages on Cara's answering machine reiterating how badly she needed a job that *suited* her, Cara felt she ought to at least come up with something. Only Betty's test wasn't much help, of course. Part One contained a list of occupations each preceded by the circled letters *L I D* which stood for *Like, Indifferent,* and *Dislike,* to be filled in accordingly. Not content with these three choices of reply, Betty had invented a new category of her own, an *H* that stood for *Hate,* which she had calmly added to the other notations at the top of the page. A brief scan of Betty's test read something like this:

Actor/Actress	I
Architect	I
Artist's Model	D
Bank Teller	D
Bookkeeper	D
Chemist	I
Children's Clothing Designer	D
College Professor	I
Dentist	H
Drafting Tech.	D
Hospital Administrator	H
Life Ins. Agent	H
Nurse	H
X-ray Tech.	H

"Hate, hate, hate, hate," Cara read out loud, nearly flinging the papers out with the birdseed. It all seemed so impossible at first, and so peevish and pinched, like Betty herself, but this was Cara's job, and she was good at it, and in just a short while she saw a solution, and slid the papers from her lap, and imagined with a smile Betty's peevish acquiescence to Cara's politic suggestion. Now, if only Cara could administer such a test to herself, and fill it out and read it and know what to do.

ARE YOU MINE?

Do I want another baby? — No.

But do I want *this* baby? — Yes.

And would I consider putting it up for adoption? — Certainly not.

Why? — Because if I carried it, and gave birth to it, I'd be in love with it, and then I'd want to keep it.

And do I want to be pregnant again? — No.

And do I want to nurse a baby again? — No.

And do I want a baby clinging to me the way babies do—the way Max does now, the way I love that he does—a year from now? — I don't know. Maybe. Well, no, I guess not.

Why? — Because that phase of my life is over. Because I've done that already, twice. Because if I do it again, just because I like the feel of it, just because I'd love that little baby in my arms, then I may as well keep doing it the rest of my life, and have sixteen babies, or twenty or twenty-one, and I don't want to do that.

Why? — Because I've got my body back now, almost, and I want to keep it.

And then the question became, *If I think about a pregnancy I don't want to have, and about an infant I don't want to raise out of infancy, then, do I have a right to abort it?* And the answer was yes. *But if I think about the child that that infant would become, and if I think about the adult that that child would become, and if I think about the life that it would lead, on its own, the way I live my life now, the way anyone does, then, do I have a right to abort it?* And the answer seemed to be no.

So the question became, again, *What should I do?*

She posed the question aloud. Max gave a little jump and then settled again into his birdseed game, tossing and sifting. The back of his neck was exposed. The back of the neck is the center of the body, Cara said to herself, seeing what a vulnerable spot it was. It made her want to reach out and protect it. But from what? This crazy weather? Georgie was at school, and Cara thought she'd walk early to meet him, before he had a chance to take the bus, and bring his roller skates along so he could skate beside the stroller, hanging on for balance. They'd make a spectacle like everyone else, embracing the summery climate so fiercely that it would surely back away, and then it would be winter again, and the seasons would follow their ordinary course, the way secretly everyone wanted them to, because this was too strange, too sudden, eveyone dressed in shorts and barbecuing chicken while near the door sat last week's boots, last week's woolen socks, next week's hats and gloves and scarves. The very oddest thing was that the mosquitoes were out. Cara watched one land on Max's neck, not believing it would bite. It bit, and then the telephone rang inside. It was Cara's mother calling from her home in Toronto, where she was growing impatient with Cara's dad. Cara's dad was getting old while her mother stayed young; that was the problem, and Cara had long seen it coming. Not that he was feeble, he was just happy to be out of touch. Since retirement, he'd cultivated a hobby, producing oil painting after oil painting of airplanes in flight that he managed to sell now and then to travel agencies and airline offices.

"He's like the son every mother wishes she had," Cara's mother once lamented. "Very studious, never gets into trouble, just surrounds himself with Piper Cubs and Cessnas and DC-10s and Lear Jets and 737s."

"How's Dad?" Cara asked now.

"He's fine."

Sigh.

Which meant he was the same. Which meant he didn't seem to notice what a lot of other people did about Cara's mother. That she was youthful. That she wasn't bored, that she "refused" to be bored. And that she was more and more lovely and exciting to look at. Nearly sixty, she had a soft, blonde serenity with a dose of flushed impatience burning underneath, and when she flipped through the course catalogs of the University of Toronto, or picked up her stack of sociology textbooks and walked out the door, it was with a blend of furious zeal and delight. Head bowed toward the buses on Yonge Street and her "academic" fascination with the women who stripped for a living at the Brass Rail, Cara's mother was nearly electric, charged with a curiosity that hadn't been there at all while Cara was a child. No, this was relatively new, Cara's mother like a house with the windows and doors thrown quiveringly open.

"And how are *your* boys?" she asked Cara.

"Georgie's getting very popular," Cara answered, "only he hasn't figured out yet how to talk on the phone. He gets all of these calls, kids wanting him to come out and play, and he gets so excited he just blushes and stutters, and I have to get on and say that he'll come, unless it's one of the kids who will make fun of him for having his mother get on the phone."

"You're a good mother."

"So were you," Cara said.

"I was?"

"You are."

"When I want to be. Am I a good grandmother, too? Can I talk to Georgie?"

"Georgie's at school."

"How 'bout Max?"

"Max was bitten by a mosquito."

"A mosquito! In February!"

"Say hi, Max. Say hi to Grandma."

But Max was sucking on some milk, now that they'd come inside. He had weaned himself suddenly at the age of ten months, but now at eighteen months they couldn't wean him from a bottle. In truth, Cara didn't try very hard to wean him, because she liked this intermediate stage—the way he leaned against her as he sucked, the way he wouldn't hold the bottle by himself, the way he wrapped his fingers round her thumb as they rocked, and the way he raised his eyebrows in order to look at her, just as if he were still breast-feeding. Except she didn't have to hike up her shirt and she never felt sore or put-upon. Now she shifted her weight, repositioned the bottle, and held the telephone receiver to Max's ear.

Cara's mother said, "Tell Grandma what a duck says, Max."

Max kept on sucking.

"Tell Grandma what you say when you're done eating dinner," said Cara.

"Burp," said Max, milk on his chin.

"What was that?" said Cara's mother. "Say that again."

"Kack kack," said Max.

"Tell your mommy we're coming out to visit next week," Cara's mother said, loud enough for Cara to hear.

"What?" Cara said. She took back the receiver, stood Max on the floor, put her elbows on the counter, and waited. She was thinking maybe this was just her mother's way of saying how much she *wished* they were coming.

"On Tuesday," said Cara's mother. "Arriving at three."

"No," said Cara.

"No?" said her mother.

"Just a minute," said Cara.

She put the phone on the desk top, then on second thought gave it to Max to mew into so her mother wouldn't hear only Cara's own silence. It wasn't usual for Cara to say not to come. In fact, she'd never said it before. She'd never had to. But now. The very thought of her parents walking in the door bearing shopping bags of tee shirts and kids' books and toys . . . the idea of them crouched on the floor of the living room playing with

Georgie and Max ... the very notion of Cara making her decision, or, if it had already been made, living with it awhile in peace and meditation like the grace period she imagined she would require, but in secret from the affectionate, unknowing gaze of her parents—that was unbearable. Unbelievable, too. For she had never kept a secret from her mother, at least not since adolescence, when her secrets were of the kind that her mother knew about anyway and kept her mouth shut about except to Cara's father, who kept his mouth shut about them in turn, for his own bewildered reasons.

No, Cara thought, she didn't want her parents here. She didn't want their support, and she didn't want their sympathy, and she didn't want their worries, their apprehensions, their foresights, their sorrows, their skewed misunderstandings. For everything would all get mixed together, Cara feared; her secrets, their needs, her needs, their secrets. Besides, her mother knew her too well, and always knew just what to say, and what she said was always right, in a way, in the long run, and Cara didn't want to hear it. No, this was muddy ground, for sure, and Cara could already feel herself slipping.

"I'm sorry," Cara said, when she took the phone from Max. "It's just not a good time. It's a bad time, Mom. Come next month, or I'll call you, or—"

"We won't disturb," said her mother. "We'll be just a few days, visit with the children, keep ourselves entertained. If it's a bad time, we'll make it better. We'll babysit. I promise. Daddy can set up his easel."

"No," said Cara, "really, Mom. I don't want you to have to—" and then she stopped, at a loss, not knowing what to say. She felt hot all at once in the face and neck, wondering, and she could see, in her mind, her father's canvas on his easel in her own living room, a jet that didn't look like it could possibly be airborne.

"If you and Douglas are having a problem . . . ," Cara's mother began.

"Nothing you need to know about," Cara said gratefully, in what she hoped was a gracious tone. Maybe this was the way out, then.

"Company sometimes puts things into perspective," suggested Cara's mother.

Cara said nothing.

"Just by the sound of things, Cara, it doesn't seem like your heart's really in it. This problem, I mean. It might vanish by Tuesday. Has it been going on long? Have the kids noticed? Georgie?"

"It's not anything like that. It's not fighting, Mom. We're getting along fine. It's just not a good time. I'd rather you and Dad didn't come, that's all. You can come another time. In a month or two. When all this is over. When this is resolved. I'm in love, Mom," Cara heard herself blurt out. "I've fallen in love."

"Oh," said her mother, and in the shared, awed quiet that followed, Cara didn't think to find a way to hang up. She only felt calm, relieved, light-headed, and safe. It was the truth, after all, she was in love, only not in the way her mother thought.

"Who knows about this?" asked her mother.

"No one," said Cara.

"Douglas?"

"He suspects, but not exactly."

"Not exactly?" said Cara's mother.

"He knows there's a bond, yes, developing, but he doesn't know how strong it is. Not quite, I think. I *think*. He doesn't see the depth of it, the color. Maybe he doesn't want to. Maybe he doesn't have to yet, either, I think."

"What do you mean, the color? What color?" said her mother, because no matter how frightened she might be of knowing, she always wanted to know more, and more.

"Oh," said Cara. "Red. And pink. Intense pink. Lots of shadows. I don't know why I feel it, really. This person, this other person, is actually very—" Here Cara paused and considered. She might say the other person was unformed, unfinished, innocent, *babyish*. "This other person," she said at last, "is sort of sleepyheaded. And I don't think they know I exist. I think they have a feeling, a sense of me, but that's all, to tell you the truth."

"Oh, Cara, if that's all, that's nothing, that happens all the time, to everyone, darling. It's no reason to feel guilty. It's natural. It's healthy."

"Who said I feel guilty?"

"You sound like you do. Calling him *they*, for instance. Really, Cara."

"No matter where I am, in my house, at work, in the super-market, in Produce, you know, comparing cantaloupes and things, I can feel it. That presence. It's there," said Cara, having fun, because it all seemed so easy, the way the story took shape out of nothing and then had its own sudden logic, its own sudden force.

"That's normal," said Cara's mother.

"And so it's not a good time, at all, for you to come, because of everything and all my confusion, and especially now that you know. See?"

"I see. And I'll try to understand how you must feel," said her mother, sounding not hurt and upset as Cara thought she would be, but breathless and unnerved. Excited. "And I'll cancel the flight, of course. And I know that you'll be keeping the children in mind, and Douglas, and what's best for the four of you, because you always do. You always think of the future, Cara, I know, as well as the here and now, but just promise me you'll—"

"I promise I'll think of the future," said Cara.

2 ❧

To Betty, Cara said, in a tone of voice ordinarily reserved for Georgie when Cara didn't want him to know, just yet, that she was losing patience, "Well, we've both had a look at your test. And what I like to do at this point is ask the client to point out any patterns they might see, after which I point out any patterns I might see, after which we talk."

"Client?" said Betty, gazing reproachfully at Cara from under her knitted hat. "You'd be out of a job if you didn't have *clients*, and then you'd be somebody's *client* yourself, and what would you think about that?"

"It wouldn't bother me," said Cara. "It's just a category, Betty, not an indictment. If it insults you, I'm sorry. But if you're fond of semantics, maybe we should talk about that, because it might help a little. It might redirect us, you know? Except it says here under School Subjects that you dislike language studies and under Occupations that you dislike the idea of becoming a linguist, which brings us back to what I was saying before, that is, do you see any patterns, or not?" Cara breathed deeply. Her use of the word *redirect* was an act of generosity; so far, their talks had had no direction whatsoever. Also, she was taking a chance and she knew it; there was nothing anywhere in the Strong Interest Inventory about either linguistics or language studies. Why, she didn't know. In fact, she didn't think very highly of these sorts of tests at all, they were only a starting point, and only that if the *client* was willing to discuss them.

"It's not necessarily true that I wouldn't want to be a linguist,"

Betty objected. "It says here under Occupations that I'm indifferent to the idea of being a college professor, and since most linguists are college professors, that means I don't dislike the idea of becoming a linguist, I'm only indifferent to it. And I don't like language studies, per se, because of the way languages are taught in this country. But I wouldn't have anything against going to a foreign country and picking up the language while I was there, naturally. So if you have anything in the Netherlands, for instance—"

"Maybe we should open a whole new category," Cara suggested. "*Like, Dislike, Indifferent, Hate,* and *Have Nothing Against It.* I kind of like that, Betty. Maybe we could get you a job with the people who make these tests. And what also interests me . . . under Activities, you answered that you're indifferent to debate. It seems to me you like it well enough. And why the Netherlands, of all places on earth?"

"No, I don't."

"You don't what?"

"I don't like debate."

"You seem to."

"Well, I don't," Betty said.

Cara smiled. Ordinarily a client smiled back, enjoying the tease. Smiles broke the ice, made them less earnest, less nervous, more relaxed, more truthful. Actually, Cara knew why Betty had chosen the Netherlands. Squatting was legal there. If you found a house with nobody in it, it was yours—for the time being, anyway.

But Betty didn't smile back. Her gaze became firmer and more impossibly stubborn. This discussion was beginning to remind Cara of the staring contests she had with the children, or of some of the arguments she had with Douglas, when the whole point seemed to be to see who could last the longest. And that was fine in a marriage, when you had a whole lifetime for working things out, but now it was wasting a good half hour.

Still, Betty surprised her. "Of course there's a pattern," she said indignantly. "I like nothing, I hate everything, I'm a pain in the ass."

With many clients, a sudden revelation like this was the moment for tears. In her desk drawer Cara kept a box of tissues, and on her desk an empty coffee mug and a full glass of water. If a client started crying, Cara handed him or her a tissue and then tried to discern whether the client was the kind of person who, when distraught, wanted to be comforted or the kind who preferred being left alone. She was very good at figuring this out, in fact. If the person crying was the kind who wanted comfort, she offered water and held the glass as he or she sipped, but if the client was the kind who preferred being left alone, then Cara took the coffee mug into the office, filled it from the pot, and stood awhile sipping from it outside the door, waiting for the right time to go back in.

But Betty was neither. Betty remained perfectly in control. The notion that she hated everything appeared not to bother her at all and was, in fact, one of the few things she seemed to enjoy, in her eye-glittering way.

"It's true you're indifferent to a lot of things," Cara offered finally, "and you dislike a lot of things, at least you say you do—"

At this, Betty bristled.

"—and you hate some things, sure, but you don't hate everything. You only hate certain things. Certain types of things," said Cara.

"I knew you'd get around to your version of the pattern before I got around to mine," Betty said.

"You don't seem to have a version."

"I have many aversions," Betty said haughtily. "Too many, I thought we'd agreed."

Cara raised her eyebrows. Why don't you take my chair and I'll take yours, she was thinking, and you can tell me what to do about this baby.

But instead she said, "Your strongest aversions, your *hates*, that is, are as follows." She read from a list she'd prepared in the margin of Betty's test. It was a doctored list, somewhat, and she was stretching things, anyway, but maybe Betty wouldn't notice. Anyway, it was all Cara had to go on.

"So?" Betty said, when Cara was done.

"So they all have to do with illness, sickness, bodily functions, one way or another," Cara explained. "Hospital Administrator, X-ray Technician, Physiology . . ." While she spoke, Cara looked out the window above Betty's head. Most of her clients blocked the view, but Betty was tiny, and Cara could look past her into what looked like a perfectly ordinary, hopeful summer day—people strolling past in shirtsleeves, and the windows open on the upper floors of the police station, and the door propped open at the cleaners, where a cat lay basking—except it wasn't summer, of course, it was February, it was lovely. If it were summer, Cara realized, then her decision would at last be behind her; she'd be pregnant, or grieving, whichever. And poor Betty. Why shouldn't she enjoy the weather like everyone else? She wore her usual coat buttoned up to the collar, along with her look of sour displeasure enlightened by a self-congratulatory smirk.

"I like the part about how I said I don't like fishing," said Betty. "Except the reason I don't like fishing is not that they die when I catch them, but that I don't. Catch them, I mean."

"But still, you have to admit—"

"Even if I do admit," said Betty, "I don't see the point. We're not here to find out what I hate, we're here to find out what I like."

"You like health," Cara said. "You must. You're not *that* different from everyone else. You like cleanliness, you like beauty. . . ." She spoke sarcastically, gesturing with mock enthusiasm, which was one way to keep Betty listening, at least. For there was actually a job, not a great-paying job but a job, at Pfeiffer's Flowers, delivering bouquets.

"But it says here I dislike the idea of being a florist, and I dislike the idea of having a garden, under Activities, and I—"

"Because of the dirt," said Cara.

"The dirt."

"If you're delivering flowers, you don't have to have anything to do with the dirt," said Cara. "I'm not talking about gardening or running a business. And you can't tell me you don't like flowers. How could you not like flowers? But if you don't, then there's nothing I can do for you, I'm sorry. But if you do . . ."

Betty raised her eyebrows even with the hem of her cap, skeptically.

"You have a driver's license," said Cara.

Betty said yes.

"You have a job, then," said Cara.

Betty shifted in her seat and gave a mischievous smile.

"What about my brother?" she asked after a moment.

"What *about* your brother?" said Cara.

3 ✳

One of Cara's favorite Saturday-morning hobbies was to drive to the flea market with Georgie in search of evidence of her childhood—books she had read, toys she'd grown up with, clothing that resembled the clothing in which her mother might have dressed her. The clothing—the decomposing velvets, the impractical, scuffed patent leathers, the dusty white eyelets—she held up for Georgie's blue-jeaned disbelief; the books and toys she bargained for and finally bought. In Georgie's room was a shelf lined with nearly spineless replicas of the books of poems Cara's parents used to buy her on her birthdays, and in his closet sat a shoebox full of assorted trolls and Gumbies and even a set of Beatles dolls, minus Paul McCartney, still smudged with what Georgie liked to imagine were his mother's own girlhood fingerprints. In her own bedroom closet, Cara kept other, more dangerous items— the Porky Pig Pez dispenser with its cargo of petrified candies, the giraffe-necked Barbie with its torpedo breasts, and a copy of the "Mystery Date Game." Cara had been allowed to play this game only at the houses of her friends, her mother having objected either to the very notion of dating at such an early age—Cara was ten when the game came out—or to the perversely arbitrary nature of the small plastic door with its spinning knob; turn the knob, swing open the door, discover who's standing there starry-eyed and eager to get married. For that was the point of the exercise; marriage, starting a life together, hopefully with the preppy one everyone wanted, although the others were acceptable, too, not including the nerdy one, whose awkward, hesitant lankiness Cara had secretly favored. Now, years later, his resemblance to the good-hearted Douglas, with his serious brow and studious, vulnerable posture, was a secret she carted out for the amusement of her friends in Group, who insisted, now and then, on a game for the sake of old times.

This morning's flea market yielded yet another memory, a wig of poured, molded plastic in the shape of a bouffant hairdo, to be fitted like a lightweight helmet over the head of a child. Amid the crammed, nostalgia-laden tables, Cara fitted it delicately onto Georgie's surprised head along with the frames from a pair of rhinestone-studded glasses. She tapped the wig with a finger, having remembered the dull, hollow sound it made and wanting Georgie to hear its echo. Somehow it seemed to Cara that even the most commonplace experiences of her childhood should be visited on her children. In fact, she'd begun to realize, the more commonplace the better, as if it were in the commonplace that the essence of those days— their unhurried, innocent goodness—resided. The subdivision in which she'd spent the first ten years of her life was bordered by fields of potatoes, and in these fields, Cara and her friends hunted potato bugs and turtles, which they carried home and kept in large, open cardboard boxes stuffed with handfuls of grass, weeds, and dug-up soil. The potato bugs gave off a repulsive, invigorating odor, but the fact that the boxed pet turtles were actually called box turtles assured Cara of the essential, sensible nature of the planet. Nothing irredeemably bad had ever happened to Cara in her childhood, or since. No tragedy, no grief, no setback, no consuming, terrible worry. Perhaps this apparent blessedness, then, was what she meant to bequeath to Georgie and Max along with the splintered replica of the magician's box she had owned at age six. It was smaller than a shoebox. Inside was a mirror at an angle down the middle. If you dropped a ball through the painted door in the top of the box, and then shut that door and opened the painted door on the side, then the ball would seem to have vanished. How many hours had she spent opening and closing those doors, gaining comfort from the trusted, reliable disappearance and reappearance of the ball inside? And how many hours had Georgie spent opening and closing his own little box? Well, not very many, actually, Cara reflected, although more than once she'd found herself idly repeating the process. Open, close, appear, disappear—with a feeling of purpose in the tips of her fingers as if what she had come to regard as the uncommon peacefulness of her life depended on this simple illusion.

Having removed the wig indignantly once Cara knocked on it, Georgie kept the glasses in place and still wore them that evening when he, Cara, and Douglas filed into their seats at Public Hall for a Pete Seeger concert. The trip was a present to Georgie, whose music of choice for two months running had been an in-concert recording of one of the singer's earliest tours. Until tonight, Georgie had not realized that there *was* a Pete Seeger apart from the voice on the tape, and now, at the prospect of a whole human being, he looked stunned and a little subdued. The spread wings of his eyeglasses kept sliding off the end of his nose, where he would catch them with a well-timed tilt of his head and poke of his tongue, then shove them back on. Maxie was home with a sitter, and Georgie sat between his parents in rare, undivided attention.

Cara was feeling a little weary, and not only because of the cavernous vastness of Public Hall, whose high vaulted ceiling, crisscrossed with cables and lights, echoed each scrape and thump on the wood floor below. That morning, returning from the flea market bearing not only the wig but a tiny, potted orange tree, she had stopped unannounced at the home of a woman she knew who had recently given birth to a third child. Not a close friend at all, but a woman Cara recognized to be living a life similar enough to her own that any major disruption in it would portend equal disruption in Cara's. Cara told Douglas after a late Saturday lunch, "I didn't say why. I just wanted to snoop around. I wanted to see if she was the same old Kerry or if she was living in total chaos. The thing is, she likes to live very much the way I like to live. Part-time work, and she doesn't like cooking, particularly, and she likes to keep things simple but good for the children, and she likes reading books, and she can't stand for her house to be messy or for things to seem out of control. Her kids are close in age to Georgie and Max; at least, close in age to what Georgie and Max will be a year from now, so I wanted to see what having another baby had done to her. You know, made her crazy or something. And I knew that if everything there was a total disaster, or even half a disaster, like if she was all frazzled and said that everything was falling apart and that she didn't know what she was going to do, then I would decide not to have this baby, just like that, all at once, as easy as . . ." Here Cara trailed off, thinking of the open and shut of the magician's box.

"But she was the same old Kerry, and the house was the same old house, and everything was going perfectly smoothly," Douglas guessed.

"Right," said Cara.

"And that was a shock," said Douglas.

"Well, more of a rude awakening," said Cara, "only not so rude because I guess I've grown accustomed to it. Every time I think I've found something to help me decide, it doesn't quite work. Sure, if Kerry was in a straitjacket rather than a nursing bra . . . I'm beginning to think that the two decisions are mutually exclusive, anyway. They don't seem to have anything to do with each other. I mean, if I decide to have the baby, then that doesn't mean, necessarily, that I'll decide not to have an abortion. And if I decide to have an abortion, that doesn't mean, necessarily, that I'll decide not to have the baby. If there were two of me, one of us would have the baby and one of us wouldn't. And if there were three of me, one of us would have the baby and one wouldn't and the third wouldn't know what to do, she'd just talk her head off about it the way I'm doing now, hoping the right words will come out instead of all this gibberish."

"It's not gibberish," said Douglas. "It makes sense, in a way. It's like what this neurobiologist was talking about the other day on the show, when you can't tell your body what to do anymore. You might want to move your hand, but your hand doesn't move, or you might want to shake your head, but there's no way to make your head do it. No connection, no mechanism. Simple voluntary actions shot to hell. Only here it's not a simple action but a complicated one. You can make your decision, but you can't make that decision apply to your body and to your behavior and to what you are going to do. You're split."

Cara thought about this for a minute and said, "No, it's not like that really, at all. I'm not split. I'm merged. There's no distinction between body and soul and heart and mind, it's all mixed together, so my mind can't have thoughts that are independent of the thoughts of my body, and my soul can't have thoughts independent of the thoughts of my body, and my body can't have thoughts that are independent of the thoughts of my heart. I feel like a turtle, carrying my home around on my back. Because my body is my home. And my past, and my present, and my future. A body's all you have to get through life in. You know how people say you can't tell what a person's like by looking at them? Well, that's bullshit. You can. The way they hold themselves, the way they dress, the way they move through space, if they're dirty or clean, if they take good care of themselves, all else being equal, I mean."

"But all else isn't equal," Douglas pointed out.

"I know that," Cara said. "So maybe this is all just a way of saying I'm confused."

"You have a right to be confused. You have a reason to be confused," Douglas said.

"Yeah. But everything I said still holds, anyway," said Cara. "And I don't feel confused. Whatever I say feels absolutely right for the moment in which I say it, and then I say something else and that feels right, too, for that moment."

"So tell me more about Kerry's," said Douglas after a while. They had both stepped onto the porch, where the afternoon sun was dim but warm. He funneled thistle seeds into the feeder, hoping for finches. They'd get house finches, Cara thought, but not gold. There'd been fewer goldfinches last year than the year before that, and this year she'd seen only one. Also, fewer juncos, fewer chickadees, fewer everything, really, except house sparrows. When Georgie and Max were grown, maybe all that would be left of birds would be a few flocks of dingy, lonely pigeons. But that was an ancient argument—the world is in rotten shape, why bring another person into it? And even if things were worse than before, Cara couldn't quite make that argument fit. After all, she'd had Georgie and Max, hadn't she?

"I gave Kerry an orange tree," Cara said finally.

Douglas nodded.

"I watched her feed the baby, and then she had to bring little Michael upstairs to change his diaper, and then she had to go back upstairs to find a book Erica wanted, and one time, when she was changing Michael's diaper, she brought the baby upstairs with her, but the other time, when she was getting Erica's book, I said I'd hold the baby so she wouldn't have to carry it upstairs."

"So . . . ," said Douglas.

"So I held the baby. Georgie was upstairs with Erica, and Max was just watching me, making me give him sips of my cooled-off coffee. He looked a little suspicious, you know. When the baby started whimpering, Kerry was still upstairs but I knew she could hear it, and the only thing I could think of was that it had nothing to do with me. Nothing. None of it. I tried to make it have to do with me, because I thought it would help, but I couldn't. I just sat there feeling how much I wanted to come home."

And to come to this concert, she remembered now, although she couldn't stand Pete Seeger. His goodness was too much part of his act. But she hadn't expected him to be so old, and his blend of feebleness and warmheartedness and humor and courage ended up affecting her. He couldn't trust his voice, he wanted everyone to sing along. He'd chosen songs that were largely chorus, to save his voice the embarrassment of breaking on-stage. Cara, holding Douglas's hand in Georgie's lap, wondered if her son was disappointed because his favorite singer wasn't singing the way he sang on the tapes at home. Instead his voice cracked or faded to a coarse, amused whisper as he beckoned the crowd to join in. But Georgie didn't seem disappointed. He was sitting very quietly, Georgie was, not like other children. Occasionally he mouthed the words, and he always clapped politely at the end of a song, and sometimes Cara thought he looked genuinely moved. The big rhinestone glasses had slipped from his face and now swung from his tiny crossed purple-socked ankles. Georgie favored socks in unusual colors, just as he favored unusual songs. He was rapt; Cara could feel it, and Douglas could feel it, too. Had they brought Maxie along instead of leaving him home with a sitter, then this moment would have been lost, this moment of quiet privacy with Georgie, alone among the crowds and crowds of people on the high tiers of seats.

Except they weren't alone, not quite, and that was the secret that Cara was keeping from Douglas even though she knew that he would try to understand. He might say—he might insist— that nothing was there, and then he might wave his hand around and he would be right—there would be nothing there, just the high beams and spotlights and vast, shifting pockets of blackness—but still he would sympathize, one way or another. There was a face above the crowd, floating like a moon, half in darkness, just the image of a face, really, but not flickering, not fading, a mask of a face gazing placidly at Cara.

Cara sat up straight, arched her neck, and stared back, not frightened or surprised or even confused, but only contemplative, and suddenly, terribly sad. The sadness hit her like a wave, and at the moment of impact, Douglas squeezed her hand and then held on tighter than ever. Somehow he knew what was happening. He knew she had made her decision, and the pressure of his fingers told her he would be patient; he would wait till she was ready to tell him. They would talk about it later, past midnight in bed, the way they'd lain talking each time she went into labor, quietly, carefully, his hand on her belly but their legs and bodies separate, so only their words intertwined. Now Cara's eyes filled with tears, but she kept them back. Pete Seeger was singing some kind of love-after-trouble song about a boat for two people, and for once his voice was strong and didn't break.

Cara tried to sing along but couldn't, and instead felt the crowd swell around her, then drop away until there was only herself and the high, floating face above a crowd so remote it seemed to have a horizon, across which she would follow the face if she had to, so it wouldn't have to be alone. For it was like the face of a person who has died. It was like the memory of a person you had loved, a memory you carried around and looked at when the grief meant you couldn't help looking away. Then, when you looked, the gaze was like a visit to a grave, a moment set aside for sorrow and for whispering good-bye, or like the moment when you looked around the dinner table knowing someone was gone, like a shadow hanging over an empty chair. No one else would have to know. Cara would carry the face with her always—in the car in the summer, speeding the length of a highway, discreet and contained, Cara and Douglas and Georgie and Max, and then, beside them, in the privacy Douglas allowed, Cara and the memory, Cara and the face.

Later she would say to her friends, "It was like a page turning inside me, like those old-fashioned movies they made out of books, when the page turns on-screen and you see it happen. And then I knew what to do, and Douglas knew that I knew, because all this talking and not deciding had been flipped to another page behind us, all at once, just like that, when I wasn't expecting it, and I was on a new page going forward. Only it wasn't as if all that stuff wasn't important to me anymore, because it was, it is, but it's on another page, and I can flip back and look at it now and then, but it has nothing to do, really, with what comes next. Because that's how you make up your mind about something like this. You don't. I haven't made up my mind, I've made up my body. I've just set myself in motion. I have to act, I have to *do*, I just have to start moving again."

Next morning Cara was sick, which wasn't a big surprise, but as she retched over the toilet, it felt like one. Somehow she hadn't expected this, or the numb-brained fatigue when she climbed down the stairs, or the fuzzy-headedness as she munched on a slice of toast. Not that she hadn't felt tired last week, or dizzy, but she hadn't succumbed, and she hadn't quite believed it would happen now. She had supposed it would just go away or dissolve, but it wouldn't, of course, there was still this little matter to be taken care of, she said to Douglas sarcastically as she rushed for the toilet again. This little matter of the pregnancy. The clinic was in the city, forty miles away, not far from the radio station, but Douglas was prepared to take off work so they could drive in together tomorrow, Monday, if Monday could be arranged, or Tuesday, if tomorrow couldn't be. Saturdays were to be avoided, they'd agreed, because of the likelihood of protest, of a line they'd have to cross, of people who might shout out, "Murderer! Baby-killer!" Elizabeth's boyfriend was a member of a group of men who called themselves Church Ladies for Choice, who dressed up like the Church Lady on "Saturday Night Live" and wagged their fingers at the picketers while ushering the patients inside. Of this, Elizabeth was affectionately proud, so Cara didn't tell her that the thought of being ushered into the clinic by a line of young men dressed in wigs and thrift-shop lace-collared dresses was as humiliating and as distressing as the thought of being called a killer by somebody else. She only wanted to be anonymous, as she said to the woman who answered the phone Monday morning. She only wanted to be left alone.

"Well, anonymous you can be, but you can't be anonymous today," said the receptionist.

"Tomorrow, then," Cara said.

"Well, no, not tomorrow either, sweetheart. You'll be coming in end of the month."

"End of the month!" Cara said.

"The first day of your last period was December 28, is that right?"

"Right."

"Yes. February 22, because you have to be eight weeks along, because we won't do the procedure before eight weeks, and if you find someone who will, don't do it, because it isn't safe. There's a risk of infection, a chance they won't get it all out."

"I thought the earlier they did it, the better."

"The earlier after eight weeks, the better."

"Oh," Cara repeated, and then, "But that Louisiana law, the one they actually passed last summer, but it was vetoed, thank God, but if you were raped you had to report it within seven days and have the abortion that very same week!"

"Honey, if you live in Louisiana you better move to another state, that's all I can say about it. So how's February 22?"

"It's okay," Cara said. She had a vision of the long days stretching ahead of her—each one beginning with queasiness and vomit, and her pants not fitting, and her legs so tired she could hardly stand up, and the feeling of her belly growing hard underneath her when she lay down in bed, and the shrinking of her bladder, and the waking up at 3:00 A.M. to pee, and the dizzy spin of hormones keeping her sleepless and fretful. And excited, she amended. Well, maybe not. But there'd be nerves and impatience and the drifting, high forgiveness of the face.

"Now," continued the receptionist, "if necessary, can we send an unmarked envelope to your home?"

"Yes," Cara said, still in a daze.

"And should we need to get in touch with you by telephone, and should we have to leave a message, can we say who we are?"

"Yes," said Cara. "Wait. No." Because the sitter might answer, and Cara might be out, and Cara didn't know how the sitter felt about abortions. As if that should matter, she thought, in my own goddamn house. But still she said no, and the woman on the phone said in that case if they had to leave a message, they would leave it in code.

"Do you know anybody named Connie?" the lady asked.

Cara said yes. She had an old friend from college named Connie, living in Tallahassee.

"Do you know anybody named Vicky?"

Cara said yes. Vicky was the name of Georgie's kindergarten teacher, who phoned now and then to talk about Georgie, whose new hobby was counting all the words that rhymed with *bat* on all the pages of all the books on all the shelves in the kindergarten classroom.

"Pamela?" asked the receptionist.

Cara thought for a moment and answered no, she didn't know any Pamelas, and then yes, wait a minute, her mother's sister was Pamela and although Cara hadn't spoken to her aunt in years, there was no knowing. . . .

"Maybe you should come up with the code name, then," said the receptionist, laughing. "I can't think of any more names but Candy, my daughter."

"I don't know any Candys," said Cara, so it was arranged that if the clinic had to phone her and if she wasn't at home, and if they had to leave a message, the message would read that Candy had called.

"And that's it," said the lady. "No telephone number, no other message, no nothing. Okay? And then you call us back and we tell you what we wanted."

"Okay," Cara said, mock-seriously, as if this were some kind of game. Except it wasn't a game for some women, she had to remind herself. She hadn't thought of such women before. Now she imagined them with their hands cupped over their telephone receivers, and with the doors shut tight in the bathrooms in the mornings and the water running hard in the tub, if they even had tubs. There are women in this world who don't have tubs, she had to say to herself with the impatient amazement she felt whenever she needed to remind herself of such things, women without any money, women with eight kids, women with no chance to work, women with husbands who beat them, women who can't read, women who can't drive, women who don't have cars, women with no place to go, women with bad backs, women without running water, even, to drown out the noise of their morning sickness.

To the receptionist's further questions, Cara answered yes, she had someone to stay with her at the clinic the whole five or six hours, and yes, she had someone to drive her home, and yes, she understood she was not to eat or drink anything other than clear liquids after midnight of the night before her appointment, and yes, she would wear a two-piece, loose-fitting outfit with short sleeves so they could take her blood pressure whenever they needed, and yes, she would bring in a urine sample. Also she would bring a money order for two hundred and thirty-five dollars, unless she wanted to be sedated, in which case it would need to be for two hundred and fifty-five dollars, unless she wanted anesthesia, in which case it would be—

"What's the difference between sedation and anesthesia?" Cara asked.

"The sedation is mild. The anesthesia puts you out."

"I'll take amnesia, then," Cara joked. "No. Really. Does it hurt?"

"Does what hurt? The anesthesia? Or the procedure?"

"The procedure."

"Yeah, honey. It hurts."

"The anesthesia puts you out completely? Like, asleep?"

"Yeah."

"What about the sedation?"

"It's just a pill. It's a Valium. It relaxes. That's all."

"So you can still feel the pain? And you still know what's going on? And what about after?"

"You know exactly what's going on. It just relaxes you, honey, that's all. Afterwards you feel a little wiped."

"I'll do the sedation. The Valium. How much does it hurt? What will it feel like?"

"Like very heavy cramping, but just for a couple of minutes. You've had children, you can handle this."

"Okay," Cara said, and then there was a silence meaning it was time to get off the phone, but Cara didn't want to say good-bye. She found this person's voice a comfort, like the presence of the nurses when she lay giving birth. They were kindly, knowing, and impersonal all at once. They made it plain that they cared, and equally plain that the caring was part of their job.

The appointment was two and a half weeks away, and Cara wondered if after all that time, the two of them might recognize each other, she and this soothing, commonsensical voice.

✖

Group met on every other Sunday, or less frequently if Cara's and her friends' lives got too complicated, but never less than twice in two months. Men were not permitted, although occasionally there were children, who, when tired of their toys, crept into the circle to squirm on their mother's laps. Once, little Max toddled off into Liz's back bedroom and knocked over a full-length mirror that had been propped against a wall. When he screamed, Cara ran back there and found him squatting on the floor amid giant shards of smashed mirror, where he could have been beheaded, or lost an arm or a leg. Then and there Cara wrote Liz a check for thirty dollars for the mirror while allowing her friends to assure her that even if there *had* been a tragedy, it wouldn't have been her fault. *Tragedy* was the word Cara used for it, but only in the back of her mind. It was a word distinct from others, mainly because she and her friends had thus far been immune to it. Not that bad things didn't happen to them. Bad things did. Liz's ex-husband was crazy, and the other Elizabeth's mother had a tumor that kept recurring. The idea was to talk about these things—the time Jack threw a frying pan at Liz's daughter's friend's head (it missed), the time Elizabeth's mother, from her bed in the hospital, begged Elizabeth to get married (Elizabeth didn't)—in such a way that the discussion might veer into weightier subjects. Violence, illness, aging, motherhood, fatherhood, parenthood, childhood, dreams, sex, fairy tales, money—they had a list typed up on a piece of paper, as if discussion of any one of these issues might not include discussion of the others, as if it weren't a big whirlpool of ideas, anyway. There were times when they decided to do things more systematically, when for two months they Xeroxed magazine articles for all of them to read and discuss, but then they always got sidetracked—Jack had followed Liz to her boyfriend's house, or Elizabeth's mother had found a fingernail in her eggs on her hospital breakfast tray.

Anyway, it was all very casual, and there'd be beer or cider or decaffeinated coffee depending on whose living room they met in that week. Sometimes there was a basket of fruit on the carpet in the middle of the floor, or a tray of cheese and crackers on a table, or a bag of store-bought cookies. Once, there was a cervical cap dusted with cornstarch that Cara nearly popped into her mouth, thinking it was one of those German Christmas cookies. The cap was Liz's, and she had had to drive nearly two hundred miles to get it. Cervical caps weren't used very much anymore, which was why Liz, who had a thing against the medical establishment, had gone to such trouble to get one.

"You can keep it in for weeks," Cara explained to Douglas, "you don't have to take it out until you have your period. The problem is, it doesn't work. At least, not very well. When I brought this up, Liz said she didn't care if she got pregnant anyway, she kind of wants to, in fact."

Such remarkable exchanges Cara made a habit of sharing with Douglas even though it was all supposed to be confidential. Telling him made Douglas feel included and calmed his not-so-openly-confessed worry and suspicion that Cara's attendance at Group would lead to her wanting to get a divorce. Sometimes he asked, jokingly, "Who's getting a divorce this time?" and Cara would have to answer quite honestly, "Well, Liz is seriously considering it."

"Which Liz? I didn't even know either one of them was married, these days," said Douglas.

"She's not, but she is sort of, but he hasn't talked about anything but cycling in months," said Cara. "He's a mountain cyclist, and he's running tours and publishing a newsletter, and last night over dinner he talked about trail maintenance for two hours on the phone with some other biker, while Liz sat and ate her spaghetti. Liz. Not Elizabeth."

"And what did *you* tell them about?" Douglas would ask, meaning, *What did you say about* me?

"Nothing really."

"Come on."

"I told them how great it was in bed last night," Cara said.

Douglas thought she was joking but it was usually true, she *did* say good things about him, except for the times she complained about his housework, and even then her complaints were affectionate ones. After all, he was a man, he couldn't help it, he wouldn't change, his mistakes were so consistent, his lapses so predictable. When it was Douglas's night to cook dinner, there was always something burned or overcooked or underdone, or the forks he set out on the table weren't quite perfectly clean. And when Douglas did the laundry he forgot to change the towels, or folded Max's pajama bottoms into the sheets and left the folded wash piled on the bedroom floor so if he vacuumed, he vacuumed around it. Anyway, among all of these women, Cara was the only one who was actually happily living with a man, and sometimes she joked she had to keep living with him if only for the sake of everyone else; when they thought it was impossible to live with a man, they had only to look at Cara to know that it wasn't, and when they thought that all men were useless and irresponsible and mean and neglectful, they had only to look at Douglas to know that they weren't. The thing was, Group had been meeting for so long, in such a contented, fruitful, satisfactory period in Cara's life, that she almost felt obliged to play the part, no matter what. She was the one to whom good things happened, she was the one who remained in control. She had a good, strong, slender, healthy body, and late at night, when the children were in bed, if she didn't have to cook tomorrow's dinner, and if she didn't have to scour the tub, and if she didn't have work she'd brought home from the office or a patch she had to sew on Georgie's school backpack, then she had time to read the books she liked to read or to take a solitary, exhilarating walk with the dog, or even to sit around with Douglas reading the paper. Of Douglas, she liked to say that their marriage was like a third person between them, that there was Cara and there was Douglas and in between them was their life together, which needed nourishment in order to survive, as if a marriage were a living, breathing being with needs of its own, independent of Cara's and Douglas's needs. The only thing she wasn't absolutely happy with was work, but she was happy to be unhappy with her work, she had a way of saying giddily.

So she knew she wouldn't talk about her pregnancy at all, for her troubles would disrupt the balance. She'd never sought the advice of the group before, and now, surprised, she found she didn't want it. No matter that she'd spoken already with both Wendys and Elizabeth, none of whom knew that she'd spoken to the others; for in a way it was those disclosures that caused her to see what she was seeing now, that is, that she really didn't want to disclose anymore. While in the several days following the Pete Seeger concert she'd told all three friends that she had made her decision—like a page turning inside her—she hadn't told them what that decision was. She wasn't ready to talk about it yet, she said. Secretly, it embarrassed her to think about how much she had talked about it already, and how little the talking had accomplished, and how it seemed unrelated to what she was going to do, as if there were two of her, two Caras, one who talked with her friends and the other who lived her life, privately, the way it was meant to be lived, with Douglas and the children. When she went to Group this mid-February Sunday, it was with her usual expectation of hearing what everyone else had to worry about and to tell them, simply, that she had decided to take a Strong Interest Inventory test after all, not for herself, really, but for the benefit of her clients, so she would sympathize with what it was like to take one.

But as it turned out, she didn't have an opportunity to talk about that either, because Liz had brought a friend.

The rule for bringing friends was that everyone had to be asked in advance if the friend would be welcome, and that, once Group had begun, she had to be made to *feel* welcome. And in fact, the new woman always managed to feel right at home, and listened and talked along with everyone else as if she had been there forever.

So today when Liz's friend was asked to tell about herself, and when she'd told them how she'd met Liz and how she came to be visiting her this weekend, she went on to talk about her work (she was a speech therapist) and about her lover, Jonathan (who was a therapist, too), and about how her parents didn't know that he wore an earring, because she'd managed all along to keep them from actually meeting, only now it had reached the point where they all should get together. She was eager and intense, drawing her feet up under her on the couch, then spreading around her the fringed, embroidered hemline of her skirt, then reaching underneath to pull off her shoes and let them drop one by one to the floor, all the while wondering aloud about whom she should tell first about the earring, her mother or her father. Not to mention her sister, who would come to her defense even if there wasn't anything that needed to be defended, and her own feelings of confusion about her attraction to this man, because he really wasn't the kind of man with whom she had ever imagined herself being in love—he was okay in bed, but his hobby was splicing home videos with scenes from television sit-coms, which he watched with the sound turned off.

"At least he doesn't wear skirts," said one of the Wendys, to which Teresa replied that he did, sometimes, when he was just hanging out.

"No pun intended," said the scholarly Wendy.

"He says they're more comfortable," said Teresa, with a shrug and a smile, after which Cara thought they'd start talking about other things, but the minute she turned to Wendy to ask about Wendy's classes, Teresa started in again, this time about a dream she'd been having about a baboon. She worried that the baboon had something to do with masculinity, which was why she hadn't told Jonathan about it even though it was kind of funny, especially the part when the baboon started climbing the—

Cara shifted in her seat, glancing surreptitiously at the other women in the room to see if they felt as she did: bored, amused, indignant, even. The baboon spoke only with its hands, dis-played a puzzling aversion to sexual intercourse, and was fright-ened of rain. The thing was, Cara knew just how Teresa must feel; that this kind of divulgence was what was expected of her in Group even just for one meeting, so that when she was done, if she ever was done, she would have earned her place as someone who could be trusted with whatever anybody else might want to say. If they had a chance to say it, Cara thought. No one else looked impatient, however. Everyone looked ea-gerly sympathetic and seriously attentive. It seemed to Cara that any woman could walk in off the street at any minute and start talking about her life, about anything at all, for that matter, and all of them would sit there and listen just as intently as they were listening to Teresa, as if what really mattered wasn't whether they cared about the person who was speaking but simply that they listened and responded to whatever was being said. But Teresa really did look grateful, and more animated even than she'd been when she started to talk. Over prominent cheekbones her translucent skin was flushed with exhilaration, and if in thought she pressed a fingertip to one of those cheeks, and then took it away, a pale spot remained as if in fleeting, bruised evidence of her pained concentration. Now and then she paused, pursed her lips, cocked her head, and then started right in again, but with a fresh, surprised cunning. Cara might have liked her, might even have admired her, if she hadn't suddenly found this whole thing so ridiculous; a coven of unshaven legs (although Cara shaved hers), of dangling, beaded jewelry (although Cara wore no earrings), of advice, consolation, and complaint (although Cara had no complaint). They might as well put a classified ad in the newspaper: AUTOMATIC FRIENDS, REFRESHMENTS SERVED.

Suppressing a smile, Cara reached for an orange and a square of paper towel. Elizabeth reached, too, and in the bowl their hands made contact, knuckle to knuckle, and stayed that way for a shared, brief fraction of a moment. Cara's smile escaped as she met Elizabeth's eye, and Elizabeth smiled back conspiratorially as if in special knowledge of Cara's pregnancy and dilemma. Earlier, one of the Wendys had given Cara the same kind of smile. It made Cara soften up a little and stop feeling so annoyed. Teresa was still talking about the dream—or was it another dream this time?—but in any case, the dream was responsible for the fact that she had decided to introduce Jonathan to her parents. She'd have to tell her mother first about the earring, Teresa decided on the spot, but then her mother would realize that she hadn't been told about it before, which might hurt her feelings.

"Maybe I could tell her that I broke up with the other

Jonathan, and that this is a new one," Teresa wondered aloud. "Only what if he wears his skirt? I can't tell him not to, can I?"

"Amazing the trouble we go to, to avoid hurting our mothers," Cara broke in.

Everyone turned to look at her. She popped an orange slice into her mouth and chewed regretfully, because in spite of everything, she found herself warming to the notion of talking, as if she really could be two Caras at once, the one who did and the one who didn't. It was like quitting cigarettes and then, in the presence of someone who smoked, bumming a cigarette and lighting up while thinking, even then, how glad she was to have kicked the habit.

"I just told my mother I was having an affair, so I wouldn't have to tell her what was really bothering me," she blurted out when they continued to look at her.

There was a loud burst of laughter and surprise.

"An affair!"

"If I told my mother I was having an affair—!"

"Jesus Christ, Cara!"

"Well, not an affair, really," said Cara. "And I didn't really come out and say it. Not really. I mean, I told her I was in love with someone I run into now and then in the supermarket, or something. Which I'm not, by the way. But that's what she ended up thinking, which was fine with me, because it got her off my case. She wanted to come out and visit. Now it's postponed. And that's what I wanted, that's what I knew would happen. You have to know my mother. She has deep admiration for that kind of thing, big, romantic secrets, and she understood that I wanted to get off the phone, I didn't want to go into it with her, I wasn't ready for her, I had to let it stew. Also, she likes the idea that she knows what I'm stewing about, so she can be tactful about it. Or maybe that's not quite fair. Not tactful. Respectful. She likes me to know she respects me."

"My mother would have respect for my love life, if I had a love life, that is," said one of the Wendys thoughtfully.

"My mother doesn't want to know a thing about my love life."

"My mother doesn't even know what a love life is."

"You know, it's easy to be *in love*. Too easy, I think. It's easier to be *in love* than to come to love a person. Maybe we should talk about that next Group. I don't mean to change the subject. That's just something I've been thinking about. Sorry."

"So did it work?"

"Did what work?" asked Cara.

"Did you end up having to tell her what was really bothering you, or not?" asked Liz.

"No way," Cara said, laughing.

"So what was it that really was bothering you, that you didn't want to tell her about?" asked Teresa.

The room grew quiet, suddenly; there was only the poke of Wendy's needle through cloth and then the long, quiet pull of the thread. It was a question no one else would have allowed herself to ask, for Cara hadn't indicated that she wanted to be asked it. In fact, somehow she had signaled otherwise. For there were clues, they all realized right then and there, subtle messages evolved over time at these Sunday gatherings: Ask. Don't ask. Tell. Don't tell. But Teresa could not be expected to know this, or to recognize. So she had asked. And all eyes dropped, to a lap, to a spiral of orange peel, a cracker, the blonde, polished wood of the table, but all ears were trained on Cara.

Cara was listening, too, for she didn't know what she would say.

"It's just that . . . ," she faltered, "I wasn't feeling well, I was getting a cold or something, and I didn't want her to know, because my mother's a worrier, and the slightest thing that's wrong with me she gets hyper-concerned about and starts recommending doctors in Toronto as if I'm supposed to fly up there every time I have to blow my nose. You know how mothers are. She'd want to check my temperature herself, because she knows I never do it. I don't even have a thermometer in the house. Well, just an anal one, for the children."

"You had a cold, and you couldn't tell your mother you had a cold, so instead you told her you were having an affair," said Liz. It was over now, the silence, Cara had spoken, her words were free game.

"I didn't exactly tell her I was having an affair," said Cara, improvising. "Just that I was falling in love. And it wasn't a cold, actually, I had a growth, a tiny growth, but my mother would have totally freaked out anyway. She would have come out to stay with me."

All this time, Cara avoided looking at either one of the Wendys or at Elizabeth, but now when she glanced around the room she saw that Elizabeth was nibbling the white fibers off her orange and that both Wendys were staring at Cara as if trying to decide whether she really had had a growth or if she was covering up. Wendy knotted her thread, bit off the end, and held the big crimson leaf completed in her lap. It was quilted on one side, corduroy on the other; it bore no more resemblance to a leaf than to an oven mitt. She folded her hands on top of it, fingers outspread, waiting.

Cara grinned, and Wendy raised her eyebrows, then put the giant leaf on the couch beside her and got up to brew another pot of tea. Group was in Wendy's house tonight, and Wendy always kept the teapot full and steaming under a cozy she'd made, an exact, quilted replica of the teapot itself. When she stood up, it was with a glance at Cara as if in invitation for Cara to follow and join her in the jasmine-scented quiet of the kitchen, but just then Teresa started saying something, staring meaningfully, insistently at Cara.

"My sister once had a growth like that," she said sympathetically. "They had to do a biopsy, but it turned out to be a virus. It was under her arm, and they thought it might be cancer of the lymph node. That was the scariest, most horrible thing, waiting to find out what it was. It must have been really hard on you, and on your husband, not knowing what to expect. Not to mention all the doctors you probably had to see, and then your mother calling in the middle of it, and having to hide your worries from your children. Children pick up on those kinds of fears, and then they bottle them up and have nightmares. My sister acted very brave, but we all knew inside she was terrified."

"It's not easy," said Cara, taking another orange and holding it unpeeled in the palm of her hand as if to signify that she was finished. She was mortified, really, having elicited confessional sympathy from a woman she had never seen before and probably would never see again, about an illness she had never even had. She felt her face growing warm, and she wanted to go home and tell Douglas about it so they could laugh about it together, except that she had never told Douglas about the thing she'd told her mother in the first place. And now it would be too late. Wouldn't it? Well, maybe not. But maybe yes. He would think she had been hiding it from him and that therefore there was really something to it, so they would need to talk about it. He would ask if it were true and she would have to say it wasn't. She would have to tell him *No, I am not in love with a person I met in the supermarket, or in the hardware store, or at the public library.* The very thought of having to say such a thing to Douglas irked her considerably—it would be an injustice, a slap in the face of that patiently needy third creature that was their marriage, if she and Douglas became the kind of couple who needed to have discussions about infidelity in order to stay true to each other. He would take it very seriously, Douglas would. He would take firm hold of the white lie she'd told her mother and dig and dig underneath it as if for a treasure, for that was the way he was. He believed all deceptions were lies and thus masked a corresponding truth. He was firm in this belief. Unyielding, actually. It was his radio philosophy, his radio technique; take any dissemblance, give the interviewee a few minutes alone with it, soon the dissemblance becomes a lie, and the lie assumes the shape of the truth underneath it. So even if he believed she had made it all up, he would think that deep down she was in love with someone else without knowing it, or that subconsciously she wanted to be in love with someone else, or that once, years ago maybe, she had been. And then she would never hear the end of it, he would joke about it so much, or worse, maybe he wouldn't say a thing about it, just go on believing it, keeping his knowledge of her under wraps as if it were his secret, not hers.

I just want to get home, Cara thought to herself, and lie down in bed with a book and him next to me, and curl up, and never talk to anyone again. She wasn't geared up for this—for the confusing, pressing company of all of these women. She wanted to be in her house, full of purposeful, peaceful domesticity. She'd brought a week's worth of papers home from the office so she could work at her own pace and be fresh and attentive to the children. One afternoon last week, sorting through a batch of resumes, job ads, and letters, organizing the lives and careers of her clients, sipping her coffee, considering, for the third time that afternoon, a foray into the pantry, where she hid her cigarettes, she had glanced up and seen the face again, floating near the ceiling, looking at her. Cara had turned away, but then she made herself look back. When she did, the face was unmistakably a woman's. So it's a girl, Cara had said to herself, the baby's a girl. Then when Georgie ran in, needing some help with his reading, she was surprised that he didn't notice, that he didn't stop short, that she could hide from him this unexpected flood of doubt and sorrow that she had thought would be over and done, not something she'd look up and catch sight of again and again. When she told Douglas about how sad she still was, he reminded her gently she could still change her mind, she could change it whenever she wanted.

"And then I can change it back again," Cara had said. "I might be changing my mind for the rest of my life. But I want you to promise me something."

"What?" Douglas asked. They were watching "L.A. Law" the way they always watched TV, in bed with the newspaper spread out around them, shushing each other every time the pages crackled.

"That if in the future I want to grieve about this, you'll let me."

"What do you mean, *let you*? How would I stop you?"

"I mean, you'll respect it. You'll respect the grief. And you won't tell me I'm being silly and get impatient with it."

"I might be feeling it myself," Douglas answered.

"You won't be."

"I might."

"So help me God," someone said on TV.

"Because I want us to remember this baby," Cara said. "I've named it, you know. Do you want me to tell you the name?"

"You'll tell me anyway," said Douglas. "But I want you to promise me one thing, too. That you recognize something. That it's not a baby, that it's only a clump of cells, and that doing what we're doing is really no different from what we always do when we use birth control."

"I'll take that under advisement," someone said on TV.

"I'll take that under advisement," said Cara.

"And one thing I want to know," said Douglas. "Did I force you to come to this decision? Was that how it felt? That you're doing this for me? Or is it really what you want?"

"It has nothing to do with what I want," said Cara. "It has to do with what I don't want. I don't want another pregnancy, I don't want another labor, I don't want another delivery, I don't want another baby, I don't want another member of our family, I don't want another this, I don't want another that. But still it doesn't seem fair not to give it a name. Everyone should have a name. I owe it that much, at least."

"Alright," said Douglas.

"Alright, what? Alright we owe it a name, or alright I can tell you what it is?"

"You'll tell me the name eventually," said Douglas, his way of telling Cara not to tell it to him now. It was a risky name, anyway, an unusual name, a name she didn't know that she would give to a girl were the girl actually to be born. Also, Douglas didn't know that the baby was a girl. He was innocent of that, Cara had thought gently and a little reproachfully, gazing at the hollow of his throat.

At ten o'clock, when she stood up and put on her boots, and threw a nod and a smile to Group, Wendy got up, too, needle in hand, and stepped into the hallway behind her.

"How *are* you?" she asked quietly.

"Oh, I've been really tired," Cara replied in a near whisper. "This one is much worse than with Georgie or Max. Maybe I'm getting old. I can hardly make it up the steps in the afternoon— you know, that time in the afternoon, around four o'clock, when you hit a low and then you need a second wind. You know what's happening already—I can't believe it—my pelvis is stretching."

Wendy made a face as they stepped out the door.

"It's normal," Cara said on the landing outside. "It happens with every pregnancy but usually not this early, at least not with Max and Georgie. But I'm okay, otherwise."

"You are?"

"Yes," Cara said a little secretively, because she knew that what Wendy wanted was for Cara to tell her what she was going to do. And Cara wasn't going to tell her. Not yet. For she could see, in Wendy's heavy, pale, troubled face, that same hint of censure that she had seen before.

"Emotionally . . ."

"I'm just trying not to think about it," Cara said. "Except I feel so pressured. Not by you, I mean, oh, no, not by you, but even when I pass people I've never seen before in the street, I feel like they're paying attention, I feel like I'm driving a car and I've come to a four-way stop, and it's my turn to move and everyone's waiting. I remember from way back in high school, in driver's ed, the instructor kept saying, 'When you're on the road, you're not alone, you can't be solitary, you're part of a community, and you have to act accordingly.' That was the instructor's refrain for the whole semester, *You're part of a community of people*, *You're part of a community of people*, and I don't think I've ever gotten in the car without thinking of that, but now I think of it all the time, in the supermarket, at work, in the shower, in bed, everywhere."

"Welcome to adulthood," said Wendy.

For a while they stood silent in the cold that was like a summer chill, not like a usual February night. There was a street lamp close by where the road made a fork, and on either side, the yellow lights behind the curtains of the houses, and the blue flickering gaze of the television sets. Some of the curtains were trembling, the windows open a crack, and Cara swore she heard her husband's voice coming faintly from over the radio, although of course that couldn't be, he wasn't on the air at this hour, but she could hear him signing off, wishing sweet dreams, saying good night to the neighborhood.

4 ❧

Over the weeks the face receded, until it wasn't a face any more than the face of the moon was a face, but just a dimly glowing circle on the farmost edge of Cara's vision if Cara chose to look at it at all. Which she didn't. Not really. Just a glimpse now and then to remind her it was there, but never for more than a fraction of a second, never long enough to give it time to float closer and look back at her.

For she had resolved not to recognize it, and not to be challenged by it, and not to answer to it at all until the day of the procedure, when she and Douglas would be driving to the city. She still had not revealed to him that the baby was a girl. She was protecting herself. He would say there was no way of knowing, and he would be right, but she would know it anyway.

The woman on the telephone had referred to the abortion as *the procedure*, a term for which Cara was grateful because it allowed her not to think about what was involved, for the time being. When she was in the car, sitting next to Douglas, and they were driving toward the clinic, *then* she would think about it. They might pull off the highway, sit talking under an underpass, then pull back on the road toward the clinic, feeling suddenly, indisputably right. At least, this was what Cara hoped. Driving to the clinic would be like the flip of a coin, and that split second when the coin somersaulted in the air and you knew absolutely what you wanted it to be, heads or tails— that would be the moment when Cara would make her peace with it.

So the face became a circle like a dimly glowing coin, suspended in air, not somersaulting, not yet falling, just hanging there patiently waiting.

And the baby was a baby no longer and not even a cluster of cells or a curled-up, eyeless thing, but just a pregnancy. Just a condition. And it was not an easy pregnancy, Cara realized soon enough, for it was full of all the bad symptoms along with a curiously heavy love that Cara lavished desperately on Georgie and Max as if to expend it.

Once, she gave Georgie an apple for lunch, but Georgie put it on his plate and sat looking at it until she noticed.

"Why aren't you eating your apple?" she asked. Georgie loved apples.

"I can't."

"You can't?"

"Because it hurts," said Georgie.

"Oh, it does, does it?" said Cara. "That's sweet, Georgie, that's really sweet, but it's just an apple, it doesn't have feelings, it doesn't have nerves, and if it did, it would want to be eaten because that's what it's for, like I told you that time, it has seeds in it, seeds from the apple tree, and if you eat it the seeds are dispersed."

She held it up and, turning it admiringly, took a bite from it herself just where Georgie's teeth had made a dent but not pierced the skin.

"It's delicious," she told him. "It's made to be eaten. Really. But if you don't want it, you don't have to eat it."

"I do want it," said Georgie. "But that's not what I'm talking about. You don't understand."

"It's okay if I don't understand. Your mind just works differently than mine does sometimes. And there's nothing wrong with that. It's just the way people are. Even if you're my child. There are things that you'll think about, that I won't understand, and things that I'll think about, that you won't understand, but then, if we accept that, we'll understand each *other*," said Cara, proud of herself, looking at him indulgently from over the table.

He was fidgeting.

To Cara's right, in his high chair, Max squealed and reached for the apple.

"I'll cut Max a piece," Cara said, "and then I'll save the rest for you in case you change your mind, and in the meantime you can eat your yogurt. Do you want your yogurt? Maybe you're just not hungry."

"It doesn't have anything to do with me changing my mind," said Georgie impatiently, lifting his spoon, "and if you'd listen for one split second, you'd know what I'm talking about."

Cara smirked. He was five years old and he was talking as if he were twelve.

"I'm listening," she said.

"It's not the apple that hurts. It's me."

"You?"

"It hurts my teeth," Georgie said. He opened his mouth and showed her where a tooth was loose on the bottom row in front. It was his first loose tooth; beneath the pressure of his finger it wiggled and jerked. Oozing out of the margin was a viscous sheen of blood.

"And I was shocked to see it," Cara was saying to Douglas. "I practically screamed. I'd forgotten all about that, about their teeth falling out. I was sitting there making such a fool of myself, being such a good mother, and he sits there so patiently, and then he opens his mouth and shows me all this blood. For a second I thought he was disintegrating. I thought he was dying. I thought his body was falling apart. It still bothers me to see it, even when I know it's supposed to happen. But it makes him look so fragile, as if at any minute anything could—"

"That's not what bothers me about it," Douglas broke in. "What bothers me about it is really stupid. I'm afraid of what he'll look like with a mouthful of gaps. He won't have such a beautiful smile anymore."

"That's what you said when his teeth first came in," said Cara. "He had such an open smile, and then you said it would be crowded with teeth and he'd look like the monsters in *Aliens*."

"I guess I did say that," said Douglas.

They were heading for the clinic, on a bright Friday morning, along the highway past the airport, where a jet was descending more slowly, it appeared, than the cars were driving on the road. "Clear as the eye of a storm," Douglas said in his bygone traffic-reporting voice that managed always to be provocative no matter what the news. "Humming like a tuning fork," he added nostalgically, which was the way he always sounded when he spoke about flying. These days they bought the road reports daily from Kerne Aviation, and Jenny read them on the air in a mock soulful way.

The jet could have been a glider, Cara thought—the way its big wings alone seemed to hold it aloft. But soon it was behind them, and there was nothing to distract her except the steady flow of traffic that seemed only to bear them relentlessly forward. They wouldn't pull off the road, they wouldn't have their discussion, they wouldn't make up their minds anew. All she wanted was to know that what she was doing was right, but there seemed no way to make herself stop doing it long enough to know it. Instead she felt helplessly, relentlessly propelled, like a fast-spinning top. She had set herself in motion, then lost control. She was reminded of being in labor, riding the waves of contractions and sometimes falling between them upside down and backwards, not knowing what was what until a new wave crested and she knew *that* for sure. She was wearing her skirt with the stretched-elastic waist and a tie-dyed tank top sweat-stained at the armpits, exactly the skirt and shirt she had chosen to wear to the hospital while in labor with Max, except that then, she'd worn sandals instead of boots, and now, she'd stuck a safety pin through the skirt's worn elastic, hoping to keep it in place. These were clothes so loose and soft that she felt naked and covered at once, clothes you wouldn't have to take off if things started happening fast. She'd resurrected this costume the night before, unpremeditatedly, amid confused moments of equal certainty and sorrow while sweeping the bedroom floor. Across the room from the bed was a fireplace, and round the flat brick hearth lay the many scattered corpses of ants, a common find in the summer but never at this time of year. Through a

chink in the brick she felt the night breathing in at her. Max
and Georgie were sleeping, together in their ever-shrinking
room across the hall, Max in his crib and Georgie in his bed and
between them on the floor a throw rug piled with tossed stuffed
animals. What a moment of peace this should be, thought Cara,
sweeping and sweeping, then pulling closed the curtain and
lying down on the bed, the broomstick across her legs. How
she wished Douglas were home. Each night this week he'd
turned to her and asked her if she wanted to talk, and each night
she'd said no, she was fine, she was ready. How she wished he
might ask her again, so they might start anew discussing and
debating, if only to be convinced, she thought, if only to know
she was right. But Douglas had had to stay late for a conference
at the station, and Cara found herself imagining another meeting a year from now when he would be out of the house and
she'd be sitting at home with a new baby in her arms, nursing,
while the children lay asleep in the room next door. When she
thought of it that way, it seemed not only possible but pleasant
and downright cozy. The baby's sweat would smell of milk, and
in the corner of the room would be the diaper-changing table
and the smell of soiled sleepers in the blue laundry bin. The
baby would be dressed in a kimono, and if she wanted she could
lift the skirt to look at its pink, bowed knees. Then would come
the nights of fragmented, grateful sleep, the long passage of
time measured in feedings and diapers, the disconnection, the
dreamy unreality of it all. In the first week following Georgie's
birth, when he was suddenly, unbelievably there, Cara cooked
herself an egg but forgot all about it. The water vanished from
the pot, the egg sat on the bottom and roasted and cracked
apart and sent up a sulfurous, bitter smoke that Cara didn't
notice. She was in the living room with Georgie in her arms
when a friend came by and said, "What's that smell?" and went
into the kitchen and found it, and it became a big joke, Cara
and her burned, exploded egg and the daze she was in, half-
naked under one of Douglas's unbuttoned shirts. It was a pleasant way to be, not responsible for anything except for the child,
letting everything else go to hell. And being fat and not caring,

and lopsidedly big-breasted, and rocking back and forth habitually even when there was nothing in her arms, and smiling back at everyone who smiled into the stroller, and not keeping up with the news, and playing with the toys that the baby didn't know how to play with yet by himself. And turning on some music, sitting in the rocking chair, and rocking the baby to sleep so when Douglas came home, he'd find them, Cara sleepy from the baby's sleep against her, Cara's heartbeat mingled with the baby's. She'd send Douglas outside with the dog, whose walk had been forgotten, and through the closed-tight window she'd hear the progress of their walk and how the dog took off around a corner so Douglas had to chase it. Then the door would swing open, pushed by the wind, and Douglas and the dog would rush in with the cold, and that would be her taste of the outside world, her only taste, enough to last until the following night. With the cold, the baby might stir against her but wouldn't wake up, or would wake just enough to need another suck, for which Cara would part the folds of her shirt and arch her back against the cushion and start rocking again.

Having imagined all this, Cara still was caught off guard by the simple argument of the clothing—the stretched-out skirt, the stained tank top—that she'd pulled out of her closet and laid neatly on top of the dresser in preparation for the morning, for the procedure. No spoken words could make so eloquent a case, she thought, and for a long time she stood still looking at them. The skirt's hem was frayed, and she remembered its caress when she'd lain on the table and spread her legs for the nurse to check the dilation with Max. The nurse hadn't thought that there was much going on, but then it all had happened at once, as it could happen again, so easily. Before she knew it she might be sitting with the baby in her arms and her head in a spinning, hollow whirl above the frightful, vast excitement of her body.

Had he been home, Douglas would have reminded her, "And then the baby would shit in its diaper and you'd have to get out of the rocking chair to change it, or more likely you'd be so sleepy that you'd hand the baby to me and I'd have to change it, but then you'd get up anyway to watch me change it because every time we have a new baby you're afraid for a while that I won't change it right, that I'll forget to put the plastic pants on under the pajamas, and then I'd get upset because you don't think I know how to take care of my own baby, which I do, and then you'd get upset because you'd think I was getting mad at you although I wasn't, but then we'd start fighting, and you'd start crying because of all the hormones, and Max would wake up needing to be sung to and rocked, and then the dog would get excited and have to go outside again, by which time it would be past one in the morning, and neither one of us would sleep because we'd know that the baby would wake at two-thirty for a feeding, and our life would change again, and you would change, and I would change, in ways we can't predict, but still we'd love that new baby to pieces, so if you want it, we can have it, I've already said that, Cara."

"I don't need your permission," Cara would have replied. "I don't need anybody's goddamn permission to have a baby, thank you."

And had he been home, after a while Douglas would have asked gently, "Are you deciding? Are you thinking about this again? Do you want to talk about it?"

"No," Cara would have said, nuzzled against the pillow.

"You can call Elizabeth if you want to, and talk to her about it. She's still awake, I saw her light in the window, if you don't feel like talking to me. Or maybe you don't really want to talk, Cara, maybe you just want to change your mind. Is that what you want?"

"I really don't think so. I'm okay. Don't worry," Cara would have said, for she'd be thinking about the car ride and how it would be like a flipping coin. And how when the coin came somersaulting down, she would know what she wanted it to be, heads or tails, and she would know that she was right.

But now here they were in the car, and it wasn't like a flipping coin at all. They were talking about Georgie's teeth falling out, and about how much money the tooth fairy left these days. A dollar a tooth, or maybe two for a molar. They might have been on their way to the art museum, for all they were talking about.

"Why don't we just skip it and go to the art museum," Cara said.

"If you want to, we can," said Douglas.

After which neither one of them spoke for a while and there was only the rush of the tires on the pavement underneath. Not far off was the familiar, peaked sprawl of the downtown skyline, but the only thing Cara could recognize about it was that it was getting closer. She had a funny feeling, watching its approach. She felt that the car was taking them into the future, rather than into the distance. They were moving not through space but through time, and there was no stopping time, so they had to go on, it was inexorable.

And if they were moving through time and not space, Cara thought, then their destination must be not a place but a moment. And if their destination was a moment, thought Cara, than that meant they would stop when they got there, and be allowed to look back and ahead, and have a past and a future again.

This would happen when they were talking to the counselor, Cara thought with relief, surprised she hadn't thought of that before. There was a counselor at the clinic, trained to talk about doubts, about fluctuations of spirit, about the sudden, erratic swings between confusion so insistent it felt like pain, and certainty so arrogant it felt nearly ecstatic. The counselor would put things into perspective, the counselor would make things make sense. On this, Cara depended. With the help of the counselor, she would have her reckoning. She would have her flipping of the coin. It would be like seeing God before you died, Cara thought, but the idea struck her as so ludicrous that she started to laugh. She put her face against her arm on the window and laughed, in such a way that Douglas wouldn't hear. If he heard, he would think she was crying. She was still suppressing laughter when they came to their exit, on a street renowned for shootings through the windows of passing cars. Really there hadn't been a shooting in years, as far as Cara knew, but everybody thought of it that way and said to lock the doors, as if a lock would make a difference. The street did look bad. They passed a gas station with inflated plastic animals strung by their necks around the parking lot, and then some vacant lots choked with dead weeds, and then a strip of boarded-up stores with a bar and grill still open in the middle of it all, flashing a sign in the taped-up window. But there were saplings newly planted on the sidewalks, and no one picketing the clinic, Cara was glad to see. It was a large, anonymous, dirty-looking office building with a coffee shop on the ground floor next to the elevator. All this they could see as they drove past into the parking lot, along with another couple in another car that followed just behind. When Cara and Douglas sat in the parked car, not quite ready to get out and enter the building, the other couple sat in their car, too, looking at the windshield and talking a little. After a while Douglas took Cara's hand, and Cara took off her sunglasses and slid them into the glove compartment as if to signal her readiness. They stepped out of the car into the sun of the parking lot, and the other couple stepped out, too, and followed them into the elevator, where Cara pushed the button for the fourth-floor clinic. At once, the other woman started to giggle, embarrassed that it was the same button she needed to push. She was younger than Cara, with a sharp, blonde face, and high-top sneakers crisscrossed with Day-Glo laces. Her boyfriend looked like a rock star. When the giggling subsided they were holding each other in the same way that Cara and Douglas were holding each other; two hands around the back, and two hands around the front with the fingers interlocked. It was a slow ride up. At the top was a hallway, and a woman at a desk behind a pane of Plexiglas. She said "Okay, Honey," to the blonde woman, and "Go ahead, Honey," to Cara, before buzzing them all through a door.

"She called me Honey on the phone, too," said Cara to Douglas. It gave her a warm feeling. A second woman at a desk on the other side of the door called her Honey, as well, and gave her some papers to be filled out. There was a large waiting room with a maze of couches, and several smaller rooms off to the side with more couches, and then some other doors you couldn't see beyond. About fifteen women were in there, and a third as many men. Cara led Douglas to a room in the back where the blonde couple already sat with their questionnaire. The blonde woman giggled again, and then got serious just as she had in the elevator. It was the standard questionnaire with a few ominous questions thrown in, like, *Do you have someone to drive you home?* and *Are you likely to faint?* Cara wrote that she was likely not to faint but to scream, which made Douglas sigh with his head on her shoulder.

"Are you going to cross that out?" he asked.

"Should I?"

"Are you?"

"Am I what?"

"Are you likely to scream?"

"No. Not in this place."

"Then cross it out," Douglas said.

"Maybe," said Cara.

It was a romantic moment. The couch cushions were deep, the room smelled of coffee, and the blonde couple was nuzzling, too. Through the gray, dusty glass of the window could be seen the bare tops of some buildings and then the sun low in the sky.

"I don't want the sedative," Cara decided. "I want to know what's going on."

She meant she wanted to feel how much it hurt.

"You'll know what's going on anyway," Douglas said. "It's just a relaxant."

"But I *really* want to know what's going on, and I don't want to be nauseated when it's over, and tired."

"You'll be tired anyway," said Douglas.

"But not nauseated," said Cara. "But what if they don't let me not have the sedative? They asked me on the phone, and I said I wanted it, and the money order includes it . . ."

"We can pay for it and not have it, if you want," said Douglas. "You're beginning to get sort of worked up, Cara. Calm down. Okay?"

"But on the phone they made it seem as if I couldn't change my mind. They made it seem as if—"

"Just go to the woman at the desk and tell her that you don't want the sedative, and see what she says."

"But maybe I should have it," said Cara, "if I'm getting uptight."

"Okay."

"Except I don't want to be nauseated. But I don't want to be too relaxed, either."

"Okay," said Douglas.

"Are you getting mad at me?" she asked. She meant, *on a day like this?*

"No," Douglas said. "But I'm not really pleased."

"With what?"

"With the way you're acting. You're getting yourself into a snit."

"I always do," said Cara.

"At least you *know* you do," said Douglas. "That's something, I guess."

He crossed the room to where the coffeepot and paper cups sat on a table, and poured Cara a cup the way she liked it, with just a small amount of milk from the half-pint container wedged in a bowlful of melting ice. Then he stirred it up gently with a plastic spoon, wiped the spoon on a napkin, and slid it back into the box. He did this all very calmly, in a measured, careful way that meant he knew Cara was watching and that he was trying to say, "Chill out, Cara."

Cara didn't know if she wanted to chill out or not.

"I can't drink it," she said when he brought her the cup. "They said only clear liquids."

"That's if you have the sedative," said Douglas.

"How do you know?"

"I just know."

"Wait a minute," said Cara.

She left the room and asked the woman at the desk about the sedative. The woman took the questionnaire, said fine if Cara didn't want the sedative and that they'd refund twenty dollars at the end of the procedure.

"She called me Honey again," Cara said to Douglas on the couch, sipping her coffee. The blonde couple had gone into another of the waiting rooms, where instead of coffee on the table there was a stack of magazines. They held a *Newsweek* open on both of their laps while the boyfriend flipped the pages, not reading, just staring together at the shifting technicolor. Now on the couch next to Douglas and Cara were two women with permed hair and cigarettes, quietly talking. Everyone looked low-key. Occasionally a nurse came in and ushered someone through a door for a blood pressure check and a brief physical, but other than that it was quiet except for the ringing of the telephone up front. It was not yet midday but a number of patients lay down as they waited. A few of them slept. Some had taken off their shoes and propped their feet on the worn, tumbled cushions of the couches or on the laps of their husbands or boyfriends, and curled up resignedly like people stranded in an airport. Nearly all of the staff and most of the patients were black. There were two young women who had come in together in baseball uniforms, the knee pads still strapped into place, and another, older woman, tall and big-boned, in a tailored purple dress and lots of heavy brass jewelry. She wore stockings and heels, and her hair in beaded cornrows, and her eyelids densely shadowed in extravagant turquoise. But there was something not quite right about her, too. Something alarming that Cara couldn't identify. Maybe it had only to do with how big she was, how high her forehead, how broad in the shoulders and hands, and how tall and erect her posture. She looked utterly composed, and she was gazing past the blonde girl's rock star boyfriend, who now sat alone on the couch. Apparently the blonde girl had gone in for her blood pressure check, leaving him nervous. His nervousness made him embarrassed, and his embarrassment made him more nervous, so while he fidgeted in his seat, he pretended not to fidget, sitting forward and flipping through the same magazine again, and then meeting Cara's eye and looking away, until finally he gave up pretending and jiggled his feet and kept his face strained toward the door, where the tall, well-dressed woman was gazing as well, but with an air of serenity on the impossible curve of her forehead.

At that moment the nurse came through the waiting room again and beckoned Cara for her temperature and blood pressure check, after which Cara and Douglas were to join some people sitting on card chairs in one of the rooms in the corner, where a video was to be shown.

It was then, linking her arm through Douglas's as they left the waiting area, that two things dawned on Cara. One was that she felt neither nervous nor serene, so that while she wasn't jittery like the rock star, neither was she as calm as the well-dressed woman. And neither was she as sleepy as the women who seemed to want to forget everything, dozing in the waiting room at eleven o'clock in the morning, their arms folded under their heads. Instead, Cara only hovered alertly at the edge of what she thought must be a deep, seductive pool of emotion, waiting for someone to push her in. She'd caught glimpses of the counselors at the far end of the waiting room, near the entrance to a hallway, leading patients gently by the arm or with a hand at the small of the back, down the hallway into rooms where they would have their reckoning. The floating coin would spin and suddenly drop, and Cara would reach out and catch it and reel with the surprising weight of it but know how to live with what she was going to do.

The second thing that dawned on Cara as she left the waiting room was that the reason the large woman in the purple dress and costume jewelry looked not-quite-right and a little alarming was that she wasn't a woman at all but a man in women's clothing.

And the video, too, was nearly surreal, like something out of a dream. On-screen was a bare, round, surgical amphitheater and in the middle of it an examining table fitted with stirrups near some other equipment on squat, wheeled carts. The doctor wore a white lab coat and rubber gloves, and the patient was pretty and blonde and Swedish and appeared as bored as if she were having her legs waxed. She lay down on the table, placed her feet carefully in the stirrups, and raised her face to the ceiling reposefully. When the doctor held up a syringe, explained that he planned to anesthetize the woman's cervix, and slid the instrument between her labia, the woman blinked at the ceiling but stayed unruffled as before. Then she blinked again and disappeared, and for a second Cara thought it was over, it wasn't so bad, it was easy, it was nothing, it was simple, only of course it wasn't over, for there was still the dilation to be done. It hadn't occurred to Cara that her cervix would need to be forcibly opened the way they diagramed it on-screen, centimeter by centimeter. But the vacuuming looked soothing by comparison, and when it really was over and the woman reappeared and brushed a hair from her eyes, the doctor helped her off the table with a chivalrous manner, the sleeves of his white hospital coat falling delicately around his wrists. Walking out, the patient appeared to be floating, head high and unperturbed. Cara felt a mixture of admiration and disbelief, the same way she felt about the movies she'd been shown before giving birth, in her Lamaze classes in the gym at the high school. There never seemed to be too much panic or pain in those movies and Cara, skeptical, was certain they were fakes until they showed the baby actually crowning. Perhaps it was the presence of the film crew that made these women so unbothered, Cara thought, feeling glum about the fact that for a week after the procedure she was forbidden to swim or to have a bath. She never swam or took tub baths, anyway—she jogged, then showered—but still the very risk of infection seemed unjust. In the front of the room, a white-haired nurse displayed a model of the reproductive tract, her gloved finger probing the plastic opening of the cervix. Cara felt a twinge in her own, real cervix, and squeezed Douglas's fingers. The fallopian tubes resembled wilting, regretful blossoms, and looking at them Cara could imagine a corresponding regretfulness in that part of her body where her fallopian tubes must be, but she couldn't bring herself to imagine those organs themselves. She didn't want to. They looked too fragile and lovely to be part of a person's body. They looked like creatures of the sea. The transvestite wouldn't have them,

Cara found herself thinking, and when she went out into the waiting room it was to look at this person with nearly breathless wonder. How like a woman she looked, and yet how like a man, with her plucked, penciled eyebrows and lavishly hennaed hair. The more Cara looked at her, the more grotesque she became, and the more enviable. How nice to be so womanly and yet not be a woman, Cara supposed. How nice to be feminine without having to be female.

How pleasant, Cara thought. How inviolate.

And yet, how naive.

For what an idealized notion of womanhood this person must have, because despite what was on the outside—the makeup and the beaded braids and the heavily dramatic costume jewelry and the shoes and the clothes and the posture and the way she crossed her legs and pursed her lips—despite all that, underneath was a body that was closed to the world, not a body that was open like a woman's.

The transvestite had put on fresh, wet-looking lipstick, and crossed her legs, and tapped a painted fingernail against one of her earrings so it swung to and fro.

"She doesn't know," Cara thought. "She doesn't know. She doesn't *know*."

"Who doesn't know what?" Douglas asked, for Cara must have been saying it under her breath.

Cara shrugged and didn't answer, certain that if she told him, then it wouldn't be so; there would be no transvestite, but just a woman overdressed in costume jewelry, with overdyed hair and a sculpted mouth. Just an ordinary woman and inside, in warmth and darkness, the fallopian tubes like regretful, wilting blossoms.

"What were you thinking about?" pressed Douglas.

"Oh, just that it's funny that they named it Ginny."

"That they named what Ginny?"

"The plastic model, back there. Of the reproductive tract."

"Oh," said Douglas. "Why? What's funny about that?"

"Ginny," said Cara. "Short for Virginia. Long for vagina."

"Oh," said Douglas, laughing. His response made her giddy

and the giddiness made her a little unstrung, and she was still
half floating when one of the counselors approached her, a
clipboard extended like a hand in formal greeting.

Outside the counseling room was a carpeted hallway, where
Douglas was told to wait while the counselor led Cara inside.
There wasn't a chair; he had to stand near the door. The whole
thing was a surprise, because Cara had imagined it would be the
three of them. Still, she supposed it made sense this way, in case
the patient had a secret. Cara had a secret, too, but it wasn't
what the counselor thought it might be. It was her own disappointment. For this wasn't the counselor that Cara, from her
seat at the far end of the waiting room, had picked out for
herself, with the open, affectionate face and demeanor. Instead,
this woman's sympathy looked blunt and aggressive, like a
badge she'd pinned on.

"So," said the counselor. "Tell me why you're here."

"I'm pregnant," said Cara.

"How did you get pregnant?"

"We had sexual intercourse," said Cara, who could feel herself
retreating, closing up.

"I mean what were you using?"

"A diaphragm."

"And what do you intend to use now?"

"I intend to continue that discussion with my doctor," Cara
answered pointedly.

The room was tiny and close. On the empty chair, the chair
in which Douglas would have been sitting had the counselor
allowed him inside, perched a carton of tissues.

"What I really meant," said the counselor severely, drawing a
breath, "was what brought you to make this decision to have an
abortion, once you found that you were pregnant?"

"Well," Cara said, and then she found herself stalling for time,
for this was the question that she had been waiting for. This was
the moment. *Here* was the counselor, and *here* was the question,
and *here* was the moment when Cara would have her reckoning,
when the counselor would listen to what Cara would say, and

then the counselor would nod, or smile, or whatever else the counselor with the open face and listening expression would have done, and then, magically, what Cara had said would be real and immutable, like an object that Cara might wrap up and take home with her and put on a shelf for safekeeping.

On the counselor's lap lay the clipboard, a sheaf of papers, and a pen. The counselor raised her eyebrows encouragingly, and Cara thought she discerned a spark of warmth.

"Well," Cara repeated, "I found myself pregnant, and it was such a surprise. Such a surprise, I mean, to find myself not knowing what to do. To have it or not. Because we'd always said, I mean up until the day before I knew I was pregnant, we'd always said we wouldn't have another, there wasn't any question. We have two, and we both have jobs, and four is such a good number, although that's what I thought about three before we had Max, but anyway the very idea of having a third child was not something we even thought about, and then suddenly I was pregnant and my body *wanted* it. My body made me fall in love with it. And if I . . . well, I've done a lot of talking. With my friends and my husband, and myself, and sometimes when I think of the child, I think of it as a face, as a person, you know, someone who would or wouldn't have a life, and then I think I can't do this, I have no right to do this, but then when I think of it as a baby needing to be nursed and needing diapering and needing holding for another two years and when I think of my other children and when I think of our life, which is so good right now, so under control, then I think I do have the right, so that's what I've decided to do. And it hasn't been easy. Really. It hasn't."

"It never is," said the counselor a little too apathetically while offering a tissue from the box between them on the chair, a gesture familiar to Cara-the-Career-Placement-Counselor as one of etiquette, for surely Cara could have reached out herself and taken one. Anyway she wasn't crying. She had thought that she would, and there had even been a moment in the middle when she thought that she was, then and there, but it never quite broke, it never quite rose to the surface.

"So you have doubts about this . . . ," said the counselor when Cara had composed herself again.

"Yes," Cara said. "Of course. I'll always have doubts. For the rest of my life I'll have doubts."

"No, I mean about being here. About having an abortion."

"That's what we're talking about," said Cara.

"Well, maybe I'm not making myself clear," said the counselor. "Tell me how you feel *now*."

"I just told you how I felt."

"That was then. This is now. You've stopped—" She waved her hand in the air. She meant to say, *You were almost crying, now you're not*.

"I feel the same," Cara said.

"No," said the counselor. "That's not quite what I mean. I mean how do you feel, now that you've said it."

"Now that I've told you how I feel, how do I feel?" Cara asked. She wished Douglas were here. Douglas would get a kick out of this.

"Yes," said the counselor.

"The same," said Cara.

"So you do have doubts," said the counselor, who raised her eyebrows again, so that again Cara thought she discerned a spark of warm encouragement.

"I'll always look around my dinner table and wonder who's not there," Cara said. "Yes. If that's what you mean."

"I mean doubts about this," said the counselor. "About the abortion."

"Everyone's been calling it the procedure," said Cara, stalling again. "No. Well, yes, I have doubts. But I came here, didn't I? I'm here. I don't want to be pregnant again. That's a lot to ask of a person's body. Not too many people think about that, you know. Or talk about it, anyway."

The counselor was nodding.

"That part of my life is over," said Cara. Douglas had said this, earlier, in the radio station on that first evening when they sat side by side near the turned-off mikes. "We're in another phase now. We don't want to go backwards."

"So you do feel different now," said the counselor. "Different from the way you felt when you were trying not to cry, I mean. That's what I'm hearing. You're feeling better now, Cara."

"No, I'm not at all," Cara said, amused, chagrined. This wasn't working out. This wasn't what she wanted, this wasn't a catharsis, there was no pool of emotion, only a muddy stretch that she had somehow to cross. This was only some kind of exercise, but she didn't understand it yet, not quite. For there was something going on, something that was expected of her, of which she was ignorant. Or of which, anyway, she must pretend to be ignorant, in order to keep being truthful.

The counselor wanted her consent. It was as simple as that. This was a formality. This was protocol. The counselor held the papers in her lap, and the pen, and she was waiting for the proper conditions, for the moment when Cara could sign.

"What I mean is," said the counselor, her forehead creased, "you're happy with your decision."

"No," Cara said. "I'll never be happy with it."

"But you're not as unhappy with it as you were before."

"I had a choice," said Cara, who even now was still hoping for that revelatory moment, like something shattering between them. "I could choose to live with the complications of a third pregnancy and a third child, and this is not an easy pregnancy, I know that already, or I could live with the decision. With the necessary grief."

"Grief?"

"I'm not doing this lightly, I'm not going to let myself forget it, it's not like clipping a fingernail. But it's not as if people never have doubts about things that they do. It's not like everything that everybody does is done contentedly. People make hard decisions. They make difficult trades. They weigh things, you know," meaning, *You* should *know, shouldn't you?*

But the counselor was at a loss. In the window behind her the sun had risen just a little higher above the glittering roof of the neighboring building. One of her arms lay in sun on the arm of the empty chair but the hand with the pen was in shadow.

This is ridiculous, Cara was thinking. This is the most absurd situation I have ever been in in my life.

"I feel better," she lied. "I have fewer doubts now than I had before, about doing this."

The counselor looked at her, hard, leaning forward in her chair.

"I don't want to be pregnant," said Cara. "I don't want to have a new baby."

The counselor leaned closer still, the hand with the pen just barely upraised.

"I want this abortion," Cara declared, dry-eyed. "I want it now. Today. This minute."

The counselor gave her the papers. She signed.

"So it wasn't at all what I needed," she said later to Douglas, when she had finished telling him all about it and when they were done laughing about the absurdity of it. "I wanted to have some kind of catharsis."

"I know," Douglas answered. "Me, too."

"So, I guess we'll have to have our catharsis in there," Cara said, gesturing toward the hallway where the doctors were.

What Cara imagined about that hallway was a scene similar to that when she'd given birth—herself on the table, and between her knees the ushering faces of the doctor and nurse, and at her side, Douglas with his hand on her forearm, stroking it gently from wrist to elbow. Cara would be crying and murmuring, "No, no, no," as she had cried out in labor with no thought of actually stopping what was happening, and then when it was over, maybe they'd be allowed to look at it, just her and Douglas, alone in the room with their born, unborn child, just to gaze at it, apologize to it, tell it good-bye.

None of which seemed ludicrous to her in the least. It would be like a scene from the Bergman films she hated; terribly, devastatingly intense, and real and unreal at once, after which, having walked out, she'd feel refreshed and reinvigorated by no more than the sight of a pebble in the parking lot, something bright and incontrovertible. It would be like seeing the trans-vestite, and pointing her out to Douglas just to hear Douglas argue, *No, Cara, that is not a transvestite, that is a woman wearing too much makeup.*

So she found herself longing for the parking lot, and for the ordinary sight of their car, and for the moment when they'd climb into it and start home in their ordinary, comradely way, when they could talk about Georgie's teeth and Max's impish-ness without the guilty suspicion that such talk was a way of avoiding talking about something else. Maybe the blonde woman and her rock star boyfriend would be starting home, too, at that very same moment, and finally they'd all four acknowledge one another with fleeting nods and waves and smiles, or more likely she and Douglas would go on acting like the other couple wasn't there at all, just as the blonde couple would act like Cara and Douglas weren't there at all, because shared privacy was the contract they'd made.

For the moment the blonde couple slumped indolently on the couch, all four sneakered feet on the table, four ankles crossed one on top of another, Day-Glo laces intertwined, lemon on lime. Around them the waiting room murmured and dozed beneath a haze of cigarette smoke and the murky undula-tion of tired voices. Only the transvestite was fresh and deliber-ate, taking a paperback out of her purse, flipping it open with one neat flick of her too-braceleted wrist. There was the dull clink of copper on silver. And Cara watched her in silence, and didn't point her out to Douglas, and snuck a glance at the title of the book, to see what such a person would be reading.

The transvestite, in fact, was the first to be called into the back hallway where the doctors were. She slid the book back in her purse, slung the purse over her shoulder, and picked some lint off her sleeve, then disappeared like a breeze through the door.

Then, soon after, it was Cara's turn.

It was the counselor who came for her, then laid a protec-tive hand on her shoulder as Cara stood up from the couch.

Cara resented that touch. She wanted Douglas to be the one to do the touching. He wanted it, too. He got up and started with them for the door.

"Oh, no," said the counselor.

Cara and Douglas looked at each other.

"Spouses aren't allowed in the procedure," said the counselor.

Procedure again, thought Cara, before realizing fully what the counselor had said.

"I was with her when our children were born," said Douglas evenly.

"They didn't say this on the phone," said Cara.

"It's policy," said the counselor. "They won't let him in. I'm sorry."

"Why not?" asked Douglas and Cara at once.

Policy, thought Cara.

"Some of the patients get upset if their spouses are in there with them."

Upset? thought Cara.

"And we've had a few spouses faint."

"They didn't say this on the phone," Cara protested. "They asked me, they actually asked me, if there was someone who would stay with me the whole time."

But Douglas already had kissed her and stood back as if to say they'd make a fuss about it later but not now. And Douglas so rarely did this, so rarely backed down, that Cara, too, acquiesced and followed the counselor with her head held high. She'd forgotten the counselor's name the moment it was told to her, and she knew that if she asked, she'd forget it again. This made her proud.

"Are you nervous?" asked the counselor.

"No," said Cara firmly. She marched ahead of the counselor straight through a door into a room that seemed ready for her except that the counselor told her to go to the bathroom first. The bathroom was at the end of the corridor, and when Cara shut the door and the fan came on, she felt suddenly acutely alone. Gone were the other women lounging on couches, gone was the noise of the telephone ringing, gone the cluttered, tired feeling of the waiting room and the sight of bare ankles and bared sleeping midriffs amid the slick, nervous whisper of magazine covers. All morning in the waiting room, she'd met eyes and looked away, and each time there was an instant of recognition of the kind passed among the people crowding the lobby of a theater after the show. But the bathroom was narrow, tall, windowless. Standing inside of it was like standing in a chimney, and looking up at the ceiling was like seeing that thin slat of sky at the top of the chimney that was utterly unpeopled. She was lonely in there. And she wasn't a lonely person, ordinarily. Ordinarily she sought out moments of solitude as a way of keeping hold of herself, as a way of shielding her thoughts and feelings against the disparate needs of her children and Douglas and the dog and her friends. But she hadn't had that kind of solitude—hadn't sought it, hadn't missed it—since the night she'd walked the dog to the store downtown in search of a pregnancy test. And that seemed like years ago, now. And since that time, when she'd learned she was pregnant, those thoughts and feelings she'd once treasured as her own seemed tangled and fused with the feelings and thoughts of others, as if no one ever could quite pull away from other people or society, no matter how hard they tried or wanted. "When you're on the road, you are part of a community, whether you like it or not," the driver's ed instructor had warned, and now the warning had borne fruit and the fruit was somehow bitter and glorious at once, and Cara had grown accustomed to the taste of it.

Then when she walked out of the bathroom, she found she was walking not as tall and proud as she had before when the counselor had been following, when she had felt so self-protective. Now her step was more tentative. For what had seemed to be a choice between feeling scared and feeling not-scared seemed suddenly less cut-and-dry, as if there were possible some middle ground to which she didn't even have to be committed. As if she could be neither, or both. Scared, and not scared. Not scared, and scared. It was like being a child, walking to school on a still-dark morning when a car slid from behind and slowed to a crawl alongside. It was like that—not knowing what to expect, and not knowing quite how to feel. *Feel vulnerable,* something whispers in the child. *No. Feel exhilarated, feel brave, feel proud. No, feel small.*

The procedure room was cramped, so the counselor stood by the door in a narrow, angled space at the side of the bed, clipboard in hand. She told Cara to undress from the waist down, to leave her skirt on if she wanted but just pull it up, to cover herself with a gown, to climb onto the bed, to lie back, to put her feet in the stirrups. The bed was hard, like a table. The counselor asked Cara if she wanted to hold her hand.

"No," Cara said, and then, for the sake of politeness, "not yet."

There was nothing on the ceiling, no picture, no diversion. On the ceiling of her own doctor's examining room was a picture of a loon on a lake; but here, only yellowed tiles. There was a thing on the floor she wanted to tell herself wasn't a vacuum pump, except she knew it was. Somehow she had imagined the machine would be disguised. But it resembled what it was, just a hose and a squat, heavy bucket.

When the doctor walked in, the counselor put her clipboard on a stool near the door. The doctor was young, thin-haired, spectacled, sour-looking, not courtly at all, like the one in the video. Cara smiled at him bravely, but he wasn't looking at her face, he was looking at her feet and at the space between her knees behind the paper of the gown. He reached for the dispenser, pulled on some gloves. He wheeled over a cart. He selected an instrument and stuck it into Cara's body and cranked it open as abruptly as if he were turning a key in a door.

Cara's legs and arms twitched.

I want to know, she was thinking. I want to follow step by step, I want to feel it, I want to look it in the eye, I want—

But it was happening so fast. The doctor prepared the injection, there was the deep, biting sting of the needle. Then the doctor stood back and started cranking again. The metal speculum was cold but the pain was red-hot. From a hook on the wall hung a blood pressure gauge, and Cara found herself staring at that, at the arrow pointing north like the arrow on a compass.

"Hold my hand," Cara made herself say to the counselor, because she didn't like the feeling of the air between her fingers, how sterile it was, and yet how stale, how dingy yellow.

"What is the doctor doing?" she asked.

"He's opening the cervix," the counselor told her, as if the doctor were a thing and not a person who might answer for himself. For that was what he seemed to want. That was what he seemed to command. He was a pair of hands, gloved in white plastic, and the hands moved as if from a distance or across a barrier of glass, like the mechanized hands in amusement arcades that closed so disinterestedly over their prize.

"And what is he doing now?" Cara yelled, because it felt like the hands were pumping her with air, pumping and pumping. All the while, the doctor was silent, his mouth set in a line, his eyes on his hands, where she couldn't see them.

"He's vacuuming the pregnancy," the counselor replied.

"How much longer?" Cara yelled, above her pain and the strange sucking sound of the bucket and the tube and the gaze of the doctor that wouldn't meet her own. Meaning, *Enough time to change my mind if I wanted?*

"He's done," said the counselor. "It's finished."

Thank God, Cara thought.

He walked out of the room with his gloves still on and the tools on the table needing to be cleaned. The bucket was quiet, the hose lay limp, and there was only the counselor again and some crumpled paper towel at the edge of the sink. The door shut with a click behind him.

Cara lay staring at the pocked, yellowed ceiling. It hurt too much to sit. It was better to lie still awhile and let the pounding come to a halt.

"It helps to sit up, believe it or not," said the counselor, while the pounding was still in full force.

Cara pulled herself dizzily forward. She took her feet from the stirrups and let her head hang down.

"How do you feel?" asked the counselor.

Cara said nothing. At least sitting was better than standing. If she stood up, she knew she would vomit.

But the counselor was already saying, "You can go to recuperation now. They'll have a couch and a heating pad. You'll need to get dressed."

She gestured toward Cara's tights. Cara said, "That was horrible." The counselor put a hand on her arm, gently, the way a teacher leads a pupil down the hall.

At the sink, Cara heaved up a mouthful of bile. That was all that would come out. She was glad she hadn't eaten, but the dry heaves made her eyes water anyway.

"Are you forcing yourself?" asked the counselor after several more heaves.

"No," Cara said. She wanted to kick this woman in the stomach and then ask her how it felt and if she was forcing herself. She ran the water in the sink, splashed her face, rinsed her mouth, spit, and rinsed again. Then she slid past the counselor out the door to the recuperation area, where a nurse stood ready near a couch with a heating pad already turned up high. Cara felt blank but grateful. She was still in pain, and dizzy. She lay down on the couch with her head on a couple of pillows, surprised to see the counselor with her clipboard less than a foot away again.

"How do you feel?" asked the counselor. Cara could see the pen poised over the clipboard.

"Like I've been run over by a truck," said Cara.

"How do you feel, now?" asked the counselor, when a couple of minutes had passed.

"Like I've been run over by a Volkswagen Bug. Better," lied Cara.

"Okay?" said the counselor.

"What?"

"You feel okay?"

"I said better," said Cara. "Not okay. What's your name again, please?"

"Rebecca." The counselor smiled. Cara shut her eyes. When she opened them again, the counselor was gone and Cara had a look around. The transvestite was on a couch perpendicular to hers, smiling as if with a secret, the heating pad over her belly. She was reading again, but also toying with one of her earrings. Cara stared at her in wonder until a nurse came over with the offer of a drink and a list of instructions to be followed at home.

"Now," she said to Cara, pointing to the bathroom, "go in there, and if there's a spot any bigger than a quarter, call me."

"Can I wait a few minutes?" asked Cara. "Can I have another drink and an aspirin?"

Later, in the bathroom, there was a spot of blood but no bigger than a quarter, so she didn't call the nurse. When she came out, there was the counselor again.

"How are you feeling?" she asked.

"Okay," Cara said.

The counselor checked something off on her clipboard.

"You can leave whenever you're ready. Just go out through that door, and they'll buzz you back into the waiting room. I told your husband you were fine. Good luck, Cara."

Cara turned away. The nurse was telling the transvestite that if there was a spot any bigger than a quarter, to call her, and the transvestite stood serenely for the bathroom, letting her heating pad slide from her lap to the couch. Cara gathered herself and stood up, too, and made her way shakily toward the waiting room and Douglas.

"It was a violation, Douglas," Cara said in the car. "The doctor hated me, I swear, that's the only explanation, I kept looking at him and seeing just hatred, Douglas, I swear I could see it in the top of his head."

"Probably the only kind of doctor that would work with all these patients he'll never see again, he has to be the kind of guy that doesn't give a fuck about being nice," said Douglas angrily. "I would have thought it would be different. I *did* think it would be different. You know, everything calm and together, and the doctors careful and friendly the way doctors are, the way—"

He groped for words. He meant, *the way they are when you're having a baby*, Cara thought.

"But this place is just a factory," he said. "It shouldn't have to be that way. It shouldn't be so iron curtain. It shouldn't be so underground."

"No," Cara said. "You know that question we always ask each other, about the ugly wallpaper, you know, who do they make it for? Why do they make ugly wallpaper to begin with? Well, it's for places like this, that think they deserve it. They operate under that assumption, you know, there's no reason why the floor has to be gritty, why the windows have to be dirty, why the couches have to be falling apart, why the ceiling has to look like, well, my ceiling looked like it had had matches held up to it, you know, on purpose, to make it uglier than it already was. And it was horrible, really, the way they did what they did, as if they didn't think they should be doing it, as if they had to keep the lights dim so no one could see. Or maybe I'm just, I don't know, worked up. I wonder what other people think. I wonder what that blonde woman thinks, right now."

"That's what I meant to tell you," said Douglas. "Something weird happened. She gets up, she goes into the hallway, then she comes back about two minutes later and gets her boyfriend and they leave."

"They left?"

"Yeah."

"Was she upset?"

"No, they were fine. It was nothing. They just left. They seemed perfectly happy. I think she was laughing, even."

"That's weird," Cara said.

"It was," Douglas said.

They were quiet for a moment, and Cara knew they both felt equally betrayed by the blonde couple's easy departure. In the waiting room after Cara had been buzzed through, Douglas had risen and come forward to give her a hug, but Cara had said, "Not yet, wait till we get in the car, wait till we get out of here." She was making herself very stiff and composed, but then in the elevator she let herself flop against him. In the car they held each other, and now she slid her hand under his on the seat between them. They were driving not west, toward home, but east into the city, toward a deli they liked. It seemed ludicrous to go out for lunch as if in celebration, but equally ludicrous to drive home at three o'clock in the afternoon when there was already a babysitter at the house and they were free of the children. In a way it seemed to Cara that they couldn't return home now even if they wanted—they still had to go forward. Cara couldn't tell if she was hungry or not, but she knew that she wanted to eat. The deli had Belgian waffles, and she had been in the mood for one for days. She felt weak and exhausted, and she wanted to be able to convince herself, when she got home and climbed finally into bed, that it was evening already and that the day was over.

When she'd ordered a Belgian waffle and changed her mind and ordered instead a bowl of mishmash soup with its comforting mixture of matzoh balls, rice, noodles, and kreplach, and when she'd fallen asleep in the car with her head on Douglas's shoulder, and when they'd pulled into town and she'd wakened and told him to stop at the store for milk and ice cream for the children, and when they'd pulled into the driveway and, having switched off the engine, sat looking at the paper bag of food at Cara's feet, then Cara said to him, a little coyly just to take some of the weight off her sincerity, "I haven't had my catharsis yet."

She could say that to Douglas and not feel ridiculous. She was grateful for that, for the way he just sat still and listened and never cut her off, even though he already knew exactly what she was talking about.

"You know," she explained, although she knew he *did* know, "what I told you about. That it would be like a coin flipping and all of a sudden I'd be able to make peace with it, with the heads or tails of it, with whether it was right or wrong, but then it kept getting put off and then it didn't happen, and now I'm too tired. I'll have to do it tomorrow. Or maybe the next day. Or maybe if I just wait, it will happen by itself, eventually."

"Or maybe it just won't happen," said Douglas.

"What?" Cara said.

"It might never happen," said Douglas. "And that would be

okay, too, Cara, you don't have to plan for it or worry about it, because it might happen and it might not."

"But that would be terrible, if it never happened," said Cara.

"No, it wouldn't."

"It wouldn't?"

"I don't think so."

"But it would be so open-ended," said Cara.

Just then there was a coughing in the street and a florist's truck pulled into the driveway behind them, and out climbed someone with a bouquet of flowers wrapped in heavy, bright lavender paper.

"Oh!" Cara said. "Flowers! Douglas!"

"Don't look at me," Douglas said, pulling open the door and giving a low shout to the person delivering the flowers, who was just now climbing the steps to the house. It was a small person dressed in a long coat and a round knitted cap of the most awful, familiar color, a mustardy mixture of browns and yellows and on top of that the faded gray look of age.

"Oh, God," Cara said.

For it was Betty, her client, looking more shrunken than Cara could remember, smaller practically than the bouquet of flowers, although she held it quite proudly, the way she held up her head, regally almost, except for the hair that stuck out at the sides. Cara hadn't seen her since the day the job was offered. She had that same look of accusatory intelligence, which she fixed on Douglas as she handed him the flowers and started into one of her usual expostulations, gesturing here and there as Douglas stood there with the flowers, his nose buried in the folds of the paper as he listened. He was so polite, he might stand there forever, Cara knew, and considered getting out and rescuing him by pretending the ice cream was melting. But then she would end up standing there, too, for too long, talking to Betty about the ChemLawn the neighbors used on their grass. And the thought of standing there nodding her head self-righteously for not using ChemLawn herself when all she wanted was to be in bed between the coolness of the sheets, with Max quiet in her arms and Douglas and Georgie at the foot of the bed, reading a book together—that thought was enough to make her stay in the car and even hunker down lower so she wouldn't be seen. Besides, she didn't want to have to act grateful to Betty for the flowers when Betty had failed to be grateful for the job of delivering them, when all Betty had had to say was could her brother read Samuel Beckett aloud to her en route so she wouldn't have to vegetate in a truckful of carnations. Now Cara propped her knees against the dashboard and let her butt slide out over the edge of the car seat, so if her pad leaked through it wouldn't stain the upholstery. She was bleeding quite steadily now, and she expected it was nearly time for a change. Maybe she could change it in the car, except the pads were in the hatchback behind the back seat and she imagined that if she climbed through the car to get to them, there'd be a deluge of blood all over the place. Anyway, Cara was comfortable like this, hunkered down with her neck bent against the back of the passenger seat so she could gaze at her hands on her belly, contemplating. Her belly felt empty, suddenly, but not empty like a box. It felt empty the way the body of a person is said to be empty when that person has died and the soul has floated off. She had lifted her shirt and with her hands caressed the skin that had a shadowy ache behind it. For a moment she thought about the bodies of people who died, and how the bodies seemed to grieve in this lonely, silent way. Her belly grieved, too, she could tell by the soft, loose curve of it, but she thought this only natural and proper, a fact of life. Even animals other than humans grieved, sometimes, and their grief was a beautiful fact, not one to be lamented.

So it was sad and not-sad at once, not one or the other. It was one of those things for which sadness takes on grace and even loveliness, like in a photograph.

Still, she didn't know if she could keep this up, this looking at things objectively, philosophically. After all, this was her own belly she was looking at, and her own feelings hidden underneath it. She didn't know what those feelings were, exactly, and she was frightened of them. Douglas had said they might never come out; she might never have to look at them directly. But they would be there either way, forever. At this notion she looked at her belly again and then pulled the shirt over to cover it, and kept her hands where they were, laced on top of the cloth. This is how a pregnant woman keeps her hands, she realized, laced like this for protection.

Later that evening, Douglas said yes, Betty *was* a little strange, but not as strange as Cara had always led him to believe.

"She's eccentric," he said, "and down on her luck, and maybe kind of haughty, but a lot of people are haughty—you're haughty, Cara—and that doesn't make them deranged. She was telling me about her brother, about how he was working on some mathematical formula that would solve some impossible shape or other, I don't know, but it sounded interesting. I might use him on the show sometime."

"Oh, that would be fascinating," said Cara. "If he's in his shy mood, he won't open his mouth, and if he's in his despairing mood, he'll think he has nothing worth saying, and if he's in his arrogant mood, he won't deign to say it. He was sitting in the truck, waiting for her. He's this guy with Einstein hair and a shiny dinner jacket he wears every day and a long-lost look on his face, unless he's trying to make you uncomfortable, in which case he stares. Besides, a person can be deranged without being totally out of it. A person can be on-the-edge. That's why he stayed in the truck."

"And why did you stay in the car?"

"Because I don't like her. And it's not because I don't like her poverty or her neediness or her weirdness," said Cara, shooting him a look, "but because I don't like *her*. She doesn't want me to like her, so I'll do her that favor. Anyway, I didn't want to talk about what I knew you were talking about. ChemLawn. Right?"

"Well, a little of that," said Douglas.

"And she said how it's not fair for people to use ChemLawn because that means she can't collect dandelion greens for her salads."

"She did mention that," said Douglas, smiling.

"And for stew," added Cara. "With black-eye peas she cooks up on a sterno."

She reached out and touched a flower, and pulled the long stem out of the vase and slid it back in, in another spot where the flower would seem more solitary. It was a red poppy in a bouquet of all kinds and all colors, although of course the red was the most brilliant and the most false-looking with its papery texture. Whoever had selected it had intended for it to be that way, Cara was certain, and she took this as a clue, of sorts, meant to help her identify the responsible party. Because there wasn't a card. The problem was that any single one of her friends might have chosen the poppy thinking they were giving Cara just such a clue, thinking their style to be unique. Wendy would have chosen it for the way it made the bouquet resemble one of her more grotesque sculptures, with its shock of bright color amid muted creams and lavenders, while the other Wendy would have chosen it to commemorate what she knew Cara liked to think of as the violence of Cara's own nature. Elizabeth would have chosen it to represent blood, while Liz might have chosen it certain that it would demonstrate her own impulsive spontaneity. However, Liz didn't know about the abortion unless Elizabeth or one of the Wendys—certainly the beautiful one, because the chubby one would have told Cara had she betrayed Cara's confidence—had let it slip out. Unless Liz figured it out just by looking at Cara and guessing. For a long time Cara had imagined her resolution to be visible on her face, the way pregnancy itself was said to be unmistakable. It wouldn't take that much intuition to see it, especially for someone who had had an abortion herself. But Cara didn't know all that many people who had had abortions, unless some of them kept it a secret, and this didn't seem likely. Maybe it was someone she didn't know so well, then, who had sent her the bouquet of flowers. Maybe a neighbor, or maybe even the babysitter had picked up on things, or maybe Douglas had actually talked to somebody about it, although Cara thought this the most unlikely possibility of all.

"Did you tell anyone we were having an abortion?" she asked him.

He fixed on her a look of tolerant amusement. "Who would I tell?" he asked.

"Oh, I don't know. Maybe Estaban. Or maybe someone else you play darts with . . . ," Cara trailed off. Douglas was too discreet. He and his friends didn't talk about things they considered to be "personal." He had a friend named Steven who once went with someone to Club Med in Acapulco, and when Cara asked Douglas who, Douglas said he didn't know, he hadn't asked, it was none of his business. If he had talked to anyone about the abortion, it would have to have been a woman, and if it was a woman, it was probably Jenny, because Jenny liked to flirt with him and Douglas didn't know how to flirt back.

In any case, Cara decided, it wasn't the beautiful Wendy who had sent the flowers, for Wendy, who had stopped by an hour ago with her usual kind words and her tall, stooped posture of concern, had stood for a moment over the poppy, handling its delicate tissue between long, admiring fingers. Under her arm she carried not a plug-in heating pad but a hot-water bottle in the shape of a frog that they joked about because, frog or not, Cara had never used a hot-water bottle before in her life. It was already filled, and its heavy, sloshing legs outspread on her belly made Cara sleepier than she was already.

"You look fragile and romantic," Wendy told Cara, smiling.

"I know," said Cara. "Like—who was that woman again?"

"Henry's delicate sister, Alice. Alice James."

"Delicate, my ass. I feel like a hypochondriac," said Cara. "But really, Wendy, it was awful. It was horrible. It was disgusting."

"I know," said Wendy.

"You knew?"

"I knew it would be, for *you*. Because of how you feel things," said Wendy, bending to give Cara a kiss.

So Cara continued to wonder who might have sent the flowers, and that way, they provided distraction along with everything else flowers were meant to provide on such an occasion. It interested Cara to find that they cheered her up. Just to look at them made her feel better than when she wasn't looking at them, and to touch them seemed an act of communion with whatever nameless person had sent them.

So those flowers became the center of the room, a kind of focus that wasn't on Cara herself. She was sitting up in bed, reading, with her head on three pillows, and the hot-water bottle on a towel on her belly and the book in her hands above it, but if anyone were to come in, they would see the flowers first, for the red poppy would claim their attention. But after Wendy and the frog, no one did come in, and with that she was satisfied, too. Douglas had fed the children and bathed them and put Max in bed, and now he and Georgie were downstairs playing their ongoing game of Monopoly. When the telephone rang, first it was the other Wendy, and then it was Elizabeth, and both of them insisted that they hadn't sent the flowers although they wished they had thought to do so. Cara told Elizabeth that the doctor had been horrible and the counselor a sham, and that the pain had been stronger than she had believed it would be. She said, "I've had such a good life, such an easy, pampered, lucky life, that I have to say that this is the only time I've ever felt—well—violated. And it doesn't have to be that way. I mean, you wouldn't go to a doctor for any other procedure and get treated like a piece of shit. If you did, the doctor would be out of work in a second. But this doctor . . . it was as if he still thought he was illegal, like it was all he could do to wipe the rust off the coat hanger before he stuck it in. And all the while, the counselor's holding my hand in this 'comradely' way, as if even the people who spend their lives with this thing can't bring themselves to treat it like an everyday, necessary, civilized event; instead they have to carry the baggage of it with them everywhere they go. So here we are in this little procedure room, and on the one hand there's the doctor making sure that I know how inconvenienced he is by the fact that I've gotten myself into such a fix, and on the other hand there's the counselor acting stoic like a missionary, and in the middle there's me, just me, just wishing they would treat me like an ordinary patient with ordinary pains and misgivings and an ordinary body impatient to get off the table and get the hell out of there and get on with my ordinary life."

Cara took a deep breath and was done, relieved to have

found a way of talking about the abortion without having to mention the face, and the flipping coin, and the dispatch and loss and finality of it.

But the third phone call, after Georgie was asleep and while Douglas was in the shower, was Cara's mother, and since Cara was still a little high from all the talking, she told *her* about the flowers, too; about how someone, she didn't know who, had sent them, and how there was a red poppy she was moving back and forth in the bouquet to see where it looked the brightest. Somehow it seemed to Cara that not to tell her mother about the flowers would constitute more of a dissemblance than the fact that she wasn't telling her about the abortion, as if her mother might smell them over the phone and know there was something Cara wasn't saying.

"Oh," said her mother. "He must be very brave, your man. Brave or careless. Which do you think?"

"What do you mean?" asked Cara.

"Or do you think he could be trying to cause trouble? Cara, is he capable of that? Is he impetuous, Cara? Because that's a scary thought, especially so early on in . . . That would be something you might want to start thinking about."

Oh, thought Cara.

Oh.

"No, I don't think he's malevolent," Cara said carefully, because that would make for an easier way out than saying he was. A less convoluted way out, she thought. And she knew she wanted to get out of this somehow, and soon. "And I don't think careless, either. I think innocent is more likely."

"But you know innocence isn't really trustworthy in grown men," said Cara's mother. "Except in your father, but that's, oh, you know . . ."

"I know," Cara said, thinking of the clouds reflected in the windows of her father's airplanes. There were never any people, only a moist view of whipping cream spread out across the sky.

"But really, what is this man like? And what's going on? I thought you said it was still very much under control. In the supermarket, I thought you said. And you said, at least I thought you said, you didn't think he knew what was happening, you said he was in the dark about how you were feeling. But do you mean innocent, or naive? Because naivete in grown men, I never know quite what to make of that."

"I don't know anymore how *I* feel about *him*, it's all very confusing," Cara said obtusely, still wondering if maybe she should come out with it right now and tell her mother the truth. But the truth would mean telling her everything wrapped up in a haze of apology that would lead to proclamations on the part of Cara's mother followed by an offering of comfort. Even over the phone, her mother's comfort smelled of Night of Olay, powdery and sweetly seductive. And Cara didn't want to be seduced on this matter. It was hard sometimes, when her mother offered solace, for Cara to remember what the solace was about; there was only the delicate fragrance of it and Cara being the daughter again, nestled inside. Tonight she didn't want to have to do that, to sob numbly, unthinkingly, uncomprehendingly through the phone into the arms of her mother.

Besides, it had not escaped Cara that her mother liked this idea of a man in the market, this brief fabrication, this lie. For it *had* become a lie, no matter what it had been before. Where there had been an unformed presence bathed in deep pinks, now there was a grown man, naivete, flowers, carelessness, trouble, the threat of revelation. Her mother fed on these things, really. She was like a person with a spoonful of stew, savoring, evaluating, trying to identify its most secret ingredients. How exotic Cara felt to be the object of such speculation on the part of her mother. She had to admit it. Yes. *Exactly who is Cara?* That was what her mother was trying to figure out.

"These flowers he sent me—" said Cara after a moment. "That one red poppy in the middle is supposed to symbolize arrested passion, I bet."

"I thought you didn't know if he sent you the flowers."

"Then who did?"

"Tell Douglas I told you *I* sent you the flowers," said Cara's mother. "That way if Douglas is beginning to suspect, that will dispel it. No reason to upset him. At least I take it from what you're saying that there's no reason yet to upset him, Cara."

"Absolutely not," said Cara. "He's a minister," she added jokingly, but then she found she liked the joke, it felt so reassuring. "He wears a clerical collar. And I know I heard him singing 'Swing Low, Sweet Chariot' when he was over near the squash, once. Like a lullaby, you know. The whole thing's very gentle, very soft, understated."

"Except for the flowers," her mother said brightly, though in the silence that followed, it seemed Cara's mother was waiting for some further admission.

"What?" said Cara, exasperated.

"Nothing," said her mother.

"I can tell that you're trying to tell me something," said Cara. "Or that you're thinking there's something I haven't told you."

"Of course there are things you haven't told me. At least I hope there are. I don't expect to know everything. I've never felt I had the right, or even the desire. When you were a child . . . I liked it that there were things I didn't know about you, about your private, inside life. Not knowing and somehow not wanting to know—that's another kind of knowledge, in and of itself."

"Yes," Cara said, surprised by how deeply she meant it. Yes, like *Amen!* It was a little embarrassing, really, so to cover up she said, "Yes, I'm beginning to feel that with Georgie. That there's a part of him that I can't—that I shouldn't—understand."

"Although I'm happy to know whatever you want me to know . . . ," said her mother.

"See? That's what I mean. You're suggesting there's something that I want you to know but that I'm not telling you because I don't think you want to know about it."

"I'm suggesting nothing of the sort," said Cara's mother, "but now that you've brought it up for the third time, it's beginning to seem you have a guilty conscience."

"Well, I don't."

"Good," said Cara's mother. "I love that song, 'Swing Low, Sweet Chariot.'"

"Me, too," Cara said, and this time there was only a pause before she added, "Douglas just got out of the shower, I think."

"Oh? Tell him hello."

"My mom says hello," Cara called to the bathroom.

"Hello," Douglas answered.

"Tell him I sent you the flowers," said Cara's mother.

"She sent me the flowers," Cara called out, shocked to find herself lying to Douglas as automatically and necessarily as if the flowers *had* been sent by a carelessly innocent priest who had fallen in love with her across the sad, yearning strains of a gospel tune. She'd never lied outright to Douglas before that she could remember. Well, it could be cleared up later on.

But later on when Douglas said, "I didn't know you'd told your mother about the abortion," Cara found herself replying protectively, "I didn't. I only told her I haven't been feeling so well. She called one day when I was really, really tired. She has a demonstrative heart, you know that. Only I never asked her why she chose that outrageous poppy. Probably thought I would like it, I guess."

"You do," said Douglas, touching a finger to one of the stems.

A single petal fell off and twirled to the floor in a slow, floating, mesmerizing spiral.

5 🖎

Several days later, around dinnertime, Cara set out from home along the road to the public library, with Max in the stroller wanting to climb out and walk, and Georgie alongside her grumbling because he was tired and wanted a stroller for himself, and the dog on a leash pulling this way and that. Douglas was at the library preparing for an interview with a woman who had written a book about twins, but the library would be closing at six and Cara hoped to meet Douglas at a halfway point and accompany him the rest of the way home. This was a risk, because if Douglas found a ride, or walked another route home, then she'd have walked all the way to the library and would have to walk all the way back, which was fine when she was alone but not fine with the dog and the stroller and the kids, who begged to be carried, or who dawdled behind with their hands in the cracks of the sidewalks, digging up beetles and dried earthworms. If they met Douglas, Douglas would take charge of the dog or the stroller, and then Cara would take hold of his arm or Georgie's. She'd worked at the office this afternoon, and had walked there hurriedly, afraid she'd miss her meeting, and had walked back hurriedly, too, worried she'd be late for the babysitter, and wondering what on earth she could cook for dinner without needing to go to the store, and thinking she should have taken the car, and deciding on a curry of carrots and onions and whatever other vegetables were lying around, although there wasn't any rice, but there was cornmeal and cheese, so she would make polenta, which the children would sprinkle with sugar. Now, with dinner prepared, needing just a gentle heating on the stove, she felt buoyant, efficient, and free, and hoped the feeling would last through the children's bedtime, because there was a book she wanted to read.

Some of the trees were flowering, and some of the old people who had been sitting out on their porches and had nodded when she walked by earlier, and to whom she hadn't nodded back, now nodded again and smiled at the sight of the children.

At the halfway point there was still no sign of Douglas, but then around the bend she saw him from far off. He had a characteristic gait. Neat, graceful steps, but with a certain floppiness about the upper body that made her heart ache when she saw it.

The heart is the center of the body, she thought, and then she remembered something.

After the abortion, when she'd left recuperation and gone back through the hallway and been buzzed through into the waiting room, she had caught sight of Douglas sitting on one of the couches, not the same couch he'd been sitting on before, but one closer to the water cooler. He twirled a coffee cup slowly in the palm of his hand, and he hadn't seen her yet; he looked worried. Watching him, Cara found herself thinking quite matter-of-factly, that man is my husband, that man with the cup, that worried-looking man with the jeans and red hair who resembles the husband you get if you spin the knob wrong in the "Mystery Date Game." He looked as usual very relaxed with his worries, and comfortable with the fact of his isolation, alone on the couch in a roomful of empty couches. For the front room appeared to have entered some kind of a lull and thinned out, as if everyone had been ushered at once into the video room or down the hallway with the counselors; aside from Douglas, there was only the woman at the telephone desk near the door, flipping through files.

"Hey, Honey." She greeted Cara with a wave of a file, and Douglas looked up and saw her, and that was that. Except, Cara had had the chance to see that he was still arresting to her, the very sight of him enough to make her pause in her step for a split, split second, as if only to register his presence. Arresting, yes, but not arresting in the way he'd been years ago in the beginning. It was not the novelty of him that made her pause to take in the sight of him, but the familiarity—the safe haven—of him.

6 ✎

*T*hen came days in which Cara seemed to exist on an incline, sliding up or sliding down (she couldn't tell which, she only knew she felt unbalanced), but in any case, sliding away from what she still thought of, mockingly, as "the procedure" and all that had come before it. For work she attended an Arts Opportunities Conference held in the basement seminar rooms of the Fine Arts Museum in the city, and while on break in the museum shop, having selected a book for Georgie and one for Max, she drifted over toward the tiered shelves of postcards, where she noticed one of an M. C. Escher print depicting the very incline whose skewed, implausible slope had become so dizzyingly familiar to her. The postcard showed a river impossibly climbing up a steep angle toward a falls. At the bottom of the falls turned a giant water wheel, and to the left of the wheel sat a house from which a tunnel led to yet another house and to a set of walled steps. On the flat, terraced roof of this second house stood a woman hanging laundry on a line, the very weight of the wet wash visible beneath her fingers. Cara felt immediate sympathy. To be going through the days, to be completing their disparate tasks, to be hanging up the wash, to be stepping out later to find it just about dry on the line, so close to the inconceivable, unnatural law of that gravity-defying river that you could feel the spray of the waterfall hitting your face—that was what it was like, going down the walled steps and then up again, or up and then down, over and over, day after day after day. Although on that morning of the drive to the abortion clinic Cara had felt herself hurtling into the future and had longed for that moment when the journey would stop, when she would exist in the present again and be allowed to look back and ahead, now she realized that it hadn't stopped at all, not in the room with the counselor and not during the procedure and not even later in bed with her book and the flowers. She'd been spun like a top and the top had kept spinning, and even the flowers seemed caught in the force of the spin. Within two weeks they had dropped nearly all of their petals, although they hadn't yet wilted or surrendered their color. Cara had dissolved some aspirin in the water, and moved the vase out of the sun when it hit too strong, and with that slight, gentle lifting of the vase across the room, more petals fell with the whisper of snow. They were soft to the touch, still velvety smooth, still blushing with pigment. She let them lie on the floor where they fell, and watched them accumulate and overlap and scatter, unable to bring herself to sweep them up or to empty the vase of the naked stems. For they belonged there, it seemed. Passing them by, time after time in the course of a day, she felt that same unnerving, magnetic pull—*sweep them up, sweep them up*—and then spun away from it only to come round again, like a planet passing the sun, circling and circling. Already she'd gotten her period again, although the nurse at the clinic had told her it might take six weeks, and already she and Douglas had used the diaphragm again, two or three times, with extra doses of caution and jelly.

"Douglas couldn't understand why I was so happy to get my period," said Cara to Wendy. "He said, 'Go talk about it with one of your little friends.'"

Wendy winced as if she'd stuck herself with one of her quilting needles.

"He was kidding. That's one of our jokes. Whenever I have something he doesn't want to hear about he says, 'Go talk to one of your little friends.' He used to say that when I was pregnant, really pregnant, I mean, with Max or Georgie, and if I wanted to tell him how I pissed when I sneezed, he'd say, 'Go talk about it to one of your little friends,' and that he didn't understand why women talk about their bodies all the time. He doesn't mind, not at all, he just doesn't understand. It's so funny, he says, 'I don't see why you have to talk about pregnancy so much.' Can you imagine that? As if it's not important. As if, if a man was walking down the street, and he ran into a man he knew who was carrying a watermelon, they wouldn't talk about the watermelon. They would, wouldn't they?"

"Cara, you make peculiar sense of things," said Wendy.

"It's my hobby," said Cara. "Or compulsion."

"Not compulsion," said Wendy, raising an eyebrow and lifting a low branch so Cara could pass underneath. Cara had run into Wendy in the supermarket, where, having finished their shopping, they decided together on a walk outside. Rain had just fallen, and the uncurling leaves staked a sudden green claim on everything. It was no longer summer-in-winter, really, because spring had slipped in somehow, unannounced. "Susan was compulsive," Wendy went on. "You can't imagine compulsion until you've seen it in action. Counting her steps before she walks in the door, having to take exactly twenty-nine steps, and if she takes twenty-seven she has to start again, and she can't put her feet on the stones of the walkway, no, she has to step on the grass, but not on the bald spots where grass isn't growing, and not on an acorn. If she steps on an acorn, she just about dies, she gets this look on her face like the world's going to stop."

The breakup had been two years ago, but the only things Cara ever heard Wendy say about Susan came out of the blue, like this, over before they began. Cara had never met Susan, because Wendy had moved to town alone, and Susan had stayed behind in Arkansas, in a small frame house that had been remodeled by a married couple named the Milners just before Susan and Wendy bought it together. About the Milners, Cara knew more than she knew about Susan, because Wendy had shown her some photos of how they'd ruined the house. The house had once been a church, simple clapboard with narrow stained glass windows, but then the Milners bought it, tore the arched windows out and put in thermal pane, tore the clapboard out and resided with aluminum. All traces of worship obliterated, all grace compressed into a windowbox full of infested geraniums. "If we had got there two years earlier . . . ," Wendy lamented, "but at least the wood floors were intact under all that wall-to-wall. But that awful dropped ceiling, and behind it who knows what, maybe the whole church is still up there waiting to be freed. We had plans to restore it, but things kept interfering."

Things, Cara thought. Things kept interfering. And now she thought of Susan counting her steps to the door, sidestepping acorns. From what little else Wendy had offered, Cara understood that Susan liked the same music Wendy liked, that she was a fabric artist, like Wendy, and that she liked to go camping, like Wendy. In Group, when someone once asked Wendy if she still kept in touch with Susan, Wendy responded by reaching deep into her scrap basket, rummaging around, and pulling out a frayed, bleached waistband of blue denim with the snap and belt loops still in place. "This is about all I've got left of her," she said, and held it up so everyone could see how terribly skinny Susan was, then basted the scrap, as if casually, onto the sculpture she was making. When a month later the piece was finished, Wendy brought it in to show. Swirls of pale greens and browns made the image of a whirlpool, while the scrap of blue denim, not so artfully placed, was not quite enough to suggest Susan's small, clenched body trapped underneath.

"This place makes me dizzy," said Wendy now.

"I've never been here before," said Cara. "Imagine. Eight years in this town and there's a spot I've never seen."

"I like it here," said Wendy.

"Me, too."

It was a rocky escarpment over the creek, with enough woods around that you could just see the flat, bright colors of the surrounding houses. They'd been following the cut beneath some powerlines, adjacent to the sloping backyards of Wendy's neighborhood, and then they'd turned off where the creek ran through some woods, and ended up at the top of the escarpment.

"This town is so flat, it's nice to run into a place where if you fell off, you'd die," said Cara.

"Or at least get hurt," said Wendy, making her way quickly down toward the water. She'd put on weight over the winter, so the rolled flesh bulged above the cut of her overalls, but she didn't seem to mind; she carried her weight easily, even over the rocks. Cara felt clunky beside her. In her clogs, she took the steep rocks one careful knock at a time, fearful the shoes might slide off her feet and send her tumbling. From the bottom, where Wendy took her shoes off and let her big, dimpled feet skim over the water, you couldn't see the houses at all.

"So how have you been doing?" Wendy asked after a moment.

"You mean, in general? Or—"

"Last time I spoke to you was right after the abortion, and you were still trying to figure out if it was the right thing or not."

"Oh. Well, it's not something that can be figured out, I think. So that's what I've figured out, to answer your question. In a way, I feel like I'm being borne away from it in spite of myself. In spite of my intuition, I mean. Because my intuition is to be sedentary and wait it out, but I can't quite do that, for a very simple reason, and it's a reason I never thought would mean a thing to me at all; that is, time passes, and there's no getting free of it, and that's nothing new except it's scary to be so aware of it. This morning I was driving to work, after I'd left Max off with his sitter, and it was such a beautiful wet green morning, and people were walking around, and I was thinking, soon it will be night, and this day will be over, and then it will be tomorrow and the next day and the next, and whole years will go by like that, and there's nothing anybody can do about it. It just seems relentless to me."

"I think I know what you mean," said Wendy. "But I think, also, if you would just stop putting it into words, Cara—"

"And that's another thing that gets me; I haven't thought about the baby at all since then, except in a kind of objective way, like this. Did I tell you I gave it a name? Well, now I can't even remember the name I gave it, and I haven't felt at all what I thought I would feel, I haven't looked around the table and wondered who's not there, and I haven't grieved really except in brief flashes of feeling, and what scares me is I never will, and I don't want to be one of those people who puts tragedy behind me as if it never happened. I don't want to be one of those people who tries to forget. But maybe I am and I just never knew it because nothing bad ever happened to me before. So I think I have to set up some kind of location, like a shrine, you know, only private, secret, really, that I can go to in order to force myself not to forget it. Anyway, you're the one who asked. And you haven't told me, either, whether you think it was the right thing for me to do or not."

To this, Wendy was silent, and Cara was thankful. She shrugged, took a breath, grabbed a handful of dead leaves and let them drop over the water. An airplane passed overhead, and then there was the dim muffled bounce of a ball in somebody's driveway. Douglas was home with the children, and the groceries were wilting in the trunk of the car. Cara felt a tug toward home and dinner, and then bedtime and breakfast and lunch again. She'd bought a week's worth of groceries, and now the force of their pull was so strong it was like the whole week yanking her forward.

"This could be it," Wendy said, when Cara stood up to go.

"What could be what?"

"This place. Right here. Or up above on the rocks. Your shrine."

Cara looked up at the rocks, at their damp, jagged edges and insensible, unbalanced formations.

"You're right," she said. "I can come here and think."

"Or not think," said Wendy. "There's nothing so terrible about not thinking, you know. You might try it a little, once in a while, Cara. It can be kind of liberating."

Max had invented a game of walking back and forth among the fallen flower petals on the floor, trying not to crush them with his tiny, sneakered feet. At this game he was as gentle as if

the flower parts were butterflies he didn't want to kill, sometimes, the very tip of his sneaker poised over a petal, he'd falter,
lose his precarious, one-and-a-half-year-old balance, look helplessly up at his mother, and fall.

"Oops," he always said then, and climbed up on his knees to
survey the damage. Cara taught him a trick, put your chin to the
floor and blow gently at the petals to scatter them out of the
way. He couldn't blow, however. He sprayed, coughed, spat,
giggled. Cara gave him a drinking straw, taught him to aim it. At
this he was more successful, and he chased a fragment of mum
round and round on the floor among the legs of the table and
chairs. At last he squatted to pick it up, very delicately between
thumb and index finger, then peered at it as if it were a moth he
held by one fragile, trembling wing. Cara smiled. Her little son.
He recognized all of her friends, and said hello to whomever
they passed on the sidewalk, friend or not. He embraced small
children, petted cats and dogs, demanded access to the telephone whenever it rang, demanded proper good-byes, proper
hellos. Every day at the sitter's house he stood waiting at eleven
for the newspaper delivery, and then at two o'clock for the
postman, and then at three for the school bus bearing his
brother. Sometimes, when Cara was at work, he showed up at
her office, babysitter in one hand, pretzel in the other, waving
hellos to the secretaries while offering grains of salt from his
pretzel. What a gregarious creature Max was, their little accident of nature, their unexpected pleasure. His brother was
quieter, more intense, always watchful, always careful about
what he said. Georgie had been conceived during one of Cara
and Douglas's summertime trips, and Douglas liked to say that if
they'd stopped the car for gas in Limon instead of Colorado
Springs, and if the wait had been longer in Limon, and if the
motel they'd found finally later that night had been booked, and
if they'd had to drive on to another motel, then Georgie would
not have been Georgie but somebody else entirely, someone
they couldn't imagine. And if the Georgie who wasn't Georgie
had spilled his milk on the day that Maxie was conceived, and if
Cara had squatted to mop it up, and if everything had taken just

that much longer, then Max wouldn't be Max, either, but someone maybe not as mischievous, not as much a joker, not as much
a wit. All of life is like that, Cara thought in awe; you might be
downtown buying a carton of milk, and step into one store
instead of another, and never know what you'd missed, either
falling in love, or dying, or anything in between. Now Max
caught Cara's eye, stuck out his tongue, held the flower petal
over it, grinned, raised his eyebrows.

"You can't eat that, Max," said Cara, laughing. "Flowers aren't
edible. Well, some of them are but some of them aren't, and I
don't know if that one is or isn't. So don't eat it."

Max put the petal carefully back on the floor, precisely in the
spot where he'd found it.

"No flowers are edible," Georgie commented dryly. He was
sniffing the tips of his Magic Markers, which smelled like their
colors. Red was cinnamon, yellow was banana. There were little
polka dots of color on the tip of his nose.

"Some flowers are," said Cara.

"Like what?"

"I don't know, but some of them. Violets are. We can look for
some sugared violets, and if we find them, we'll buy them and
you can have a taste."

"I don't think so," said Georgie. "Anyway, these flowers are
dead. Why don't you throw them out?"

"Why don't *you* throw them out?" said Cara playfully, tous-
ling his hair. Except his hair was all ringlets; it wouldn't get
tousled.

He went back to his sniffing. His favorite marker appeared to
be the brown one—root beer—although mango inspired, over
and over, a look of puzzlement and disbelief.

Cara lifted the vase off the speaker and carried it into the
yard. She pulled the stems from the vase and was tossing them
onto the neighbor's compost heap when she found the gift
enclosure card in its miniature envelope wedged among the
long, dry, rotting stems.

The card was blurry but still readable. In her memory, later,
whenever Cara reconstructed this moment, she remembered

standing for a minute, card in hand, not quite reading it but knowing what it said, looking around at the neighborhood. Hers and Douglas's was a postage stamp yard, but no fence divided it from that of its neighbor to the south, and though the rear boundary of Cara's property was blocked by a row of evergreen trees, now immense, the rear boundary of her neighbor's property was open. Her neighbor's was a corner lot, and the view was of the deep backyards of the houses on the street perpendicular to theirs. Swing sets, sandboxes, vegetable plots, rose gardens, torn sewer lines, picket fences, wash lines, garden sheds—all formed an endless muddy corridor of disheveled, springtime domesticity. Evenings, children played along the length of it, woodpile to woodpile, and sparrows flocked at one feeder, then another and another. At the far end was nothing but sky. To Cara it all looked mysteriously inviting, like a door left ajar, yet she stayed clear of it, stepping past her own evergreens only to feed her peelings to the neighbor's compost, or to call Georgie home to dinner, or, occasionally, and with a feeling of great trespass and self-consciousness, to chase the dog. She didn't recognize, when she passed them on the street, most of the adults who lived in these houses, and they didn't recognize her. In fact, she was grateful for the sharp density of evergreens and the privacy it offered.

Her neighbor with the compost heap was in her sixties and tended her vegetable garden with dignified stiffness, the result of two hip operations; both hips were synthetic. She was widowed, with a daughter in Salt Lake City. This was all Cara knew about her except that she appeared to be some kind of computer buff; Cara frequently caught sight of her seated at a table in the second-story glass-enclosed porch of her house, intent on her monitor. Her name was June Adams, and the flowers, it turned out, were meant for her.

For Betty had made a mistake, of course.

Will you allow me to take you to dinner? is what was printed on the card, and then the name *Wallace Caldwell*, a name that Cara had never heard before but whose rich, formal, melancholy syllables seemed already to forgive her.

❧

*T*hat night, Cara sat in the kitchen at the desk near the open window, feeling the wind and rain on her skin. She was wearing not her robe but the thin, gauzy caftan-type thing that her mother had bought her years ago before Cara went away to college. Cara was to be living in a co-ed dormitory, and while it was understood that in such a situation the men and women were to live affectionately like brothers and sisters and cousins, it was equally understood that there would be the possibility of sex in the air and even the possibility of romance, so while the baby doll pajamas were definitely out, so were the homely, velour, zippered robes and the boxy quilted ones. What remained were some sashed flannels and then suddenly this caftan that Cara's mother grabbed off the hook in one of the dressing rooms to show her. It was pale blue-green and soft as air; wearing it, Cara had felt like someone costumed as the wind for a school play. Now, nearly fifteen years and two children later, it made her feel the same way, graceful and tall and discreetly romantic, as if her life in this house with Douglas and their children required of her the same cool self-possession required by life in the halls of the co-ed dorm. Which in a way it did. But in more ways it didn't, of course. Still, sometimes she and Douglas grew remote from each other, out of necessity, Cara believed, and tonight felt like the beginning of one of those times. She hadn't told him, for instance, about the card hidden among the stems of the flowers, or about what she imagined to be their neighbor June Adams' suddenly apparent loneliness. Douglas, if she told him about Wallace Caldwell's invitation, would expect—would insist—that she tell June as well, and Cara didn't want to do that. She *wouldn't* do it. The whole thing seemed too much an invasion of privacy—Wallace Caldwell's, June Adams', Cara's. Besides, there was no way to tell Douglas about the card without also admitting that she had lied when she told him the flowers were sent by her mother, unless she invented some new lie to go with it. Which would be easy to do, come to think of it—Betty and Sam confusing the bouquets, maniacally, even, their eyes gleeful beneath their mustard-colored caps as they switched the cards and envelopes. How easily one lie slipped into another! Cara and Douglas had friends who knew a man who kept lying like that. He was teaching at a university, on faked credentials. He invented publications, doctored his c.v., confessing to no one, not even his wife. For years this went on, and when finally the lies were discovered, when he lost his job, he told his wife he was going on a lecture tour, left home, made phone calls with lies about Oklahoma, lies about Texas, lies about California. After that, no one heard from him awhile, and then they found him hanged not five blocks from home in a one-room rented apartment. Cara wondered if he remembered what his first lie had been— the lie that started all the others, that fed into them like water into a river—and if he thought it had been worth it, even at the end. So far, Cara's lie *had* been worth it. The whole thing had a simple, reassuring kind of inevitability—she had told a white lie to her mother, the white lie had turned to a lie, the lie had gained her a degree of harmless and delightfully mischievous privacy that she intended to preserve one way or another even if it meant telling small untruths to Douglas in order to protect him. And protect her, too. Privacy, after all, was another part of the equation of marriage, the one she set forth for Group— herself on the one hand, Douglas on the other, and in between them their marriage like a living, breathing thing that some- times walked off as if to brood in peace and quiet, leaving them separate, apart, *private*. Douglas didn't worry, but stayed out of Cara's way just as she stayed out of his. There was no malice in this, no insult, just a shared recognition of the need for self- sufficiency of spirit. Douglas, when this happened, played Nin- tendo, ordinarily the Legend of Zelda, long after the children had gone to sleep. Controls in hand, he lay on his side at the foot of the bed, flipping desultorily from map to maze and back again, trying to negotiate a pathway from here to wherever. With the music turned off the way he liked it, there was only the noise of his fingertip hitting the trigger with a nearly inaudible click. That click was distracting to Cara, even to- night, when all she was doing was busywork for the school

PTA, cutting circles out of sheets of paper. The circles, no bigger around than the bottoms of teacups, were printed twelve to a sheet of nine-by-eleven-inch paper of varying pastel colors; if there were a hundred sheets of paper, then that meant Cara would have to cut out twelve hundred circles, and if there were three hundred sheets of paper, thirty-six hundred. Cara didn't know how many sheets there were but it seemed like a lot, and though she cut through six sheets at a time, the stack had shrunk barely at all since she'd started. The completed, flimsy circles she put into an envelope marked for the PTA, to be used for button-making at the school carnival. It seemed an honorable way to pass some time, doing good for the public schools. In any case, just cutting the circles gave her a queer sense of satisfaction. She enjoyed the simplicity of it; the dependable utility of the scissors, the slow, definite accretion of blue, then green, then yellow circles in the marked envelope, and the way Georgie, earlier, had crept up behind her and watched in admiration as the neat shapes dropped from the blades of the scissors.

"I could never do that," he'd said matter-of-factly.

"Someday you'll be able to," Cara had said, although she had her secret doubts. He was as uncoordinated as he was intelligent. He could not cut a circle if his life depended on it, and he could not ride a bike even with the training wheels attached, and he was frightened of the water. He had started swimming lessons just today, in fact, with an instructor named Biff at the YMCA. Biff looked like a Biff, well-made and good-natured, and Georgie clung with all his strength to the comforting, fraternity-nourished confidence of Biff's broad neck and shoulders as they bore him out into the pool. Cara had been moved, for there was something characteristically masculine about this kind of intimacy and this was Georgie's first young taste of it. He seemed to welcome it. Later, blue-lipped, walking home from the pool, Georgie commented, "Biff had a nice voice."

"See? It wasn't so bad," Cara admonished.

"It *was* bad, but he had a nice voice," Georgie countered. "Did you think he did?"

"Yes," Cara said, because it was a nice voice, just the kind of boyish, enthusiastic voice you'd expect of a person like Biff. She put a hand on Georgie's wet curls, a little jealously, guiding him home. He was tired from the lesson and fell asleep early, and slept right through the start of the storm with its clapping of thunder. Now the rain fell hard in the darkness, and the wind blew wild in the tops of the trees. Cara's caftan had grown damp, and having put the scissors down, she was reaching for the window when she heard it, a child calling out in the night and the storm.

"Mom!" the voice called, and then again behind the pounding of the rain, "Mom!"

Cara stood up, walked purposefully through the house to the bottom of the stairs, and listened. There was the clicking of the button as Douglas played his Nintendo, and the deep, hushed soundness of her own children's sleep.

In the kitchen she opened the door just as the cry cut again through the storm, but when she stuck her head out, there was only the noise of the wind. For a whole two minutes she stood there, getting wetter and wetter, listening hard. When there was nothing, she shut the door, but then she opened it again to be sure.

Still nothing.

And nothing again.

But she was not comfortable.

On the phone with the police dispatcher, Cara was calm.

"I have a strange thing to say," she began.

"Say it," said the dispatcher.

"I'm sitting here with the window open, and it may just have been somebody calling a dog, but I thought maybe I heard a child calling for its mother. I could have been wrong. I mean it could have been anything, but it sounded like that."

"Where are you calling from?"

Cara gave the address just as Kato came into the room, eager to know what was going on.

"When?"

"Just now. I mean I heard it a minute ago, and then I stepped outside for a minute, but I didn't hear it again."

"What did you hear, exactly?"

"I thought it was somebody, a child, calling for its mother," Cara repeated, not really surprised to find herself growing less calm, more anxious by the second.

"How old a child would you say?" asked the dispatcher.

"Not little. Not a toddler. About eight or nine."

"Where?"

"Behind my house. Well, way behind my house, in one of the neighbors' backyards. Those would be the backyards of the houses on Jefferson Street, not Monroe. There's a little strip of pine trees, and then there are the yards."

"And what did the voice say, exactly?"

"'Mom.' Just 'Mom.'"

"And did it sound frightened?"

"No," Cara answered. "Not really. It sounded the way you'd sound if you were calling for a dog, but it said '*Mom!*' I'm sorry. Maybe someone has a dog named Mom. That would be a great name for a dog, wouldn't it? Or maybe it just sounded like *Mom* over the noise of the storm. I don't know. Maybe I should just sit here and call you back if I hear it again?" asked Cara, thinking all the while that there was something else she should tell the dispatcher—that she had recently had an abortion, that the decision had been traumatic, that any of her friends, that even her husband, might associate her hearing of the child's cry with her uncertainty about the abortion, and that therefore maybe both of them should hang up right now and just forget about it although she was quite certain she had heard it, she knew the second she heard the cry that it might only have come from her mind and heart, yet here she was on the phone, in spite of that. . . .

"Yes, you should definitely call me right away if you hear it again," said the dispatcher, and that seemed to be all until a few minutes later, when, still sitting at the desk near the open window, and not having picked up her scissors again, Cara was startled by the appearance of several flashlight beams criss-crossing her lawn, and then of two uniformed police officers hunched in matching ponchos under the rain as they made their way back past the house.

"Oh, my God," Cara heard herself say, and then in no time she really was shaking, because the presence of the police had a way of making it all seem so real, as if there really was a child in the rain and the darkness, crouching among the boughs of the dripping-wet pine trees, soaked, chilled, and afraid.

As maybe there was.

But it seemed unlikely.

From the open kitchen doorway she looked out at the police officers and gave a little shrug designed to hide the fact that the very sight of them in her backyard had rendered her practically speechless. Kato was speechless, too; she only barked when she felt like it. Now she felt like going out, but Cara blocked her with a foot and a fold of damp caftan.

"It was you who made the call?" asked one of the officers, a woman, whose radio at that moment bleeped forth a garbled message about some other person's trouble—a skidded Toyota on Nickleplate Road, license plate such and such, driver hysterical, hazards flashing.

"Yes," Cara said.

"When did you hear it?"

"Just before I called. About ten minutes ago. And I haven't heard it since. It might have been anybody calling a dog."

The policewoman nodded, then followed the beam of her flashlight across the grass toward the strip of pine trees, where the other officer waited. They looked wet and resigned. The rain had slowed. The radio repeated its message. The wind had slowed, too, but the blood in Cara's ears was fierce and determined. *You should know that I had an abortion,* she very nearly shouted out, *this may be . . . I might have . . .* but at that moment the policeman ducked cautiously into the trees, then stepped back into the yard gripping gently the arm of a boy Cara recognized as one of Georgie's playmates from the strip of backyards behind the compost heap. It was the boy with problems, the one who tried to hit the sparrows with badminton rackets. The other children called him names but only when he wasn't around. Even in the rain she could see his face was tear-streaked, awash with mud and shadows. He wore a bathrobe, slippers, a too-small raincoat not buttoned up, and he carried, by one finger hooked under the fender, a toy cement mixer.

Later, even after the police car had pulled away and the swish of the tires on wet pavement had faded, instead of going inside, Cara stayed on the front steps staring at the road. It was late at night, and next door even June Adams' glassed-in-porch lamp had been shut off. Kato had gone back to sleep. Douglas hadn't come downstairs. He might have been sleeping or in the shower. Rain fell on Cara's caftan and soaked immediately through to the skin, but Cara didn't mind. The name she had given the baby was Lark, she remembered, and the thought of it filled her with a luxurious sadness recognizable as the same kind of sadness she felt for anyone she'd ever loved in this random world of accident and glorious chance. How lucky she felt, her body eager and strong beneath the folds of wet cloth, the rain misting her upturned face. It made her think of the postcard of the woman hanging laundry. Cara wasn't there anymore, on that weird incline. She had stepped off it barefooted onto wet wood. It seemed to happen so gradually, then all at once, and now there was nothing she would trade for the promise of this particular moment, for the way it would hold still until she chose to turn away from it. Which she didn't. Not yet. She felt proud just to stand there soaking up rain. She thought she must tell her friends about it, and she must tell Douglas, but not tonight, and maybe not even tomorrow.

THE
SECRET

M uch later that year, at ten o'clock in the morning on the day after Halloween, having fasted since midnight not because anybody advised him to but because he is afraid, and because fasting will make him clean, and because he associates cleanliness of body with cleanliness of spirit and a lifting of the heart, and because he believes that a lifting of the heart might coincide necessarily with a lifting of fear and apprehension and worry, Douglas rides a bus alone to the hospital not far from the radio station and undergoes a vasectomy. He is pleased to be doing this on the day after Halloween because the holiday furnishes him with a joke he can tell himself, a joke he believes in, a joke pertaining to the notion of himself as a soon-to-be-changed individual.

"Yesterday was the last day I wore my costume of myself," he says to Estaban, who is on the phone on hold with National Public Radio in Washington, trying to schedule Douglas's interview with an Amish ostrich farmer from Charm, Ohio. "Today I turn this old costume in for a new one."

"Oh, bullshit," says Estaban. "We'll still recognize you when you hobble in the door. Yes? Yes? Yes!" he adds into the receiver, raising eyebrows at Douglas and then swiveling to his blackboard and chalking sloppily the offer he made earlier that morning, that he would drive Douglas to and from the hospital if Douglas wanted him to. Douglas shakes his head no, knowing even as he does so that his fantasy of walking bravely and gingerly back from the hospital is as absurd as it will be impossible. When Douglas told Estaban that he was having a vasectomy, Estaban replied simply that one of his brothers and three of his brothers-in-law had finally had vasectomies and that only one regretted it. He didn't say why the regret, but he looked at Douglas in a way that showed he understood how scared Douglas was, even though it was outpatient. Mild. Douglas is terrified, of course, just as Douglas has always been terrified of doctors, hospitals, dentists. It is true that he will change, he is utterly convinced. If today he is whole, then by nightfall he will have become the sum of his parts. Visits to the doctor always do that to Douglas. Remind him that he has parts. Tender parts, wet parts, parts smaller than the eye can measure, drifting parts, parts that hurt. If this morning he is flesh and bone, then tonight he will be flesh, bone, tendon, nerve, spinal column, plasma, and saline. He'll be urine and saliva, tooth and nail, hemoglobin and testosterone.

He will no longer be entirely, completely himself.

Already Douglas has managed to convince himself that of the 60 percent of men who following vasectomy produce antibodies to their own sperm, he will be one of only a handful who develop a full, allergic, sneezing, itchy-skinned, swollen-tongued reaction.

So from now on he will choke on his own lovemaking.

His own orgasms will cause him to break out in hives.

His own desire, even, will send him rushing to the pharmacist for a dose of antihistamine.

Also he might suffer hematoma, whatever that is.

And in addition, inflammation of the epididymis, a part Douglas hadn't known he possessed before he scanned the literature and found it sitting like a shock absorber on the dome of a testicle.

He does not expect hair loss, premature aging, change in vocal pitch, narcolepsy, or multiple sclerosis. The death rate is 0 percent, but Douglas isn't afraid of death. He is frightened of the doctors, frightened of the razor, the scalpel, the needle, the tweezers, the hot lights, the cauterizer, the metallic clips, the probes, sponges, hands, fingers, sutures, even the Xylocaine, even the cold, stinging absence of pain. He is frightened of being a body, just a body supine on a table, oozing or not, eyes open or not, tongue moist or not, fingers clenched or fingers open and all the while the masked face of the doctor peering critically at the exposed loops of Douglas's vas deferens.

He's familiar with the word *vas deferens*, although he's never really thought about it before. He's never recognized its beauty, or looked it up in Jenny's little *Pocket Oxford Dictionary* to find that it isn't included. It's Latin, he decides, although why it should be one of those rare Latin words that has never achieved proper English substitution is a question that irks him considerably and makes him even more afraid. Already he has determined that this is a question he will put to the doctor while on the operating table. Also, he will ask whether medicare covers vasectomies and what percentage of the doctor's patients are on public assistance and how the doctor feels about the recent federal ruling barring doctors at federally assisted clinics from discussing abortion and what his position is on socialized medicine and whether he himself has ever had a vasectomy. And he will interject, among these weightier topics, questions concerning the specific nature of the procedure at hand, for instance: *How do you disinfect the scalpels?* and *For how long will the Xylocaine keep it from hurting?* In short, he will interview the doctor just as if their two voices are being recorded, as a way of keeping himself less afraid, and all the while he'll be glad that Cara isn't present because if she were present, she would know that that was why he was doing all that damn talking. She would know it absolutely even if they didn't allow her to accompany him into the operating room.

If they do it in an operating room at all.

He doesn't know how long it will take. He supposes he should have asked Estaban to find out from his brother. He only knows he's scared shitless and he doesn't want Cara to see him so scared that he can't shut up. He hopes this has nothing to do with the fact that he's a man and she's a woman. He doesn't like to have to think of himself as a man who doesn't want his own wife to see him afraid. He prefers to believe he's protecting her; she wouldn't like to see him scared, so he won't let her. Cara has never seen him afraid before, except for the times he's been frightened for *her*. And that fear was solicitous. But this fear is naked. This fear makes him skinny and cold and pale, and there's no reason for Cara to have to see him like that.

There was a day early on when he thought he would tell her, and then another day early on when he believed she would talk him out of it, she would do it herself, get her tubes tied, why not? *Doctors don't scare me the way they scare you*, she would say. But it didn't take long for him to know she wouldn't say that, either, no, she'd be thrilled with the idea of his vasectomy, that was the hard, indisputable truth, and she'd be gentle in the face of it, comforting and proud. She'd tell her friends. She'd cook a pot of chicken soup with all the bones taken out the way he liked; he'd find her standing in the kitchen peering into the pot, reaching in with her spoon, peeling hot meat from between steaming ribs. In bed, she'd put her tongue to the place they would cut, breathe moist air against it, tease it, love it like a baby, soothe it with a lullaby. The thought made him shiver, so he never did tell her. The day grew nearer and nearer, and he grew more and more afraid and more and more glad she didn't know what he was planning. He would surprise her with it afterward when it was over and done and he was no longer quite exactly himself.

And that is why he is alone, passing through the spinning glass doors into the hospital lobby and then pausing and glancing back to see the door still revolving with nobody in it—around, and around, and around.

The abortion still surprises him. All during the days of Cara's hard deliberation he expected that when the moment came to walk into the back rooms of the clinic, she would change her mind and turn around and walk out again. They'd have driven home into seven and a half months of pregnancy, and then the baby would have been born, in the Blue Room this time, not the rose-colored room because some teenager would have been in labor in it. Cara would have grown yet darker in the nipples, softer in the hips; both her smile and her frown would have broadened accommodatingly, and so would the depth and complications of her feeling. The baby would have been a girl, Douglas is certain. He hasn't said this to Cara; he knows it would pain her. Dark hair at birth, then red like the boys' hair, a shade at once brighter than Cara's and softer than Douglas's red. Brood red, he and Cara like to call it. And unlike the boys, who are handsome like Cara, the little girl would have most resembled Douglas. His freckles. His bony wrists and neck. His face too pinched at the temples, too long in the jaw. A little gangly for a girl, but touching, disturbing, with Cara's bright, angry eyes that would have made up for everything and made her look womanly even when she was two years old. Like her father, she'd have been duck-footed when she started to walk, dressed in her brothers' outgrown overalls except for the flounce and the eyelet that Douglas's sister Susan would have insisted on sending, along with a doll that pooped in her own little diaper. Both Cara and Douglas would have been mystified and then in awe of their daughter's practical, maternal attention to this doll and to the other dolls that would have followed. There'd have been a roomful of well-dressed, well-scrubbed, well-fed dolls all with unlikely names that Douglas can't begin to imagine. He can't imagine the bedroom, either—the curtains, the nightlight, the bedspread he knows she'd have wanted to choose for herself—or where in their too-small house it might be. But he isn't in love with this child. He doesn't miss her or grieve. He only thinks of her as something that never happened and never will; it's like the feeling he gets when he watches the Talking Heads' *Stop Making Sense* and wonders what it would be like to be buttoned into David Byrne's giant white suit. *Intense*, he always thinks, *Brilliant, a trip*, but his fingers never itch to put it on.

He tells all of this to the nurse, who turns out to be someone who occasionally bakes cookies with Estaban's mother. Douglas might even have eaten a few of those cookies himself. The connection inspires his confidence. That, and the nurse's air of sympathy and calm. She just goes about her business—taking his blood pressure, taking his temperature, flipping her long braid over her shoulder, shaving the hair off his scrotum, clipping a pen into place in her starched white pocket—in such a way that each small gesture seems a gesture of understanding about the tiny red-haired nonexistent girl.

"Nervous?" she asks. Her face is simple and uncomplicated, open to him. "A lot of guys are. A lot of guys get so freaked by the shaving that everything else seems easy. Also they get freaked by the idea of being sterile. Just the idea. They feel guilty about it, like if there were only two people left in the world and they were one of them, they wouldn't be able to repopulate. See? All done shaving. Now we inject a little Xylocaine into the skin. Then we do the incision. Here, we only do one, a midline scrotal, less than an inch. Some doctors do two, one on each side. That? That's a tantalum clip, what we seal you up with, right at the ends of the vas deferens. Don't worry. Lie back. You won't feel a thing, you'll be out of here in no time. Well, just a poke, maybe. Get ready for a poke, right now."

Douglas is unnerved. Maybe it's her uncommon sympathy that ruffles him; he actually has considered, if only for a moment, the abstract possibility of being the last man left on an empty, infertile earth. Still, the small talk is reassuring to a degree he hadn't expected. Doctors always small talk, but it has never worked before. Nor had he expected the nearly imperceptible but elegant arch of the nurse's eyebrows each time the razor missed nicking his scrotum by what seemed like the width of a hair. He hadn't expected the razor to tickle, nor that the stuff she swabbed on afterward with a few balls of cotton would be so outrageously cold. Frosty, like a spoonful of sherbet. He hadn't expected to laugh. *My prick pricked*, is what he will say to Cara when he tells her about it later. Then the doctor comes in, and they are covering his lap with a sheet so he won't have to see what they're doing. He is grateful for this, because the anesthetic isn't doing what he thought it would do. He had thought it would make him feel at a distance, as if the operation were happening to somebody else, someone far enough away that if he reached out a hand, his fingers wouldn't quite touch. And he had thought that the sheet draped over his lap would make him feel like half a body gazing at somebody else's half a body, but really what he feels is the cool, soft presence of the cloth and his own sharp awareness of the doctor's hands fussing on the other side of it. If he tries, he can almost imagine it's the nurse down there and not the doctor, giving him a blow job under the sheet, the heavy rope of her long braid coiled on his thigh. How good that would feel if he could feel it, so good that when the doctor asks him if he wants to look at the pulled-out loops of his vas deferens, he almost doesn't say no. But he catches himself. He puts both hands on the sheet and holds on tight and tells the doctor about Georgie and Max's new rivalry. Max has bad dreams, but he thinks they're funny, and he laughs when their details frighten his older brother. This happens night after night at two, three o'clock in the morning. The dreams, if Cara and Douglas understand correctly Max's some-what garbled attempts to communicate them, are about some-one called the Crying Man, and it is always the part about what seems to be the Crying Man's truck that makes Georgie hide under his pillow, wide-eyed and tense and trembling, while Max laughs all the harder in his high-pitched, two-year-old way. It's amazing how different they are, says Douglas, the older one careful and intellectual, the younger one mischievous, funny, and mean. The doctor shakes his head, amused. The nurse removes the paper from a roll of gauze as attentively as if she is hoping to save it for Christmas wrapping. The doctor has two sons, also, but twins, with rivalries of their own. One night years ago, each son set the other son's rabbit loose and left the hutches lying open. By morning the rabbits had both returned and sat hunkered in the far corner of each straw-smelling hutch, munching rinds of zucchini. This happened for two more nights and mornings, but on the third morning only the cotton-tail came back. She sat in the pygmy's hutch, eating nothing, her round eyes milky with thirst. But she wouldn't touch water. She drank only flat ginger ale out of an eyedropper. They kept an open can of ginger ale perched on the kitchen window sill, and one day when one son climbed up to get it, dropper in hand, he slipped off the step stool and hit his chin against the sink. The cut required nine stitches. In retaliation, the other twin slit his own chin open with a razor. The eye dropper got trampled. Thirty days later the cottontail gave birth to a litter of six blind babies that she kept in a huddle in a depression in the straw. Now both boys are in medical school trying to grow enough facial hair to camouflage their scars. It's a joke they've grown tired of: Identical Chins. Their failed beards are oily with stubble. One's girlfriend refused to kiss him, and then the other's moved in on the vacant position, filling two spaces at once, so to speak, says the doctor with a chuckle. His voice from behind the draped sheet is like a genie rising out of a bottle.

"Clips," the doctor says. The nurse passes the clips on a tray, then places a sponge on a second tray near the sink. The sponge oozes red, and Douglas swears he feels the clips pinch hard and sudden. His eyes burn, then well with tears, then spill over. He hadn't expected blood. The nurse finds a tissue and presses it into his hand, smiling warmly, flipping the braid off her shoulder again.

"That's a sad story about the rabbits," she offers.

She puts a hand on his arm, squeezes, sets her fingers adrift beneath the wide, loose sleeve of the gown.

"Kids," says the doctor, shaking his head.

"Yeah," Douglas gulps. He doesn't know if he is crying from the story or the surgery. Or maybe the fear. His legs are like rubber, his raised knees flopping apart.

Or maybe embarrassment. What if he has an erection? He can't tell if he does or not. Anyway, it's humiliating lying there with his balls in the doctor's face.

Or maybe he is crying about the red-haired never-to-be baby girl with her never-to-be flounces and eyelets and lace, but he really doesn't think so.

Or maybe he is crying about his two boys half-asleep in their bedroom, laughing and crying over the same bad dream. Everything's all mixed up. He once interviewed a wrestler whose pet bear drank grape soda whenever he won a match. It's funny that both the bear and the rabbit should be fond of soda, so funny that Douglas starts crying again. But just a little, in a way no one will notice. A tightness in the jaw, a swimmingness under the eyes. He is delightfully and horribly confused. He can feel the needle going painlessly in and coming painlessly out and then the long dry pull of the thread through the loose pouch of his scrotum. It's enough to make him make himself faint.

When he comes to, he feels the heat of the stitches and the nurse's hand cool on his shoulder. Which is funny because she isn't touching him. She isn't even standing close. Having opened the curtain in the corner of the room, she stoops gathering together all the nickels and keys and a rosary that fell out of Douglas's pocket when he slung his jeans over the chair. The rosary isn't his. He found it in the stairwell at the radio station and plans to lay it on Estaban's desk as a joke. Probably it slipped off someone's Halloween costume the night before. He relates all this to the nurse even as he thinks, what difference does it make? He'll never see her again. Her braid appears to have grown several inches since he arrived; it reaches all the way down to her beautiful ass. Below her earlobe is a birthmark resembling the sharp, chiseled point of an arrow. It occurs to Douglas that if she bakes cookies with Estaban's mother then she and Estaban must have met. The thought makes him jealous. Cara would never believe this, Cara who jokes about the fact that Douglas never gets attracted to anybody but herself, to which he protests in a way that reassures her it's true.

The rosary slides off the nurse's open fingers into the pocket of his Levi's, bead by bead. Soon he will have to sit up. But it's easier than he fears, just a pull in the groin and an ache he doesn't notice until he puts his weight on his feet. If he falls, the nurse will catch him, he knows this absolutely. He isn't dizzy, just uncertain, but he feels it in his legs as he dresses himself and follows the nurse down the hallway, where she gives him some pills for the pain. No aspirin, she instructs, no athletics, no sex for seven days and then only with a contraceptive until he's emptied his ejaculate of sperm. That means fifteen ejaculations followed by a checkup. Now that it's over, she's matter-of-fact. He knows he should have told Cara, she should be here with him now, the knowledge hits him in a way that makes a sound in his throat. He'll let the sound spill out later when he's with Cara again; he imagines complex loops of syllables twirling between them all during the night as they talk it through and through. For a moment he wonders if men and women do these things— have babies, abortions, surgeries—so they can talk about them intimately after and before. That seems as good a reason as any to do them.

Estaban doesn't come to get him. Jenny does. Her earrings are miniature wraparound sunglasses that flash mirror images of the city as she drives him through the streets. Those earrings would look funky and crazy, just the way Jenny wishes they looked now, in the kind of big crowded city in which she wishes she lived, but in this city where there are barely any people on the sidewalks, they could easily be mistaken for the kind of dress-up earrings displayed in the toy aisle of a drugstore. The funny thing is, Jenny knows this; her subdued disappointment is part of her act. It's an act to which Douglas warms; he can't keep himself from confessing to Jenny's earrings that the vasectomy is intended to be an early Christmas gift for Cara. He hadn't thought of this before, but it seems just right. This evening when Cara gets home from work, he'll tell her Merry Christmas, she won't know what he's talking about, he'll let her unwrap the bandages over the stitches, see for herself.

Jenny winces when he says this, the miniature sunglasses barely trembling, and insists on driving him all the way home.

*E*ager for company, the dog is waiting at the door when Douglas steps inside. He's not afraid of her jumping against his bandages, for she is not the jumping type, not a barker, not a whiner, not skittish or hyperactive as other dogs are. Instead she follows him discreetly to the tape player, toenails clicking gently on the living room floor, tail wagging as he slides the tape Jenny gave him into the machine. It's an accidental recording—Cara talking to her mother on the telephone in the studio yesterday evening during the station's Halloween party—and since Jenny didn't feel she could erase it without listening to it, and since she certainly didn't feel she could listen to it, she saved it for Douglas to take care of. At first he thinks he'll erase it himself right away—he doesn't want to eavesdrop—but then the notion of Cara's voice washing over him seems a soothing rehearsal for their long night together when he can hold her and say Merry Early Christmas and tell her about the razor and the nurse's long braid and how he felt Cara's hand on his shoulder when he came to after a faint. Not the nurse's hand but Cara's, and if he says it, then it will be true, and if he says it longingly enough, then it will be as if Cara had actually been there with him in the procedure room during the operation. They'll look back on it as something they went through together, and then they'll look ahead of it into their altered life. He is no longer afraid, he discovers, of developing an allergy to his own sperm. He isn't prone to allergy, and anyway he feels too good for such a thing to happen. He feels good and in pain at once; that is, it's a pain that makes him want to be good to himself. He's never done this before, taken care of himself in this way. In the closet in the playroom he finds two down pillows, fresh and bare, the ticking yellowed but smooth to the touch. Also a blanket, and on reflection, the spotted green frog-shaped water bottle that Cara has never returned to her friend; it really does feel like a frog, when he fills it with ice-cold water. The dog watches quizzically as he arranges these things on the couch, as if she knows as well as he does this isn't his style; the way he's settling in, coddling himself. He steps gingerly, slowly out of his blue jeans, checks his bandage for blood (there's none, just a faint pink streak he can swear he sees glowing under the layers of gauze), adjusts his jockstrap, takes the phone off the hook, and lowers the blinds past the shimmer of pale green toilet paper someone wove last night through the branches of the trees in the front yard. Not for a minute does he consider pulling the toilet paper down. Not today. Not now. It is two in the afternoon, Cara is due home at half past five, he'll pick up the children at Deena's at four-forty, which is when he ordinarily gets home from work on Tuesdays. In the kitchen he fills a tall glass with orange juice instead of his usual after-work beer, thinks for a minute of dinner, dismisses the thought, thinks it guiltily again, decides he'll take care of it later. He pulls his watch from his wrist, places it on the kitchen counter, not thinking to set its alarm in case he falls asleep. He realizes this the second he lies down among the pillows and even mentions it to the dog, who raises her near-naked eyebrows and tries to climb up next to him. Neither Douglas nor Kato is surprised she can't make it, nor is Douglas surprised she doesn't notice the smell of the Xylocaine. Instead she noses her head along the couch to his feet, nuzzles the arches, a memory of smell. Her nose has grown old along with the rest of her; Douglas wonders when it happened, stroking her ear with his toes. He hears his heartbeat keep time with Cara's voice on the recording Jenny gave him, and feels the haze of his own warm pain and cool comfort mingle with the whirring of the tape. Yet, how impatient he is. He can't wait to talk to Cara, can't wait to tell her not only what he has done but that he has told Estaban, told Jenny, had to stop himself, even, from telling the boy he sat next to on the bus on the way to the clinic. "I did it how you would have done it," he'll tell Cara, meaning, he talked himself into it like painting himself into a corner, he said the word *vasectomy* so many times that he didn't have a choice, as if talking were doing, the way smiling produces endorphins, and the endorphins, in turn, produce smiles, and the smiles, in turn . . . He remembers reading this about endorphins in one of the term papers Cara got paid for writing for someone else; possibly that's one of the things she made up. He used to think it was hilarious that she made things up; in fact, he still does. How audacious she is! He'd do anything for her. He had the surgery for her, though he'll never be so crass as to put it that way. Still, she'll know it, and she'll say to her friends, *No more pills, no more goop, no headache, no worry, no more not fucking because we don't feel like turning on the light to find the damn diaphragm, no more counting back the days on the calendar, no more this, no more that*, in her proud, singsong voice that on the tape Jenny gave him sounds characteristically elated. He can feel her words enter him, beat by beat, like touching pulses wrist to wrist, or like his temples to the insides of Cara's thighs. It's like whispering into the small of her back, or her saying "Fuck me" into his mouth. It's like the two of them suspended in bed, treading sheets like water, his body confused with her soul and vice versa. It's like his ear against the zipper on the pillow at his neck, and feeling the catch in Cara's voice on the tape when she tells her mom the children will be okay. Okay about what? Douglas wonders as usual. Balloons? Grapes? Sunlight? Icicles? To Cara's mother, every simple, lovely object is a tragedy waiting to happen to her grandchildren. But Cara stays patient, telling her mother what she's learned about children's medications—no bottle is ever large enough to hold a fatal dose. So that's why the bottle of grape-flavored Tylenol is no bigger than a thumb, Douglas realizes contentedly.

But now the subject changes, and so does Cara's voice, which grows airy at the edges, wistful almost. Something about a priest. A black priest she met one afternoon in the supermarket. Or maybe not a priest, but with a clerical collar and a quietly confidential priestly bearing, who taught her how to cook an unusual pizza, in his own pink kitchen the size of a confessional. The strange flavors of the pizza, the sharp unpredictable texture, remained with her throughout the affair as a kind of reminder that it couldn't last. She uses that word, *affair*, although she lies to her mother they did nothing but kiss, the priest's tongue with that flavor still on it. Douglas doesn't believe that, not for a second. Cara doesn't kiss and run, Cara's kisses don't stop at the mouth. He believes he's been a fool and he's a fool right now, naked, wrapped up in a blanket, the dog kissing his feet, his forehead shocked pale between the too-orange fuzz of his eyebrows in the mirror. It's the mirror he bought for their fourth wedding anniversary, and now it frames him as he rises from the couch, folds the blanket, nearly uncorks the frog while slinging it over his arm along with his discarded clothing. He pops the tape from the player then slides it back in till it's over. He can watch himself walking right out of the mirror, and it seems a final exit, like walking out of his life. Upstairs, he puts the still-sloshing water bottle away in a drawer, pulls his jeans up over his bandage and jockstrap, then on second thought, pulls them down again and puts on a pair of underwear and the jeans on top of those, too tight with the bandage but he zips them up anyway and lies on the bed with the TV on. He had thought he would go, but finds he doesn't want his body to move, he just wants it to lie there and forget. He forgets about dinner, forgets about fetching the children. The dog has followed him to the base of the steps, and the thought that she might stay there unfed, unwalked, her thirsty nose raised toward the shadow of his bedroom, is a comfort to him until he hears her walk away and settle her weight in her usual corner. The pain is no longer a comfort, no longer good, no longer the kind of pain that makes him want to be good to himself. And the thought of Cara ministering to him—he can't stomach that. "I despise you," he says, to the priest, to Cara's mother, to Cara. Especially to Cara. "I hate you," he says. He's never said these things before in exactly this way, alone, out loud, his lips pursed around the last word as if in a kiss.

O IN THE
MORNING,
O IN THE
EVENING,
O AT
NIGHT

✳ ✳ ✳

1 ❧

The dog started life as a foundling.

Occasionally Cara, explaining how they'd found her, referred to her as a stray, but then she always took it back or regretted it later, the way you'd regret an unwitting insult. For the dog *hadn't* strayed; indeed, after a few days of phone calls and newspaper announcements it seemed to Cara that there had been no place from which the puppy could have strayed had she been so inclined—no person phoned the paper saying yes, they had lost a puppy, and no pound within a fifty-mile radius had received a report of such an animal. And since the puppy couldn't speak, and couldn't tell them what her life had been like in the approximately three months between the day she was born and the night she was found, and since she came equipped with no obvious memories the way other lost-and-found dogs did—no bounding enthusiasm triggered by the sounds of cans of dog food being opened, for instance, and no fear of cars or of large, bearded men—Cara liked to say that Kato had had no past at all, and that her time on earth had begun, at three months of age, on a cold, rainy midnight in the parking lot of the truck stop where Cara and Douglas stopped while driving home from a camping trip aborted by rain, toward the end of the very first year of what they would someday call their life together.

Cara drank coffee, and Douglas a Coke. Their conversation was lively for this time of night not only in the hope that they might keep themselves awake but because of their twin needs to convince themselves that the trip had been anything but a failure. This was the third night of rain, and while the tent had held up through the first night, it started oozing in the second, and although by morning moisture had crept through the seams of their zipped-together sleeping bags, they still rose optimistically, cleared camp, and set off for Mingo National Wildlife Refuge, to walk the network of creaking boardwalks through a half-submerged forest of cypress trees. Neither Douglas nor Cara had seen a cypress swamp before, and the broad, spreading skirts of the tree trunks, disappearing under black water only to send up knees and knobs and elbows, looked murky and eerie and made Cara long nostalgically for the shelter they'd found from yesterday's rain, a tiny bar with a dart board and a game of table soccer. Between games, they'd eaten corn chips at a lopsided table, nodding now and then at the other customers while stepping to the door to see if the weather had changed, even though if they just sat still and listened for a minute they could hear the rain plunking on the corrugated roof. At Mingo, fog floated on the water in a low, flat cloud that kept yawning and swelling, until finally the knees and the knobs were obscured and there was only the boardwalk vanishing between the tree trunks not five feet ahead and the loud, wet suck when they walked along it.

At midnight farther north, in the truck stop over coffee and Coke, Cara said to Douglas, "Just imagine that if by accident I stepped off the boardwalk into that swamp and never came up, and you went home alone and called your sister with the news that I'd been eaten by an alligator, how happy your sister would be."

"Christ, Cara. Is that why I have bruises on my elbow from how hard you were hanging on?"

"Sorry," said Cara. "But I didn't want to give your sister that pleasure. She'd get to ask you what parts of me they recovered, and if there was a head left or only a chewed-up torso. Oh, God, that reminds me." She reached into their knapsack to fish for her packet of pills. In the past five years she'd switched from pills to diaphragm and back again more times than she could remember; in the single year she'd been with Douglas, she had already made the switch once. Good health or convenience, one or the other, over time Cara figured she'd strike a good balance. Tonight's pill skidded across the table when she popped it from the case; Douglas caught it with his spoon and flicked it back to her, table soccer style.

"But there aren't any alligators in Missouri," he was saying. "At least not anymore. Years ago, maybe. Hundreds of thousands of years."

"Oh," said Cara, disappointed, although she'd suspected as much. Already she'd allowed herself to nurture this memory of the boardwalk as something they had endured together and survived, like an earthquake or a car wreck. They'd been living together for months, easily, contentedly, and Cara worried that for the romance to endure, it would need to be tested somehow. So far they hadn't even had a memorable fight, and the worst they'd been through were a few sleepless nights in a bedroom no bigger than the shaft of moonlight falling through its window, kept awake by the tortured, emphysemic cough of an elderly neighbor. And even that didn't count, for with each new phlegmy, hacking episode Cara and Douglas only burrowed more deeply into each other's welcome, needful bodies, then finally dressed and went for a walk, out on the vacant streets. This was in the mid-1970s, when Cara, having dropped out of school for the second time just several months short of a college degree, had found a job writing other people's term papers under the shady auspices of a resume typing service run by a man in plaid business suits who seemed at last to have given up putting the moves on her. That it was this item on Cara's own resume, rather than her ultimately and laboriously acquired degree in philosophy, that she managed to parlay into a position as director of Career Counseling and Placement at the community center several years later didn't surprise her in the least. Even then, researching someone else's term paper on "The Angle of the Gaze in Hieronymus Bosch's *The Seven Deadly Sins*," or detailing someone else's summary of the secretions of the anterior lobe of the pituitary, Cara had had the feeling that she was preparing herself for something else, although she couldn't imagine what. At the time, hunched over a table full of overlapping reference books, her pen to paper, her shoes askew on the library floor, her bare feet tucked under her ass, she felt only a curious blend of mischief and accomplishment. Not yet having had her own children, still she likened the moment in which she handed a finished paper into the flushed, eager grasp of a student to the moment when a newborn is slid from the arms of its doctor into the arms of its mother; for that long, fraught second, the paper seemed to belong to both of them at once.

"Nothing ever happens *to* us," Cara said to Douglas in the midnight glow of the truck stop, tipping the salt shaker over her coffee and then righting it before any spilled. "We *do* things together, and we *go* places together, but then we come home and we're the same people we were before and our life just goes on."

"I thought that was the point," Douglas argued. "That part about life going on. Survival. The future. *Our* future. That's what it's all about, right? If we like our life together, and if we like who we are, and if you like me and I like you. On the other hand, if we're miserable . . ."

Douglas often said *we* when he meant *you*, then gazed at her with an intense, meaningful squint. Tonight his face was so pale it looked practically blue, and his hair stood up straight all around, as orange as could be. Even camping out, he'd been as earnest as Wally Cleaver, and now he sat on the literal edge of his seat, watching her as closely as if she were a movie. He wants to know me, Cara thought, he wants to know what's going to happen in me next. But at the same time there was a curious edge to his absorption, a kind of restlessness that made him turn around if anyone opened a door. He was jumpy yet resolute, devoted but impatient. Already that year, Cara had developed the habit of gazing at him the way she always would, with surprise, that this was the man with whom she was so happy to be. She never loved him right away when she looked at him like this; it always took a minute or two before the feeling settled in.

"You're not going to get me to tell you I'm not miserable by squinting at me like that," Cara said. "I'm not falling for that trick. You know damn well I'm not miserable, but—"

"Hah!" Douglas said, raising his eyebrows.

"But I just don't trust my happiness," said Cara. "Not that I don't think it's real, but it's always come so easily, nothing bad ever happens, even when you spilled the Wesson oil on the kitchen floor it was the funniest thing in the world, falling on our asses every time we needed a glass of orange juice for a whole goddamn week, and that was the worst thing that happened to us all year except when the John Updike novel got stolen out of the car. And anyone who steals a John Updike novel, well, they didn't even take the camera, I didn't even feel violated the way you're supposed to feel when someone steals something from you. I felt lucky, actually. I'd already finished the book, even."

"Me, too," said Douglas. "But a lot of people wouldn't look at us and say, 'Hey, they're lucky.' We're broke. We eat tunafish six times a week. You hate that."

"I know. But I like hating it. I don't mind being broke. Do you, Douglas? Are you unhappy? Have you been unhappy all this time and I've been too happy to notice?"

"No. Just sick of tunafish."

"So cook spaghetti. But that's the problem. Spaghetti's too simple. Nothing's complicated enough. If life keeps going like this, and if nothing ever goes wrong, then I'm afraid that when something *does* go wrong, we won't be able to handle it. We won't recognize each other."

Douglas drained his Coke, tipping the ice cube back into his mouth just so he could squint at her from under his lashes. "Should I choke on this ice cube? Would our life be more exciting if I died, Cara? Is that what you're saying?"

"Don't. I guess not. But if only things could get a little more complicated. Yes. I want *complications*," said Cara expectantly, for the instant she said it, something changed in the air around them. It took her a moment to figure out what it was. There'd been a puppy outside, rain-drenched and howling, when she and Douglas had driven up earlier. Suddenly the howling, a high-pitched bark-and-squeal fully audible even from inside the restaurant, ceased.

They both sat still a minute, listening to the slapping of the rain on the windows and to the steamy, clanking noises of the truck stop kitchen, where someone was running a vacuum cleaner. Oddly, now that the puppy had stopped its howling, everything else was noisier than it had been before.

"I thought it was pretty complicated sleeping last night in that puddle," Douglas suggested after a while.

"Not complicated enough," said Cara.

"I thought it was complicated when you dropped the binoculars."

"They didn't fall in the water."

"I thought the Wesson oil on the linoleum was complicated enough."

"It was slapstick, and it was only for a week," said Cara, reaching into their knapsack for her wallet and plunking down the money for their drinks and the tip. Outside, the lot was empty except for their car and a canister of Cheez Whiz that rolled back and forth in a puddle. In the distance, the Ozark foothills hunkered dark and wet around the curve of the highway. Later and forever, Cara would imagine in those foothills a low white farmhouse where the litter of pups had been born and where the mother lay curled on a bathroom rug with the one damp puppy left to her, suckling and sleeping in turn. But for now Cara wasn't thinking of the puppy at all, so when Douglas paused at the car and said, "Hear that?" it took her a moment to figure out what it was.

She put her knapsack on the car hood and squatted near the fender for a look underneath.

Cara saw the tail, not wagging, and Douglas saw the nose. When he reached under the car to touch it, it was dry in spite of the rain.

"Come here, little doggy," said Cara, from her side of the car.

"Over here, monster," said Douglas, from his.

The dog stayed put.

"Sweet little doggy," said Cara, as Douglas patted the pavement, then reached out a hand, palm up, for sniffing. The dog backed farther under the car. Cara grabbed hold of its tail.

"We might offer it food," Cara said, feeling the rain on the back of her neck. A drop of it snaked down under her shirt collar and traveled the length of her spine.

"We have that salami in the cooler in the trunk," Douglas said.

"No, we don't. I threw it out. It got disgusting," said Cara. "We have that chocolate bar."

"I ate that," said Douglas. "I'll go in and get some crackers or something."

When he vanished through the truck stop door, Cara let go of the dog's tail and went around to Douglas's side of the car, so she could look into its big brown eyes.

"You poor thing," she heard herself say. "You sweet, adorable, scared little thing. Don't be scared. I won't hurt you. Come out and I'll kiss you and hug you, and wrap you up in a towel and dry you."

Cara had never spoken like that in her life. She had never had cause. In fact, baby talk had always filled her with mistrust. But now her wrists tingled with the sugariness of it, her neck blazed even under the drip and slide of the rain. Still the dog only gazed at her and whimpered all the more plaintively.

"I can't believe it's scared of us," said Cara to Douglas, who waved a hamburger under the fender. The dog strained forward, sniffed, and ate, bite after bite until its nose was in the rain. Douglas wrapped his arms around its neck, and Cara took hold of the collar, but not a second later Douglas had his arms around nothing while the empty collar swung from Cara's fingers. This was a moment they would always remember—their four hands cradling wet, dark space—although neither of them knew it at the time.

The dog slid under the car again, and the rain was falling faster.

"If we could only start the car," Cara said mournfully.

But the starter was broken, and they had taken to parking on hills so they could jump start the engine, only now there was no way of releasing the brake without running over the dog.

"If I could run it over just a touch," she added speculatively.

"Try honking," Douglas offered. "Is this complicated enough, Cara?"

"Honking won't work," Cara answered, but she honked anyway until the waitress stepped out with a broom and a dustpan, to see what was going on. It was the waitress who poked the broom under the car and soon burst into laughter as the puppy lunged backward onto the slickness of the parking lot, then skidded around the building into the night.

The waitress went inside, forgetting the dustpan she had propped against the brick. On the pavement fell the glow from the restaurant windows, which seemed to hold in blurred green-ness the echo of the shape of the dog. They'd seen it only for a moment, but that was long enough to see how delicately the animal was made. It was tinier than they had thought. Cara slid the collar over her wrist; it fit like a bracelet. No tags.

"I don't think you could choke to death on an ice cube," she said. "I think it would melt before."

They sat quietly in the parking lot a moment, patting their necks with the ever-damp towel. Douglas took an extra long time, drying his hair, but the puppy didn't reappear around the corner of the building. Finally he cranked open his window, stuck his head out, and whistled. That whistle—two high staccato notes and a third note extended, allowed to fade between pursed lips—became Cara and Douglas's special signal from that day forward. Not only did they use it to summon the dog, who never obeyed it anyway unless she knew they had something to give her to eat, but they used it in crowded supermarkets as well, if they had lost each other among the aisles. And sometimes they whistled it at home, softly, if one wanted the other's attention. Now it only hung in the air between them, the third note vanishing into the night, and the dog not appearing, and still not appearing. Just then another car pulled into the lot and parked. Someone belched as the doors swung open.

"It might only have been disoriented," Cara suggested, "and then when it ran around back, it saw its house down the hill or something and knew where to go."

She threw the car into forward and coasted downhill to the road until the engine kicked in. The dog was waiting on the berm of the entrance ramp, not wagging its tail and not howling, but looking matter-of-factly expectant. When Douglas opened his door, it stepped eagerly forward and waited to be lifted onto his lap, where he wrapped it in the towel, lifted each soaked, floppy ear, and swabbed the pink whorls dry inside. Then he parted the dog's legs and looked between.

"It's a girl," he said to Cara.

He was beaming. He wanted to name her Katie. Cara said no, she'd known too many Katies in starched pink dresses, too many Katies in Mary Jane shoes. Not until they'd reached home nearly two hours later did they remember the knapsack—the camera, binoculars, toothbrushes, wallet, and birth control pills—that they'd left on the hood of the car. It was gone, of course.

Those early years in Missouri, most of Cara and Douglas's friends had dogs, and the dogs were included in the things they did together. They picnicked, they hiked, they swam, they stopped over for beer at one another's houses, and always there were the dogs to be watched over with their helpless canine politics and four-legged antics. Kato was smallest, but she was also the dominant one. Lance was sleepy, Jamie stupid, Rose stout and un-roselike, always farting under the table and then snapping at the other dogs who came sniffing at her tail. Rose was stubborn, Lance amiable, Jamie too carelessly enthusiastic. Among them Kato was the one who seemed most commonsensical. Being the most independent, she was also the most sly, and it was she who made everyone, dog or otherwise, wait while she chased a squirrel or rabbit and then moseyed around awhile where no one could find her, digging up smells. More than once she got carried away, forgot to think where she was going, stayed missing for hours. Several times she got picked up by the city truck and delivered to the pound. Several times she arrived home after two in the morning, nosing her way past the door Cara and Douglas left open for her in case they both fell asleep. They never did sleep, though, not while Kato was gone.

They worried and fumed, went naked to the door, whistled two short notes and one long, pretended indifference, switched off the porch light, came back to bed, then went to the door and whistled again. More than once they reported her missing to the police, and more than once she finally showed up not at home but outside the rear door of the radio station, where Douglas, who did classic rock and offbeat city news with a little talk show mixed in, had started dreaming of what he hoped would someday be his show, a series of weekly interviews with people chosen at random off the buses and streets; sometimes a drug dealer, a bus driver, a zookeeper, a keyboard operator, anybody who might be enticed into conversation and then into the recording studio itself, where Douglas, with his blend of gentle sympathy and sharp impatience, might draw forth confessions, recitations, tics, and regrets. He joked he would interview Kato, too. To Cara and Douglas, their dog's personality seemed but a more reticent, sneakier variety of their own.

"She understands everything, in her own doggy way," they boasted to their friends, while privately they worried over what they called Kato's essential humanity. It seemed too much of a burden for a dog to have to bear. Just the lingering scent of Cara's plaid-wearing boss was enough to make Kato circle Cara warily when she got home from work; until Cara changed her clothes, Kato wore a look of mistrust and supplication. When Cara and Douglas made love, Kato left the room discreetly, then came back when they were finished. When they played chess, she licked the captured pieces clean then stood them carefully in a row. When they did the wash, she went with them to the Laundromat, carrying her own bedraggled towel between her teeth, then snuck out the door while they loaded the machines. It did no good to call her name or try to track her down, for having tasted for a moment the pleasure of stealth, she was all too happy to indulge herself in it; they knew she hid herself purposefully from them, darting strategically behind the carts to make her way around the corner of the supermarket, or slipping deliberately farther into the alleys, silent as a cat.

"She loves adventure," Douglas marveled, but Cara argued that what she loved was disobedience, pure and simple.

"She likes to worry us. It gives her the advantage," complained Cara, whose worry turned to indignation the minute Kato finally came home. They always gave her the cold shoulder when she walked in the door, although it broke their hearts to watch her get so desperate for attention; tail between her legs, ketchup on her nose, a low, tremulous whine escaping from between clenched teeth. At last, when enough time had passed, they patted the bed and let her jump up between them, where, while Cara petted and kissed her, and nuzzled Kato's ruff, and lifted the flaps of Kato's ears and blew teasingly into them, Douglas asked Kato questions about where she had been and how she felt about what she had seen, exactly the sorts of questions he might have asked had he been interviewing Kato on his would-be radio show. Throughout, Cara and Douglas shared their relieved amusement with covert glances over Kato's glossy head. Years later they'd look back on these shared glances with awed embarrassment: how could they not have recognized what it was they were doing, when in retrospect they saw it all so clearly? Indeed, it was as logical as if it had been planned. Having learned to love each other, they now learned to love, in unison, a thing outside themselves, so that their two distinct emotions, Douglas's and Cara's, might assume a shape between them, a shape with body and soul and its own queer, compact energy.

Which is why it was so frightening when Kato ran away. For it wasn't just a dog that had escaped them but this thing they had fashioned together unbeknownst to themselves, this mechanism they had created in the service of their hearts' educations.

When they had left Missouri, and Cara had conceived and given birth to Georgie, Kato had been living with them for seven years. And when Douglas came home from the hospital that afternoon after Georgie had been born, to take Kato on the morning walk of which she'd been deprived, he found the dog on her side unwilling to get up, and unable to stand when he lifted her and set her on her legs.

Each time she fell, her legs skidding sideways and apart, she looked at him with a mixture of anger, pain, and sorrow.

She was a barrel-chested dog, short-legged, long in the torso. She had a star on her forehead, the way some horses do, and another at the tip of her tail. Her chest was freckled, her belly practically hairless, the pink skin exposed but the nipples coyly hidden under whorls of fur. Her brown eyes were large and thickly lashed for a dog's, and her face was of definite female appearance. Actually, she was pretty. Doe-eyed, gently whiskered, narrow of skull. Although Cara often said, "She's just a hound, part beagle, part something else, like all farm dogs in that part of the country," she believed Kato to be special—less bluntly made, and with delicate feelings to match. Despite her stubbornness, her impertinence, her bland self-assurance, Kato had developed a fondness for baby talk; she liked to be sung to, cooed at, and called by her nickname.

"C'mon, O," cajoled Douglas, sliding one arm under her haunches and the other under her forelegs, then making his way through the door and down the steps of their building. "Stop playing games. You'll feel better outside."

He stood her gently in the grass. She took a step, peed, sank to her belly, glanced at him briefly over her shoulder, then turned to the grass and started nibbling. Grazing, Douglas knew, was something dogs did when they needed to vomit, but Kato grazed defiantly. When she retched something yellow back onto the lawn, it was as if to say, "Try and tell me everything's alright, and I'll prove to you it's not."

"What happened then?" asked Cara, from her bed in the hospital later that night. She hadn't yet slept deeply, so excited was she, so wide-eyed and astonished at what they had made. She felt uncommonly alert—to the cries of the newborns from the nursery across the hall, to the queer sensation of her breasts filling suddenly with food, to the ache between her legs, to the unfathomable waves of new emotion she had for their baby— and yet she couldn't quite take in what Douglas was talking about. With Georgie so close, Kato seemed distant, far off. It was as if Douglas were coming to her with news of some worldly event—a coup, a hijacking—that she simply didn't want to have feelings about in the face of all the feelings she was having already.

"And then I carried her upstairs and laid her on the bed in the guest room and tucked her in," Douglas said.

"It's not the guest room, anymore," Cara corrected. "It's the baby's room. Georgie's."

"But the baby will be sleeping in our room for a while, I thought we decided," said Douglas. "I set the crib up in there."

"With the bumpers?" asked Cara.

"Yes."

"And the comforter?"

"I couldn't find the comforter," Douglas admitted.

"It's folded on the radiator in the guest room. In the baby's room, I mean," said Cara, who found that her awareness of this small detail—the purple alphabet comforter warming on top of the radiator—brought with it an awareness of the dog as well, asleep on the bed, half in and half out of a tangle of army blanket, the tags on her collar jangling fleetingly with each fit and start of a dream.

Except the dog didn't dream on Cara's first night home, or on the nights after that. Nor was she content with her place on the bed in the guest room. Fitfully, Kato slept on the floor next to Cara and Douglas's bed, not a foot from the crib, her dry nose turned toward and then away from Georgie's strange mixture of smells—the milk, the lotions, the diapers, the vernix still cling-ing to the creases of his underarms and neck—as if she were trying to make up her mind. The question of whether Kato's illness was psychological or entirely physical had not satisfac-torily been answered by a day of tests and X-rays at the veter-inarian's, nor would it ever be. But she was making life miserable, that was for sure. If the baby woke fiercely at two in the morning, then the dog woke at three, crying to be carried downstairs and outside, and if Georgie woke hungry again around four, then Kato woke whimpering with pain at four-fifty, just as Cara had finally coaxed Georgie to sleep. Stumbling out of bed to quiet her, Douglas would step barefoot in a spreading pool of urine that had crept beneath the bed or among the four legs of the crib. Night after night passed like this, and day after day—a confusion of whimpers, burps, bathtimes, and feedings in a house that smelled alternately of dog piss and Murphy's Oil Soap. Photos from this time show Cara and Douglas, Georgie in arms, sagging lower and lower with the gravity of their own exhausted sleeplessness. Years later, Cara still remembered saying to Douglas, in all earnestness, "This is it. Our lives are ruined. I don't even know what I was like before this happened. I don't remember myself. Do you? A colicky baby I could handle, I think. And a sick dog. But not both all at once. Not now," and her utter relief when Douglas replied, "There's always the vet. We can board her. Right away. Just a week. Maybe two."

"Maybe three," Cara said.

But they had lost track of time. Of whole days. It was seven o'clock on a Friday evening, and the vet's was locked and shuttered. From inside came the yowling of cooped-up dogs. For a panicky moment they considered leashing Kato to the door with a note for the following morning, but then, resigned, they brought her home, carried her upstairs, laid her on the bed in the guest room within reach of her twin bowls of food and water. That night, the dog slept through, and in the morning she could walk again, shakily at first but with enough determination that she made it down the steps and then up. After that, there was gradual, steady improvement. She didn't whimper in her sleep, she didn't pee in the house, she even stopped grazing when she went outside. When Cara and Douglas woke in the night with Georgie, there was only the contented thump of Kato's tail and an occasional, decorous visit; if Cara sat nursing Georgie in the rocking chair, for instance, Kato might pad in quietly, sniff the runners, wag her tail, circle once, then disappear back into her room.

All was peace and quiet again. At least it seemed like peace and quiet. Freed of the endless demands of the dog—her incontinence, her suffering, her sad, indignant glances—even the most chaotic moments of new parenthood felt calm, methodical, richly satisfying.

Not until years later were Cara and Douglas able to recognize precisely what they had permitted to happen. How the dog, no longer a menace, or a threat to their new contentment, became instead a kind of shadowy nuisance but never the companion she had been before. No longer did they comment on her humor, her intelligence, her remarkable powers of understanding, for the more they reveled in these qualities in Georgie, the less they noticed them in Kato at all. When she was hungry, they fed her. When she was dirty, they bathed her. When she needed to go out, they walked her. When she got fleas, Douglas took the children away from the house, out to dinner, maybe, while Cara donned rubber gloves, chained the dog to the tree in the lawn, and sprayed her with poison, then sprayed the carpet and the dog's jumbled bedding and the couches on which the dog occasionally climbed and the drapes against which Kato occasionally nuzzled. Escaped fleas, Cara pinched between thumb and middle finger, then flushed down the toilet. No longer did they save for Kato choice scraps from the table; instead, as the years went by, she learned to sit patiently near Georgie's and later Max's high chair for whatever fell her way. And no longer did Cara and Douglas wait up for her, worrying, when she managed to escape on one of her adventures. Instead they left the door ajar so she might slip in unnoticed, without even having to wake them up.

That was the dog's middle age.

2 ✖

On Halloween nights, Jenny was in the habit of throwing a little party at the station. There'd be a punch bowl, a cake or a tray of doughnuts, depending on whether people were feeling industrious or lazy, and some decorations pulled hastily out of the closet from among the reels of tape. Jenny might be wearing a witch's hat, and one of the technicians a full, rented costume, and then, after the feeling of festivity had begun to wane and the empty candy wrappers to pile up in the ashtrays, Estaban's mother would arrive and gather everyone around and intone a ghost story that Douglas interrupted to cajole her into the recording studio, where she would tell it to the mike, live, every year, the same soft-spoken, credibly matter-of-fact delivery, the same changeable, always unpredictable tale, about the ghost of her grandmother, who in the years since her death by shooting at the polls in Haiti had grown ever younger and younger until now she was a girl ghost not much older than Georgie, in a pink ruffled skirt too short over too-long legs that followed you everywhere you went. Georgie and Max sat together on Estaban's mother's big lap while she related the antics and adventures of the ghost, their quick breath mingling with her voice in the mike and getting carried out into the night over the air, so that to the people listening to their radios on the other end, Georgie's and Max's breathing must have sounded like the swish of the girl-grandmother's skirt as she settled coyly among the cushions of the couches in their living rooms. At six, Georgie understood that Estaban's mother did not really believe in the ghost, but he understood as well that she wanted very much for *him* to believe it, so out of generosity he convinced himself and was afraid. That was Cara's interpretation, anyway. How tender she felt for her son at these moments, watching him bury himself quaking in the folds of Estaban's mother's lap while clapping his hands over Max's tiny ears even though Max enjoyed the story of the ghost, seemed actually to enjoy being frightened, and Cara wondered, should she shield Georgie? Shelter him? Keep him innocent of the things that would scare him?

Cara's mother said no, don't shield him, don't keep him away, that will only make it worse, he'll be insulted, he's too smart for that, Cara, and then she asked Cara a question that Cara didn't hear and didn't really care to hear either because she wanted to get off the phone. Halloween was her mother's birthday, which Cara had forgotten till now, and since she always phoned her mother on her birthday, and since their birthday talks were usually on the long side, and since in any case their talks often veered toward the personal, Cara had chosen to place this call from the safety of the studio and not the busy open cubicle where Douglas had his desk. Gloria was turning sixty-one years old, and having borne her sixtieth birthday last year with utter grace and dignity, Cara thought she might reverse herself this year and get petulant about it and start feeling sorry for herself. But that wasn't the case. Her mother seemed determined to age with equanimity, to hold herself straight, to wash her face with creams instead of soaps and pat dry instead of rubbing, her sole concession to vanity. And just a wash of blonde highlights every so often, and pretty underwear, a big expense but worth it for the way it made her feel. She felt exactly how she looked, "young but mature," and regal in the way small women can be regal, and serene of spirit. She had gone out and bought herself a woven silk jumpsuit and boots and long earrings, and she and Cara's father would be going out for dinner to celebrate. They'd walk the long way to the restaurant, down to the water, then up again, unless they took the ferry in between and forgot about dinner entirely; it was a beautiful evening. Cara's gift to her was just what she needed, a bag of supple, dark leather big and sturdy enough to carry her schoolbooks, which led to a discussion of the classes she was taking—statistics, and a survey of third-world health issues for which Cara's mother was reading a paper called "An Overview of Sanitary Conditions as They Relate to Human Fecal Matter in Tropical Barrios," which led to a discussion of Kato and the messes she left nearly every morning lately in her usual corner of the dining room.

"We don't know if it's senility or just plain old age," Cara said, aware that it might be considered a breach of tact to be discussing incontinence on her mother's birthday. But she went on anyway. She was at a loss about what to do about Kato.

"She went on one of her outings the other night; she was gone so long I thought maybe she wouldn't come back, at least I hoped she wouldn't, anyway, though Douglas still thinks she'll get better, I think. At least he thinks he should *hope* she'll get better. Anyway, finally she drags herself home, it's obvious she's been on a binge—she's just an eating machine these days, just an eating, shitting machine—and she drags herself into the house with her belly touching the ground, I swear, like she swallowed a whole garbage truck full of rotten hamburger because that's what keeps coming out of her, from one end or the other, she's just lying in the corner of the dining room too full to move, but every time I go in there she's belched more of it up—"

"Oh, Cara, please!" interrupted Gloria.

"But it's so disgusting. It's like brown, lumpy oatmeal, it—"

"I know it's disgusting, that's why I want you to spare me the particulars, thank you very much."

"But you were the one talking about fecal matter—"

"Human fecal matter, not dog."

"Oh."

"But I'd be interested to know . . . or in any case, I think you should find out if there's a threat posed to children, to Georgie and Max. A parasitical threat. Because that's one of the . . . but I don't know if humans can get parasites from dogs. Can they, do you think? That's a huge factor in malnutrition, parasites."

"Georgie and Max aren't malnourished," said Cara defensively and with great amusement, because it seemed to her that the paper "An Overview of Sanitary Conditions as They Relate to Human Fecal Matter in Tropical Barrios" was one she herself might have written for one of her frantic graduate student clients so many years ago, when she worked for the man in the plaid business suits. On second thought she was sure she had written it, she was absolutely certain, she could remember what it said, that studies of helminthic infections tended to focus on biomedical rather than socioeconomic factors—but she couldn't remember if she had made that up or read it in some journal. She must have read it, she would never have come up with the word *helminthic* on her own, unless she'd invented that as well, which would have been risky, sure, but she remembered being thrilled by such risks in those days. Anyway, the outrageous coincidence—her own mother reading her own paper nearly a decade after she'd faked it—fit in perfectly with the way she had been feeling lately about her life. Namely, that there was too much going on in it at once, and hardly a moment when she wasn't doing at least two things simultaneously— giving Max a bubble bath, for instance, while reviewing someone's water-spattered Strong Interest Inventory, or cooking supper while watching the news on TV. And the news seemed more than usual to demand her close attention; that is, the buildup of troops in the Persian Gulf region, the invasion by Iraq of Kuwait, the young men and women executed in Kuwait, the young men and women donning gas masks in the Saudi desert, the children left behind or taken forever away from their families—all of this was part of Cara's life, too, wasn't it? Or was it? *Shouldn't* it be? For there were children involved, children who might as well have been Max and Georgie, who needed love, who needed safety and drinking water and blankets and compassion. Shouldn't she cry? Wasn't it useless to cry, but wouldn't it be horrible not to? she wondered, crying, not crying, staunching the tears, then watching them fall on the omelet pan as if to test the heat of the cooking surface—if the teardrop exploded and vanished, then the pan was hot enough, but if the teardrop pooled up, it wasn't. Sometimes when Cara saw on the news the smudged, frightened faces of abandoned children, she had a vision of herself reaching into the television screen to embrace and comfort them, but then just as quickly she saw how acutely the facts of her life contradicted that vision; she was a woman in her kitchen with her sleeves rolled up amid rings of green pepper spread apart on the cutting board, tossing Greek olives into the salad bowl. *That* was Cara, *that* was her, the one rinsing the lettuce, the one wiping her hands on the dishtowel in order to answer the phone, the one who listened patiently and politely to the entire recitation of the magazine salesman before saying she wasn't interested and then realizing the message was taped, the one wiping Max's nose with the hem of her blouse, the one who once squirted dishwashing liquid instead of salad dressing on the salad, *that* was Cara, not the one willing her caresses to travel via satellite halfway around the world, not the Cara brushing sand from the eyelashes of children fleeing through the desert. Still it seemed there were always three or four of her; the one who was thinking, and the one who was thinking about what she was thinking, and the one who was crying, and the one who flipped the omelet too abruptly so part of it broke, flew off the spatula, missed Max's face by an inch. So when she phoned her mother from the recording studio in the station, and when she'd said Happy Birthday, and when her mother said, "Happy Halloween. How are you? What have you been up to?" Cara didn't know which answer to give. This? That? The other? There were too many words, too many possibilities, she felt like one of Georgie's *Choose Your Own Adventure* books, and when she talked, the talking only made matters worse, because then on top of everything, there was the Cara that was talking, the Cara who couldn't shut up about kids' Tylenol and how her mother shouldn't worry about the children getting into it because . . . and it was just by accident, really, that she'd chosen to talk about that, when just as accidentally she could have picked the answer about Elizabeth's trip to Mexico and how Cara had been entrusted with the care of Elizabeth's houseplants and mail, and how every couple of days,

240

when she found herself alone in Elizabeth's third-floor apartment with the doors shut around her, Cara felt that she had taken a vow of silence. It was there, in Elizabeth's untraveled hallways, that Cara admitted to herself that she had quit going to Group forever, that all the Sundays when she told her friends she was "just too busy" were really Sundays she just didn't feel like doing all that gabbing and sympathizing and posturing and evaluating. She felt lighter, somehow, once she'd figured this out. She felt freed, as if she really could reside in more places at once, here, and not here, like the ball in the magician's mirrored box, when in fact what she was doing on the Sundays when there was Group was sitting either inside the car or out of it, depending on the weather, smoking cigarettes and considering taking in typing again now that Max went to bed at a reasonable hour, or even writing other people's term papers again even though it was unethical, sure, but in the scheme of breached morals it was modest, a luxury, like a stubbed toe, something to feel good about when you knew how much worse it could be.

Douglas didn't know she was considering doing term papers again, or that she sat alone in private cogitation. Sundays, Douglas thought she was at Group. She hadn't told him otherwise, for it seemed unfair to ask him to stay home with the children while she went off somewhere for two hours of peace and quiet, smoking cigarettes, which was another thing he didn't know she did.

So, since Douglas believed she was at Group, and since the women of Group believed she was running errands with the children, and since she actually was sitting on a bench or a tree stump, sometimes with a book, sometimes not, sometimes in darkness, sometimes in daylight, then she really *was* in three places at once, wasn't she?

It perplexed her that Douglas still hadn't figured this out. But she was grateful for it, too. Grateful to him for being who he was; so firmly rooted in the moment, so confident of the limitations of space and of his own place in it, and of the true, fixed nature of his blue jeans and black Chinese slippers, his too-narrow chest, his too-orange hair, his big ears and long neck, his very gangliness that Cara and her friends have remarked is like the gangliness of a tall wading bird. A heron, say, a gangliness that when the animal is in its proper element, poised for a glimpse of a fish under water, isn't gangliness at all but grace and surefootedness of spirit. And then a fish would dart by and the heron would spear it at once. Douglas would figure her out, soon enough. He just liked to stay cool, before he got hot. It was a game they played, because she liked his attention and he liked sneaking it to her.

Her mother might find this alarming. But her mother had asked Cara a question again, and again Cara hadn't quite troubled to hear it, and there was silence until her mother commented, "Why not keep the dog on the leash when you take her outside? Then she couldn't run away the way she does. Or, when she gets back from one of her binges, as you call them, why not keep her outside until she stops making messes? Make life easier for yourself, Cara. Why not?"

"Because she won't do what she has to do, when she's on a leash. She won't shit, I mean. She's too well brought up. She's too discreet when she's out in the world, in public. She has to find a spot a quarter of a mile away before she squats. She's very ladylike when it's in her best interest. Anyway, she needs the freedom. She needs the exercise. These days if she doesn't get enough exercise, she gets stiff and falls over. One leg or the other just goes, and then her body kind of rolls on top of it. And if she didn't make messes, I'd have nothing to complain about. My life would be too perfect, without Kato shitting all over the polished floor of it," Cara said resolutely, leaning back in her chair and propping her feet among the knotted black cables and the blunt, lowered heads of the mikes.

"Would it be?"

"Absolutely," said Cara.

"Which brings me to my next question," said Cara's mother. "How's Douglas?"

"He's fine," Cara said. "He's got a good show tonight, recordings of a couple of his interviews with parapsychologists talking about cake plates falling off tables when there's no one in the room, and ballet slippers dancing up steps when there's nobody wearing them."

"I thought Douglas had no patience for that kind of thing," said Cara's mother.

"He doesn't," said Cara. "But on the radio he does, especially on Halloween. He's very open-minded on the radio, until it's time to show somebody up."

"And when he's not on the radio?"

"Oh, you know. He's usually right about things. And if he isn't right, he probes until he is, or until the other person gives up arguing, whichever comes first," said Cara, although she knew this wasn't fair, not at all, to take the thing most admirable, most lovable about Douglas—his very stubborn delight in his own very sensible nature—and turn it into something helpless and laughable. She could see him through the glass, bent patiently over the children in their weird, uncomfortable-looking costumes. They had dressed themselves up, and Cara had forgotten what they were supposed to be. But Douglas wouldn't have forgotten. Douglas would know exactly why they were wearing inverted metal mixing bowls on their heads. She could be sure of that, and she felt a surge of affection for him as he hunched before the children in the darkened sound room, among the gentle to-and-fro-ing of the orange paper streamers. She felt a surge of affection for the children, too, a familiar, inspired beneficence that for the moment made her think that it really was enough, in this world, just to love your own children.

Gloria had asked her a question again.

"If you don't want to talk about it, don't," she was saying.

I don't want to talk about it, Cara thought, but then the other Cara, the one who was doing all of the talking, said, "Repeat the question, please."

"I just asked how he was doing these days, that's all."

"Fine, I said," said Cara, her eyes still on the children, on the careful way they held their papercups full of punch, as if the cups were lighted candles. If they grew up happy, if they admired themselves, would that be enough?

"Just fine?"

"He's doing great, Mom," said Cara impatiently.

"So you're still . . ."

"Excuse me?"

"Things have progressed?" asked Cara's mother. "I know it's been a while since we've talked about this. I've tried to be discreet. I hope—"

"I put a stop to that," said Cara. "It didn't go very far. No. Things stayed pretty much the same, just as I told you."

"That's funny."

"Why?"

"Because you never told me much of anything at all," said Cara's mother. "I don't know the slightest thing about this mystery man. He could be a Southern Baptist, for all I know."

"He is a Southern Baptist," said Cara smoothly, not even surprised by how easily—how naturally—she allowed herself to slip again into the lie. How accessible it was, and how novel an offering, that she might open very slowly, peel back the layers, see what was inside. And how harmless it was, less harmful, actually, than spending Sundays on a rock near the creek with a pack of cigarettes. It was like another world, and she was like another Cara living another life inside of it. And it was *that* Cara whose mouth was moving ninety miles an hour. The produce aisles of the supermarket, the small black man in a cleric's collar in careful examination of the violet heads of elephant garlic and then his first direct question to Cara, a question either terribly suggestive or terribly ordinary, but in any case, perfectly obscene when you looked back on it.

"Do you know where they keep the yeast?" was the impertinent or possibly quite innocent question, and then he confided that he was making a pizza, an unusual pizza with endive and radicchio chopped up and sautéed and sprinkled on top of it, Cara said to her mother, having read about just such a pizza in the food section of the newspaper. And that was how the affair had begun, if you wanted to call it an affair, Cara said, which it wasn't, because all they did was kiss, reverentially. They went to a restaurant once, Cara said to her mother, for coffee, but it was closed, so they went back to his house and had coffee there and made out in the pink kitchen while the pizza sizzled in the oven, and then ate a little of it and made out again, standing up against the table, practically. Cara's mother said that she didn't know what it meant to be practically standing up against a table or against anything else for that matter, and that she wondered if Cara didn't mean *reverent* instead of *reverential*.

"Is *practically standing up* standing up or lying down?" asked Cara's mother, and the funny thing was, she wasn't being sarcastic or snide, she simply wanted more than anything to know.

"I do like flirting," Cara said, by way of reply. "But sometimes it's hard to separate feelings from feelings, you know, you play around with the idea that you're attracted to someone and then before you know it, you are. Or you imagine what it might be like to love someone and then you do love them, or rather you're *in love*. It's so easy to be *in love*. It's easier than just coming to love a person," said Cara, just letting herself talk, just speaking, listening, speaking again. She was fascinated, really, by what she had to say. Where had she dug this stuff up? "I can see that as a danger now. Yes, it's a danger."

"Is it a danger to your marriage?"

"*Was* it, you mean. *Was* it a danger. No. Not really. No. But he's an interesting man. He sings in some kind of ensemble. Once when I was there, he got a telephone call, he had to teach someone the bass to 'Jesus, Lay Your Head in the Window.' He has a gentle, floating voice. To think what an imbecilic notion that is, that of all the billions, the *billions* of people in the world, each of us should be expected to fall in love with just one of them. So I was just, I don't know . . ."

"Acting out," said her mother.

"A little. It was just . . ."

"Entertainment," said her mother. "But you sound as if there's something you're not telling me."

"I thought you didn't want me to tell you everything. That's what you said last time, remember?"

"Well, okay. But did you ever point out to him he should never have sent you those flowers at home? Really, Cara."

"Oh, he didn't send me the flowers, it turned out. Douglas

did. He finally admitted, when I told him *you* sent them. He thought I was testing him. Anyway, I forgot to tell you. He was very proud of that red poppy. He knew it would interest me, like when you give somebody the perfect book, it kept me distracted. It occupied me."

"Douglas is very smart that way," said Gloria wistfully.

"Yes," Cara answered, glad to have managed this plug for Douglas, not wanting to leave him out. Douglas was amazingly, penetratingly smart about her, and she loved him for it absolutely.

"Your father's not," said Cara's mother.

"He's not what?"

"Smart that way. About me. Sometimes I think that I got him too used to the look of me. Too accustomed. He thinks he knows me. He *did* once, believe it or not."

"Oh," said Cara, and thought of her father bent-kneed at his easel, applying with concentration the airline logos on the vertical stabilizers of his airplanes on a sky bluer than lapis. Cara, who kept his painting of a Continental 727 above the dresser in Max and Georgie's room, occasionally tried to convince herself that he'd meant it to look the way it did, surreal, motionless, trapped in impenetrable color. But he hadn't, certainly. He was as proud of his airplanes as if they might actually take him somewhere.

"Is this something old that you're thinking, or something new?" she asked her mother.

"Or something blue," answered Gloria. "Let's just say it's something blue for now. Okay?"

"Okay. Tell me about the outfit Daddy bought you," Cara said breathlessly. She felt winded by all of this talk, and unhappy, as if she had taken a risk. And maybe she had, although she couldn't put her finger on the nature of the danger. She only knew it was time to hang up. Through the dark plate glass of the recording studio window, she saw that Estaban's mother had arrived in the sound room, bearing a plate of her strange, sweet, syrupy cookies. Everyone clustered around her, sucking the tips of their fingers.

"Daddy didn't buy it. I did. It's elegant in a way I wouldn't have liked a couple of years ago. I would have thought it made me look old. It has that certain kind of draped, loosefitting look about it. It's teal. And it's sexy, Cara, believe me, in its way. In its not-quite-over-the-hill kind of way. And now tell me one thing. How was the pizza?"

"What pizza?"

"With the endive and radicchio."

"Oh," Cara heard herself exclaim. "It was delicious."

3 ✐

*H*alloween was bad to the neighborhood that year, but not until Cara was finished picking the bits and streamers of pale green toilet paper off the branches of the trees in their front yard did it strike her as odd that Douglas hadn't done it before her. On Tuesdays he got home before five o'clock, while Cara came in just in time for dinner. Ordinarily Douglas would have been the one to do it—grumbling, yes, and then he would have left the wadded tissue not in the trash but in the house somewhere obvious where Cara would see it and know that he was one up on her as far as cleaning messes went—and ordinarily on Tuesdays he would have shopped and made dinner as well. But he hadn't, not tonight, not even store-bought sauce and a pot of spaghetti.

The TV was on in the bedroom upstairs, and that's where she found him, propped up in bed against the armchair pillow, doing the newspaper Cryptoquip. The children were watching television, their bowls of cold cereal side by side on the floor, their two spoons colliding in midair between as each of them reached for a taste from the other one's bowl. The lamp in the corner was on, making shadows of the children's cast-off shoes and sweaters, and Cara swore she could see the shadows of their cast-off toys as well, although the toys themselves were gone; apparently the children had put them away, in a haphazard pile in their room across the hall. Douglas wasn't feeling well. The children were being cooperative. That was the situation as Cara understood it, standing in the doorway for a moment, looking in.

Douglas was pale, no fever, a little shocked-looking around the eyebrows the way he got when there was pain. Of course he hadn't thought to take off his clothes; he had his shoes on, still, and even his tie, on top of his sweater the way he liked it, a joke. But tonight it looked limp, not funny. When Cara sat on the bed and put her finger to a stripe, he winced as though she'd touched a nerve.

"You have a headache?" she asked him.

"Not really."

"Stomach?"

"Not really."

"What then?"

"I'm just not feeling so well," Douglas said, just like that, and went back to the jumbled-up words in the paper, pen poised over the clue.

AOP XGIB WEVB AOP XGIB LB EPAB PZ GFFB, Cara read, as Georgie came over to give her a hug.

"Deena had to bring us home. Daddy forgot," Georgie volunteered.

"I didn't forget. I was asleep," Douglas said.

"You didn't set the alarm?"

Silence. The newspaper was brittle to the touch of Cara's hand, and unyielding when she tried to lift it off his lap.

"Under here? You got kicked? You pulled a muscle?" Cara said. "You should take off your jeans. Or at least undo the fly. You won't feel better all zipped up, whatever it is."

"Thank you for your advice," Douglas said.

"Did you hurt yourself there? Can I see?"

"No," Douglas said bluntly, and put the newspaper aside and climbed gingerly, stoopingly, out of bed for the bathroom. When his sweater rode up, Cara could see the jockstrap poking out from under the waistband of his jeans.

"Oh," she exclaimed. "You played squash! You got hit with the squash ball. In the balls? Douglas? Poor baby."

"No, I didn't play squash. Jenny found a fairly interesting recording," he said offhandedly. "From last night," he added, closing the door between them.

Still she might have supposed it was only his illness shutting the bathroom door in her face if, when he'd emerged from behind it a few minutes later, he hadn't started watching her the way he did. It was a sideways glance, slightly hooded. Every time it slipped her way, no matter what she was doing— dressing the children in their pajamas, combing their hair, watering the dog, ironing her skirt for work the next time— she felt a momentary jolt, as if she'd caught sight of him spying on her in a mirror. This was not an entirely new phenomenon; his eyes had tethered her this way before, but when she tried to remember when, and what the sideways glance had meant, the only thing she came up with seemed too farfetched, years ago when they'd first met, or rather, between the evening they'd first noticed each other and the evening they'd first slept together, when Douglas hadn't known if she was falling in love with him the way he was falling in love with her. For those couple of weeks (Cara remembers two, Douglas remembers five), they encountered each other only in the vast, ugly game room, where Cara liked to study amid the drop-ceilinged echoes of pool and Ping-Pong and the white, neon drone of the vending machines. Douglas, who had time to kill between stints at the radio station down the hall, was playing darts. Of course, darts was something he was good at. He was limber and intense, and what Cara first mistook for loose-jointedness she soon recognized as choreography. He played darts as if he were voguing; every flap of the wrist, every buckle of the knee, every drop of the shoulder served its discrete, careful purpose.

Cara didn't play darts, or pool, or Ping-Pong. That first evening, while hanging flyers advertising her per-page typing rate, and having tacked one over the couch in a far corner of the game room as well as on the pillar where the cues were stacked, she discovered she simply liked it there. It seemed like a good place to study. The tock of the Ping-Pong, the thwock of the pool balls, the whiz and thwack of the darts converged in a kind of noiseless cacophony that reminded her of the clanking, grunting echoes in the weight room at the gym, except she couldn't very well bring her books into the gym and sit and spread them around on the slick new finish of the floor.

"Why not?" asked Douglas, who kept his Coke can perched on the arm of the couch and came over now and then for a swallow.

"First of all, shoes," said Cara, displaying the wood soles of her sandals. "And because I know how those weight lifters are. They would think I was getting a high off their sweat." Cara breathed deep. She thought she smelled rum in his Coke. She had thought she smelled it the previous evening, too. When he was back at his darts, she put her nose to the can and sniffed, then stole a drop with her tongue. It *was* rum. Pleased, curiosity aroused, she went back to her studies. Sometime later, glancing up, she was jolted by the first of his sideways, hooded gazes. Embarrassed, she decided he must have seen her sneaking a taste of his drink. So she snuck another, right then when he was looking. He hadn't seen her the first time, he told her much later. He was only trying to figure her out, and he was scared.

He was scared tonight, too, but he was angry as well, and less approachable than he'd been all those many years before. Still she had the feeling that he wanted her to try, so when the children were in bed, she said to him gently that in all the nights they'd been together they had never once skipped dinner, and that if something was wrong, it would only get worse if they didn't sit down and eat something together. She said this in the kitchen, having followed Douglas's pained, hunched progress downstairs, past the dog asleep on the fourth step, to the sink, where he squirted soap on the day's assortment of dishes. There was laundry on the counter, unfolded but clean in the basket.

"What would you like to eat?" he asked. Such a straightforward question seemed a good omen and made her feel better at once.

"I don't care. Whatever you want," she said, rolling socks into a ball.

"How about we call out for a pizza?" he asked.

"Okay."

"How about pizza with endive and, what do you call it—"

"Radicchio," said Cara, because the word rang a bell even though she'd never eaten either endive or radicchio as far as she knew. She didn't even know what radicchio looked like. "But I don't think they'd have it. I could call up and ask, but they wouldn't, I bet. We could eat it in bed. You shouldn't be out of bed, you look miserable, Douglas. Why don't you go upstairs? I'll finish the dishes."

Douglas ignored this.

"Surely you know *someone* who would be likely to have pizza with radicchio and . . . what's it called?" he asked.

"Endive," said Cara.

Douglas aimed at her a look fiercer than the looks he'd been sliding her all evening long. But Cara saw only how the look contrasted with the rest of him; how unusually vulnerable he seemed tonight, barelegged now in his bathrobe with the sleeves rolled up to his elbows, his cowlick trembling as if with exertion, his shoulder blades rigid under red flannel. It seemed to Cara, at that moment refastening the buckles on a pair of Max's overalls, that another Cara crossed the room and fitted her face between the angular peaks of those shoulders, cheek to hollow, nuzzling the soft, fuzzed colors of the fabric of his robe. But he went on washing. He was terribly efficient. He washed dishes the way dishes were washed on television commercials; a sinkful of suds, then a sinkful of clear water for dipping, then the rack. He didn't know there were two of him, the one dutifully washing dinner dishes so the sink would be ready for breakfast in the morning, and the one who might stop washing dishes to turn and make love, the soap suds sliding from his elbows to her belly, the floor gritty and unswept beneath them. He didn't like to think that way. It was a concept he might entertain with patience and some amusement on the radio, but at home in real life it would make him testy and uncomfortable. With forbearance he would ask her to explain. She would tell him that every moment had a parallel moment, and that a single gesture might, in less than a second, pull him from one moment into the other, like being yanked through a mirror into its opposite side. She would say he might be driving down the street and swerve into a tree—*smack!*—or he might keep on going and never know what he'd missed. "Smack?" Douglas would say, chagrined. "What does that have to do with making love on the kitchen floor?" and there might be a minute, several minutes, even, when he would truly want to comprehend. But then he'd lose patience, shrug it off, chalk it up to a difference in temperament, get back to the business at hand.

Anger in the kitchen, then anger in bed; apparently that was the business at hand. Cara might have found it childish if he didn't seem so hurt. So wounded, actually. He was lying on his back with his hands on the pillow under his head, staring past his elbows at the ceiling. He didn't want to be touched, but she was touching him anyway. She stroked his thighs and his chest but not his belly. He still wore his underwear and even the uncommon jockstrap as if for protection, and if her fingers grazed the waistband, he jerked hard away from her. What's wrong? Cara wondered. It was as if his sex was hurt. His *manhood*, Cara thought, a little amused, and then she remembered what he'd said in the kitchen.

"Surely you know someone who would be likely to have pizza with radicchio and endive," he had said.

And then, earlier, that thing he'd said out of the blue about a recording, *"Jenny gave me a recording,"* or something.

And the way he'd sat there listening to her all through the night, in the way he listened when he was angry that was like a black hole in space, so whatever she said became final and irretrievable all at once, like a rock smashing glass.

Smack! Cara said to herself.

Her fingers circled his nipple, then stopped, pulled away, tapped a message in the air as if they were trying to tell her.

"Oh, Douglas, *no!*" Cara shouted, but just then there was a thump as the dog rolled off the step, and the scrape of toenails as she tried to catch herself, and then a longer thump and scuffle and the click of her nails as Kato half dragged herself across the floor below and lay down in her usual corner with a terrible, heart-stopping sigh.

*W*hat was clear from the start was that the truth sounded more like a lie than any lie ever sounded like truth. Not even Cara's body, a rush of nerves and heat and sweat, seemed to believe what she had to keep saying. Yet still she insisted, over and over, "Douglas, believe me, there's no preacher, no Baptist, I made him up, there's no pizza, it's a lie, well not a lie but a story, well not a story but a habit I got myself into, with my mother, a diversion, on the telephone, all these months, it was getting to be funny, Douglas, really, not funny *ha ha*, but out of control." And it *was* funny, Cara thought, it was like a nursery rhyme, it was like "The House That Jack Built." The more she recited the truth, the more ridiculous it grew, the more she seemed to be lying, the more hurt he became, the more damage was done, the more difficult it would be to extricate herself. It would be easier to lie about it had she actually *had* the affair, she believed. Had there actually *been* a man in a clerical collar, had he actually *asked* her where they kept the yeast, had they actually *crossed* the parking lot to a restaurant for coffee, had the restaurant *really* been closed—then each lie would have value like cards she could lay on a table, saying, *Look, here they are, count them.*

As it was, her denial was shapeless, vast, confused, and incredible.

Douglas argued, "Then who sent the flowers? You told *me* your mother sent them. You told *her* I sent them. Well, Cara, in case there's been some misunderstanding, I didn't. So that leaves somebody else."

Those last couple of words—*somebody else*—he delivered as if they were darts and Cara the bull's-eye. When they struck, they quivered. For a second she was speechless. Then she said, "I don't remember his name."

"You don't remember whose name?"

"Wallace something, I think," said Cara.

"*Wallace?*" said Douglas. "*Wallace?*"

"Yes, but the flowers were for June. June Adams. Not me. I was throwing them away, and I found the card wedged in the—"

"This is a man with broad tastes," Douglas said. "You and June

254

Adams, kisses for you, flowers for her. Just tell me one thing. Did you use protection? That's what I need to know."

"No."

"No?"

"I didn't need to, Douglas. There was nothing to protect. Nothing to protect against, I mean. They have nothing to do with each other, Wallace and the man in the supermarket. The one with the flowers, Wallace, he's in love with June Adams. I got the flowers by mistake, Douglas. It was just a mistake. A mistake."

"I don't want to know about mistakes," said Douglas. "I don't want to know if there are two men, three men, four of them, five. I don't want to know how it got started. I want to know what's happening now."

"Nothing," Cara shouted. "Jesus, Douglas, five!"

"I want to know who you're in love with," said Douglas. "Well, frankly, I don't want to know that right now, either."

"I'm in love with you," said Cara.

Downstairs the dog dreamed fitfully, in yips and starts that drifted through the floorboards and the walls of the house. With each new whimper, Douglas seemed to tighten just a little, so Cara thought of screws turning, fixing objects into place.

"It was during the abortion," Cara began. "During that time we were deciding, I mean. My mother called and said they were coming to visit, and I didn't want them to come."

"So you told her you were having an affair," said Douglas incredulously.

Cara was incredulous, too. Helplessly she said, "It wasn't really an affair."

"It wasn't? Really? Now we're getting somewhere, Cara. What else wasn't it? How wasn't the pizza? Wasn't it delicious? Wasn't that what I heard on the tape? I've never had pizza with cheddar cheese on it."

"Not cheddar," said Cara. "Blue."

"Oh, wait! It wasn't blue, or it was blue? I'm getting confused. You're confusing me, Cara. Which lie do you want me to try to believe? The one that he doesn't exist? Or the one that you didn't have an affair with him? Or the one that, regardless of everything else, you didn't really tell your mother it's imbecilic to love only one person. Imbecilic, Cara."

"That wasn't quite what I said."

"I have it on tape."

"I told my mother I was falling in love. I was talking about the baby, but I didn't want to say that because I didn't want her to know. I told her that there was this bond, between me and this person, and that it seemed to be growing stronger and that I didn't know what to do about it."

"And that he sang gospel music and that he taught you how to make pizza."

"No, that came later. I got carried away. That's why the kitchen is pink, Douglas. I didn't notice that till now. That's amazing."

But Douglas wasn't amazed. Instead, he was more hurt than ever. Blurry-eyed, diminished. Even his freckles had paled. Having fished the tape out of his bedroom drawer and held it up for evidence, he now seemed reluctant to part with its weight, and flipped it over in his fingers, this way and that. Cara thought of pointing out that they could tape this conversation, too, if that would make him believe her. She actually meant this in earnest but was able to stop herself from saying it when she realized he would think it was cruel. Anyway, it was clear he was trying very hard to accept what she was saying. He just found it impossible. He couldn't help it. She couldn't blame him. After a while he said, "If everything you're telling me is true, and if you really did tell your mother you were having an affair because you didn't want them to visit, then that really is kind of funny."

"I know," Cara said, ready for forgiveness, leaning forward as if to offer it to him so he could give it back to her.

"Because what I'm getting at is, if it was so funny, then why didn't you tell me about it?"

"I don't know, exactly," Cara said gently. "First I forgot. And then I didn't get around to it. I'm sorry. And then it was too late. Because I knew what you would think. And also, Douglas, really, we can't expect to know everything there is to know about each other. Can we? I mean, should we even want to? I mean, when one of us gets off the phone with somebody else, and the other one says, 'What did you talk about, and what did she say, and what did you say, and what did she say,' that gets kind of old, doesn't it? I don't mean we shouldn't know about each other's lives, but still, isn't it natural that—"

"And what are some of the other things I don't know about you?" asked Douglas, so suddenly, so desperately, really, that before she could stop herself Cara answered, "I haven't been going to Group, Sundays. I've been going somewhere else."

"Where?" Douglas said, as he pulled himself very carefully, very painfully, into a sitting position, which caused Cara to pull herself into a sitting position as well, so they could see eye-to-eye even though he wasn't looking at her. He was looking only at the tape.

"I've been taking the car out and reading and driving and just sitting somewhere by myself," Cara said. "I've been thinking."

"Prove it," said Douglas.

So Cara climbed out of bed, went downstairs to the baking powder tin in the rear of the spice cabinet where she hid her cigarettes, and brought them upstairs to Douglas.

"What does this have to do with anything?" Douglas said with contempt.

"I smoke. On Sundays, when I sit down and think, I smoke."

"Smoke one now," Douglas told her.

"I don't have my matches."

"Go get them."

"No," Cara said. "That's humiliating," although she knew he didn't mean for it to be. He only wanted to see her smoke in order that he might be able to imagine her doing it on Sundays the way she said she did. Somehow, if he could study the gestures—the flick of the match, the angle of the cigarette as she held it between her lips, the way the first match invariably never lit right and had to be replaced by a second—if he could follow it through from beginning to end and hear the sigh of her last exhalation when the ashes had been stubbed out, maybe then he would believe her.

But still she couldn't do it, she couldn't light up in his presence, she was too ashamed, she told him, and as the minutes ticked on and they sat side by side, Douglas palming his tape and Cara her pack of cigarettes, it seemed they had reached a stalemate. And because they'd reached stalemates before, in other disagreements, it seemed to Cara that this one might end as the other ones had, imperceptibly, so that by morning, the night would appear to have passed like any other. They might even make love, she supposed. And as soon as she thought it, she wanted it. Because as long as this was going to be over, why not let it be over now?

So she slid her hand under the bedclothes and over the thick, soft cotton of his underwear. Fucking would help matters, she couldn't help thinking, fucking would break the ice, fucking would be like two cars screeching toward each other, then breaking into shards across a stretch of scorched, steaming wet pavement.

Looking back on this moment, what struck her most forcefully was her absolute faith in the healing power of her own desire as she leaned to kiss his eyelids, and then her shock when he stood to get away from her. He seemed to have difficulty pulling on his jeans, but then they were zipped and he was combing his hair with his fingers the way he always did, the red tufts furrowed like crops when he was done, and she wondered when she'd see him do it again. Or if. Outside, the moon breathed a haze underneath the chilly darkness, but since the idea of Douglas walking out the door in the morning was so much easier to bear than the idea of him leaving in the middle of the night, Cara let herself believe that it was dawn already, just the barest, faintest opening of a new day, no different from any early Wednesday morning except he wouldn't be around to kiss the children's cereal spoons good-bye as usual.

When he left, the dog accompanied him out the door, but Cara could see through the window that they ignored each other, that the dog hung back among some smells beckoning to her from the rear of the house while Douglas limped for the car and wouldn't let himself look behind.

4 🪶

Cara didn't want the dog to come home at all. All morning, having brought the children to school and to the sitter's, having sat at her desk to prepare a schedule for a Careers in Public Relations conference to be held in January, it frightened her to think that if she heard the dog's paws scuffling on the porch, she might fool herself for one split second that they were Douglas's feet. And it frightened her that if she heard the dog's cold nose pushing against the door, she might fool herself that it was Douglas's gloved hand inserting the key. How awful that would be, to think that Douglas had come home when it was only the dog, and how awful that even if Douglas did come home first—if it *was* his foot she heard on the landing, and if it *was* his gloved hand at the door—still there would be a moment of anxiety when she wouldn't let herself believe what she was hearing, when she would make herself believe that she was hearing the dog. So there was no way out of it, it would be horrible no matter what, and ludicrous, and to save herself the possibility of hearing the door open and not knowing who it was, she propped it open herself with a basket of shoes. So the morning went by and the November air blew into the house, and the afternoon passed and the rooms grew colder, and then the children were home from school all bundled in sweaters and there was noise in the house again, for they were making a spider's web in the playroom. This was their favorite game. They had a ball of twine and skeins of colored yarn and scissors. The tiny room doubled as a guest room in which a twin mattress took up whatever space wasn't crowded already with toys, and which the children crisscrossed giddily with lengths of string knotted here and there with bits of yarn and paper streamer, floor to ceiling, a cocoon of tangled yarn and vectors of twine strung taut and firm so there was no chance of strangulation. By dinnertime the web was completed, so Cara served dinner on trays so the children could eat inside it. They sat together on the bed, spiders eating flies. They slept there, too, in the light from the hallway under layers of blankets. To give them their good night kisses, Cara had to crawl through the holes in the web to reach them, just as she knew she would crawl in later, in the middle of the night, when Max woke from one of his dreams. And though she'd tried not to show them how worried she was about Douglas, Georgie seemed to have figured it out. He tugged gently at a lock of Cara's hair until her face was level with his, then stared into it beseechingly.

When after a while he asked, "Are you going to sing Max his lullabies?" Cara said she'd sing them later in the shower and Max would hear them in his nightmares.

The shower was a good place to be because she couldn't hear the telephone not ringing and she couldn't hear the porch not creaking, so she stayed under the roar of it a long time and then switched on the fan when the water turned cold. This was the guest bathroom; in the cabinets were all the toiletries they gathered now and then from motels and airplanes, along with other, extra items for people who arrived unprepared. Cara even kept a tube of spermicidal jelly in there, and a packet of condoms, and some extra socks in case one of her guests got cold. Tonight, she washed her hair with shampoo from a bottle the size of a chess piece, brushed her teeth with a collapsible toothbrush, shaved her legs with the disposable razor from some airline's bonus travel kit. Now she sat on the too-narrow lid of the toilet, longing for a miniature bottle of whiskey and a dark, oblong window to lay her head against. If she were flying, if she were traveling, at least she'd know where she was going, where she'd end up. She felt lonesome and scared, and then in a daze, and then she found herself thinking how childish it was for Douglas to have run off like this, like a three-year-old who packs a suitcase and sits stubbornly on his perch on the back-yard swing set not allowing his parents to coax him back into the house, and it was then that there were footsteps in the hallway and the bathroom door swung open.

"Douglas," Cara whispered, and in that split second, she had a premonition of the way their life would be. All around there'd be a rushing like the echo of the shower, and in the middle of it would be Douglas not quite ready to believe that he trusted her, and Cara not quite trusting what appeared to be the fact that in spite of himself, he believed her. Then years would go by, and over time the blend of trust and mistrust would stop rushing and just lie flat and familiar and even necessary like a thing of sustenance.

And it would sustain them. Yes, of course it would.

Cara rose to greet him and tell him this, but in the door stood only Kato, who had a new twist in her spine that made her look like she was trying to catch her tail between her teeth to stop herself from falling. She curled up under the sink in the puddle of water she knocked out of her bowl, while the steamy room filled with the bitter smell of dog. Not tired dog, exactly, and not wet dog, but old dog, a smell Cara recognized even though she'd never smelled it on Kato before.

5 ❧

*E*very now and then, no matter where she was living, but in particular at night or at dusk when all was quiet, Cara paused in her step midway across a room and just stopped and stood still and admired. She'd done this even as a child, when the home for which she felt such a sudden onslaught of proprietary fondness was her parents' house and not something she had made. Over the years in her own house there was a certain spot that drew her in these moments, just halfway up the stairs, where if she propped her chin slantwise on the banister, she had a wide-angle view of the small, curved living room and its nearly imperceptible boundary with the dining room beyond. The dining room was not used as a dining room but rather as a front hallway, of which the house had none; there was the basket of shoes, a cushioned rocking chair stacked with the week's unopened mail, and an old Quaker hutch lined with mismatched pottery. Also there was the corner where the dog slept on a throw rug, and a heating vent that in the winter seemed to murmur with the noises Cara's children made while sleeping; a soft rustle of blanket, a squeak, a settling in. The whole scene had an aura of peace and close comfort and scattered, happy domesticity, and sometimes Cara even poured a glass of wine and carried it purposefully to her place on the step in order to indulge herself in it.

But this first week in November, when she looked down from this spot, she saw only that the front door was closed and that Douglas wasn't opening it and stepping inside. Then, in the bedroom, she put her face to the window where she'd watched him limp away across the driveway that first night, and remembered a little shrug he shrugged just before climbing into the car, when he must have known that she was watching. It was a pained, formal gesture, a quick dip of the chin, the palms slightly upturned as if he were taking a bow. Since then he'd been silent and cool. Every evening he ate dinner at home so the children wouldn't feel abandoned and as a way, Cara thought, of demonstrating certain feelings of ambiguity, but once the children were in bed, he went back to the radio station to sleep. If he phoned during the day, it was to ask about the children and the dog. The veterinarians blamed the sharp twist in Kato's spine on her fall down the steps and on her other, recent spells of falling. The falling they blamed on an inner-ear infection further evidenced by an apparent decrease in hearing, and the inner-ear infection they traced back to what appeared to have been an inflammation either of sinus or tooth, evidenced by a lumpy protuberance in Kato's jawbone. Cara didn't buy this explanation. For one thing, the protuberance had been there for years without anyone saying a word about it. For another thing, the dog's falls were too consistently executed—the right rear leg gave way, the spine curved to follow, the body fell and rolled backwards along the curve of the spine in a soft rocking motion that left Kato at rest on her side—and for another thing, Kato always stood up right off, with no apparent dizziness or pain. The lack of pain, Cara reasoned, was because the twist in Kato's spine had been caused, ultimately, not by injury to the bone but to the brain itself.

"She's fourteen years old," Cara insisted to the specialists who alternately appeared in the clinic's examining room over the course of several visits. "She's been acting kind of vague. Kind of simple, actually. She's been deteriorating for a while. Physically, and more recently, mentally, I think. Also, she has these fatty tumors under the skin on her belly, see? You've noticed them. And she has spells of incontinence, too."

"We might order a biopsy of one of her tumors," said the vet.

"As for the incontinence, that's very likely caused by the antibi-
otic we're giving her for the ear infection."

"But it's been going on longer than that," argued Cara.

"We could order a CAT scan," said another vet.

"And an angiogram," said yet another, younger vet.

The other vets demurred. Cara made a face. She longed for
Dr. Carpenter, whose simple practice she and Douglas had
boycotted years ago because the examining rooms always stank
of flushed anal glands and because he wouldn't acknowledge
that Kato was female. Dr. Carpenter would say matter-of-factly,
"You're exactly right. He *is* getting old. We can either speed him
up or slow him down, the way I see it."

By mid-November, Kato had become almost entirely deaf,
but having feigned deafness so often on earlier occasions, she
seemed hardly to notice or care, and she seemed only a little
troubled, now that deafness gave her license to ignore Cara's
calls, that her legs no longer carried her as far as she wanted to
go. No longer could she slide under fences, dart beneath the
cracked-open doors of garages, escape after squirrels through
the dense woven branches of yews and low hedges. Having
come to the edge of a wood, she would stop, not trusting her
body to carry her safely into and out of it, and sometimes even
the vast stretch of backyards behind June Adams' compost heap
seemed too daunting an adventure. There O would stand,
straining forward for a sniff, her nose like an arrow, her body the
bow that would not release it. Watching her, Cara all at once
remembered an open, leafy place in the middle of some woods
where she'd been shocked one day to discover, of all things, a
goldfish in clear water in a goldfish bowl. It had been Kato who
led her to it, years ago on a morning when Cara was late for
work. When the dog shimmied backwards out of her collar,
Cara chased her down the road into a strip of woods. Branches
caught at the hem of her skirt, while the flapping leash lassoed
her ankles. How angry Cara was, and how she just wished the
dog would drop dead out of their too-busy lives, and how she
sweated under her jacket and swore at the dog and was aware, in
her anger, of saliva frothing in the corners of her own mouth, so

when she saw the goldfish swimming placidly in shimmering circles, she kept right on swearing, and chasing after the noise of the dog's footsteps through the undergrowth, and getting tangled in the leash, and sweating and frothing, while at the same time a part of her hung back in silence and reverie to stare at the gauzy undulation of the fish and to wonder how it got there. But by the time she'd caught the dog and buckled her tightly into her collar and dragged her furiously back home and rushed off to an office meeting, she'd forgotten the fish, so now it came back to her along with a feeling of grief, because Douglas didn't know about it. She'd never mentioned it, somehow, and now it was too late, for now he would hold it against her. In spite of herself, Cara found herself dredging up other accidental secrets, things she knew that Douglas didn't, like the time in Missouri at the resume service when, while crossing the hallway past the office of her plaid-pants-wearing boss, she caught sight of him absently caressing the naked hips of the Barbie doll he used as a paperweight. Or like the thing she'd just learned about the sinoatrial node, the heart's natural pacemaker, a bundle of modified heart muscle without which the heart's muscle cells would contract anarchically, one here and one there, this way and that without order or reason like a marching band gone out of sync. How small this thing was, no bigger than a lentil, too small to make her wake in the middle of the night feeling sad and guilt-ridden because she knew about it and Douglas didn't. She nearly phoned him at the station to tell him.

Except she couldn't tell him about the sinoatrial node because she hadn't mentioned Julie Tremor or the fact that she was writing Julie's undergraduate honors thesis, entitled "Characteristics of the Right Atrium of the Vertebrate Heart." Cara herself hadn't known this before three days ago, when Julie called in response to her ad. Douglas didn't know about the ad, either, although Cara really had planned to tell him. She just hadn't planned when. She didn't know if he had a cot at the station or even a sleeping bag. He had blankets he'd taken from home, and the guest towel and washcloth, and the pillow that

Cara had forced on him several days earlier. Every night after dinner, Cara wondered if maybe this was the night he would stay home. But once the children were asleep, he left. On laundry nights, when he stayed a little longer, Cara clung to the sight of him pulling his things from the dryer, folding them more meticulously than he would have had he been living at home as usual, then sliding them neatly into his gym bag and zipping it shut. Three tee shirts he had with him, two pairs of jeans, three pairs of underwear, three pairs of socks. Cara knew from having peeked at his laundry that he was still wearing his jockstrap, for there were two that came out of the dryer each night he did it, one old and one new, or two new, depending on which he was currently wearing. The new ones were whiter than anything else in all of the family wash, and she believed that he wore them in order to keep her away, like the light shined in the face of a vampire to make it shut its eyes. His neckties he kept at the office, slung over various doorknobs. His hairbrush—well, Cara didn't know. There was one in the bathroom she'd thought all along was his hairbrush that she used, but now that he'd left it in its customary drawer, she thought maybe all along it had been hers that *he* used. In any case, he'd been brushing his hair with his fingers and letting Jenny muss it the way she liked to do, most likely.

He never left home without saying good-bye, and he never slammed the door even though both of them, Cara and Douglas, wanted him to. If they could scream at each other, or cry, then they might get this stalemate over with. Instead, they were civil and aggrieved. Secretive. He had secrets from Cara, as she had from him. She could see it in his face, and she could hear it on the air when he did the late late show. No matter what he was talking about, no matter with whom—the lispy astronomer, the masseuse with the fake British accent, the teenage-philosopher-car-thief—the real point seemed to be that he wasn't talking to Cara and that she wasn't talking to him. If Douglas knew how dangerous this was, he wasn't saying. The danger was that secrets were seductive, Cara was learning. They gripped and held on, they had siren calls. The more secrets you had from a person, the harder they were to disclose. And the harder they were to disclose, the more important they became, the more silence they demanded and the more company. More secrets. New secrets, to camouflage the old. Sneak a cigarette, and then you had to hide the matches, the ashes, the odor. You hid the can of fresh air spray behind the washing machine, you filled the bottle of mouthwash with measures of water so he wouldn't know any was missing. In fact, Cara wasn't smoking anymore, at all; she'd thrown the baking powder tin away without even checking to see how many stale cigarettes were still nestled inside. She had never been much good at smoking, anyway. Someday she would tell Douglas how easily she had quit. For the moment he thought she still smoked. He might be dreaming about it now; on his face would be a look of righteous rebuke, as if he'd rounded a bend and come upon the sight of her coughing out smoke, the spent butts in a cluster in an ashy cleft of rock. But his dream was a secret, too, from her, because she couldn't see his face to decipher the clues. Perhaps he didn't dream at all in the radio station, perhaps the floor was too hard, perhaps he wasn't even sleeping, perhaps he was too sad to sleep. Perhaps she wouldn't even wake him if she called him now, at nearly three o'clock in the morning. She would tell him she was moist between the legs, wanting him. They hadn't had sex since before Halloween. She'd remind him of that. No, she wouldn't. But she would tell him she was lonely. She would tell him please come home. She would tell him she'd arranged to have a tubal ligation, even though they weren't having sex.

Yes, she would, absolutely. She would tell him that.

The telephone sat askew on the pillow next to hers. For a minute she propped herself on one elbow, looking at it as if it were Douglas and she were deliberating whether to wake him or not. One touch and he'd open his eyes. One kiss.

At last she dialed, deliberated, got scared, hung up. But it had already rung, so now Douglas would be cruelly awake, trapped with his dreams on the floor of the station or maybe on the couch in the conference room, tiny lights blinking all around. In the station there were always lights blinking no matter what time of day it was, and a vast, empty humming of speechless mikes. Sleeping in the station must be like sleeping in outer space, Cara thought. Waking in the station must be lonely as hell.

So she dialed again.

She would tell h.m she had made an appointment for the week following Thanksgiving, to have her tubes tied, and that he could come with her if he wanted. She had a vision of the two of them tussling in bed without consequence, their bodies rolling through space like the bodies of children, uncompli- cated by anything but desire. She would tell him this, and it would be like a threshold over which they would step together, unharried, into their future.

And, thinking about it, he would have a chance to stop thinking about the things that had made their life so strained and unhappy—the pink kitchen, the pizza, the priest, Cara's unreal, untrue kisses.

She could feel his sadness through the ringing of the phone. It rang twice, and then he fumbled when he picked it up; there was the disconsolate rumble and scratch of the receiver on the floor.

Some music was playing, very, very loud.

"Hello?" someone said.

"Oh. Estaban?" said Cara.

"Dee," said one of the overweight technicians she could never keep straight. Dee and Bobbie, one a man and one a woman. Dee was the man, then.

"Oh. Hi, Dee. It's Cara."

There was a hoot, loud laughter, more scratching and thump- ing, then Douglas. The music stayed loud, and there was some kind of party going on on top of it.

"What's going on?" Cara asked.

"Estaban's forty."

"Happy birthday," Cara said.

"What do you want?" said Douglas.

"I want to talk."

"About who?"

"No one. Nothing. Just talk."

"Fuck you, then," said Douglas, and hung up the phone.

Cara called right back, and he picked up right away. If he wanted her to talk about the priest, then she would talk about the priest. She would say the only thing that could be said about him.

"Douglas, I told you the truth. I swear."

Douglas stayed mute. In the background someone hollered, popped open a beer bottle, and slammed a door.

"I was lying to my mother, not to you," Cara said.

"You didn't tell me about it."

"That's an oversight, not a lie, Douglas. When I told Group about it, that's when I realized that you didn't know."

"You told Group about it."

"Not exactly. I lied to them, too."

"What do you mean? Just a second."

It was his turn at darts. She could hear him take aim. That was strange, and endearing. She knew his dart posture—his choreography, his poses, the way he held his wrist, the very British-tea-like angularity of his fingers—so well that she could hear it.

"Yes?" Douglas said when he was done.

"Douglas, tell me what you love about me."

"What?"

"Tell me if you love me, just me, the way you loved me when we first met in Missouri, when we had no life together yet but were just beginning to see in each other the things we would fall in love with, or if the thing you love about me is the way I function in our life together all these years."

"Cara, get to the point."

Cara heaved a sigh and tried again, wishing she could put it into technical terms—the sinoatrial node, the Purkinje fibers like an inverted tree—any of which would be simpler to talk about than love.

"I mean, which do you love? Me? Or our life together?" she insisted, making that gesture she had come to use when referring to what she called their life together, that sweeping motion of her arm that included the house and the leaky ceiling under the flat part of the roof and Georgie studying his books and Max learning the parts of the body and the ever-more-weary dog and their arguments and car trips and assorted shoes and spoons and even the chopsticks the children used in their parades, for banging on pot lids, and their past present future all seeming to happen at once.

"I don't know if I can tell the difference anymore," Douglas said matter-of-factly.

Cara said she didn't know if she had heard him right over the music.

Douglas said he couldn't lower the sound, it was Estaban's party. "Cara, listen to yourself. You tell your mother, you tell Group, but you don't tell me. And now you ask me about *our life together*," he finished sharply, and she could feel, over the phone, that he made the gesture, too, that sweep of the arm, but mockingly. She could imagine his beer bottle arching through space when he did it, then the way he caught the spilled foam on his tongue. But he was trying, he really was, he hadn't hung up the phone, he was still listening.

"Max knows elbows and knees now," she offered, buying time.

"And nipples," said Douglas.

"And he's very big on *penis*," Cara said, laughing.

"Cara, I don't know if you know what you've done."

"I did nothing," said Cara.

"Prove it."

"How?"

"That's just it. There's no way," answered Douglas.

"So you just have to believe me. Please. There's no affair, no black priest, no pink kitchen, no pizza, I swear. If I could touch you . . . if we were in the same room, if I could touch you . . . I want you in bed, Douglas. I want you close to me again. This is crazy. I don't know what to do. I don't know what to say. Can't you see that this is funny? Can't you see this should be one of our private jokes, one day, maybe twenty years from now, it will be funny?"

"No. I keep thinking about the baby we aborted. I think I'd die if you told me it could possibly be his."

"It wasn't his. It didn't happen. He doesn't exist. Don't you know why you don't believe me? Because I can't say it hard enough. I can't. If I were lying I would say it much harder. If I *did* have an affair, then you would believe that I didn't," said Cara, not aware until she said it what harm it would cause, what terrible, irreparable harm. And she couldn't un-say it, of course. And there was no way of taking it back. For she had said it so unhesitatingly. It was like a door, and she had breezed right through it as if Douglas had held it open for her.

"So you would lie to me," Douglas said, satisfied. "Given the opportunity."

"But Douglas, there's always opportunity. Always. I could say to you, right now, I could say, Douglas, I don't love you, I don't want to be your wife, I don't know why I married you, and it would be a lie. It would be the biggest lie I've ever told. Or I could say—"

"Cara."

"Yes?"

For a moment there was only the party music blaring at the station. Then Douglas hung up. Cara didn't. Not yet. She laid the receiver gently on the pillow next to hers, where Douglas would have been if he were there, on a dent in the fabric where his face would be, a ridge in the tight weave of linen, then a shallow depression. She put her tongue to it.

6 ✦

Climbing along the edge of a steep cliff.

Forget it.

Taping a sprained ankle.

Indifferent.

Where does a body start?

In the center. Of the heart.

Not the womb?

No. The heart.

What is Max's favorite word?

Penis. No, *dog.* No, *penis.* And if he tells you he loves you, you have to say it right back. It's like throwing a ball high up and waiting for it to come back down.

So where does Max's body start?

In his penis. Or in the dog. Or in love, depending.

To whom does Max belong?

Only to himself.

And to whom does Georgie belong?

Only to himself.

And what is the center of Georgie's body?

The brain. The eyes, for reading.

And what is the center of Douglas's body?

The dart board. The target. Whatever he's after.

Is it fair to him, to say that?

I don't care.

Did you tell him that you're planning on having a tubal ligation?

I tried.

And what did he say about it?

None of the above.

Experimenting with new grooming preparations.

Once a year, maybe.

Looking at things in a hardware store.

A fine way to pass time with Dad.

Does Douglas love you?

He loves our life together.

Is that what he said? Come on now, Cara.

Come to think of it, he didn't say what he loved, at all. He said he couldn't tell the difference anymore, between me and our life together.

But can you tell the difference?

Shit, yes.

7 ✢

Cara's mother refused to say, exactly, whether she believed that Cara was telling the truth, when Cara confessed she had made up the story about the priest. Truthfully, Gloria admitted to Cara, she preferred to believe that the story had not been invented. She liked the idea of her tall daughter—her daughter who had been somewhat awkward during adolescence, her daughter whose sixteenth year had been marked by a gaze so intense and so stubborn that the only thing that could make it flinch, even for a second, was for someone to ignore it—kissing someone in a pink kitchen languorous with the smell of tomato sauce. She liked the steam of it, the very sexiness of it, she said to Cara, she herself had never had that in her life—pure sexual attraction, brief, distracting intimacy so distilled it was pure, so pure it was innocent—or at least, she had never indulged it. She wanted it for her daughter, who had aged gracefully if not beautifully, whose awkward, too-long limbs had turned at once fluid and angular, a startling combination and very original when most women were either one or the other. Cara's mother had been watching women closely, in fact, at the Brass Rail, where with her tape recorder and notebook she analyzed the choreography of various striptease acts—the norm and its deviations. This project was to evolve into her master's thesis, she hoped; she had a grant from the university that paid for not only her bus fare and tape player but for the beers she had to buy in order to sit undisturbed at a table, her head craned inquisitively toward the cheerleader-type on stage, who stripped to nothing but her tennis shoes and white pom-ponned slipper socks, or to the vamp in black leather who at the end wore only her whip, coiled like a snake around one arm. What most fascinated Cara's mother about these dances was the unvarying emphasis placed on gradual exposure of the genitals—the whole dance, the whole costume being nothing more than an elaborate prop designed so that a body might be disrobed piece by piece, strobe by strobe, so that at last there was only a G-string and finally only the vulva itself, undulating moistly in a spotlight from which the rest of the dancer appeared to have vanished along with the parts of her costume.

However, Cara's mother speculated that Douglas *did* believe Cara when Cara told him she'd made up the priest. That is, said Cara's mother, "He wants to believe it. He just finds it too hard. And it's inescapable that there's a certain amount of game-playing going on. He can't afford to believe you quite yet. He's too hurt. He's too bewildered. It was far too much of a shock, Cara. He has to live with it awhile, the hurt, the shock, he has to let it play out, then he'll let himself believe what you tell him," she said. "And then slowly things will get back to normal."

"Maybe," said Cara, who, as usual, found her mother to be right but beside the point. The point was not the affair, not the priest, not the kiss, not the steamy pink kitchen. Even Douglas knew that. The point was deeper now, more complicated. The point is not to get back to normal, Cara said to herself with surprise, but for normal to be different than it was before. If she and Douglas were to become just a little wary of each other, if things were to become a bit mysterious between them, if a certain amount of *not-knowing* were to become the norm, well, then, life would be more truthful, somehow, wouldn't it?

"Or if you could find some evidence, Cara. For instance, that gift enclosure card you say you stuffed into your neighbor's compost heap . . ."

"I don't *say* I stuffed it. I stuffed it," said Cara.

"Well, maybe if you could find it."

"No way," Cara said. She had already looked, late last night in the season's first brief hint of snow. And of course the card was gone, either frozen in compost or buried last summer in June Adams' vegetable garden. Decayed, turned to soil, Wallace Caldwell's hopeful invitation might have come up as a carrot, been picked, peeled, rinsed, shredded over June Adams' solitary dinner salad. Earlier this evening, Cara had led Douglas into the yard and made him look at the echoes of her footprints on the still-frosty ground, as if evidence of her search might be as definitive as if she'd found what she'd been looking for. Douglas scoffed but stayed out there a minute, studying the footprints that, though barely discernible, were so clearly Cara's. The pointed toe, the large stride, the single-mindedness of purpose. Then he sighed, went inside, washed the dishes, saw the children into bed, said good-bye, and left for the station. Yes, of course he would be home for Thanksgiving day, he told Cara, but if her parents were going to be there, then he would bring Estaban and Estaban's mother and maybe Jenny if Jenny's boyfriend was being a schmuck. This would be for ballast, Cara understood. More than anything, she wanted to touch his cowlick. The palm of her hand was still numb with that particular desire, even now as she spoke on the phone to her mother. She could hear the whisper of her mother's recipe files over the wires and then some distracted murmuring about walnuts and marshmallow topping.

"We could do one with rum, for the adults, and one with marshmallows for the children. Thanksgiving gives me a headache," said Cara's mother.

"Douglas doesn't like food with rum in it, and Georgie doesn't like marshmallows, Georgie likes his sweet potatoes baked in their skins," said Cara, wondering if she should tell her mother now about her plans for the tubal ligation or if she should wait until her mother arrived. It would be her mother who would drive her to the clinic and sit with her, Cara decided, and then they'd go out for a drink afterward and pop pain pills together.

"He does?"

"Yes," said Cara. "He's a purist, remember? They both are. Douglas doesn't like sweet potatoes at all, come to think of it; he likes regular, baked, with butter melted in the cracks."

"Of course I was thinking maybe I wouldn't do Thanksgiving at all this year," said Cara's mother. "I was thinking I could cook for a shelter, or I could stay home and work a little and have a bath and a glass of wine, but then I realized that the only way I want to do that is if your father isn't here, so maybe he could come to you and I'll stay in Toronto. There's something about a bath in an empty house, and wine, and everyone says if you're alone on a holiday, that that's the worst time, the most pungent kind of loneliness. And I know it sounds strange, but that's what I want. I want to see what I'll be lonely *for.* Or, *who.*"

"You might not be lonely for anything, or anyone. You might just be lonely, period," Cara speculated. "Whatever you do, I don't think you should work on Thanksgiving."

"I'll light a candle, I'll cry, then maybe I'll feel silly. As far as work goes, Cara, I'm just sitting around with a paper and pen, it's not like I'm hauling bricks or anything. And what you just said, I don't want to consider that, Cara, I don't even want to think about that. Because that would be horrible, really, the most horrible thing, after sixty-one years, not to know who you were lonely for. Or not to know what you regretted having missed doing all those years, when you were doing the things you were doing instead. You make choices, you have regrets, the very least you can do is know what they are. Otherwise—"

"Otherwise?" asked Cara.

"Otherwise, what's the point? Thirty-seven years of Thanksgivings with the same man," said Cara's mother. "I want to know why human beings do this. Pair up. Couples. What does it *mean* about people? Has your father changed over the years, Cara?"

"He seems more naive, somehow. But that might just be that I'm less naive, myself."

"No, I think he is more naive. Is that possible? People say that when people get old, they become more who they are. Less faceted, somehow. Has that happened to me?"

"No," Cara said.

"Good. I didn't think so. Yes, I think I'd like to have Thanksgiving by myself. You're responsible for this. I'm not accusing. I'm grateful, but scared, just a little."

"Okay," Cara said.

"You don't sound like you like the idea," said her mother.

"It has nothing to do with you. It's just that—"

"We can tell your father I'm doing the shelter. That way he won't be hurt. Only bemused, you know, in that way he gets . . . On the other hand, it might be good for him to know that I should want one holiday by myself after thirty-seven years. He should be able to handle that. In fact, I want him to know, I insist that he know. And Christmas, too. I think I'll go to an island. What do you think, Cara?"

"Oh, I was getting used to the idea that you were coming here, that's all. I had plans for the two of us."

"What plans?"

"Oh, we could go out for a drink together. Just the two of us."

"That's a nice idea," said Cara's mother wistfully.

"Want to hear something about Norplant?" said Cara. "You know, those birth control rods they stick in your arm that release estrogen?"

"I was thinking that would be a good option for you, when I saw it on the news. And now that Souter's on the court . . . the thought of all of those men, Cara, the nerve of those men . . ."

"I know. It's amazing. Imagine what would happen if it were the other way around, what an uproar there'd be. So, Norplant. But hardly anybody ends up doing it. It makes you irregular. You could go five years without a period."

"I've gone twelve years without a period," said Cara's mother. "It's not the end of the world, believe me."

"You might have a period, then not have one for six months, then have one, then not have one for three years, then spot for three months, sporadically. They don't say that on the news. But my doctor says it's what you can expect, on Norplant, that you'll be totally, completely out of whack."

"Out of whack, but you won't get pregnant. But with Douglas sleeping every night at the radio station . . . ," Cara's mother

278

added with a sigh, and then a whisper of recipe files again. "I can make a big casserole, rum on one side, marshmallows on the other. I'll send it with your father. Douglas can bake his own potato. Kato can lick the pans. How is Kato, by the way? And what's wrong with the pill? And what's wrong with an IUD?"

"The pill makes me nervous and lethargic at the same time. IUDs cause cramping, anyway I don't trust the way they keep going off the market, then coming back on. Kato's unhappy," said Cara. "It's very sad, actually. I feel sorry for her. She just lies in her corner, decaying."

*I*t was true, the dog really did seem to be decaying, slowly but surely, from the inside out. There was a heavy gray odor that lived in her corner with her, that seemed to hover around her like the dry, living smell of a cellar—stale mildew, wood already rotten, hardened mouse turds—but sadder than that, deeper and more precarious. Kato herself seemed wary of it, as if the smell were a hole that she was too close to the edge of, trying not to look down into it, her front paws skidding, her rump in the air. Sometimes, just lying in her corner, not asleep, her fur ruffed up along the whole curled length of her spine as if something had threatened her. Sometimes she groaned. Or she sighed and then groaned. Cara found it strangely disheartening that the sigh turned into the groan, rather than the other way around. There was a bowl of water in the dining room corner, too, to save Kato the indignity of somersaulting whenever she got thirsty, although she drank very little, and a throw rug for her to lie down on, although she rested just her chin on it, and some treats Max liked to give her, even though she didn't eat. Cara kept the throw rug vacuumed of hairs, changed the water every morning, tossed the treats back in the box so Max could pull them out again. Throughout, the dog managed to look both thankful and annoyed. She was clever, O was. She refused to eat her pills. She licked the peanut butter off the spoon, then let the pill drop from the end of her tongue. Every so often she might kiss Cara's wrist as Cara knelt tucking the blanket around her, but then her tongue lingered so hungrily, Cara knew it was the flavor of salt she was after.

Evenings, after dinner, Douglas led her out where she could squat among the dry, blown leaves on the lawn. If she wanted to walk, he allowed her to, and when she fell, he waited patiently for her to pull herself up. It took longer and longer, day after day, for her to arrange all four wobbly legs in their proper places again under her belly. Then she swayed like a loose-jointed table and sometimes fell a second time, or third; when there was frost, the grass broke under her weight. She scorned help, pulled her haunches away from any steadying hands. The vet said it was pain, but Cara thought it was pride. Douglas said it was both. Georgie wouldn't let himself watch the dog struggle. Max said "Throw up," which is what he said whenever anybody got sick.

O stopped eating, generally. She chewed grass and dead leaves, then shat them out amid transparent tendrils of mucus. One evening, she refused to come back in the house. Her tail between her legs, she backed away from the threshold, wedged her body on the porch in a corner of railing. Cold air whistled among the slats. Every night before he left for the station, Douglas rigged up a tent of blankets and folding chairs. He was clumsy at this but he didn't want Cara to help, so she stood on the porch and watched, and discovered on the porch a kind of no-man's-land, a safe zone where she might say to him things she couldn't say to him in the house. For one thing, he could pretend he wasn't listening. So when she said to him, "Douglas, there are things you don't know about me, and there are things I don't know about you, and there always have been, and there always will be, but that doesn't mean that we're lying to each other, it just means that we're two different people," Douglas went on draping blankets and knocking over folding chairs and refused to acknowledge that he had heard her. But he had, of course. And when she said, "The thing is, I liked telling my mother that story, I felt possessive of it, it was like another life, but not one I wanted to be living, exactly, just one I could imagine, like any number of lives, like you thinking you could be a pilot, you could be Estaban, you could be wearing Estaban's flight jacket, but you don't, because, well, you just don't," Douglas didn't even raise an eyebrow, but went on with his clothespins, fastening the corners of Kato's tent. By morning the blankets had fallen, the chairs collapsed shut; the dog lay underneath them apparently undisturbed, not asleep, not twitching, not whimpering, not peaceful but quiet, not tranquil but dispassionate, watching Cara pull the night's blown tent away from her. Morning by morning, O's look of thanks and annoyance vanished. Her tongue grew dry. She seemed never to sleep. Her eyes grew wider than ever, like wet brown globes in dry sockets. Douglas said it was pain, Cara said it was fear, the vet said it was probably both. Secretly, Cara was glad to have the smell mostly out of the house so she might work undistracted, unrepulsed, unsympathetic, even, for with the smell out of reach, the dog might as well have vanished during one of her walks, the way she always had before, when she would always come back and there was no use fretting. Cara brewed coffee, pulled her hair into a knot, fitted the proper tip onto her Rapidograph then set it to paper conscientiously. DETAIL OF THE ACCELERATOR NERVE OF THE RIGHT ATRIUM OF THE VERTEBRATE HEART, she printed in the upper left corner of the page. The paper was rag of the highest quality; the graceful shaft of the neuron first swelled, then tapered, then swelled again like blown glass into a cluster of circular knobs. *Boutons*, they were called. French for *buttons*. Cara saved the dendrites for last; the tiny hairlike projections seemed to waft in her breath as she bent close to the paper. In the stippled, shaded curve of a bouton she concealed her own initials, then she printed Julie Tremor's name on white underneath it, fully exposed. She was sorry when the drawing was finished. She considered phoning Julie Tremor to convince her that it was worth paying for yet another diagram—a neuron in context, perhaps, bunched together with hundreds in the sheath of the accelerator nerve. When Julie Tremor's line was busy, Cara dialed the doctor's office and spoke to a nurse practitioner to confirm her appointment for after Thanksgiving. She'd go in

Monday morning, she'd come home four hours later. The procedure—a laparoscopic tubal banding—would be relatively simple; a probe through the navel, a telescope, a single incision below the pubic hairline, the nimble work of the doctor's practiced fingers. No longer was it considered necessary to clip or cauterize the fallopian tubes; instead they would be looped, the twin kinks sealed with tiny plastic bands. Cara sipped coffee and asked a few more questions, moving her pen on paper again. Beneath her pen, the boutons blossomed and elongated; the swollen end of the neuron seemed to wave and undulate. Her abdomen would be pumped full of carbon dioxide. If she opted for a spinal instead of general anesthesia, she might watch the operation on the video screen. Recovery was simple; she would feel a little pain. Twenty years ago, added the nurse, Cara would not have been permitted a tubal ligation at all.

"You would have failed your 120," she said.

"My what?"

"Your 120," said the nurse. "Your age, multiplied by the number of children you have. You're 34, you have two kids, you'd get a score of 68. Not enough, by far. If it was less than 120, they wouldn't give you a tubal. That was the standard. They'd send you back home to bed, so to speak. This was happening in 1970 right here in this very clinic."

"No," Cara said.

"Cross my heart," said the nurse practitioner.

Cara hung up the phone and took a sip of her coffee. Surprised that the heart's accelerator nerve so resembled a sea anemone, she slid the drawing into Julie Tremor's folder, and the phone book into the drawer. No more headache, no more worry, she was thinking; one day the ligation would already be done, a thing of the past although Douglas wouldn't know about it yet, so she would climb upstairs to tell him, slowly because of the pain. She was confident that he would be upstairs, that she would climb toward him. She would have had the surgery for herself, but his gratitude might convince her that she had done it for him. In bed she'd let him fit his cheek into the space above the bandage, not quite touching the gauze. She'd snake her hand between his legs and massage his balls and penis for the first time since Halloween, but then she'd fall asleep before she brought him to climax, the medication drowsing through her fingers while his penis swelled inside them, then shrunk, then slipped free still pulsing. She was confident of this, that he would be in bed with her again, and no more goop, and no more pills. She thought of phoning the station to tell him this. She would tell him that sperm had olfactory powers; they smelled the egg, they swam toward it. She would tell him she was longing for him again, the longing numb in the palm of her hand even as she cleaned the nub of the Rapidograph. She would tell him that every abortion clinic advertised in the Yellow Pages includes among its list of services tubal ligations, but that not a single one of them actually performs such a service. She would say this made her angry at the clinics not because they lied but because they cowered and were complicitous with the people who made them cower. She would tell him she loved him, she would tell him Max and Georgie had discovered his carton of old 45s. She clicked the cap into place and the pen in its box, caught the phone on the very first ring, looked up just in time to see the dog on the sidewalk, loping away from the house. Funny, but what appeared to be keeping Kato from falling over was the weakness in her legs. She'd be listing to one side, her spine so twisted that her feet were on top of each other, so low to the ground that one ear almost dragged, but then the second she lost her balance, her rear legs gave way so she fell backwards instead, or almost, the two falls, forward and backwards, just catching each other, canceling each other out. The dog looked confused to be moving at all, her gait like the gait of a slow pendulum, a series of falls and rebounds, rebounds and falls. Still, Kato kept moving forward along the curb lawn, around a ginkgo tree and then around the same tree again and again because her body was stuck in tight circles, the narrow tree in the center, the circles shrinking around it. It was Wendy on the telephone. Cara hadn't spoken to Wendy in ages. Wendy, it turned out, had stopped going to Group as well.

Every other Sunday, Wendy imagined Cara sitting at Group wondering where Wendy was, while Cara imagined Wendy sitting at Group wondering where Cara was. That was their way of missing each other, Cara and Wendy both said at once.

"Oh, God." They both laughed.

And then, "What's going on?"

Wendy said she had completed a sculpture, *Tank Tops*, made of camouflage fabric and bunches of mosquito netting, "and something else, Cara, but I don't want to tell you. I want you to see it. You'll be honest with me, I know. . . ."

"Maybe," Cara said, quite honestly, she realized.

"The whole point of it is—"

"Don't tell me the point of it," Cara objected. "Let me look at it. Let me figure it out for myself. Bring it over right now. I'll make coffee. But first I have to get the dog."

Around the base of the tree lay a blanket of frozen gold fans. Female ginkgos have an odor, but this tree was male—no fruits, no stink, just the sharp, woody perfume of winter with no trace of Kato anywhere.

8 ✺

Thawing the turkey.

Stuffing it.

Is there or is there not a black priest, preparing pizza in a pink kitchen?

What is his favorite song?

Where did you look for the dog?

Finding the wishbone so Georgie and Estaban can compete for wishes.

Cranberries.

Sex.

Max.

Georgie.

Douglas.

Repairing a clock.

Pursuing bandits in a sheriff's posse.

Indifferent.

Couldn't care less.

There is not.

"Swing Low, Sweet Chariot."

In the woods. And in the lot behind McDonald's.

Like.

Like.

Hardly remember.

Love.

Same as above.

Same as above, but different.

You've got to be kidding.

One of my favorite activities.

Where did you look for Kato?	Behind the school. At the creek. In the house in case she crawled in when no one was looking.
When will Douglas come home?	Very soon.
How do you know?	Not applicable.
Let's talk a little about your father's Thanksgiving day painting.	It's a Piper Cub, fifty years old, the plane, not the painting, blunt nosed, flaps up for soaring but of course it's not soaring, it's like something you'd see on a postage stamp, not a plane but a symbol of a plane, not flying but motionless, flat, and the sky flat, and the distance flat behind it.
Let's look a little closer.	Well, there's a pilot. Oh, the pilot is a woman. Amelia Earhart, maybe? An Amelia Earhart doll, the little visor in place on her hat but uplifted so you can see that her face is serene, a touch sad, a touch amused by its own sadness. Oh, my! It's my mother's face, it's my own mother flying the Piper Cub!
Washing dishes.	Like. If the radio's on.
Dividing and wrapping the carcass for storing.	Indifferent.
Sweeping the floor.	Indifferent.
Mopping it.	Hate, except after midnight.
What are you?	Excuse me?

ARE YOU MINE?

Are you Realistic, Investigative, Artistic, Social, Enterprising, or Conventional?

There are no pure types. Results of this test can give you some useful systematic information about yourself, but you should not expect miracles.

Are you scared about Monday? About the laparoscopy?

No. I just want it to be over with. And I don't want to watch, even though the doctor says it's a beautiful sight.

And why haven't you told anybody about it?

Talking's too confusing, too problematic, opens more doors than it closes, poses inconsistencies, gets me in trouble. Besides, I might talk myself out of it. I need to do it how Douglas would do it, in silence, the way you tie a shoe or brush your teeth or anything, there's no need to make an announcement.

What's this?

Elbow.

What's this?

Ovary.

No. Try again.

Ovary.

No. Try again.

Ovary.

Are we on the air?

No.

Is the mike on?

No.

Cleaning the dog's vomit.

Detest absolutely.

The dog's smell.

Well—

Well, what?

Well, the smell has a certain integrity somehow, like the way the dog was walking, catching herself from falling, and the way her eyes got bigger, global, as if—

As if, what?

As if there's something behind them, something more than a person might expect, as if she's trapped in a body, too, like everyone else.

Trapped?

Yes, but you make the most of it. And that's the point, to make the most of it, to love it. The body, I mean. Whichever body you happen to be in.

Would Douglas understand this?

Don't know. Maybe. Probably. Yes.

9 ✖

*I*n Wendy's new *Tank Tops*, half hidden among the bunches of mosquito netting, among the folds of mottled brown-green fabric and the pale, fat female arms and legs, was sewn a blunt green object that at first glance Cara did not trouble to identify. The sculpture was better than Wendy's others, more contemplative, for instance, than *Hippos in Hose*, less overwrought than *Mainly Manic*, of more intricate design than *Lost-and-Found Lovers*. Wendy was big on alliteration, on gimmicky (Cara thought) juxtaposition. But *Tank Tops* wasn't garish like the others, or even sentimental. In fact, it was strangely, disturbingly arresting; Cara's eye hesitatingly found its way back to the green, pineapplelike object that she recognized finally as a grenade. Not a toy grenade, not gleaming but dull, and with a definite, volatile weight that bore down on the big quilted fingers in which it was cradled. The grenade was fastened by its pin. Wendy wouldn't say if it was live or not, in fact, she claimed not to know, there was only one way of being absolutely certain, is what she said.

The whole thing gave Cara a rather uncomfortable sensation in her nipples. A tingling, a humming, like the feeling she got in the palm of her hand when she wanted to touch Douglas's cowlick. Her hand no longer suffered that particular longing. Douglas was spending the night at home, as he had since the Monday after Thanksgiving. Tonight was his third night home, though they were still very chaste to the point of apparent bashfulness, remaining dressed until the very last minute and then slipping to the bathroom to shower in private, emerging fully camouflaged in underwear, pajamas, heavy flannels, Cara's father's snores drifting from the bedroom below, and then, this evening, after he finally left for Toronto, his very absence like a chaperon still tiptoeing across the kitchen for a slice of pumpkin pie at 2:00 A.M. Douglas's cowlick was the only part of his body that Douglas would allow Cara to touch, and in return he touched no part of hers, not yet, anyway, though he was gearing up to do so, squinting sideways at her as if in search of someplace safe to put his finger. She wanted more than anything for him to touch her nipples. So sensitive, they were, that if he put his mouth to one of them, she'd orgasm, she told him. He said he wouldn't do it.

"Don't push me," he said, and that he doubted there was anything he could do to her nipples that would be enough, for she was always slow to come, and so particular. Cara was shocked. He'd never spoken this bitterly before about sex, it wasn't in his nature. In fact, he seemed embarrassed to have said it. He put his book down and sat up in bed, as if preparing to escape and take his shower, but then he parted the curtain and peered out for a look at the night. In the moonlight his neck was uncommonly pale and his cowlick flopped and trembled as if it wanted to go to sleep. She knew he was looking at the car in the driveway, although the car was not the object of his attention. Nor was the dog who lay in the trunk of it, wrapped in their Mexican blanket. That blanket had been Cara's favorite among all of their wedding gifts, only over the years its loyalties had shifted to Kato; its bright dyes blended by drool and wet nose, its fringe of loose yarns stiff with flea spray and grit. They might find something fresher to wrap her in, Cara suggested now to Douglas, whose concern was not the blanket but the burial itself—where would they put her? Not at the vet's, because Kato had hated the vet, and not Cara and Douglas's backyard, where the ground was too frozen to dig, and not back in the woods where Douglas had found her and from which he regretted having removed her in the first place. He should have left her there. It was a place she must have liked—far from home, private, forbidden, squirrels chirping territorially. She was buried in ice. Precisely how this had happened Douglas couldn't imagine, for there was not so much as a whisker piercing the sheen of it. She lay on her side, her brown eyes wide open like eyes under glass. She looked neither dead nor alive; to Douglas, she just looked like a circumstance that was responsible for his life being the way it was. Had it not been for Kato escaping from the motel cabin that night in Colorado, then he and Cara would not have had Georgie, and had it not been for Kato whining to go out every morning while he and Cara tried to find the time to make love, then they would not have conceived Max but some other child, and had Kato not wandered off when she did, then he and Cara would not have had to spend the weekend searching for her, fanning out to whistle their customary whistle. In the woods, the high notes of that whistle seemed to dance among the boughs of the naked trees, and on the streets, the long, drawn-out third notes faded in midair as if he and Cara whistled not for the dog but for each other. Then on Monday evening Cara lay in bed inexplicably tired, secretive, achy and doped up with Tylenol or whatever she was taking. He didn't ask her *what*, or *why*, and she didn't tell him. The hot-water bottle offered no clues; it lay flat on the floor with its legs outspread, neither hot nor cold but exactly frog temperature. Douglas nudged it with a foot, then went out searching by himself, not whistling even halfheartedly but just poking around, knowing what he would find if he found it. And if he hadn't nearly stumbled upon Kato when he did, and if the ice hadn't shattered when he kicked it, and if he hadn't then pried up the dog and carried her stiffly home in his arms, and if Cara hadn't climbed deliberately but painfully out of bed to wrap the dog in that ancient, grayed Mexican blanket, and if they hadn't sat around with a beer into the night wondering what to do with her, and if the dog—even dead in the blanket, her head and tail exposed, her eyes frozen open—hadn't seemed to know so much about what Cara called their life together, then Douglas would have returned to the station as usual and slept on the couch in the conference room.

And now he couldn't go back to the conference room, for the

couch would make him lonelier than it had before, and the loneliness would be more final, more absolute, somehow, as if *that* were his life and not *this*. Cara was stroking his hair. She didn't know it made his spine tickle or that every stroke was echoed in the arches of his feet. She seemed to find the gesture only maternal, and indeed, there was something motherly about it, but still—she reached down to his scalp, closed her purposeful fingers on a lock of red hair, and pulled hard and slow the whole length of the shaft until the hairs fell loose and separate again. The sensation, midway between giddiness and orgasm, made Douglas sit patient and still like a lump of clay that she was coaxing into being; the cowlick, then an ear, then the cowlick again. After that, her hand hovered not quite touching until Douglas released the curtain over the window; it fell shut with a barely discernible whisper.

"There's something I'm going to have to tell you," Cara said then.

"Yes. Me, too. About something I did," Douglas said.

For a moment there was quiet in which they found they had entered a contest of sorts, Douglas staring at Cara, and Cara staring at Douglas staring at her, and Douglas damned if he'd stop staring, and Cara damned if she'd stop being stared at. She could feel, in the corners of her mouth, the tension of the moment blending with the tensions of the last few weeks, and Douglas could see it there; the very margin of a crease where the skin had forever been smooth. Later he would tell her this was beautiful, and not long after, she would concur. But for now Cara said, "Well, not something I did, exactly, but something someone did to—"

Later, they couldn't remember which one of them had raised a finger. Speech was inappropriate. When Douglas climbed out of bed, Cara climbed out, too, and they began to undress themselves, a wary removal of tee shirts and socks and the faint snap of Douglas's jockstrap, which he still wore these days out of what seemed to him to be fear—fear of pain, he supposed, of stuck zippers, of standing up too soon from the table, of children climbing on his lap all sharp knees and elbows. The staring contest had ended, and both of them watched as the folds of their clothing pooled up on the wooden floor. Not for years had they stood before each other disrobing in this mute, expectant fashion, their heads nearly knocking together as Cara stooped to pull her blue jeans off her ankles just as Douglas leaned over for his. There was something shy about it, and amusing, too, and Cara found herself embarrassed by the same thing by which she'd been embarrassed before, years ago at the very beginning—the fact that she saved her bra for last, as she did if she undressed when she was alone, but which, with a man in the room, seemed awkward and not in good form. Georgie coughed into his pillow in the room across the hall, and then Max began making his wake-up sounds, the frightened chuckle of his bad dream surfacing and finally subsiding in renewed, contented slumber. It was the first night ever that the dream failed to wake him, that he managed to make himself stay asleep, but neither Cara nor Douglas remarked on this fact. When they raised their heads at last, they did not meet eyes. The shared gaze was eye to groin, groin to eye, and the funny thing was that when it came time to look, both of them knew exactly what it was they would discover.